Praise for
MICK FINLAY

'Think Sherlock Holmes is the only detective working
in Victorian London? Meet William Arrowood, the
hero of Mick Finlay's series of absorbing novels'
The Times

'A fantastic creation'
Spectator

'Outstanding'
Publishers Weekly

'Gripping'
Daily Telegraph

'A gripping historical crime novel … book clubs
will love it, especially fans of C. J. Sansom'
NB Magazine

'Loved it – the sights, sounds, smells, and horrors of
Victorian London are so vividly portrayed'
Roz Watkins

'Mick Finlay's richly told story evokes the bustling all-encompassing
worlds of C. J. Sansom and Charles Dickens. I loved it'
Lesley Thomson

'A book with enough warmth, charm, humour, and
intrigue to signal the start of an excellent new series'
Vaseem Khan

'The new master of gritty, gruesome and
gripping historical crime fiction'
Lancashire Evening Post

'Readers of historical detective fiction will enjoy this
well-set, darkly humorous addition to the canon'
Historical Novel Society

Mick Finlay was born in Glasgow but spent his childhood moving between Scotland, Canada and England. Before becoming an academic, he ran a market stall on Portobello Road, and has worked as a tent-hand in a travelling circus, a butcher's boy, a hotel porter, and in various jobs in the NHS and social services. He teaches in a Psychology Department, and has published research on political violence and persuasion, verbal and non-verbal communication, and disability. He now divides his time between Brighton and Cambridge.

🐦 @mickfinlay2
f /mickfinlayauthor
www.mickfinlay.com

Also by
MICK FINLAY

ARROWOOD
THE MURDER PIT
ARROWOOD AND THE THAMES CORPSES

Arrowood

and the

Meeting House

Murders

MICK FINLAY

ONE PLACE. MANY STORIES

HQ
An imprint of HarperCollins*Publishers* Ltd
1 London Bridge Street
London SE1 9GF

www.harpercollins.co.uk

HarperCollins*Publishers*
1st Floor, Watermarque Building, Ringsend Road
Dublin 4, Ireland

This paperback edition 2021

1
First published in Great Britain by
HQ, an imprint of HarperCollins*Publishers* Ltd 2021

Copyright © Mick Finlay 2021
Mick Finlay asserts the moral right to be identified as the author of this work.
A catalogue record for this book is available from the British Library.

ISBN: 9780008324551

MIX
Paper from
responsible sources
FSC™ C007454

This book is produced from independently certified FSC™ paper
to ensure responsible forest management.

For more information visit: www.harpercollins.co.uk/green

This book is set in 10,7/15,5 pt. Sabon by Type-it AS, Norway

Printed and Bound in the UK using 100% Renewable Electricity at
CPI Group (UK) Ltd, Croydon, CR0 4YY

To John and Maya

Characters

William Arrowood – private investigative agent, Ettie's brother, Isabel's husband

Norman Barnett – Arrowood's assistant, was married to Rita (Mrs B)

Ettie Arrowood – nurse, mission worker, William's sister, Mercy's mother

Mercy – Ettie's baby

Isabel Arrowood – applicant for medical scholarship, Leopold's mother, William's wife

Leopold – Isabel's baby, his father is a lawyer (deceased)

Neddy – eleven-year-old muffin seller, helps Arrowood from time to time

Flossie – five-year-old street child rescued by Arrowood and Barnett in a previous case

Lewis – William's best friend, runs a second-hand weapons shop, one-armed, lives with Willoughby

Willoughby – works for Sidney as stablehand, lives with Lewis, has Down's syndrome

Sidney – Rita's brother and Norman's brother-in-law, runs a cab yard

The visitors from Natal, South Africa

Thembeka Kunene – ex-servant to English family in Natal, ex-beerseller, S'bu's aunt, Senzo and Musa's cousin

Senzo Nyambezi – younger man from Natal, ex-convict, Thembeka's cousin, Musa's nephew

Musa Schoko – older man from Natal, ex-convict, Thembeka's cousin, Senzo's uncle

S'bu Kunene – fourteen-year-old boy, Thembeka's nephew

PC Mabaso – police constable from Langlaagte Police, Natal
Princess Nobantu – young woman, doing Zulu exhibitions around
    Britain with two companions, a man and a woman

Scotland Yard police
DI Napper – detective inspector, Scotland Yard
PC McDonald – young constable, Scotland Yard
Sergeant Farmerson – one of the two desk sergeants, Scotland Yard,
    suspended by the superintendent

Capaldi and his men
Bruno Capaldi – the family boss, showman
Ermano Capaldi –Bruno's brother
Ralf Capaldi –Bruno's son
English Dave – guard, works for Bruno
Nick – guard, works for Bruno, in love with Sylvia

Capaldi's Wonders
Leonie – Pig Woman, English
Gisele – Lobster Claw Lady, French
Sylvia – Baboon Girl, American, in love with Nick

The others
Madame Delacourte – showman, rival to Bruno Capaldi
Polichinelle – famous clown, appears in theatres and variety shows,
    sometimes works for Capaldi, friend of Madame Delacourte
Ma Willows – owner of Willows' coffee shop
Mr Deakin – manager of York Hotel, Waterloo
Mr Lilly – office manager of Coastal Steam Packet Shipping
    Company
Reverend Hebden – runs the mission where Ettie works
Reverend Jebb – runs the women's sanctuary (part of Reverend
    Hebden's mission)

Note on Terminology

All historical fiction is a compromise between historical accuracy and the needs and values of the current day. This compromise is particularly difficult when attitudes that were common then are recognized as offensive now. Racism was a widely accepted feature of white Victorian society. Since this book features a number of black characters from Natal, it was important I represent the language and attitudes they faced, but in a way that tries not to cause further damage. It would have been historically inaccurate to have all white characters, even those who were openly racist, use only terms we would today see as acceptable. For this reason, a range of terms are used by white characters in this book when they are talking about the South African characters, and in several places those with openly racist attitudes use less acceptable terms. However, I made the decision not to have any character use the four or five most offensive terms that were commonly used in England to refer to black people in the 1890s. I thought this was the best compromise for this book at this time, although I understand that some might disagree.

Chapter One

South London, December, 1896

All my life we'd been at war. This year alone we'd had the Ashanti campaign, the Jameson Raid, the bombing of Zanzibar Town, and Kitchener's battles with the Mahdis. Over the last two decades we'd fought the Boer, the Burmese, the Afghans, the Marri Baluch, and the good old Zulus. War had become our way of life, and how we loved opening the paper every morning for news of our adventures. Empire made the reputation of many a fine fellow and the fortune of many others. It made for songs and toys and ceremonies. It made for an army of broken soldiers and a city awash with guns.

The storm pounded on the narrow street outside the tailor's shop, corralling the soot on the window into ragged lines and dams as maggots of grey rain made their way down the glass to collect on the sodden sill. Me and the guvnor, our clothes soaked through, stood before Forbes Rucker as he inspected a pistol at his cutting table. Around us on rails hung the jackets and suits made in the sweat shop above. The tailor ran his nimble red fingers up and down the barrel once more. He opened the chamber and held it to the lamp.

'It wasn't in this condition when it was stolen,' he said at last. He nodded at my swollen lip. 'I can see you've been in a fight. The handle was damaged then, I suppose?'

'The gun's exactly as it was when we retrieved it,' said the guvnor.

Rucker put a monocle to his eye and studied the chip on the wooden handle. It wasn't any old pistol: it was the one General Pennefather used in the Battle of Inkerman, and worth a lot of money to a collector. Finally, he threw it down. 'It's worthless. The initials are gone. There's no way of identifying it as Pennefather's.'

The guvnor glanced at me.

'I'm sorry to hear it, sir,' said I. 'Now, if you'll just pay us what you owe, we'll be off.'

'It's damaged.'

'As Mr Arrowood says, that's the way we found it. We did what you asked. Four days at twenty shillings an hour, plus the two shillings we gave Mr Creach for the information. You paid one day in advance. That makes it sixty-two shillings, please, sir.'

'I'm not paying,' growled Rucker, rising from his chair and holding out the gun. 'You can have the pistol instead. Now, get out.'

'Not until you pay us what you owe, sir,' I said, stepping towards him.

In a flash, a knife appeared in his hand. 'Out,' he snarled.

'You owe us.'

'Out, Mr Barnett. I will hurt you, have no doubt.'

I looked at the guvnor, who gave a great, weary sigh and shook his head. The both of us knew there was nothing we could do, least not then and there. I took the ancient gun and slipped it in my pocket.

'We won't forget your debt, sir,' said the guvnor as we backed to the door. 'And we will collect.'

Money being tight, we had to walk all the way to the women's sanctuary in Kennington where Ettie, the guvnor's sister, had asked us to deliver a bag of Christmas gifts. As we hurried through the storm, he cursed.

'Will this rain never stop? We should have listened to Lewis, damn it. He warned us about that hound.'

'We needed a case, sir,' I said. 'We had to risk it.'

'I lost my best umbrella for that blooming pistol.' We stepped into the road to let two old women dressed in black pass on the pavement. Each was dragging a bulky sack through the puddles. 'That money would have paid for Christmas. I was looking forward to a good bit of beef. Ettie wanted a bird. Some good brandy. Damn it! I was even going to visit the bath-house this evening. Isabel does prefer me washed at Christmas. What about you, Norman? Why don't you join us?'

'Sidney's asked me. But thanks. You might be eating bread and cheese, anyway.'

'Lewis can pay this year,' he said. 'I think I paid last year.'

'You didn't, sir.'

'No?' said he, disappointed. 'I thought I did.'

Reverend Jebb opened the door to us. We'd just stepped into the hallway of the sanctuary when his eyes widened. 'Good heavens,' he said.

We both turned, and there, climbing down from a four-wheeler in front of the building, were four Africans. At the front was a short woman wearing a rough woollen coat and a pair of coachman's gloves. Behind were two tall blokes. The older wore corduroys and an Italian hat, to which he'd stuck ribbons that hung down limp and wet. The younger, who wore military overalls, was only a young lad. Last out of

3

the carriage was a broad, strong fellow, dressed in a moleskin suit and a necklace of feathers. Each one of them, man and woman, wore earrings.

'Good afternoon,' said Reverend Jebb as they walked up the path towards us. He bent his neck as he always did when greeting people he wasn't sure of. 'How can I help you?'

The lady came to stop on the doorstep. 'The chaplain sent us, Father,' she said, taking Jebb's hand. She shook it hard, staring up at him. 'We're in trouble and need sanctuary. We're good Christians, sir. We don't know anybody here in London.'

'Well, I'm afraid you cannot stay here,' said Jebb, pulling away his hand. 'Have you tried the seamen's mission in Poplar?'

'We aren't seamen, sir,' said the short lady, her nose twitching like she was about to weep. Her voice was deep, her speech more proper than mine, with an accent that was upper class in some ways and foreign in others.

'I'm afraid this institution's only for women,' said Jebb. 'No men are permitted.'

'We need help, sir,' said the older bloke, stepping up level with the woman.

'I am sorry, sir,' said Jebb. 'As I said, only women may stay here.'

'But we're in great danger, Father,' said the lady, gripping the young pastor's arm so hard he grunted. 'Please. Please let us in.'

'Well,' said Jebb. Behind us, the kitchen door opened and Mabel, the matron, poked her head out the kitchen door. 'Well,' said Jebb again, scratching his chin.

The four of them just stood there as the rain fell down. Not one of them had a waterproof or brolly.

'Jebb,' hissed the guvnor, giving him a jab in the back.

'Yes, yes, of course,' said Jebb at last. 'Please come in. You're soaking wet.'

'We'll let you get on with it,' said Arrowood, clutching his raincoat to his throat and stepping outside. 'Come along, Barnett.'

'Stay, William,' said Jebb quickly. 'You might know something useful to them.' He looked at the short lady. 'Mr Arrowood's an investigative agent. Something like the police.'

'Ah,' said she. 'Then you can help us, sir.'

'Well, I can listen, madam,' said the guvnor with a little bow. 'I can at least do that.'

The fire was out in the parlour, and the thick net curtains let in little of the grey that passed for daylight in London that winter. The three men rubbed their hands together and shuddered: without gloves or proper coats I could see they were frozen to the bone. Jebb invited them to sit on the couch and we made our introductions.

'I'm Thembeka, sirs,' said the woman. She nudged the youngest one. 'The boy's S'bu.'

Though he was tall, the expression on his face and the uncertainty of his movements told you he was younger than he looked. A smile appeared on his lips but there was pain in his eyes: he seemed innocent, too innocent for whatever journey he was on.

'Good morning, sir,' he said, taking care over the words.

'Good morning, S'bu,' answered the guvnor. 'And how old are you?'

'Ah,' he said, looking at Thembeka.

'Fourteen,' she said, her face grave. 'He doesn't speak English.' She jutted her chin at the muscular one. 'That one there's Senzo. He doesn't speak it either.'

'I Musa,' said the older one, holding out his hand. His accent was rough, and it was clear he didn't speak so well as the woman. 'Good day.'

We each in turn shook his hand, then shook the others' too. When we'd given them our names, Jebb asked, 'Now, what seems to be the trouble?' He stood by the mantel, me and the guvnor in the chairs.

'There's a—' Thembeka began, but stopped when the parlour door opened and Mabel stepped in, her brow drawn low, her eyes darting across the four visitors.

'D'you need anything, sir?' she asked like she was in half a temper.

'No, Mabel. Thank you.'

Still she stood staring at the Africans, who shivered and stared back at her.

Jebb walked over, took her arm, and turned her out. He shut the door.

'Please continue, miss.'

'There are some men chasing us, Father,' said Thembeka, sitting forward on the seat. 'They want to kill us. We'd be happy sleeping anywhere you'd let us. We don't need beds. We'd be no trouble. We can work. We'll do anything you want.'

'Who are these men, Miss Thembeka?' asked the guvnor.

'The Capaldi family, sir. D'you know them? They're showmen. Into all sorts of illegal business. Mr Capaldi wants to exhibit us at the Aquarium here in London, then he's got an idea to take us all round the country. Here.' She got up and collected the *Standard* from the side table. 'Look in the notices. Royal Aquarium.'

She gave it to Jebb, who opened it. His eyes travelled up and down the columns. '*Capaldi's Zulus,*' he read after a few moments. '*Performances 5.30, 7.30 and 9. The only ones that have ever left their country. Two months only. First performance Sat 21 December. One shilling.*' He looked up at Thembeka. 'Is that you?'

Thembeka nodded. 'We don't want to perform, but Mr Capaldi won't listen. He's sent two men with pistols to hunt us down and take us back.'

'Please, sir,' said Musa, with a scratch of his grey moustache. 'You can help?'

'We'll take you to the police,' said the guvnor. 'You must report this to them.'

'Mr Capaldi said he has a man in the police,' said Thembeka. 'He said they'll arrest us. They'll make us go back.'

'I don't think they can do that,' answered Arrowood. 'How is it you speak so well, if I may ask, ma'am?'

'I was a housemaid for the Sinclairs in Johannesburg. An English family. Mistress Ann taught me from when I was six.'

As she spoke, there came a knock at the front door. Mabel must have been waiting in the hallway, as a moment later we heard the swoop of the door being opened and a few words exchanged. Seconds later three coppers burst into the parlour, each holding a truncheon afore them.

'On your feet, you lot,' said the sergeant to the Zulus. 'You've got an appointment with the magistrate.' He turned to Jebb. 'Begging your pardon, Reverend. I need to take these Africans.'

'On what charge?' asked Jebb.

'Contract-breaking.' The sergeant poked Musa on the shoulder with his stick. 'You, get up.'

'You can't arrest a person for contract-breaking, can you?' asked Jebb.

'Don't know, sir,' said the copper. 'The owner of the Aquarium's reported it, and my inspector give me the orders to bring them in. Whether I can or can't ain't my business.'

The four Zulus remained on the sofa. 'We've done nothing wrong, sir,' said Thembeka to the copper. 'It's Mr Capaldi you should be arresting, not us. He imprisoned us. He said he'd kill us if we didn't dance.'

All of a sudden, Senzo leapt from his seat and lunged for the door. Before he'd got halfway, the other two coppers were on him, wrestling him to the floor. He tried to get up, but one of the police walloped him in the arm with his truncheon while the other shoved him to the floor again. Senzo lay there on his belly as they put wrist-irons on him, a tear in his eye, his head at a painful angle.

'Anyone else want to try?' asked the sergeant.

'Sergeant, be reasonable,' said the guvnor. 'You can't arrest a person for breaking a contract. It's not legal.'

'You'll have to raise that with the inspector,' said the sergeant. He looked at the other three and raised his truncheon. 'Now, get up or you'll taste my woody.'

The three Zulus stood.

'We're Christians, sir,' said Thembeka, as the coppers put her in irons. She looked at Jebb with proud eyes. 'We're Christians.'

'I'll pray for you, madam,' said Jebb. 'I'm sure the magistrate will be understanding.'

We followed them through to the hall and watched as the unhappy four stepped back out into the rain and trudged in a line down the street. Just before they reached the corner, the young lad, S'bu, looked back at us standing on the path. He did a weary salute, then turned and was gone.

Chapter Two

The guvnor lived in rooms behind the pudding shop on Coin Street, just down the road from Waterloo Station. There were five of them there. His sister Ettie and wife Isabel slept in the bedroom with their two babies, Mercy and Leopold. Arrowood had a mattress on the parlour floor. When I arrived at lunchtime the day after the Zulus had been arrested, Isabel was out at the apothecary. Since I'd last been there, the Christmas decorations had been put out: some holly and twigs strung up to nails on the wall, a few painted baubles hanging from the mantel, a little model of a manger with the baby Jesus on the dresser. The babies slept in their boxes on the table.

As Ettie went out back to make tea, there was a knock on the door. I opened it to find Thembeka standing in the corridor with a tall, wispy-haired gent. S'bu was behind them.

'Miss Thembeka,' said the guvnor, rising from his chair. A warm smile creased his great cod-fish face as he shook her hand. 'And S'bu. I'm so very glad to see you released.'

'Good day, sir,' said S'bu as Ettie stepped back into the parlour to see what was up.

'This is my sister, Ettie,' said the guvnor.

'Good day, miss,' said Thembeka, proper as before. She nodded at the old white bloke she'd collected. 'May I introduce Mr Fowler?'

'Of the Aborigines' Protection Society,' said the other in a breathy voice. He was a dry, dusty fellow, hollow-cheeked and leggy. He stepped over to shake our hands. 'The court's lawyer asked if... if I could assist on Miss Kunene's case. Do you know our organization?'

'I don't believe I do, sir,' answered the guvnor.

'I've heard of it,' said Ettie. 'You're Quakers.'

'We strive to protect the rights of native peoples against the colonizing powers,' said Fowler. 'South Africa is a particular interest of ours.'

'Did they dismiss the case?' asked the guvnor, pointing at the chairs around the table.

'The magistrate said we hadn't committed a crime, but he told us we ought to serve out the contract with Mr Capaldi,' said Thembeka, sitting stiffly with her coat still buttoned and her gloves still on. The fire hadn't yet been set that day. She looked around the room, at the portrait of the guvnor over the mantel, the books and tracts stacked on the shelves, the mattress leaning against the wall. Her eyes softened as they fell on the sleeping babies.

'Mr Capaldi was in court,' said Fowler, his knees creaking as he bent to fit his legs under the table. He clasped his hands in front of him, one long finger picking at the weave of Leopold's sleeping box. He seemed unsure of himself. 'He paid to... to bring them over from Paris, and since then he's been covering board and lodging. He's out of pocket. He also has to pay the Aquarium compensation if the show's cancelled. It's a significant amount. Christmas is their busiest time.'

'Can you pay him off?' the guvnor asked Thembeka.

'We've nothing,' she answered. She looked away, her lips

thin and tight, and I wondered if she might be fighting back tears. S'bu stood aside her, his hand on her shoulder. He was staring at the photo portrait above the fireplace, looking from it to the guvnor.

'That's me, S'bu,' said Arrowood. He thrust out his chin and put his hand on his chest just like in the picture.

S'bu smiled, nodding quick. 'Yes, yes. Good.' He pointed at the parrot in the picture. 'Upholi. You? Upholi?'

'He wants to know if you have a parrot,' said Thembeka.

The guvnor smiled. 'No, that was in the photographer's studio. It was dead. Stuffed.'

Thembeka spoke to the young lad in their own tongue.

'Didn't you work in Paris?' the guvnor asked when they'd finished.

'Yes, but we sent the money back to our family.'

'And you signed a contract?'

'With Mr Monteuil,' said she. 'He's a French showman we met in Africa. We agreed to go to Paris to do exhibitions. But then in France Mr Monteuil turned around and said we could earn more money in London and we should sign a new contract. I wasn't there when it was done. My cousins put their mark on it, but they can't speak French and Musa only has a little English. They didn't really know what they were signing, but Mr Monteuil said they had to if they wanted to get to London.' She rubbed her nose as she spoke, watching the babies. 'Is the child ill?' she asked, pointing at Mercy.

The guvnor peered into the box and studied the baby for a moment. Her eyes were open, her little mittened hands clenched at her sides. A bit of dried milk was crusted at the corner of her mouth. 'No, I don't think so. Why?'

Thembeka's eye twitched. 'Is she usually so stiff, Miss Ettie?'

Ettie looked down at her child. 'Is that a sign of something?'

'She might be coming down with a fever.'

'I hope not. She's only just recovered from a cold.'

'So they signed another contract with Mr Monteuil?' asked the guvnor.

'We thought so, but when we got here we discovered the men who'd brought us were Mr Capaldi's men,' she said, her voice tight with anger. 'They only told us then that Mr Capaldi bought our contract from Mr Monteuil and he owns it now and we can't leave the lodging house without his say-so. They treated us as prisoners: they wouldn't allow us to go out, nor get the food we want. They say nobody'll buy tickets if they see us in the street. We said we won't put up with it and won't perform for him. When the chance came, we escaped.'

'There's a law against imprisonment, Miss Thembeka.'

'There's a law against a lot of things.'

'How did the police know you were in the women's refuge?'

'When we escaped from Mr Capaldi we hid in a church. We asked the parson for help. He told us to go to the refuge and he even paid for the cab. But when we'd gone he reported us to the police.' She shook her head, her eyes blazing.

The guvnor sighed.

'Yes, Mr Arrowood. Is that how holy men behave in this country? Or is it only for Africans?'

'Mr Capaldi had already reported them missing,' said old Fowler. 'The police were looking out for them.'

'Can you find a benefactor to pay off the debt, Mr Fowler?' asked the guvnor.

'It's rather a lot.'

'It won't stop him anyway,' said Thembeka. 'He wants to take the exhibition all over – Wales, Scotland, Belgium. He can make a lot of money out of us. When we said we wouldn't do the show, he said he'd pick one of us and kill them and nobody would ever know.'

'But the police would arrest him,' said the guvnor. 'He knows that.'

'He says he'll drop the body so far out to sea it'd never be seen again. We told the police: they said no crime's been done.' Her words were moving quick now, her shoulders up, her hands open. 'They're criminals, the whole family. They've a freak show too, and one of them doesn't want to be on it either. We were on the boat from France with them. They've shows on all over. They've got a travelling cat-house too. And a couple of circuses. They've just brought over three lions.'

'Do you really think he'd do it, Miss Thembeka?' asked Ettie. She'd been listening carefully, a horrified look on her long face.

'We heard he killed somebody in Paris,' said Thembeka, glancing up at S'bu. 'A Frenchman who served him snails when he asked for eggs. Shot him in the face with a pistol.'

'Surely not!' exclaimed Fowler. 'Not for bringing the wrong food, Miss Kunene.'

'Yes, sir.'

Fowler sought out the guvnor's eye and raised his brow in disbelief. Thembeka saw him.

'We heard it was true, Mr Fowler,' she said.

'Why wasn't he arrested?' asked the guvnor.

'I don't know. That's all we heard.'

'A little protection would help assure them, Mr Arrowood,' said Fowler. 'Our society has a small fund to help in times of crisis. We could pay you.'

'Do you want us to protect you, Miss Kunene?' asked the guvnor, rising from his chair.

'Yes, sir. But please, call me Thembeka.'

'And you must call me William,' said the guvnor, picking up his pipe and turning to look out the little window at the sooty wall outside. The orange cat came padding in from the scullery and walked straight toward the lady, whose eyes widened. She clutched the sides of her chair, pushing back as the cat made ready to leap. I pushed it away with my foot.

'We charge twenty shillings a day for guarding,' I said. 'Plus expenses. How long for?'

Fowler looked at Thembeka. 'Do you have tickets for the boat back to Africa?'

'We're not going back,' she said, her fierce eyes still following the cat as it loped over to the guvnor and looked up at him. 'We're staying in England.'

'You're staying?' said Fowler. 'But why?'

'There's nothing for us in Natal.'

'Then why not work for Mr Capaldi?' demanded the old bloke, a flush coming over his long forehead.

'We won't work for a white man who thinks he's bought us like cattle. My cousins want us to do our own exhibitions and take the profits ourselves. Senzo thinks we can hire a manager to work for us, just as Chang and Eng did. You know about them?'

'The Siamese twins? They became very rich, didn't they?'

'Is it permitted?'

'Permitted?' asked the guvnor. 'What do you mean?'

'Are Africans permitted to do this?'

'But of course, miss. Why not?'

'It wouldn't be allowed in South Africa.'

'The Society could pay for, ah… two days,' said Fowler, writing the numbers in a notebook. 'Perhaps Mr Capaldi will give up after that.'

The guvnor gave me the wink. We needed the money, and even if it didn't solve their problem, it gave them a bit of space.

'We need the payment in advance, sir,' I said. 'Forty shillings.'

Fowler's eyes widened for a moment, then he composed himself. 'Well, I think I might just have that.'

As he fished out his purse and counted the money, Ettie asked S'bu if he wanted a biscuit.

'Biscuit?' he answered.

She went to the scullery and came back with the tin. It was full of garibaldis. 'Go on,' she said, holding it out to him. He took one and had a bite.

'Good?' asked Ettie.

'Good!' he said, taking another bite. Ettie handed him two more. As he chewed, he stepped over to the mantel and examined the row of Christmas cards Ettie had put up.

'Where are Senzo and Musa now?' the guvnor asked Thembeka when I had Fowler's money in my hand.

'The Quaker Meeting House. Mr Fowler took us there.'

'It's on St Martin's Lane,' said Fowler.

'Did anyone see you go in?' asked the guvnor.

'I don't know,' said Fowler. 'It was the afternoon. The streets were busy.'

'Were any of Capaldi's men with him in the court?'

'I don't know,' said Thembeka. 'I only met two of them, Nick and English Dave. They weren't there.'

The guvnor looked at me. 'We'll stop at Lewis's on the way.'

'You can't come now?' asked Thembeka.

'We need weapons, miss,' I said.

She turned to Fowler. 'You can buy us weapons?'

'I certainly cannot. We're Quakers, Miss Kunene. The trustees would never approve.'

The guvnor took his astrakhan coat from the hook and put it on. 'We'll meet you there in an hour or so,' he said. 'But please make sure you're not followed.'

When they were gone, the guvnor kissed Mercy on the forehead, then little Leo. Before stepping out into the cluttered back corridor of the pudding shop, he turned to have one last look at Mercy, his brow drawn low in worry. He stared at her for a few moments, then, with a final shake of the head, he pulled shut the door.

Chapter Three

Lewis was the guvnor's oldest friend. He ran a second-hand weapons shop on Bankside, surrounded on all sides by warehouses. A couple of navvies carrying a bundle wrapped in tarp were just leaving when we arrived. Seeing the packet of hot sausages in the guvnor's hand, Lewis smiled.

'A welcome sight, William,' he said, clearing a space on the table with a swipe of his good arm. The wooden one was detached, and lay serene as the baby Jesus on a pile of fiercely stained butchers' aprons that he'd had in there for five years at least without ever selling one. A half-smoked cigar rested above his ear; three waistcoats covered his bulk against the cold. 'My belly's been gurgling since eleven.'

Arrowood opened the packet and took the thickest one for himself. A gob of mustard landed onto the filthy wooden top; he rescued it with his finger and spread it back on the greasy skin. 'We need to borrow a few pistols, Lewis,' he said as he took a bite.

'I might have known,' said his friend, already chewing. Resting the knuckles of his hand on the counter, he raised himself off the chair and lumbered over to a cabinet, wiping the grease from his fingers onto his britches. There he drew a key from his waistcoat, unlocked the top drawer, and pulled out the usual two pistols. 'Isn't it time you bought these?' he asked.

'Ettie won't have them in the house, not with the children,' said the guvnor. I took a sausage. As I chewed it, I felt the sawdust on my tongue. The guvnor took another for himself, rubbing it in the mustard stuck to the wrapping.

'Well, this is the last time I lend them,' said Lewis, laying the two pistols on the counter, his hand black with gun grease and soot. He picked up the last banger. 'Where'd you get these from?'

'The fellow by the Tabernacle.'

'I keep telling you he dilutes the meat. Go to the place opposite the station. It's the same price. Now, you buy these pistols next time. This is a shop, you know.'

'Of course, dear friend,' said the guvnor. 'In fact, we've brought something for you.'

I got Rucker's pistol out my jacket pocket and handed it to Lewis. He scowled as he put on his eyeglasses and inspected it. 'Point three six calibre, Colt Navy.'

'Used by General Pennefather in the Battle of Inkerman,' said the guvnor.

'Really?' asked Lewis, inspecting the handle and barrel. 'There's no identification.'

'How much?' asked the guvnor.

Lewis cracked it open and looked down the barrel. 'Two bob.'

'For a pistol? What's wrong with you, Lewis? You'd cheat your oldest friend?'

'The barrel's twisted. Look.' He handed it to the guvnor. 'It won't fire.'

'Are you sure?' he asked, though we knew the pistol was no good even before we returned it to Rucker. 'Can't it be fixed?'

'With a new barrel, yes.'

The guvnor sighed. 'Oh, all right, then. I'll take three bob.'

Lewis went to the back of the store to find his money box. The damp little room was lit by two paraffin lamps, one on the counter, the other on a barrel of gunpowder. From the ceiling hung boxing gloves, cowls, truncheons and clubs, and stacked on the floor were open crates with knives and bullets. By the front door about fifty old umbrellas stood in a tea chest.

I took the silvery pistol I'd used before and let it fall into my pocket. The guvnor took the black Lancaster, saying: 'We need a few more this time if you don't mind, old friend. Just for a few days.'

Lewis studied him for a moment, a frown on his bloodless face. He put the three shillings back into his pocket.

'What's the case?' he asked at last.

Arrowood explained what Thembeka had told us.

'Are you preparing for a gun battle?' Lewis brushed the stringy hair from his eyes and looked at me. 'That won't end well.'

'Nobody's going to shoot,' said the guvnor. 'If the Capaldis bring out guns we only need to match them. Once they know the Zulus are armed, they'll leave them alone.'

'That's your plan?'

'I can't think what else we can do. They insist on staying in London. They'll never be able to hide.'

'Are you sure about this, William? It sounds too great a risk.'

'Trust me, Lewis. The first person who shoots in a situation like that'll get shot themselves. The Zulus are just one of many business opportunities the Capaldis have. It just wouldn't be worth it.'

Lewis sighed and took out three more pistols. From another drawer he brought out a couple of boxes of bullets.

'But these ones you'll have to hire from me. The Quakers can pay. Say a shilling a day for each.'

'We'll ask them,' said the guvnor as we put the pistols away in our coat pockets.

Lewis took the cigar from behind his ear and lit a match. 'Are you coming for Christmas?'

'Of course,' said the guvnor. 'We do so enjoy your Jewish Christmases, my friend.'

'It'll be a pleasure having children around the place for once. And you, Norman?'

'Thanks, Lewis, but I'm going to Sidney's.'

As I opened the door, the guvnor pulled out an old umbrella from the tea chest. 'Do you mind if I borrow one of these?' he asked, tapping it on the dusty floor as if to test it.

'Bring it back,' said Lewis, lowering himself onto his stool with a groan.

By the time we crossed Waterloo Bridge, the rain had stopped and a fog was falling over the city. We hurried through the wet crowds to Covent Garden, avoiding the puddles and gutters spurting their load onto the greasy pavements. Mr Fowler let us in when we reached the Quaker Meeting House, leading us through the lobby and some doors hung with heavy red curtains. In the main meeting room, benches ran along three walls; two rows of chairs were set around a long table in the middle. A piano was in one corner. Fowler'd brought a burner into the big room and the three Zulu men sat around it warming their hands. They'd taken off their earrings, Musa his ribbons, Senzo his necklace of feathers.

'Good morning,' said each in turn, shaking our hands.

'Good morning,' we said.

'How are you keeping?' asked the guvnor.

'Well,' said Musa. 'Come. Sit.' He was a fair bit older than the others, his moustache thin, his head bald but for a patch of thin hair at each side. His voice was soft, and his eyes shone with a kindly glimmer. He touched the guvnor's overcoat. 'This good. Coat good.'

'Why, thank you,' said the guvnor. 'It's my favourite.'

He'd got the coat from a second-hand barrow on Petticoat Lane a few years back, and though he loved it, with its blue bodice and furry black collar, it never fitted him right. The sleeves were over long, and the buttons had popped a few times when his wind was troubling him.

Musa ran his fingers down the soft lapel. 'What is?'

'Astrakhan,' said the guvnor.

'Astrakhan, yes. Good.'

'Where's Thembeka?' I asked Fowler.

'Ah, yes… she's in the… the…' he mumbled as he fiddled with his watch chain. 'The lavatory, I believe.'

The dusty Quaker looked older now – maybe seventy or so – and a bit out of his depth. His face was drawn, his eyes set deep in their holes.

'Go and make sure she's safe,' the guvnor told me.

I waited down the corridor from the privy until she'd finished. When we got back to the meeting room, we saw that the guvnor'd given them each a pistol. Senzo and Musa sat by the burner inspecting their guns, while the young lad lay on a bench, his pistol hung upside down, his finger stuck through the trigger loop.

'Where's mine?' asked Thembeka, dropping onto one of the chairs like she was in charge of the place.

23

'We only brought three,' said the guvnor. 'But they're not for shooting. If the Capaldis come, you just show them. They'll back off.'

The doorbell rang. Before letting Fowler answer it, I pulled the pistol from my pocket and looked through the doorkeeper's window, a bit of mirror as let you see from the meeting room through the lobby and straight down to the glass doors on the street. It was only a couple of well turned-out women, so I hid the gun behind my back and followed Mr Fowler through. When he opened the door, we could see there were two laundry hampers sat on the step.

'The bedding, Mr Fowler,' said one of the women. Though her face was set in a sneer, her eyes travelled up and down my body with a fevered curiosity. A thick scarf was wound round her neck. 'Are they really Capaldi's Zulus?'

'They're not anybody's Zulus,' said Fowler. 'They're free men.'

'Well, they're called Capaldi's Zulus in the paper,' said the woman. 'We've brought everything you wanted and a few extra jumpers and blankets. Oh, and gloves. We didn't know if they had them. They won't be used to the cold.'

'Can we meet them?' asked the other, a stout woman with a honking voice.

'Yes... I mean, well, no, you're not supposed to know too much about them, ladies,' answered Fowler. 'They're in hiding.'

'But we'd never tell anyone, Frederick!'

'Of course, Pamela. It's just our procedure. We must have rules.'

'May we come in, just for a moment?' asked the first. 'Is it true they wear earrings?'

'What have you been told about them, ma'am?' I asked.

The first lady looked startled.

'This is Mr Barnett,' said Fowler. 'He's one of the agents helping us. This is Mrs Stockton-Hugh.' He indicated the one who'd inspected me, then the one he'd called Pamela. 'And Mrs Porter.'

'What d'you know about the people staying here?' I asked.

'Only what we've read in the papers, Mr Barnett,' said Mrs Porter.

I looked hard at Fowler. 'We asked you not to tell anybody who they were, sir.'

'Well, no, of course,' he said with a shrug. He raked his long fingers through his sparse hair. 'The ladies don't know anybody connected to the Capaldis. Nobody in our society moves in those circles.'

'People talk. Don't tell anyone else, please, Mr Fowler. Not a single person. Understood?'

'Ah... well, yes... if you think it's best.'

I looked hard at Mrs Porter and Mrs Stockton-Hugh.

'Of course, Mr Barnett,' they said together.

I pulled the two hampers in and bolted the front door. As Fowler and me carried the first one through, a shouting arose in the big room ahead. I dropped the handle and bounded in to see Thembeka and S'bu in a tussle. S'bu was bent at the waist, his hands clutched at his belly. Thembeka had her shoulder under his chest, and with both her hands was trying to wrench the gun from his grasp. A chair lay upturned by their side.

'Thembeka asked the lad for the pistol but he wouldn't hand it over,' said the guvnor as we watched them grunt and wrestle. Musa and Senzo sat next to each other, a bored look on their faces.

'Now, now!' cried Fowler, striding across the polished floor. He tapped S'bu on the back. 'Stop it. There's a good chap.'

The old Quaker might as well have blown in his pocket for all the difference it made. He looked over at me for help. I shrugged: it was clear they were playing at fighting, though he didn't seem to see it.

Senzo spoke to Thembeka. She rolled her eyes, and, with what sounded like a curse, went to sit on the other side of the hall. Then she began to laugh. When she forgot her worry, you could see a mischief in her face that spoke of better times.

S'bu smiled, waving the gun at her, and they spoke for a while. After a moment or two they were both laughing.

Watching them, the guvnor chuckled too. 'What did they say?' he asked, turning to Musa.

'She say S'bu likes you look at him like um...' The old fellow's face screwed up. He put his hands on his bald head with a finger stuck up on each, like he had horns. Then he dipped his head and made a groan.

'A bull,' said the guvnor.

'A goat,' said Thembeka. 'Like a long-hair goat.'

'Oh!' said the guvnor with a chuckle. 'Yes, yes.'

'Like goat,' said Musa.

'It means he likes the attention,' said Thembeka. 'And he said I fight like a bush pig.'

We passed out the blankets and the four of them fashioned a bed each around the burner. I set myself up in the lobby, with the guvnor by the side door to the alley so we could hear if anyone tried to get in. Fowler went out for food while the four of them looked through the hamper of clothes. Thembeka picked out a thick vest, a linen undersuit, and a tasselled shawl she wrapped over her dress. Senzo and Musa each took a cable-knit jumper, and Musa found a Donegal overcoat.

'That's a good one,' said the guvnor, stepping over to have a feel of the material. It was just like one he'd been trying on the week before in Pope's. Though the coat was a few years old and had a tear under the arm, he didn't have the thirty shillings so he'd asked the shopkeeper to hold it for a fort-night. I didn't reckon he'd afford it now. This case wasn't going to earn him enough, and he owed the chandler and Mrs Pudding first anyway.

He helped Musa get it on. S'bu pulled a cricket sweater over his overalls, then put on a greatcoat over the top. Then they added scarves and gloves. Thus thickened, they sat back around the burner and crossed their arms.

The rest of the day passed slowly. S'bu spent a few hours playing with the piano – he seemed to know a thing or two, as after a little practice he stumbled over a few hymns I almost recognized. Thembeka told us he played the concertina. The guvnor found a draught board in the vestibule and played with Musa for an hour or so. Senzo lay in the blankets watching them play. When Arrowood offered around his thin cigars, Thembeka took one and had a smoke as she read the paper. Musa took one too, and the guvnor and him puffed away as they played game after game. Every now and then they'd break into peals of laughter, patting each other on the back and shaking hands.

The Quaker came back with bread, pickled eggs, and a few pots of ale. We laid it out on the table and ate. Musa picked up an egg and bit into it.

'Owf!' he spluttered, his face screwed up like a bulldog. He spat it into his hand. 'Masimbanko.'

All of us except old Fowler laughed.

'What is?' muttered Musa, staring at the brown egg in his hand.

'Pick... pickled... egg,' said the guvnor through his laughter. There were tears in his eyes.

Musa held it out to Senzo who shook his head. They spoke in their tongue and Senzo laughed again. Musa offered it to Thembeka.

'It's vinegar,' I told her. 'Keeps longer.'

She translated it for Musa, then turned to me. 'Have you ever had porcupine eggs?'

I shook my head. 'Is that a kind of chook?'

'No,' laughed Thembeka. She translated for the others and they laughed too. 'No. It's like a... like a dog with needles sticking out all over his hide.'

'Get away,' I said.

'It's true. That's right, isn't it, Mr Fowler?'

'Yes, Mr Barnett,' said the old Quaker. 'Like a monstrous hedgehog.'

'You must try the eggs one day,' said Thembeka. 'They're the best.'

The way she was looking at me with her big eyes and lop-sided smile, I didn't know if she was codding me.

'Trust me, Norman.'

'Hedgehog eggs? I never heard of them.'

She patted me on the shoulder. 'I'll find some for you.'

'If you say so, miss.'

I suppose my face gave me away, for she began to laugh again.

After eating, the Zulu men sat around quietly while the rest of us turned to the papers. Now and then they spoke to each other. Since the darkness fell, they'd grown nervy, looking up at any noise, going to the vestibule to peer out the front door. At about seven, Fowler went home, promising to return in the morning with more food.

A few hours later, the four of them lay down to sleep, the guvnor and me taking it in turns to stay awake. Towards one there was a great row in the street, but it was just two cabbies fighting over a fare. The Capaldis never came.

Chapter Four

Fowler arrived with his wife about eight the next morning. She had a basket of boiled eggs and bread; he held a couple of jugs of tea in his shaky hand. The guvnor and our friends ate quick while Mrs Fowler, who was a good bit younger than her husband, sat by the door, studying their habits closely. When we'd finished and it was all cleared away, Thembeka walked over to S'bu and held out her hand. The thin lad shook his head. She raised her voice, pointing at the pocket in his overalls where he held the gun, but the boy only rammed in his fist and turned away.

'Why don't you let him keep the pistol, Miss Thembeka?' asked the guvnor.

'He's a boy. I don't want to see him shot.'

'Senzo and Musa don't seem to mind him having it.'

'They don't want me to have it because I'm a woman.' She looked at the young lad and smiled with affection. 'He'll give it to me soon enough.'

It was queer. I didn't know what to make of Thembeka and her cousins. She spoke for them, but there was something wrong about how they were together, like they didn't trust one another. And then from nowhere you'd see something like love rise up for a few moments.

'Musa,' said the guvnor, holding his chin between his finger and thumb and examining his new friend. 'That coat's too big for you.'

'Too big,' he nodded, looking down at the new Donegal overcoat buttoned up to his chin. It was the right length but could have been tighter around the belly. It didn't matter: half of London was trundling around in clothes that didn't fit them proper. Musa shrugged.

'Why don't we exchange?' asked the guvnor, removing his astrakhan overcoat and handing it to him. 'You said you liked it, didn't you?'

Musa narrowed his eyes. 'I? I coat?'

'Yes. You take.' The guvnor plucked at Musa's sleeve. 'You give me this.'

'Ah. Yes.' Musa shed his coat and handed it over. 'Take coat.'

The guvnor put it on: it fitted him a deal better than the astrakhan that his belly'd outgrown some time ago. And the astrakhan fitted Musa better too. 'Good,' said the African, stroking the furry collar. 'I like.'

They shook hands, then, in a fit of joy, the guvnor gave Musa a great hug.

'You look like a king, my friend,' he said.

Musa laughed. 'You? Long-hair goat!'

They thought that was the funniest thing in the world, and as we watched them laugh, S'bu, Thembeka, Mrs Fowler and me found ourselves joining them. Finally, even old Fowler himself began to smile.

When we were all sitting around the brazier and smoking again, the guvnor turned to Fowler. 'The two days you've paid for will expire at dusk tomorrow, sir. What are you going to do then? D'you have a plan?'

'Oh,' said Fowler as if he'd been taken by surprise. 'Well, no, of course... Yes, but I... I hadn't...' He covered one fist with the other and pinched his nose.

'Are they going to stay here alone, or will you move them?'

'Well, I suppose they...' He looked at Thembeka with his brow raised as if expecting her to answer. She said nothing.

'We'll have to take back the guns,' I said. 'They were only loaned.'

'Well, well, yes, of course.' Fowler crossed his arms and frowned. 'It really would be safer if you just got on the next ship to South Africa, Miss Thembeka.'

She looked over at her three companions, but her eyes were in a haze, like she wasn't seeing them so much as something hidden there, a ghost or a long-lost place. 'We're not going back, sir.'

'But why? The longer you stay here the more danger you're in.'

She took in a big draught of air. 'Because we're Africans, Mr Fowler,' she said in a great outbreath.

'I don't understand,' said the guvnor.

'Don't you know what happens in your empire, William?' she demanded.

'Well... I—'

'Every year the government of Natal gives your people more of the good land so there's less for us. Not enough for all of us to live on – us, who were there before you came, and that's on top of all the problems with rinderpest and locusts we've had over the last few years. Every year more of our men must leave their homesteads to find work. Most of the jobs are in the mines, and who owns those?' She paused for a moment, looking back at Fowler. 'Your people. Many men die there. The pay's low, the hours are long, and the workers must live in compounds with guards. If they want to leave they're arrested. If an African breaks a contract or refuses when a white man offers work, he's put in prison. S'bu was five months in Cinderella prison because he wouldn't take a job in the mines when an agent asked him. He's fourteen, for goodness' sake! Senzo's been in that prison three times. Musa was flogged for not giving the Bayede salute to a road inspector.'

The guvnor shook his head. 'Is it really that bad?'

Musa nodded. 'Very bad,' he said softly.

'You don't know the native laws, do you?' asked Thembeka. Senzo and S'bu were watching: they could see from her face and the quiet anger in her voice she was talking of home. 'British laws that are only for Africans. The Masters and Servants Laws. The Pass Laws. The Compound Laws. The authorities love to make laws for us. Half our men have been in prison, and most of them more than once. Some of our men have been flogged so many times their backs are like lizard skin. Why would we want to go back? What life is there ahead for a boy like S'bu? We're slaves in our own land. Here there are no Pass Laws, no Servant Laws. It doesn't make any sense, but we're more free here than in Africa.'

'But life's hard here too,' said Fowler. 'Life's always hard when you're poor.'

Thembeka just stared at him.

'Where's your homestead?' asked the guvnor.

'Now? On a scrap of poor land in a place called Lower Tugela. The authorities moved us from our place and gave it to white settlers. Half of my people had to leave to find work in the mines and docks.'

Senzo and Musa stiffened, their eyes growing cold as they watched her.

'In Zululand?' asked the guvnor.

'In Natal. We're amaQwabe. On the other side of the river.'

'Why does it say in the paper you're Zulus?'

She clicked her tongue. 'We're all Zulus to you.'

'You said before that you were six when you left?' asked the guvnor.

'Six, yes. Could I ask for some of your tobacco, William?'

The guvnor held out his pouch and she packed her long-stemmed pipe. He lit a match for her. 'Why so young?' he asked.

'My family needed money, so an agent brought me and my sister to Johannesburg to serve with the Sinclairs, the family I told you about.'

'And you left that job to come here?'

She shook her head. 'When Mistress Ann died, the master had a new wife. She took against us and turned us out. We found work selling beer.'

'How old were you?'

'Sixteen, seventeen. We did that for a few years, then we started brewing our own isishimiyana. We didn't like working for other people.'

'Isishimiyana,' said Musa softly. His eyes gleamed.

'It's beer and sugarcane liquor,' Thembeka explained. 'I don't think you have it here?'

'No,' said the guvnor, 'though I'd certainly like to try it.'

'You'd like it,' she said with a smile.

'He would,' I said.

'You left your sister there?' asked the guvnor.

Thembeka swallowed, then quickly took a draw on her pipe.

35

She shook her head, her eyes rising to the ceiling. 'Cholera took her two years ago.'

'I'm sorry.'

She seemed to lose herself in thought for a few moments. Then she asked: 'What about you, William? How long have you been an investigative agent?'

'Only seven or eight years. I was a newspaperman before that. I must say I'm sorry to hear about your homestead, Thembeka. I truly am.'

'It's a crime,' she said, blowing out a deal of smoke. Her brow drew down. 'But they wouldn't make a colonial law to stop that, would they? Don't you read about what they're doing in the newspapers?'

'The Society tries to keep up,' said Mrs Fowler. 'But the empire seems to keep getting bigger every year.'

'We do write reports,' said Mr Fowler.

'Ah,' said Thembeka, raising her lip. 'Reports.'

After a few minutes, the guvnor turned to Fowler. 'Will you continue to help them when we leave?'

'I'm not, ah, at, at liberty to make any decisions without the committee,' said Fowler, his eyes resting on S'bu, who was aiming his pistol at a pigeon outside the window. 'I oughtn't to have brought them here, really. Not, not without a full meeting.'

'Then perhaps you could assemble the committee and decide,' said the guvnor.

As they talked, S'bu stared at his pistol. The pain that was in his eyes the first time we met was there, but his neck was taut, his hand shaking. Sensing me, he looked up. He put the gun in his pocket and smiled.

'They're busy gentlemen,' said Fowler. 'Some live a day away.'

'Perhaps you could pay us for a few more days, then, sir,' I suggested, putting my hand on S'bu's hot shoulder.

'Oh, I couldn't possibly use more money without full committee consideration. Perhaps...' He looked at his wife. 'Oh, dear.'

'Perhaps you could go home and return tonight, Mr Barnett,' said Mrs Fowler. 'I assume the danger is at night rather than the day when the Capaldis would be seen? If you only come at night, might the two-day fee stretch to three nights?'

The guvnor looked at me and shrugged.

'Well, I suppose we could do that,' I said, giving S'bu's shoulder a squeeze and stepping away.

'Yes, what a good idea, Margaret,' said Fowler eagerly. 'That would give the committee time to assemble.'

'In that case we'll go now,' said the guvnor, collecting his hat and coat from the hooks by the door. 'We'll return at half-past five. Now remember, keep the door locked. Only let in members. And summon the committee immediately.'

As I got on my coat, I met S'bu's eyes. He raised both hands to show me they were empty; the pistol was back in his pocket.

'Goodbye, sir,' he said, and, with a smile, saluted.

After arranging to meet later that day, we parted company at Trafalgar Square and I wandered back over Blackfriars Bridge. It was dry, a cold wind running up the brown river and filling the rusty sails of the barges as they cut through the water loaded with cargoes of coal and dung. I'd slept a bit on the Quaker floor, but my bones ached and I needed more. I turned down Southwark Street, heading to my new room.

'Is that you, Norm?' came a voice from the doorway of a pub on the corner.

I turned.

'It is you, mate,' she said with a smile.

'Molly,' I said, giving her a hug. 'I thought you were living up north.'

'I'm back now,' she said, her smile falling away. She rubbed my arm. 'I heard about Rita, Norm. I'm real sorry. I would've got in touch but I didn't know where you were.'

I nodded, watching the tears fill her eyes. Molly was my wife's oldest friend: grew up in the same building with her in Bermondsey, went to school together and started work in Potts Vinegar factory the same day too. First time I met my Rita she was with Molly on a night out. But Rita had been dead a year and a half now, and I was about to face a second Christmas without her.

'Where are you living?' I asked her.

'Tabard Street with my sister. Working in here,' she said, nodding at the pub behind her. She put a pipe to her mouth and took a puff. 'Why don't you come in and have a drink, eh?'

The Pelican wasn't a place I'd been in much. It was a bit bigger than a lot of them around the Borough, with a long counter and benches along the walls. A little coal fire heated the room, and keeping near it for warmth a good dozen men and women watched a game of dominoes. Molly got behind the bar and poured me a porter. I bought her a gin and water and we spent the next hour or so talking over old times. Though she was shorter and thinner, there was so much about her as reminded me of my Rita: the way she spoke, the things as made her laugh, the way she set her hair and flipped her fingers at me when I got saucy. After a couple of drinks it almost felt as if my old darling was there with us, and we began to talk about her passing, how it happened all of a sudden when she was away visiting her sister.

'You're still sad, mate,' she said, with a gentle frown. 'I can see it.'

'Just don't get the chance to talk about her much. Except with Sidney sometimes.'

She smiled. 'He still with Pearl?'

'Still is.'

'You two was suited better'n anyone back then. Everyone said so.'

'We got on.'

She laughed. 'You got on. I was jealous of you two, d'you know that?'

I shook my head.

'Thought I'd never find a bloke suited me so well as you and her. Least not from round here.'

'That why you left?'

She sighed and pushed her hair back. There was a little nick at the side of her nose that I was pretty sure wasn't there back when I knew her. Like something done by a knife. 'No,' she said soft. 'Just had an urge for going. See something new, you know?'

I nodded, looking at her kind face and feeling warmed by it. 'So, you got a bloke hanging around? You never had a shortage, did you, Molly?'

She laughed and turned her head away.

'Nobody special, Norm.'

Her voice wavered, and I wondered what she was

hiding. I bent over the bar and gave her a quick peck on the cheek.

'I got to go and get some kip afore work. It's good to see you, Moll. Perhaps I'll drop in here again, eh?'

She tipped the gin down her throat and took a tankard from a woman who'd come over. 'You better, Norm, else I'll track you down.'

'Might drop in tomorrow, then.'

'You do that,' she said, smiling to herself as she pulled the pump and the gush of black ale filled the woman's battered tankard.

Chapter Five

It was six o'clock, and night had fallen over London. St Martin's Lane was part blocked by two fire wagons, the buses and cabs toe to tail trying to get past. A smell of burning filled the air. An old fellow watching from the other side of the road told us there'd been a fire about midday.

'Flames come out over the top there,' he rasped, pointing at the printworks about two hundred yards down the road from the Quaker Meeting House. 'There was an explosion like you never heard. Made the bloody ground shake and they all come rushing out, all a-screaming and a-whooping. Like the Great Fire, it were.' He shook his head. 'Twelve of them never got out. Last count was twelve anyways. Might be more.'

The guvnor was staring at the crowd on the other side of the road. In the middle of the confusion, a woman was weeping, her face red and twisted. An older man held her to his chest. Another was arguing with a fire officer, pointing at the ruined entrance of the printworks. In the dark sky, you could just make out ribbons of a lighter dark rising to the clouds. A stream of people moved through the gaslit street, others stood about, getting in the way of the horses, their faces blackened, eyes wide with shock, asking questions to others who just shook their heads, their arms folded across their chests as the river of folk in thick coats and scarves surged past to the station.

The guvnor took my hand as we moved through the mêlée to the Quaker Meeting House.

'No lights, Norman,' he said, hesitating before we crossed the road.

'Maybe they've been moved.'

'I hope so.'

He let me step up to the door before him. It was only then I saw that one of the glass panes was bust, the broken pieces scattered on the floor inside. When I pushed at the door, it swung open. There was no sound inside. I took out my pistol and entered the dark lobby. There was just enough light from the street to see the long row of hooks held two coats: Fowler's and his wife's. A table on the other wall was stacked with tracts.

Quiet as we could, we walked forward to the closed doors of the main meeting room, where we stood for a moment, listening. All we heard was a gurgle of pipes and the mutter of the street behind us.

'Ready?' I asked, looking back to make sure the guvnor had his gun.

'Let's go.'

I raised my pistol and we stepped in.

In the dim light of a single gas jet, I could see the blankets laid out where our friends had slept the night before. An overturned chair lay by the far window. The table stood in the middle. Then, in the shadows behind the chairs, I saw something else on the floor.

We hurried over.

It was Fowler, lying on his belly, his arms and legs out like a star.

The guvnor dropped to his knees.

'Sir!' he said, shaking the man's shoulder.

The body barely moved. He turned Fowler onto his back, and we saw that his mouth was open, his eyes shut. 'Sir!' exclaimed the guvnor again.

I felt for the pulse. Though his wrist was warm, there was nothing. The guvnor put his ear above the Quaker's mouth, listening for life. Shaking his head, he checked the pulse in his neck, then sat back on his haunches. I moved around the room, turning on the other gas jets while the guvnor searched Fowler's body. He found a bloody hole through his jacket and into his chest. 'Looks like a bullet,' he murmured.

The basement door was ajar. Inside was a small, dark stairhead. I picked up a storm lamp from a corner and when I'd lit it the guvnor followed me down the stone steps to the little basement.

It was there we found Musa. He lay sideways across a mattress on the floor, his head bent back, his mouth a mess of blood and bone. On the floor next to him was a hammer.

'Musa!' cried the guvnor, pushing past me and hurrying over to his friend. He fell to his knees, feeling for a pulse. 'Musa, wake up!'

The old fellow's eyes were open. His lips were mangled and torn, his teeth shattered and broke. His wrists were tied behind his back with a cord, another binding his ankles and knees together.

I undid his clothing, searching the body for more wounds. I found them on his neck: finger marks and bruising.

'Been strangled,' I said, getting to my feet. 'They hurt him first.'

The guvnor took Musa's hand and straightened the

astrakhan coat he'd swapped with him. 'Oh, what have they done to you?' he said, brushing some mess from the lapels.

For some time, he kneeled next to Musa's body. I lifted the lamp and looked around the tiny basement. It was being used for storage: there was a pile of old curtains, a few broken chairs, a shelf of mouldy books and a stack of crates filled with empty bottles. Musa's blankets were on the floor, next to a pickle jar full of dark piss.

'We'll find who did this to you, Musa,' said the guvnor at last. 'I promise.'

We climbed back up and had another quick look around the meeting hall, then went out the side door. There was a small kitchen, a toilet, and another, smaller meeting room. All were empty. A door opposite the kitchen was locked.

'They might be upstairs,' whispered the guvnor, pushing me forward. We waited at the foot for a few moments, listening for sounds on the floors above. When we were sure it was quiet, we climbed. On the first floor were two locked doors. We rose to the next level. Another two doors. One opened into a room with a polished table and twelve chairs, a smell of cigar smoke and furniture oil. Books ran along one wall; a window looked down onto the dark back yard. The next door also opened, this time to a small office. Nobody was there either.

We climbed back down to the ground floor. In the lobby, the guvnor picked up a basket that was under Mrs Fowler's coat. In it were two loaves, a packet of beef, four onions and four bottles of porter. In the umbrella stand was her violet umbrella.

'What does that tell you, Norman?' asked the guvnor, his voice hard and angry.

'They were about to eat.'

'And Mrs Fowler left without her umbrella and coat. She must have run off.'

He picked up the umbrella and ran his finger over the fabric. 'Wet. When did it stop raining?'

'About two.'

'So the latest time she arrived was perhaps two thirty or three.' He shoved the umbrella violently into the stand and searched the pockets of her coat, pulling out her gloves, a silk hanky, a poke of acid drops and a pamphlet. 'Left her gloves, but not her scarf or bonnet. That's queer. Go and find a constable. I'll take another look around.'

I found one walking the beat on New Oxford Street. He sent a boy for a detective and followed me back to St Martin's Lane. There, the guvnor showed him the bodies and explained what we'd found. The copper, a young fellow with over-wet lips, wrote in his notebook.

'Stay here and look after the bodies,' he said. 'I'll search the building. If I call, come and help me please, sirs.'

We sat down in the circle of chairs and watched as he carefully checked the corridor, his truncheon tight in his hand. When he was sure there was nobody hiding in the shadows, he moved on.

'Fowler's purse is gone,' said the guvnor, getting to his feet and pacing angrily to the window. 'And Musa had a letter in his pocket. I've copied the words, but we'll need to get a translation. All the pistols are missing too.'

'You think the others ran off?'

'Either that or they were captured by Capaldi's men.' As he marched back across the meeting hall, he pointed at a bench by the wall: Musa's Italian hat decorated with ribbons, Thembeka's coachman's gloves and Senzo's feather necklace were still there. 'They left in a hurry.'

The guvnor continued to pace up and down the length of the hall, his arms crossed over his breast, thoughtful and unhappy. Finally, we heard a knock at the front door and the PC stomp down the stairs to open up. From the clicking approaching in the lobby, the detective who'd arrived had hobnails on his boots.

'These are the men who called us, sir,' said the young copper when they appeared.

'Thank you, McDonald,' said the detective. He was about the same age as me, a strange-looking fellow, his thin eyes gummy somehow, a bony lump the size of a Brussels sprout on his neck. Beneath his bowler, his red hair, cut tight to his skull, was the texture of a scrubbing brush. He looked at us with a scowl. 'I'm Detective Inspector Napper. Who are you?'

'Mr Arrowood,' said the guvnor, pushing himself to his feet. 'And this is Mr Barnett, my assistant.'

Napper thought for a few moments, then his eyes opened wide. 'The private enquiry agents?'

'Yes, sir.'

Napper nodded. 'I was at the Catford Murder Inquiry. You didn't get the credit you deserved, sir.'

The guvnor coloured, and a look approaching worry came across his face. We didn't hardly ever get praised by the Old Bill. 'Thank you, detective inspector,' he said slowly, waiting for the criticism. But none came. Instead, Napper marched over to Fowler and squatted.

'Who's this gentleman?' he asked as he had a poke at the body.

46

'Mr Fowler,' said the guvnor. 'He's a Quaker.'

'The African's in the basement,' said the PC, pointing at the door.

'His name's Musa,' said the guvnor. 'We don't know if he has another name.'

'Did you search the building, McDonald?' asked Napper.

'Yes, sir. Couldn't find nobody else, but some of the rooms is locked.'

Napper took the lamp and went down to the basement, the PC following him. Five minutes later he was back up again, Musa's letter in his hands. He click-clacked over to look in Fowler's pockets. There he found a bunch of keys. The guvnor looked at me with a frown: it seemed he hadn't searched the fellow as well as he could have.

Napper gave them to the PC. 'See if you can get in those rooms. And send for the police surgeon.'

He lifted the lid of the piano and began to play a slow polka, stumbling over the notes while we sat smoking. He gave up in the middle of the tune, eased himself onto one of the benches and opened the letter again. He looked up. 'Tell me everything, Mr Arrowood. Who are these people and why are you here?'

The guvnor told him what we knew. Napper listened close, fiddling with a couple of marbles he'd pulled from his pocket.

'So, what do you think happened?' he asked when Arrowood had finished.

'The first possibility is that the Capaldis came to take the Africans back,' said the guvnor, lighting his pipe. I noticed his hands trembling as he did it. 'Mr Capaldi did promise to kill one of them if they didn't perform. His men arrived, there was a fight and the two men were killed. They captured the others and took them away.'

'Or the others escaped,' said Napper. 'But how would Capaldi know they were hiding here?'

'They'd have learnt that Mr Fowler had been asked by the court to help. They might have followed him or asked one of his servants where he was. And people would have noticed four Africans coming into this building. I just don't understand why Capaldi would go to these lengths, though.' Arrowood pinched his hooter, to prevent a sneeze, then added, 'It doesn't seem very sensible, does it? He's the obvious suspect.'

'The murderer usually is the obvious suspect,' grunted Napper. 'In my experience. Doesn't pay to be too clever, else-wise you end up chasing ghosts.'

'But think of the money side of it, sir. Capaldi's got shows booked at the Royal Aquarium all over Christmas and the New Year. Tickets sold. He'll never be able to exhibit the other three now.'

'Seems like good publicity to me,' said Napper. 'People'll be flocking to see the Zulus when they read about these murders.'

'Did you see what they did to Musa? Even Barnum wouldn't do that for publicity.'

'People will do anything for money. Have you forgotten the slave ships, Arrowood?'

'Of course not.'

'D'you know what people do to each other here, in your own city? I've seen men slice the skin off a baby as revenge on their mothers. I've seen—'

'Please, detective!' cried the guvnor, holding up his hand. 'I know people can be cruel.'

'Maybe Mr Capaldi has to be seen doing what he said he'd do,' I said. 'Maybe it's as simple as that.'

'Was there any dispute between the Africans, d'you know?' asked Napper.

'There was a disagreement about who should have the guns,' said the guvnor. 'Miss Thembeka wanted the pistol the young lad had. The others wouldn't help her take it off him.'

Napper wrote it all down.

'D'you know whose coats are out there?'

'Mr and Mrs Fowler. She must have arrived when the murderer was here. The basket of food's still in the vestibule.'

'If she'd escaped, she'd have alerted the police by now,' said Napper. 'She must have been captured. But why?'

The guvnor shrugged.

'Well, as Sherlock Holmes would say, *It is a capital mistake to theorize before one has data*,' said Napper, putting on a lofty voice.

'Any fool would consider the data,' snapped Arrowood. Napper didn't know it, but unlike the rest of London, who seemed to worship Sherlock Holmes, the guvnor couldn't abide the bloke. It wasn't just that Holmes was richer and more famous than him, he didn't think the fellow was as clever at solving crimes as he made out. Even hearing his name could be enough to burst another blood vessel in his swollen hooter.

'My old man's memorized every case,' said Napper, tapping his pencil on his notebook. 'So, we've two suspects: Capaldi's people or the Africans.'

'Or Mrs Fowler,' I said.

They both looked at me.

'*When you've eliminated the impossible, whatever remains,*

even if it's not likely, has to be the truth,' I said, pleased with myself for remembering another of Holmes's sayings.

The guvnor glared at me, his lip curling. 'At least get the quote right, Barnett,' he said at last.

'Who else knew they were here?' asked Napper.

'Two ladies from the Quakers,' answered the guvnor. 'Mrs Painter and Mrs Stockton-Hugh. There may be other Quakers who knew.'

'I'll speak to them,' said the copper, writing the names in his notebook. He held out the envelope to the guvnor. 'Does this mean anything to you?'

'No,' said the guvnor.

'You're not going to read it?' asked Napper.

The guvnor shook his head.

'Ah,' said Napper. 'You've seen it already. Well, I'll have to get it translated. Must be in African, I suppose.'

PC McDonald returned. 'I've searched every room, sir. There's nobody else here.'

'Right. Go to the offices,' said the detective. 'There'll be some kind of book with the names and addresses of the members. Get the Fowlers, Mrs Stockton-Hugh and Mrs Painter. Find out who's in charge too.'

'Yes, sir,' said the young copper. He looked about sixteen years old.

'After that, you stay here until the police surgeon comes. Tell him I'll see him at the mortuary later. You'll need to give him a hand with the bodies. Now, get me those addresses.'

'Yes, sir,' said the young copper. He looked at Napper but didn't move.

'What is it, McDonald?'

'Stay here on my own, sir?'

'Yes.'

'With the deceased, sir?'

'Yes, with the deceased. What d'you expect them to do, lad? Get up and go home?'

'No, sir,' mumbled the young copper. 'Yes, sir.' He didn't look happy at all.

'And get a brush to that helmet, lad. It looks like you've buttered it.'

'Yes, sir.'

'What are you going to do now, detective?' asked the guvnor.

'I'm going to the Royal Aquarium. They must have an address for Capaldi.'

'Very good,' said the guvnor, buttoning his Donegal at the neck. 'We'll come along, if you don't mind.'

Napper laughed again. 'I'm afraid not, Arrowood. This is a police case now. Leave it with me.'

'But we're employed to protect the Africans for two more nights.'

'You've helped enough already. If you feel guilty, you may return the money to Mrs Fowler. When we find her.'

And with that he whirled on his heel and clattered out into the evening. The constable stood staring at the door, a miserable look on his wet lips.

'Why don't you let me help you find those addresses, lad?' said the guvnor.

'Yes, sir,' said McDonald. 'That'd be best.'

As the lad set off for the office, the guvnor pulled me into the lobby and drew his mouth near. 'Get after Napper,' he whispered. 'Don't let him see you. Hopefully he'll lead you to Capaldi.'

I gained the street just in time to see Napper cross the road down past the fire carts, and from there followed him across Trafalgar Square to Whitehall. Though it was cold and foggy, there were plenty of folk around. Crossing sweepers patrolled each intersection, while gents stepped out the government offices with top hats and shiny bowlers, their carriages waiting on the street to take them to their clubs.

The entrance to the Aquarium was on Totthill Street, just opposite Broad Sanctuary. I watched from across the street as Napper climbed the steps, past the queue of punters waiting to pay their shillings for the evening show. After talking to the gent on the door, he was waved through and disappeared.

'Suicide on the Southend train!' yelled a newspaper seller walking up and down the line of frozen people; 'Get your toffee apples!' cried a thin woman coming behind him with a basket under her arm. 'Get your pippins!' I remembered taking Mrs B to the Aquarium to see Carter the Great in the days before we married. It was a sight to behold: six hundred feet long, with a curved glass ceiling, winter gardens, pools full of fish and a skating rink that my old darling wouldn't try. She loved every minute of that day, and, as the bells of Big Ben sounded eleven, we walked to St James's Park, climbed over the railings and rutted in the sweet summer night. It was the best day of my life. As I stood there alone on the cold pavement, I realized I was smiling to myself. An image came to my mind of how she used to look at me, and I felt the smile fade. I shook my head. When would this wretched sadness leave me?

To move my thoughts on, I read the bills posted along the

wall telling you what awaited inside: the trained cormorants and seals fed three times daily, Captain Swan and his boa constrictors, the Honrey Brothers, Chas Dubois' Grand Promenade Concert, Polichinelle and his Laughing Cat, Professor Stokes Memory Show. Capaldi's Zulus were due to perform at 5.30, 7.30 and 9. There'd be a few unhappy punters in there tonight.

A sudden wind rushed up the street, causing all those waiting in the queue to clutch their hats and gasp. I crossed to the hotel opposite where there was a bit of shelter, and there I stood until Napper came out ten minutes later.

I dipped my head so he wouldn't see my face under my cap, but he crossed the road and walked directly toward me.

'Mr Barnett,' he said. 'Bruno Capaldi lives at 25 Albert Terrace in Stockwell. That's not an invitation for you to visit, I'm just trying to save you the trouble of following me again. I'm going to get a few constables and go there now. If he has the Zulus, I'll free them. Do not interfere. Understand?'

'Yes, sir.'

'Come to Scotland Yard later this evening and I'll fill you in.'

'Thank you, sir.'

He turned and marched toward the river.

Chapter Six

It'd been a real surprise when Isabel moved back to London that summer. She'd left the guvnor a couple of years back and found herself a lawyer in Cambridge, who caught belly cancer and died while his baby Leopold was still in her womb. When she returned to Coin Street, the guvnor's sister Ettie had also just had a baby, and for the first few months it'd worked out fine. They took turns to look after the children, and that meant Ettie could keep helping at Reverend Hebden's mission, where she and the other ladies visited the slums and ran the ragged school. But it had got strained between them over the last few weeks. Arrowood told me they'd been rowing over little things, over the towels and the tea, and that sometimes it'd moved on to the scriptures. When I reached Coin Street later that night, Isabel was vexed.

'Ettie's at a meeting about the medical mission again,' she said as I stepped in. 'I've been here on my own since midday.'

'Is she going to take the job, then?' I asked, gazing down at the two babies lying in their boxes on the table. Reverend Hebden had been raising subscriptions for a medical side to his mission, and he'd offered Ettie a position there to help set it up when enough money came in. At the same time, Isabel had put in her papers for a new scheme at the Hospital for Women to get more ladies trained as doctors, and was waiting to hear if she'd been chosen.

'Heaven knows.' She wiped her hands on her pinny. 'I don't want to look after them both. We'll have to get a wet nurse if I'm chosen for the medical scholarship. That is, if they ever get round to making a decision. I'm beginning to wonder if they've withdrawn the money.'

'Maybe a lot of women applied,' I said.

'I wouldn't be surprised. The suffragists have changed how people think, more's the pity.' She laughed, and it was good to see a little bit of light in her eyes again. 'That didn't come out right, Norman. I meant they probably all sent in their blooming letters as well.' Her face fell again. 'Oh, Lord, I hope they choose me. The more I think about it, the more certain I am I could be a useful doctor.'

I went to make the tea. When I brought in the tray, she was sitting in the good chair reading *Beeton's Medical Dictionary*, a pair of the guvnor's spectacles on her nose. I'd just poured her a mug when he came down the stairs.

'Did Napper find Capaldi?' he asked, cutting a slice from the Christmas cake that lay on the table.

'He gave me the address as long as I didn't follow him,' I answered, pouring him a mug. 'Said we should go to the Yard this evening and he'll tell us what he found. He doesn't seem a bad bloke.'

Arrowood drank down his tea in one. 'Right. Let's get to it.' He turned to his wife. 'Goodnight, my dear.'

'I did ask you not to call me that,' said Isabel, looking up from her book. 'Are you deliberately ignoring me?'

He pulled on his coat with a sigh. 'I'm sorry. It's habit. I'll try to remember.' He kissed little Mercy, little Leo, then straightened, smiling at the sleeping babies. 'Goodnight, my darlings.'

'Why do you do that?' asked Isabel sharply.

'Do what?'

'Kiss Mercy first and Leopold second. You always do it that way.'

'Do I? I don't th—'

'Yes, you do. Doesn't he, Norman?'

'I don't know.'

'He does. Why, William? Why always Mercy first?'

'But I don't—'

'You do. I'm asking you why?'

'But I don't th—'

'Is it because Mercy's your blood?'

'No! You're my wife, and Leo's my son.'

'You'd love him more if Mercy wasn't here. If you didn't have a child of your own blood you'd give him all your infernal love.'

'You're all wrong, Isabel. I didn't even know I kiss her first!'

'Then perhaps it's that primitive inside you that loves her most. You think I betrayed you and you can't forgive him for that. Just like you can't forgive me.'

'But Isabel! It's you who push *me* away! I've tried to be kind ever since you returned, but you don't want me.'

'Because I see that you don't forgive me. Admit it, you don't love me as you did before.'

The guvnor's face crunched up. His brow tightened, his eyes swivelling left and right. I stepped to the door, feeling uncomfortable.

'I do love you, Isabel. But you left me. You took up with

57

another man. I don't know what I feel until I know what you feel. And you just keep pushing me away.'

'Sometimes I think we'd be better off in Norfolk.'

'Please don't say that. I need both my children.'

'Neither are your children, William. What's wrong with you?'

'I don't understand what you're saying.'

She was pale, her face drawn. She pointed at him and said with venom: 'Neither Mercy nor Leo is your child. Now go on, run away to your little games. Try and remember to get those red candles this time. And don't go to the pub again.'

He looked at me, a confused helplessness in his eyes. I took his arm to lead him to the door. As we stepped out into the corridor, I could feel his whole hot body trembling.

Chapter Seven

We had to sit in the waiting area at Scotland Yard for half an hour before Napper came down. All the time, the sergeant at the reception desk stood behind the counter, turning the pages of the *Evening News*. It wasn't a busy night for the coppers.

'We searched Capaldi's house, but there was no sign of them,' said Napper when he finally appeared. It was nine, the gas taps lit along the wall. The detective's hands were in his pockets as he stood before us. One shirt tail hung outside his britches and his eyes were dull with tiredness. He wore no hat, revealing a bare line along the side of his head as if he had a parting, though no comb would do any good on that orange bristle he had for hair. 'The one in charge is Bruno Capaldi. He swore he had nothing to do with it.'

'Any of his men there?' asked the guvnor.

'He lives with his brother, Ermano, and his wife. They didn't say much.'

'How did he react when you told him about the deaths?' asked the guvnor.

'He wasn't too happy – said he'd paid twenty pounds to take over their contract. He blames a rival of his, Madame Delacourte. Have you heard of her?'

'Didn't she manage the bi-penis boy?' asked the guvnor.

'The bi-penis boy?' repeated Napper, his nose wrinkling. 'Not with...'

'Yes. Didn't you see the bills?'

He shook his head. 'She's exhibiting some tribesmen from Borneo in the Egyptian Hall next week. He believes she's trying to do away with the competition.'

The guvnor snorted. 'He thinks she'd kill two people to sell more tickets?'

'That's what he said.'

'Did he have any other theories?'

'He believes it was her. I asked around the detectives upstairs. She does have a reputation. Intimidating the managers of other shows, threatening theatre owners for the best bookings, that sort of thing. There was a case of blackmail, but it was never taken to court. She's a bad lot, but Capaldi's no angel. They've been feuding for years.'

'Are you going to see her?'

Napper nodded, turning his eyes to watch as a huge bear of a man was hauled into the reception by four constables. His arms were shackled to his waist, his ankles in chains. 'Capaldi said the Zulus were always arguing, that sometimes it turned violent.'

'Surely they wouldn't batter Musa's teeth out with a hammer and then shoot Mr Fowler?'

'Well, he believes it was Madame Delacourte, but I wouldn't put it past the Zulus. If they did kill Musa, maybe they shot Mr Fowler as a witness.'

'Has the police surgeon examined the bodies yet?'

'Fowler was killed with a single shot to the heart. We've got the bullet but no gun to compare it to. Musa was strangled after his teeth were knocked out.' Napper stood, looking down on us sat on the bench. The marbles had appeared in his hand, and he was rolling them around in his fingers.

'He wasn't struck anywhere else?'

'Only the mouth.' Napper sighed and when he winced it looked almost like a smile. 'It's queer, right enough. Very bloody queer.'

'We have to catch whoever did this, Napper,' said the guvnor. 'These people are monsters.'

'Perhaps you shouldn't have been handing around guns, Arrowood,' said the detective, glancing at me.

The guvnor dropped his head, his fat right hand clenched on his lap. 'I know,' he said.

I patted his knee. 'We didn't have any other choice,' I told him. 'And it could have been worse for them without the guns. Maybe they escaped, eh?'

'We've been to the Fowler household,' said Napper. 'Mrs Fowler never returned.'

The door swung open again and a constable pushed in a well-dressed woman with a head full of bees. She swayed in the middle of the small waiting area until her eyes got right again. Seeing the guvnor sitting next to me, she dropped herself onto his lap.

'Excuse me, madam!' he squealed. 'Do you mind?'

'Aw,' she cooed as she draped her arm over his shoulder. 'You're a very handsome fellow.'

'Get off him, Ida,' said the constable, pulling her up. 'I got other things to do tonight.'

Ida slapped the guvnor hard on the top of his hat as she got to her feet. 'You wait for me here, Michael,' she slurred.

'I'll be back out in an hour or two, just as soon as they've had their way with me.'

Her corn-pipe cackle echoed around the bare walls. Napper grinned as he helped the constable get her over to the sergeant's desk.

'Here,' said Napper, feeling the bony lump on his neck. 'D'you fancy a mug of ale? I'm about to knock off.'

He went upstairs to get his coat and hat, then took us to a pub down the road. It was a pub I'd been in before one time as I waited for the guvnor to come out of an interrogation. The place was full of coppers, in uniform and plainclothes, and Napper nodded and patted his way through them to get to the bar. I spied a fellow I knew sitting in a booth by the fire: Detective Coyle of the Special Irish Branch. We weren't on friendly terms, and I turned away quick from the ugly bugger, hoping he hadn't seen me.

We squeezed in at the end of a table. I rolled a fag, while the guvnor took out his pipe. Napper drank down half his beer in one.

'The police don't usually want to associate with us, sir,' I said.

'We get a lot of trouble from private agents, Mr Barnett.'

'What makes us different?'

'Just as I said. I saw what happened in Catford.'

'How long have you been a detective?' asked the guvnor, taking a great swallow from his mug. He burped.

'Six years. I was with K division before that. West Ham.' Napper drained the rest of his beer. The guvnor nudged me: I got up to buy another round.

When I got back to the table, they were working their way through a pile of winkles.

'What's the next step, detective?' asked the guvnor, his mouth full. He picked up the mug I'd put before him and sloshed it all down with porter. 'How are you going to find them?'

Napper levered a winkle out of its shell and popped it in his gob. 'It'll be in all the papers tomorrow. We're putting bills up asking for information, and all the police divisions are keeping an eye out too. If they've got any sense they'll be near the docks: they'd stick out like yellow dogs anywhere else. Even so, three Africans and one of them a woman's something you don't even see in Canning Town. Someone must have spotted them. I've asked the superintendent to put up a reward.'

The guvnor nodded as he forked out five winkles and put them one after the other in his mouth. He swept the shells to the floor. 'Any ideas about that letter?'

'We haven't found a translator yet.'

As I listened, I kept one eye on Coyle at the far side of the room. He was half-jiggered, talking loud to his mates. He hadn't noticed me. Maybe it didn't matter. But after what I did to him last time I reckoned maybe it did.

'Are you going to have the Capaldis followed?' asked Arrowood.

'I've been given one PC and told to see if we can find witnesses on St Martin's Lane. If I had another couple I'd follow Capaldi.' He looked at the guvnor and smiled. He looked at me. 'But I don't. They been cutting the money for policing these last few years. Ain't enough of us for all the crimes in this cesspool.'

The guvnor nodded. 'That's why you offered us a drink.'

'Yes, Mr Arrowood. The way I see it you've been paid for one more day.'

The guvnor nodded, a tight, unhappy smile on his face. The winkles were making him sweat. 'I like you, sir. Most other detectives would tell us to keep clear.'

'I need your help.' He nodded at our mugs. 'You want another?'

'Perhaps just one more,' said the guvnor. 'We've got things to do tonight. And perhaps a brandy and hot water to go with it?'

Ten minutes later we rose to leave. Before stepping onto the pavement, I took one more look at Coyle on the other side of the room. His mates were silent. He was watching me. They were all watching me.

Bruno Capaldi lived in a tall house on a terraced street in Stockwell. The guvnor's plan was to take it in turns watching the door, following anybody who came out in case they led us to the Africans. I arrived about half ten that night. Neddy, the little lad who helped us now and then, would take over about five in the morning, then the guvnor from midday.

The buildings on the street weren't gentry rich, but they were well-painted and lit with electricity, with maybe a cook and a maid in each one. In a few the curtains were still open, and here and there could be seen a Christmas tree, dripping with baubles and sweets. About a hundred yards down from Capaldi's house was a square with a little park, a great plane tree at each corner. There were some bushes to provide a bit of cover, so I tucked myself behind them and waited.

Over the next few hours, carriages pulled up at some of the other houses, letting out folk back from the theatres and dining clubs, but nobody went in or out of Capaldi's house that evening. Soon after the bells of St Stephen's sounded midnight, the windows in all the other houses had gone dark. Just the Capaldis' lights stayed on.

A glow from the moon only just made itself known through the low grey cloud of smoke as hung over London that night. Rats moved about in the bushes, ran along the gutters and climbed down the drains. A fox or two came and stood in the road, staring at me, then went hopping along to their dinner appointments. I paced up and down the edge of the green, puffing out my white breath, half-hid by the bushes. I had on two waistcoats, a thick overcoat, a scarf Ettie'd bought me the Christmas before, but my fingers were numb and my toes ached with the cold. How I yearned for a chair and a nice coal fire.

About three, a few workers came walking along, heading for the Locomotive Works at Nine Elms, I reckoned. By five, deliveries of milk and coal were arriving in the dark. A few folk in suits and overcoats stepped out and walked down to the trams on Clapham Road. Nobody came out the Capaldi house.

I spotted Neddy at the far end of Albert Terrace about six, skipping down the street like he had no cares in the world. I waved and he broke into a run.

'Hello, mate,' I said. 'You're an hour late.'

'I had to wait for the baker's to open. I needed get some bread in for Harriet.' He kicked out at the bushes. 'I gave Ma the money for it last night but she went and spent it all on herself.'

Harriet was his little sister. She had a bend in her leg and was slow to speak, so Neddy and his older sister, Abigail, looked after her. His ma seemed to love her gin more than she loved her kids.

'You didn't just oversleep?' I asked him.

'I wish. I can't blooming trust her with anything.'

He was so put out I thought he must have been telling the truth. Neddy was about eleven or twelve but small for his age. This was the first winter he'd got long trousers, rough, thick things run through with repairs stitched in every type of wool. A scarf I hadn't seen afore was wound round his neck and over the top of his head, with a ragged little sailor's cap jammed on the top.

He pulled a sooty muffin from his pocket. 'I brought it for you.'

'Thanks, lad. I'm hungry as hell.' The muffin was a bit stale, a bit dusty, but he knew I loved muffins. I pointed at Capaldi's place. 'That's the house there. Twenty-five.'

'Blue door?'

'That's right. If anyone comes out, you get after them, but don't let them see you. Did the guvnor give you any money in case you need to take a tram?'

Neddy nodded. He put on the guvnor's voice: '*Find out where they go and write the address down. Don't get seen. Don't try anything else.* I have done this before, y'know, sir.'

We fell silent as a couple of laundrywomen passed on the other side of the railings.

'These are nasty blokes, Neddy. You got to take care.'

He looked at me like I was a fool, his missing front teeth making his expression only more insulting.

'Get a boy to bring us a note if you find out anything.'

'What if it's a servant comes out?'

I thought about it for a minute or two. 'Don't bother with servants. Mr Arrowood'll be here at twelve. You can go home then.'

'I'm on the muffins at one.'

'Will you be warm enough?'

'Reckon so.'

'Keep moving, but don't get closer than here. Don't leave the park. You can sit in that bush. And keep hid if you see a copper. Don't want them thinking you're planning a click.'

'I'll be right.'

I shook his bony hand and walked off towards Clapham Road. A few moments later, a bloke on a bicycle entered the road. He stopped pedalling, his eyes fixed on me like he was trying to decide something. His face was square, his nose wide and flat, and he wore a flash overcoat buttoned up to his chin. A rubbery scar like a worm ran over one eye and disappeared into his ear-hole. My hand clenched in my pocket, ready in case he should stop. But just as we were level he seemed to change his mind and began to pedal again.

Something about that bloke was wrong. I watched him reach the square and turn down toward where Neddy was hid. As he reached the gate, he got off and laid his bike against the railings. I started walking back to the park, my boots crunching on the cinders. In the dark of the winter morning, I saw him step through the gate and disappear, hidden by the bushes. I broke into a run.

'Oi!' came Neddy's voice, then a squeal of pain.

I reached the gate just in time to see the bloke dragging Neddy out onto the grass, one hand pulling his hair, the other twisting his wrist up his back. The lad was trying to get free, swinging out with his other arm and stamping on the bloke's foot. I leapt forward.

Suddenly the man lost patience and lashed out, striking

Neddy across the face with the back of his hand. I flew at him, my hands around his throat, my knee in his ballocks.

He fell, pulling Neddy down with him and me on top. I remember smelling dog shit, then patchouli, then feeling the wind knocked out of me as I landed on his upturned elbow. As I gasped for breath, I glanced another bloke running up behind, a cosh raised in the air. It landed on my skull.

Chapter Eight

I came to out of a sunlit dream and for a moment felt joyful. Then I felt the pain all over my head and the cold floor on my cheek. I opened my eyes, seeing stone flags, the grease-spattered feet of a dresser, rat pellets along the skirting. I shut my eyes against the sickening dizziness, knowing the Capaldis had me but not clear enough in my head to be able to do anything about it. I felt something nudge my back.

'Wake up, Muggsy,' said a low voice.

I opened my eyes again, pushing myself up so I was sitting, my back against a cold door.

We were in a gloomy basement kitchen. A bloke on a wooden chair watched me with small eyes, a pistol in his hand. The right side of his face was purple and yellow from a recent battering. He was bald on top, an edge of oiled black hair round the sides, a neat moustache. He wore a brown suit, a thick red waistcoat, a green tie. Neddy sat on another chair, his hands under his thighs, his cap on his knee. He didn't look hurt.

'You all right, mate?' I asked him, feeling something stab the back of my head with each word.

Neddy nodded. 'You been out a few hours. Does it hurt?'

I shook my head. It wasn't a good idea.

'Who are you?' asked the bloke.

'Name's Barnett,' I said, touching the lump on the back of my head. The hair was wet and sticky. 'You?'

'Capaldi. Why was you watching us?'

'Ermano Capaldi?' I asked. It was a guess.

He nodded. 'Why?' he asked again. Upstairs I heard a door close and footsteps on a wooden floor.

'I'm trying to find the Zulus,' I said. I reckoned there was no point hiding what we were doing; there couldn't be many other reasons to be watching them. 'You know where they are?'

'We're trying to find them too. What d'you want them for?'

'Take me to Bruno and I'll tell you.'

He didn't even think about it. He got to his feet and looked at Neddy. 'You come too, Topolino. Chop chop.'

Neddy jumped to the floor and held out his hand to help me. Soon as I was on my feet the dizzy feeling came back, and I had to grab the table till it passed. Ermano waited till I'd opened my eyes again.

'You can walk?' he asked. For a bloke who'd just coshed me, he didn't seem too bad.

He directed us up the narrow stairs to the floor above, where the corridor widened. It wasn't bright, just a bit of daylight tipping in from the fanlight above the front door. A long Turkish carpet went along the hallway, the walls papered in dark wallpaper with purple and pink flowers.

As Ermano opened the door to the front room, I saw his hair formed a thin pigtail at the back that fell just over his collar. He led us in. It was a billiard room, a full-size table taking up the centre. There were electric lights, and a fire blazed and crackled in the grate.

A shortish man leant over the far side of the table lining

up a shot. He had no moustache, his thin black hair smoothed over his balding scalp. His hands were tiny, his fingers little stubs that seemed too small to be useful. A boy of fifteen or sixteen in a checked lounge suit stood by the window, a cue in his hands. Sitting on a high-backed chair was a woman of forty or fifty. A pair of marbled spectacles sat on her crooked nose.

'Mr Barnett,' said Ermano. 'The boy's Neddy. They're looking for the Africans.'

'Ah, yes,' answered the short bloke, staring at me hard. While Ermano's voice was pure East End, this one spoke like he'd been schooled at Winchester. He straightened. 'Ralf, go upstairs.'

'But we're halfway through the game, Dad.'

'I need to talk to this man. We'll play later.'

Ralf looked at me, his hands tight on his cue. He still had child fat around his cheeks, but his eyes were bright and eager, his hair combed into a wave. A few freckles were dotted across his cheek. The boy was turning into a handsome devil.

'Can't I just stay and listen? You said I should learn.'

'No, darling,' said the woman. She looked Italian but spoke like a Scouser. 'Do as Dad tells you.'

Ralf looked one last time at his old man, who shook his head. He leant the cue against the wall and left. Ermano closed the door behind him.

'So, you know who I am?' asked the short man.

'Bruno Capaldi,' I said.

'And you know why I want the Africans back, I suppose.' He leant over the table and lined up his shot again. 'But why do *you* want to find them, Mr Barnett?' He cracked the cue ball. It hit the red, bounced off the baulk, then touched the other white, leaving both on the cushion. The woman stood and took up Ralf's cue.

'I'm a private investigative agent,' I said. 'They came to me for protection. From you. Said you'd kill one of them if they didn't perform.'

He laughed, a wet crackle like a frying sausage. 'Have you ever worked with performers, Norman?'

I shook my head. I didn't know how he got my first name, and I didn't particularly care.

'I just wanted to frighten them. I've been paying their food and lodging for weeks. They signed a contract.'

'Well, I was paid to look after them. Now two men are dead.'

Neddy was over by the cue rack, fingering the polished sticks. I got out the way as the woman leant over the table, lined up her shot, and prodded the white hard with her cue. The ball hurtled down the green cloth and hit the red at an angle, sending it into the pocket. She gave a grunt of joy, then stood by Bruno, her arm around his shoulder.

'It wasn't us,' said Bruno. 'But we do want to find them.'

'So do the police.'

'We all want to, old chap. It's for their own good. There are so many dangers in the city, and they're not used to it.' As he spoke, his words slipped here and there, and I knew he wasn't all he was pretending to be. 'Tell me, what do you think happened, Norman?'

The woman lit a fag, fixing me with her bloodshot eyes.

'Could be you and your men came in and threatened them. Someone took a shot and someone else shot back. Maybe you're holding the others somewhere, maybe they escaped.'

He shut his eyes and twitched his head. 'And if it wasn't us? What other theories do you have?'

'They might have done it to each other.'

'What about your boss. Mr Arrowood, isn't it? What does he think?'

'That's all we got,' I said. I hadn't told them about the guvnor either. They must have got it out of Neddy.

Bruno picked up a small silver platter stacked with Turkish Delight. He took a dusty cube between his two middle fingers and dropped it into his mouth. As he chewed he held the tray out to Neddy. 'Boy?'

Neddy stepped over, looked at the pile of sweets, then up at Capaldi. I knew Neddy, and I knew how filthy his little fingers always were. I also knew how he loved sweet things.

'Go on, boy,' said Bruno, his voice now light and bright. 'Have two.'

Neddy snatched a couple of blocks. One he put in his mouth, the other in his coat pocket. Bruno nodded at me.

I went over and took a cube. It was like a jelly but smelt of a flower. There was a nut inside. Wasn't too bad, I tell you.

After putting the platter down, he chalked his cue and blew on it.

'Those Zulus owe us,' said the woman, leaning over the corner of the table and giving Neddy a poke in the belly with her cue. 'And, as the Lord is my witness, they do need us. They can't handle their liquor, and the girl don't understand contracts. We looked after them like our own children, and they don't appreciate it.'

'Mrs Capaldi spoils them,' said Bruno.

She smiled. 'Well, maybe a little.'

73

'Why are they so important to you?' I asked, trying not to show the anger that had risen in me. The way they talked about those Africans wasn't so far from how a lot of the toffs of this city talked about the likes of me, folk with the mark of the workhouse and the South London slums, and it vexed me, I can tell you.

'If you go out on the street in London, you can see black men,' said Bruno. He sipped his tea, his little finger pointing in the air. 'Medical students, priests, beggars, you'll see one every week. But Zulus? No. Never. People will pay to see a Zulu.'

'You know they're amaQwabe, sir? Not Zulus.'

He looked at me for a moment. 'Are they? Well, nobody's ever heard of amaQwabe. People'll pay for Zulus. And we're going to take them all over the country, then the continent. Maybe we'll even take them to Barnum's American Museum. Everybody wants to see the great warriors who've caused such trouble to the British, and the show is quite educational, you know. The audience see stick fighting, dagger throwing, native cooking and dancing. You know the giya dance? It'll scare you witless! We'll sell out everywhere, Norman. This is why we don't like our Zulus to wander about getting in trouble. We give them good rooms, good food. We look after them. And, as I said, we've invested a good deal to bring them here.' He pointed at a pile of pamphlets stacked on the desk. 'Look at all those, full colour. If they don't work, how do I pay for those?'

'So you find out anything, come tell us,' said Mrs Capaldi.

'Why would we do that, ma'am?' I asked.

She picked up a cube of Turkish Delight and held it to Bruno's lips. Her husband bit off half the cube and smiled at her as he chewed.

'Just tell us, Norman,' she went on. 'If we find out you know something and didn't tell us… Well.' She popped the other half in her mouth. 'We'll slaughter you.'

Bruno laughed his wet laugh again. 'Slaughter!' he gasped in delight. Ermano grinned, stroking his belly with his pistol.

Bruno was still laughing while he lined up his next shot. 'Slaughter!' he cackled as he struck the cue ball.

The woman bent her neck, looking at us side-on, still smiling.

I took Neddy's shoulder and pushed him to the door.

'Goodbye, Norman,' said Bruno as we stepped into the hall. 'We will see you very soon.'

As we walked to the front door, we heard the crack of the billiard balls striking each other, and the three of them began to laugh again.

Chapter Nine

'You want me to stay?' asked Neddy as we walked down to Clapham Road. 'I can go up the other end.'

'Too dangerous, mate. They know you now.'

'That's what I thought. What was the sweets?'

'Turkish Delight.'

He said nothing for a few steps. I was moving awkward: my legs were stiff, the cold still in the bones. My head was thudding from Ermano's cosh, so I popped into a little apothecary we were passing and bought a box of Black Drop, swallowing a couple as we walked on.

'Is it dear?' asked Neddy.

'What?'

'Turkish Delight.'

'Too much for you, mate. Maybe when you're a rich man you can afford it.'

'Did you hear about the lady got her foot boiled in *Spears and Pond*?'

I laughed again. 'Go on. Tell me.'

I listened to his story as we walked along Clapham Road, busy with people hurrying along the pavement as trams and buses passed them on their way to Wimbledon and the Elephant.

'I will get my money, won't I?' he asked when he'd finished. 'Even though I weren't there long?'

'You'll get it all, mate. What did they ask you when I was out?'

'What I was doing there, who sent me, who you were. Mr Arrowood told me to tell them the truth.'

'Good, lad. You did right.'

'We getting the bus?'

'Not this time, Neddy.'

When we got to Coin Street, the guvnor was eating a kidney pudding and watching Isabel rifle through his psychology books. The fire was unlit and they were both wrapped up against the morning cold, she in two shawls, he with his scarf and Donegal coat.

Isabel held out her hand to Neddy and pulled him in for a hug. Her eyes were red and swollen, her smile sad.

'Back so soon?' asked the guvnor.

'They spotted us,' I told him. 'Came just after Neddy got there. Two blokes.'

'Sorry, sir,' said Neddy, picking at a darn in his britches.

'What did you do?' barked the guvnor. 'Walk past the house?'

'I didn't, sir. I came from the other way.'

'Think, boy,' he said, the anger gone from his voice as soon as it'd appeared. He pushed the spoon in his mouth and spoke as he chewed. 'How could they have seen you? This is important. To be a detective you must learn from your mistakes.'

'I come up from Clapham Road and went to the square where Mr Barnett was. Just like you told me. He said to hide in the bushes.'

'That must be when they saw you.'

'It wasn't his fault,' I said, lowering my aching bones onto the stool. 'They'd gone round the back, came in the other side. Must have already left the house by the time Neddy arrived. It was me they spotted.'

'You weren't careful enough.'

'No.'

He sighed hard through his swollen hooter, looking long at me. 'Damn it,' he muttered at last.

'Have you seen my medical dictionary?' asked Isabel, pulling out the drawers in the dresser and poking about.

'No,' said the guvnor. 'Did you look upstairs?'

'Of course I've looked upstairs!' she snapped. 'You didn't pawn it did you, William?'

'What do you think I am, Isabel? I know you're studying it.'

She stepped back to his books and pulled one out. 'Where are your eyeglasses?'

'On the mantel,' said the guvnor, shoving the last bit of pudding in his gob and sweeping the crumbs to the floor.

'William! How many times must I tell you not to do that? It brings in the mice.'

'I'll clear it up,' he said, turning to me. 'So, they caught you. And then?'

I told him everything that happened. I knew I'd get a grilling, it was the same every time. He asked Neddy too. When we got to the end of our reports, one of the babies started making a noise upstairs. Isabel looked at the ceiling, her hands gripping the black book in her lap. Then the wailing began, and, moments later, a second little voice joined in.

'I only just got them to sleep,' she said, getting to her feet. 'They caught a fever last night. They just won't settle.'

I went upstairs to help her. The bedroom window was open, the two babies lying in their boxes under thick blankets. Their faces were red and wet with tears. Leopold's eyes were shut as he wailed, a lick of black hair stuck to his forehead; Mercy was staring at the yellowed ceiling, her fists clenched and pink, her bottom lip hiding her top. Her little body did a shiver.

'Why don't you lift the blankets?' I asked. 'They're stewing.'

'The doctor said they must be kept hot to beat the infection.'

'Does that really help?'

She put her hand to her forehead. 'I don't know. Ettie agrees and she was a nurse. They want the windows open for fresh air, but say the babies must be kept warm. It's so difficult.'

We carried the boxes down and put them on the table. The guvnor rose to have a look, shaking his head as the babies choked and sobbed.

'You want me to bring them a muffin?' asked Neddy as Isabel covered them again.

'No, thank you, dear,' said Isabel, patting his hand. 'They're too young.'

'Did you try mustard?' I asked. Mercy really didn't look good, and it pinched my heart to see her that way. Her body gave another little shiver and she fell silent. Then the crying began again.

'Yes,' answered Isabel. 'I'll put more on later. I told Ettie not to take them out yesterday, but she knew best, her and that Campbell woman. Oh, Lord, they're so unhappy. What are we to do?'

'Shall we wet them?' asked the guvnor, bringing a bowl of water from the scullery.

Though it was cold, Isabel peeled off their blankets and

raised their dresses, revealing their glistening pink bodies and grey nappies. Leopold had some red spots across his chest. The guvnor and Neddy wiped their miserable faces and patted their bodies with the wet cloths. As the babies quietened, the guvnor began to sing to them in a soft voice:

O where are you going, my pretty maiden fair,
With your red rosy cheeks and your coal-black hair?

It was a duet you'd hear in many a pub around London on a Saturday night. From the chair by the window, Isabel sang the next lines, her voice as gentle as the guvnor's:

I'm going a-milking, kind sir, says she,
And it's strawberry leaves makes the milkmaids fair.

With the cool cloths on their skin and the sweet melody, the babies fell silent. The guvnor sang the next lines:

Oh, may I go with you, my pretty little dear,
With your red rosy cheeks and your coal-black hair?

Then Isabel answered again, the faintest smile appearing on her tired face:

Oh, you may go with me, kind sir, says she,
And it's strawberry leaves makes the milkmaids fair.

And so they continued for several verses. Then, while still singing, the guvnor put down his cloth and wrapped Leopold back up, while Neddy did the same with Mercy. Arrowood straightened, rocking from one foot to the other, gazing at the babies as he sang:

Oh say, will you marry me, my pretty little dear,
With your red rosy cheeks and your coal-black hair:

And Isabel replied, her eyes shut:

Oh yes, if you please, kind sir, says she,
And it's strawberry leaves makes the milkmaids fair.

And even before she'd ended her line, the guvnor started his turn, this time the words trembling, his throat tightening:

Oh, will you be constant, my pretty little dear,
With your red rosy cheeks and your coal-black hair?

Isabel clasped her hands in her lap. The room was silent, the babies tense and waiting. Through my head ran the lines she wasn't singing:

Oh, that I cannot promise you, kind sir, says she,
And it's strawberry leaves makes the milkmaids fair.

Then, as if she hadn't missed her part, the guvnor answered:

Then I won't marry you, my pretty little dear,
With your red rosy cheeks and your coal-black hair.

He straightened. The air was cold and still. Neddy looked from Isabel to the guvnor, then to me, a question on his brow. I shook my head, holding my finger to my lips. Mercy croaked. Arrowood gazed out the window, his lips muttering something silent, then he marched through to the scullery and out the back door to the outhouse. Isabel raised her hand to her brow, and I saw the glister of a tear in the corner of her eye. Those last verses were too close to their own history, and I couldn't help but wonder if he sang it to hurt her.

Now that silence had returned, Mercy began to cry again. Moments later Leopold started up too, joining her in their own infernal duet.

'Will you go out and get me some Godfrey's Cordial, Neddy?' asked Isabel, wiping her eyes. She reached for her purse.

'I thought you didn't use it?' I asked over the storm of unhappiness.

'Ettie says we use it too much, but they need to sleep, Norman.'

I went along with Neddy to the apothecary, glad to get out of the din for a while. On the way back, I took him into a coffee shop for a bit of fruit cake, hoping Isabel and the guvnor would take the chance to talk things over. There was a lot between them that they were afraid to bring out in the open, and sometimes it seemed they just wanted to hurt each other.

By the time I returned, Arrowood was there with Mercy in his arms, pacing the floor, making low buzzing noises. She'd calmed a bit, but was gasping and grunting like she was about to go curly again. Upstairs, I could hear the sound of Isabel's footsteps, no doubt doing the same. Leopold had quieted too.

I put the kettle on the boiler and a few minutes later had

four mugs of tea ready. I found half a box of cream crackers and brought them through as well. Isabel had come down and was dropping a bit of the Godfrey's Cordial into Mercy's mouth. Leopold slept peaceful in his box.

'You'd better not tell Ettie you've done that,' said Arrowood.

'I know, William.' She stoppered the vial and hid it on the shelf behind one the books. The silence in the room was thick and lovely, and we sat for some time, drinking our tea.

'I don't like to see them ill,' said the guvnor at last. 'Poor little mites.'

'It'll break soon.' Isabel's face was as drawn as the guvnor's.

'You mustn't tell Ettie you gave them that soother,' he said again.

Instead of answering, Isabel smiled sadly at me. 'You'd better go and get some sleep, Norman. You look exhausted.'

Chapter Ten

I wandered home, cold and aching, and was looking forward to my bed when I passed the pub on Great Guildford Street where Molly worked. It was almost midday. Before I knew what I was doing, I'd stepped inside.

A bloke was kneeling on the floor before the fire, cleaning out the ash with a rusty little shovel. There was a hole the size of a penny in one of his soles. A toddler stood next to him, his pink hand on the bloke's back.

He turned his head when he heard my boots.

'Is Molly here?' I asked.

'She's sick.'

'What's up with her?'

'Message said she'd explain tomorrow,' he said, getting to his feet. 'Can I get you something?'

I shook my head, feeling uneasy. In a job like that you came in when you were sick. There were so many folk looking for work you couldn't risk it. You only stayed at home if you couldn't walk. Or if you had something on your boss.

We were back at Scotland Yard at five that evening. It was already dark on the Embankment, though the streets were crowded with vehicles and the river still busy with barges and steamers. Napper'd left a message at the front desk, telling us he'd be there at seven, so we went to a pub down the road, avoiding the one where the ogre Coyle drank with his mates. At seven we were back. A PC led us up two flights of stairs to an office where Napper sat at a desk. He beckoned us over, asking:

'What did you discover?' He wore the same suit, the same tie, the same shirt as the day before. Eight desks stood in the room, only one other being used. Three bowlers hung on the wall. Two chairs sat by the desk, waiting for us.

He leant back and crossed an ankle over his knee. As we told him about the Capaldis, he glanced at the copper on the next desk and exchanged some kind of look.

'So you can't follow them now, is that it?' he asked when we'd finished.

'They know me,' I said. 'And there's nowhere else to watch the house from. It's either the park or standing in plain sight. It ain't a busy road, and they'll be looking out in case there's anyone there now.'

'That makes things difficult,' said Napper, a curl to his lip.

'There is a way,' said the guvnor, leaning forward with both hands open. 'Get an officer in an upper room of one the houses down the road. Plainclothes. Better still, two officers so that one can follow anyone who leaves while the other stays watching.'

'I've only been given one constable. I need him.'

'Two murders isn't enough to get another officer?'

'Not for my superintendent, no.'

The guvnor sighed. 'Did you speak to Madame Delacourte?'

'Not yet. There's only so much I can do with one PC, Arrowood.'

'We'll go and see her.'

'Leave that to me,' answered Napper sharply. 'I want to search the premises. I'll get a warrant.'

86

'Mrs Fowler didn't appear?'

'No. She must have been taken too.'

The guvnor grunted. 'What did you find out in St Martin's Lane? Any witnesses?'

'A few of the printers said they saw two Africans running down towards Trafalgar Square. A man and a woman.'

'Being chased?'

He shrugged. 'They didn't know. It happened as they were escaping the fire. There was bedlam on the street.'

'Could the fire have been started deliberately as a cover?'

Napper shook his head. 'The engine driving the rotary thing exploded. Seems the workers had warned the owner about it a few times recently. The thing kept blocking.'

'Did the ones who saw the Africans running also see Mrs Fowler?'

'They only reported the two of them, but she could have been there. Folk were pouring out of all the buildings nearby lest the flames caught.'

'Where was the last point the Africans were seen running?' asked the guvnor.

'Just past the printworks, opposite the theatre. Heading towards the river.'

'Did you question the theatre staff?'

'They were watching the fire. None of them saw the Africans. We've questioned everyone we could find along that stretch.'

'How far down did your officer go?'

'Down to the bank on the corner.'

'Not Trafalgar Square or the Strand?'

Napper shook his head. 'There are three roads out of St Martin's Place, and those divide into eleven more. We can't check all of them. And Trafalgar Square's just a moving mass of people.'

'What about the vagrants who sleep there?'

Napper shook his head again. 'They're always on the move.'

'They have their favourite places. And what about the station? And the barracks?'

'Listen, Arrowood,' said Napper, a flush coming to his forehead. His finger rose to the knob on his neck. 'If I had twenty men and a month, perhaps I could've done all of those things. I've one officer and the murders were yesterday. So don't take that tone with me.'

'Three Africans in a mostly white city, Napper!' exclaimed the guvnor. 'Somebody's seen them after they left St Martin's Lane. We just have to find who.'

'Why, thank you, Mr Holmes. I'd never have thought of that.'

'Don't compare me to that charlatan, Napper.'

'Then don't tell me my job, Arrowood.'

I took the guvnor's arm, warning him to calm down. He had a habit of getting emotional when he dealt with coppers, and it never helped our work when he did. It was one of my jobs to keep the peace. 'Don't mind him, detective,' I said to Napper. 'Mr Arrowood gets too close, especially when someone's been killed. Is there anything you want us to do tonight?'

'How about *you* go and question the vagrants?' said Napper a bit too quick, almost like he'd planned it.

'That all right, sir?' I asked the guvnor.

He nodded his potato head, his fleshy lips sealed tight.

'Right,' said Napper, then sealed his lips tight too. They looked at each other with a bitter curiosity. Whatever love was between them was fading fast.

Chapter Eleven

The streetlamps cast a hazy glow over the frozen fountains of Trafalgar Square. Black pigeons swarmed across the paving, drawn in by a couple of shuffling feeders wrapped in wool and canvas. Round the edge of the square queued buses heavy with Londoners and wagons stacked with barrels and Christmas trees, pulled by slave-horses in one or other stage of ruin. A few horseless carriages had appeared on the roads that year and, though they made an awful noise, I couldn't help but think the sooner they replaced those poor beasts the better.

'Why the hell did you sing that song this morning?' I asked the guvnor as we waited for a chance to cross the road. 'Aren't things hard enough for Isabel without you blaming her for your marriage?'

'I didn't do it on purpose, Norman,' he said, a twitch to his cheek. 'I only wanted to soothe the children.'

'You should have stopped.'

'But I didn't remember how it ended until I was singing that line asking the milkmaid if she'd be constant. I don't think Isabel realized until then either.'

'I think you wanted to give her a dig.'

He blew his nose. 'It's so very hard all of us living together. She tells me our marriage is over, but that's all she'll say, and I don't know if she really means it. Oh, Norman, it's unbearable. She sits across from me as my love eats away at my guts like a blooming worm. And the way she acts, sometimes I think I actually dislike her. But how can she think straight with those two babies? And Ettie leaves her to look after Mercy too often. It isn't fair.' His jowls drooped, his dark lips in a pout. He dragged his walking stick back and forth along the edge of the pavement. 'I felt awful singing that last verse, but I thought it'd be worse if I stopped. It'd look as if I only chose the song to hurt her. I ought to have apologized, but I can't bear to face it head on, damn it. My heart would break if she told me to leave. I love those children.'

'She wouldn't throw you out. She needs you to bring home the money at least.'

'What if she gets the medical scholarship? And Ettie's going to start working as a deaconess for the mission. She says Hebden will be ready to start paying her soon. They won't need my money then.'

'Ettie'd never forgive her if she made you leave.'

'She might ask Ettie to leave as well. Isabel owns those rooms.'

I shook my head. He was facing the traffic but looking at me from the corner of his eye. 'I know things are overheated at home, William, but you surely know your wife better than that. She'd never do it.'

'I thought I knew her before she made love to a lawyer and set up home with him while we were still married.'

'You made life impossible for her.'

'I know, damn it!' he barked. 'You remind me of it often enough, for God's sake. But she fell in love with that scoundrel. That's what I can't get over. She gave him love that was mine.'

'Your marriage was over.'

'Was it? Who's to say that it wouldn't have been revived in a year or two?'

'I don't know, William,' I said, feeling tuckered out from thinking about it all.

He looked across the road at Nelson's Column rising in the sky. 'When this case is over I'm going to take her to the new show at the Polytechnic on Regent Street.'

'The moving pictures?'

'They say it's like magic. We need to make some new memories.'

'Heather, sir?' said a little girl of ten years or so. She stopped by the guvnor's side, holding out a little bunch. 'Lucky heather?'

The branches were dried and dead, with no flowers on them. You couldn't even say for sure it was heather. The guvnor got out a farthing and took the bits of stick. The girl scampered off into the evening as I felt the lump on my head. It was starting to crust over. I got out my box of Black Drop and swallowed another couple.

'We've only been paid for one more night,' I said. 'What are we going to do after that?'

'We're going to find the killer,' he said firmly. 'I promised Musa and I won't let him down. I just wish Napper was more thorough.'

'Don't make an enemy of him. He's only got one man to help him.'

He tapped his stick on his boot, pondering.

'This traffic seems to get worse every year,' he said at last, throwing the heather sticks into the gutter.

Finally, there was a space and we hurried across to the paved square. Dark bundles lay here and there in the corners and on the benches, poor souls trying to steal a little kip before the next copper came to move them along. By the nearest sleeper lay a bull mastiff, who looked up as we approached. The guvnor pushed me forward.

'Evening, mate,' I said.

The dark figure on the bench moved a bit. All that poked out from the rough blanket was a pair of old boots.

I gave it a prod.

'Mate. Can we have a quick word?'

The lump made a twist and a face appeared.

'What is it?' The woman was somewhere between forty and sixty, I'd guess, her face grubby and lined. It wasn't easy to see in the dim light.

'We're looking for some Africans, missus. Might have come this way yesterday around midday. You see anything?'

'I wasn't here,' she said, then pulled the blanket down over her face.

We had no luck with the next one, nor the next, and on it went round the square. Thirteen unlucky buggers sleeping out on that freezing December night. As we walked towards St Martin-in-the-Fields, the pigeons scattered then immediately fell back to earth to peck at the wash of bread thrown by the feeders. Moments later a group of soldiers marched across the square on their way to Soho, sending the birds up in the air again.

We crossed Charing Cross Road to the church, where a few more homeless souls lay on the steps beneath posters for the carol services they were having over the weekend. The first we reached was a young woman with two little kids clutched to her breast, the three of them wrapped in what looked like a bit of a barge sail. All of them were awake, both kiddies whimpering.

'Good evening, madam,' said the guvnor. 'Could I ask you a question?'

'D'you have any money so I can buy food for my children, sir?' she asked, her voice soft and well-spoke.

'Of course,' answered the guvnor, fetching his purse from his waistcoat and handing her a tuppence. 'How long have you been sleeping here, if I may ask?'

'Too long, thank you, sir,' she said, taking the coin.

'Don't you have anyone who could help you?'

'No, sir. We've nobody.'

'I'm sorry to hear that.'

'I'm sure you are, sir.'

'You sound vexed with me, madam. I don't know why.'

'I'm vexed with everyone except these two,' said the woman, her voice softening. 'But I know my situation isn't your fault.'

'You wouldn't consider the workhouse?'

'Would you?'

He shook his head and smiled at her. 'Tell me, were you here yesterday about midday?'

She nodded. 'But it wasn't me. There's another young mother who I've seen around. I think that's who you're looking for.'

'No, no. I'm not looking for a woman. I'm looking for two or three Africans who ran down from that road yesterday afternoon. I'm trying to find them.'

'A man and a woman?'

'Yes, madam.'

'What d'you want with them?'

93

'We're private agents,' said the guvnor. 'They hired us to protect them, but something happened when we were away. We need to find them. Are you sure it was only two?'

'I think so, but it was busy. There was a fire up there.'

'Could you describe them?'

'The man was quite broad, like you, sir,' she said, nodding at me. 'Dark suit. No beard.'

'Young or old?' asked the guvnor.

'Thirty or forty. The woman was short. She had a brown coat.'

'Did you see a young lad?'

She shook her head.

'Which way did they go?'

The infant in her left arm groaned and coughed. She drew back to see its face. 'Kingsley? What's wrong, love?'

She gazed at him for a few moments, until he took hold of her shawl with his little fists and buried his head in her neck.

'We watched them.' She squeezed the older child in her right arm. The girl was about three or four. 'Ivy'd never seen an African. She was beside herself.' And despite all her misfortune the mother smiled at the memory. 'They ran down Duncannon Street.'

'Was there a white woman with them?'

'I didn't see one, but it was so busy.'

'Was anybody chasing them?'

She shook her head. 'I don't think so. Oh, perhaps. There was a policeman running that way.'

'Are you sure?'

'He was running. I don't know if he was chasing them. I just saw him run past.' As she spoke, the baby Kingsley started to make the most unholy noise, a terrible bubbling cough that turned into a shriek.

'Oh darling,' whispered the mother, stroking the boy's hair, which was knotted and oily. 'He started making this noise yesterday. I don't know what it is.'

The baby kept making the noise, jerking back and forth against her breast. Then all of a sudden he let out a dull gasp and a big clog of mucus oozed out of his mouth.

The child's heavy head tipped and fell forward like he'd gone to sleep.

The mother cried out, pulling his head up again, but the boy made no response.

'What is it, darling?' she asked. 'What is it? What is it, darling?'

The guvnor got to his knees, feeling for the baby's pulse as the mother moaned and pulled both kids tight to her chest. Eventually he looked up at me and shook his head.

The little girl now began to wail.

The guvnor put his hand on the mother's shoulder. 'My dear,' he said as they cried. 'My dear.'

He looked back at me, his eyes asking me what he should do.

'The Woman's Hospital?' I suggested.

He stood and hailed a cab. I gave the driver the instructions as he helped the mother up. She said nothing. When she was seated, the little girl aside her and the baby's body still wrapped to her breast, I folded her sheet of canvas and put it at her feet.

'I'll make sure she gets there safely,' said the guvnor, climbing up the steps with a groan. He fell heavily on the seat beside her. 'Talk to these other people and meet me in the Lamb and Flag in an hour.'

When the cab was gone, I spoke to the other folk huddled on the church steps, but nobody'd seen the Africans. From there I walked down Duncannon Street. I talked to a coffee man, a girl selling Christmas baubles, a coster and his son with a cart of oranges, but still nothing. I had more luck with a fellow hawking ginger cake.

'Yesterday? I seen them,' he said, scratching his balls. He was a young fellow, maybe twenty years old, a loose grin on his face. His talk was slow, the words rolling around his mouth. A laudanum addict, I supposed. He pointed towards Charing Cross. 'Turned down there to the station, mate, two or three... or four of them. Quite a sight, they were.'

'How many, mate? Two, three or four?'

He screwed up his nose and looked at the sky. 'I just couldn't say.'

'Any women?'

'Oh, yeah. There was a woman too. They had black faces and so on.'

'Give us a bit of that cake, will you?' I said, offering him a penny.

'Oh,' he said slowly, like he'd only just noticed the tray was around his neck. 'Help yourself.'

I took the biggest bit and had a bite. 'Eh, that's good. That's nice cake.'

'Good, ain't it?' he said, the idiot smile coming back to his face. 'I had three bits already, since lunchtime.' He patted his belly. 'Can't seem to help myself.'

'That's 'cos you're an addict.'

'Eh?'

'Listen, mate. This is important. I need to find those Africans. Did they look like they were being chased?'

He seemed confused. 'Well,' he said. He looked up towards the church, his eyeballs following the route they'd have come till they were level with us. 'Now, they were in a hurry, I know that.'

'Anybody around them?'

'It's always busy here.'

'Anybody behind them? Following them?'

'Well, I just don't know.' He laughed. 'Quite a sight they were, you know. You should've seen them! And all the pigeons flying about.'

I knew I'd get nothing clearer out of him, so I moved on. I asked a few more folk selling on the street, but had no more luck.

The guvnor was an hour late reaching the pub. He had a quick brandy and we walked down to Charing Cross Station, asking anyone else we could find: guards, ticket sellers, hawkers, porters. Finally, one of the sweepers outside the station said:

'Yeah, I seen them. Got in a four-wheeler out front there.' He pulled a tobacco pouch from his overalls and started to roll a smoke.

'How many of them?' asked the guvnor.

'Two. A bloke and a lady.'

'And a white woman?'

'All darkies.'

'Were they being chased?'

'Don't know about that, sir.'

'Did they look afraid?'

'Couldn't say. Don't look like us, do they?'

'Can you describe the man?'

'Solid bloke, with that hair that sticks up. You know, like some of them got.'

'Was there a thin lad with them?' asked the guvnor. 'About fourteen?'

The sweeper shook his head.

'D'you know where the carriage went?'

He shook his head and lit his fag. 'Went off that way,' he said, pointing up towards Blackfriars.

'Was it a cab?' asked the guvnor.

'The driver ain't licensed, but he picks up fares here. Station master sends him away when he sees him, but he keeps coming back. It's a green one, French-made, I believe. Needs a lick of paint. Drawn by a brown mare.'

'You know his name?' I asked.

He shook his head.

'Is he here every day?'

'Few day a week. Reckon he goes to other stations too.'

'Thank you, sir,' said the guvnor, jamming his hands in his pockets. He looked at me. 'What's happened to S'bu, Barnett? Nobody seems to have seen him. Why wasn't he with them?'

'You think he's been captured?'

'Either that or he's on his own somewhere, the poor lad.' He looked up into the dark sky, the wind flapping his Donegal coat. 'He must be terrified.'

'You want to go and look for him?'

'I don't know where we'd start. At least we have a trail for Senzo and Thembeka. If we can find them, they can tell us what happened. You stay here this evening, Norman. Go home at ten if he hasn't appeared. I'll come tomorrow morning. If you don't hear from me, come and relieve me at midday.'

'Don't go to the Hog, William. You'll need to be up early.'

'I won't,' he promised with a click of his heels and a quick salute. He got me a saveloy from the station and left me there.

I waited at the entrance to the station for the next few hours, watching the cabs come and go, pacing back and forth trying not to freeze my ballocks off. My mood was sour: two nights on the watch mid-winter was hard, and my joints were stiff, my face raw. I ate a few mince pies from a cart outside the station and nursed a couple of mugs of hot wine from another, trying to swallow my way into a more seasonal mood. I paced till ten. The green four-wheeler never came.

Chapter Twelve

The Pelican was warm and smoky, a party of balding men in suits standing in the middle of the room celebrating something. Molly was bringing through a couple of bowls of soup from the back: she winked at me as she delivered them to a fellow sitting in the corner with three kids. One of the boys grabbed a bowl and pulled it to his chest.

'You share that!' barked the bloke.

I got a mug of brandy and hot water from the landlord and found a place by the fire, where I stood watching the balding men. Each had a stale-smelling cigar and a tumbler of claret. They laughed too loud, clinking their glasses. One of them spoke and there was a cheer. I watched their fat necks, their collars too tight, their sweaty faces red from the labour of being loud and jolly and with each other.

A tall, unhappy-looking woman near the door started singing 'A Violet From Mother's Grave', her back straight against the wall, her eyes fixed on the little boy with the soup spoon in his hand.

One by one the punters fell silent, all except the balding men, who were too caught up in their efforts.

'Shh!' hissed a craggy old fellow in a French cap, poking the baldest one with his stick.

The middle-aged men hushed, and we all listened to the

woman sing. She was Irish, her nose hooked, one hand lying on the table, withered and black and twisted. At the chorus, the old fellow joined in, and a short girl of sixteen or so leaning against the counter.

> *Only a violet I plucked,*
> *when but a boy,*
> *And oft time I'm sad at heart,*
> *this flower has given me joy*
> *So while life does remain*
> *In memoriam I'll retain*
> *This small violet I plucked from mother's grave*

As they sang, Molly came beside me and squeezed my belly. I put my arm over her shoulder and we listened as the woman sang the next verse alone. The second chorus came, and this time half the pub were singing.

'You know that was Black Mary's song?' she asked when the song ended and the talking started up again.

I nodded. 'Your master said you were sick.'

She looked over at the door, where a couple of shifty fellows had just come in. 'I'm good now.'

'Oi, Molly!' cried a hairy woman. 'Couple of bowls here.'

She looked in my eyes. 'They all want soup suddenly. Had to get a new pot warmed up at this bloody hour. You eaten, Norm?'

I nodded, draining my mug.

'Molly!' called the landlord.

She stepped away from me. 'Got to work. I'll be off in two hour. You staying?'

'Too late for me, mate. Been working all day.'

She took the mug from my hand.

'Take me out for cakes, sometime, Juggins?'

Juggins. For a few month one summer, back when we were young, Rita was always using that word – on me, on Molly, on her mother. It amused her. It was a word from some other place, and all the more funny on her lips because of it.

Molly smiled, a tear coming to her eye, and in a surge of feeling I remembered how strong we were bound.

I kissed her on the cheek and said I'd see her in two days.

The guvnor was sitting on a pile of newspapers outside W.H. Smiths when I gained the station next day. It was a bright, cold morning, the sky a hard blue. On his knees the *Shields Daily News* lay open, a little pile of winkles half-eaten. Four hansoms queued on the road waiting for fares.

'You look terrible, Barnett,' he said. His bowler was pulled over his ears, his scarf wrapped round his neck. He sneezed and wiped his nose on his glove.

'Any luck?'

'I've asked every cabman. The driver's name is Bill Craft. Works from here a few day a week, as the sweeper said.' He shook the winkle shells from the paper and held it out to me. 'Look at this.'

It was column titled MIGHT AS WELL BE ZULUS about a speech the Earl of Derby'd given at a school prizegiving in Liverpool. He was telling them about the criminals he'd faced in his years as a magistrate: 'Nothing has struck me more forcibly than the utter stupidity and brainlessness of ninety-nine out of every hundred of those unlucky individuals,' he'd said. 'It is not merely ignorance – that might be explained by their mostly belonging to the poorest class; but, as far as my observation goes, they are for the most part as much below the average of their own class intellectually as they can be morally. Nine-tenths of them might be Zulus for any good they have got from civilization, and that is my answer to the foolish talk you sometimes hear about the worthlessness of merely intellectual training. Civilized beings will at least not have the voices of savages or brutes.'

I looked up to see the guvnor scratching his greasy scalp furiously. 'How d'you think our friends would feel reading that?' he asked. 'People talk about those they know nothing about with such abandon and always to assure themselves of their own superiority.'

I nodded, feeling the same vexation as him. But what he'd missed was that the Earl was also talking about me and the friends I grew up with on Jacob's Island. Most of them had been up afore a beak just like him back then, and some of the things I did would have put me in prison for many years had the coppers been better at their jobs.

I threw the paper on the ground as he picked up a copy of the *Star*. 'They've got a whole column on the murders here,' he went on, turning the page for me and pointing at another column. MEETING HOUSE MURDERS was the headline. I had a quick read, but there was nothing in it we didn't know already. They were getting close to saying that it was the Africans who'd killed Mr Fowler and Musa. Getting close without actually saying it. Mrs Fowler's family from Godalming were worried that she hadn't been heard from. Detective Inspector Napper was named, but not us.

Before I had time to finish reading, he pointed over my shoulder.

'Well, well,' he muttered. 'Will you look at that?'

There, coming along the Strand, was a green four-wheeler.

Chapter Thirteen

We waited as it pulled up behind the rank of hansoms and the driver got down. He wore a long army greatcoat. His bowler was scuffed and battered, and one of his boots was missing its lace. Thick lenses sat before his eyes, and his mouth had a sour look. A coster was walking past him on the road pulling a wagon loaded with shoes. In a flash, the driver reached over, swiped a pair of boots, and hid them under his coat. The coster walked on, blind to what'd just happened.

'Bill Craft?' asked the guvnor.

'Who are you?' he grunted.

'We're trying to find some Africans you picked up here two days ago.'

'Who said I did?' he snapped, his eyes almost closing.

'All we need to know is where you took them.'

'Can't tell you,' he said, tightening the harness. 'I've a rule to protect my passengers. You wouldn't like me telling any Tom, Dick and Harry where *you* go, would you?'

'For thruppence?'

He thought about it. 'How about I take you there instead, sir? How would that be?'

'Yes!' exclaimed the guvnor, surprised. 'Yes, indeed. What a splendid idea.'

'What's the fare?' I asked.

'Let's say fifteen bob, just to be fair on us both,' said Craft, still talking to the guvnor. A tongue brown from coffee licked his black teeth.

'Fifteen bob!' cried the guvnor. 'Where is this place, Liverpool?'

'I can't tell you, as I said. Better I just take you there.'

'How many of them did you take?'

'Can't tell you that either, sir.'

'Is it in London?' asked Arrowood.

'Can't say, sir. It's my passenger protection rule, as I said.'

'You haven't got a rule. You just offered to take me!'

'I can take you wherever you want to go. That's my profession, sir. That's why I'm here. But I can't tell you other passengers' doings.'

'But how can we bargain if you won't tell me where we're going?'

'We don't have to bargain.' He slapped his horse's arse and gave it a rub. 'It's a fair price.'

'It's too much,' said the guvnor. 'Nowhere in London would cost anything like that. I'll give you two bob.'

The first hansom in the line picked up a punter and moved off. All the other cabs moved up one space. Craft led his horse forward. 'It's all the same to me if I take you or not,' he said.

'All right,' said the guvnor. 'Five.'

'Eight.'

'Seven.'

'Climb aboard, gents,' said Craft with a smile, opening the carriage door for us.

'Oi, oi!' cried one of the cabbies further up the line. 'Use the first cab, gentlemen. That's the system.'

'Ignore him,' muttered Bill Craft.

Another cabbie approached from behind. He took my arm, pointing toward the hansom at the front of the rank. 'That's the one, mate. First in line.'

'We're taking this one,' I told him.

'No, you ain't,' growled the first cabbie coming up too. He grabbed Craft's lapels and shoved him against the wheel. 'I told you about this afore, you little weasel.'

'Ask them where they're going!' cried Craft. 'Go on, ask them!'

'That's nothing to do with it,' said the cabbie. 'There's a system.'

'The thing is,' said the guvnor, 'we don't know where we're going. Only this man knows.'

'That don't make no sense,' said the first cabbie.

'I know, but I'm not going to explain,' answered the guvnor, climbing into the carriage, his great behind marking the end of the argument. It seemed to work, as the cabbie let go of Craft. I jumped aboard and slammed the door.

The bench was plain wood, crumbs on the floor among the dried mud and one of the glass panes missing in the door. The carriage moved off and we sat back and watched London through the window. Christmas geese and turkeys hung from their legs outside butcher's shops, costers stood by carts piled high with spiced apples and figs, spuds and carrots, while plum puddings and mince pies were laid in trays on tables outside the many little baker's. Posters in shop windows yelled CHRISTMAS BOOKS!, CHRISTMAS FASHIONS! In a toy shop was a bright red banner: DO, PAPA, BUY ME A TOY! It made me sad somehow.

Down we went along Whitehall, where men in toppers

chatted on street corners, past Parliament, whose lights peeked shy through its narrow windows, along by the wharves and factories of Millbank to Lambeth Bridge. On the Surrey side of the river we followed the tram lines to Vauxhall Park, down past the board school and the vinegar works, crossing Clapham Road and on towards Brixton. There, soon after the police station, we came to a stop.

The driver knocked on the roof with his stick.

'Out you get, gents.'

It was a terraced street of three-storey houses, all made of good London brick. In the middle of the row was a meeting hall, its tall windows dark. Up ahead a lad on a grocer's bike rode towards us.

'There you go,' said Craft, climbing down. 'Gresham Hall.'

'Did they go in?' asked the guvnor.

Craft held out his hand. With much groaning, the guvnor took out his purse and counted seven shillings. When the money was in his pocket, the driver answered: 'Didn't wait to find out. Now, sir, you want me to wait and take you back? It's murder finding a cab round here.'

'For another seven shillings?' said the guvnor. 'You must think we're balmy.'

'I'll do you a special price.'

'Get out of here, you blooming crook.'

Craft climbed up to his box. 'Fat pig,' he muttered as he gee-ed on the horses.

Gresham Hall was taller than the houses on either side by about a half. A sign was pasted on the wall saying:

CHRISTADELPHIAN LECTURES
EVERY SUNDAY AT 7 P.M.
Hear the momentous truth of the infallible God!
Free entry. No collections.

Up a couple of steps was a pair of heavy wooden doors. I pulled on the bell. We heard it ring inside, then silence. I tried the handle but it was locked. I pulled the bell again.

'There's a door down the side,' said the grocer's boy, who'd come to a stop to look at us. He pointed at a little path that ran down the side of the hall.

'Have you seen any Africans around here, lad?' asked the guvnor.

'No, sir,' he said. 'Not here.'

The boy pedalled off.

'I wonder if I could ride a bicycle,' said the guvnor, watching the lad bump along the cobbles.

'No, sir,' I said, fairly sure his body wasn't put together right for transport as that.

'Because of my haemorrhoids?' he asked as we went down the narrow path.

'You'd be too heavy.'

'Balderdash. I've seen heavier fellows ride bicycles. You can hire them in Crystal Palace, you know. Perhaps I'll ask Isabel when it's warmer.'

The path squeezed between the side of the building and the neighbouring house. We followed it to an annex at the back of the hall, where there was a yellow door. It opened soon after I knocked, and there stood a white woman of nineteen or twenty with the hairiest face I ever saw on a lady. She had no moustache, but the brown hair grew down the side of her face and along her jawline. She wore a Fair Isle jumper, tatty and long, her chest drooping and her hips set back like she was leaning over a well.

'Oh, hello!' she said, her voice light and bright. She was a Yank. Her eyes rolled over my body, then the guvnor's, then mine again. 'What a pleasure to have some visitors. Come in and get out of the cold, fellas.'

She turned and led us down the corridor. Her rumple was like a big balloon, and where it met her back was a ledge you could rest your mug on. The guvnor raised his eyes at me, though his was almost as big.

She took us into a kitchen where two more of the queerest-looking ladies I ever saw sat in chairs by the range. The one who opened the door was the youngest by a long way.

'Who's this, Sylvia?' asked the one nearest the door. She wore eyeglasses and a headscarf, her face a strange orange colour. She was Continental by the sound of it, French or Spanish, maybe. Or Greek. With mittened hands, she put the gin-jar she was holding on the edge of the range and closed her book.

'Gisele, this is…' said Sylvia. She looked at me again and smiled. She laughed. 'Oh, darling, I quite forgot to ask your name.'

'Norman, ma'am,' I said. 'Norman Barnett. This here's Mr Arrowood.'

'And you're with Mr Capaldi, are you?'

'Well…' I hesitated, looking over at Arrowood.

'Why are you here?' demanded Gisele.

'We've come to talk to the Africans, madam,' said the guvnor.

'Africans?' asked the third of the odd-looking ladies. Her arms were short stumps, and she had little bloodshot eyes. Over her coarse white scalp grew bits of hair like burnt straw. She wore a plain brown dress. Open in her lap was the *Star*. 'What d'you mean Africans?'

'They arrived at this building yesterday afternoon, madam,' said the guvnor. 'We were paid to protect them and they disappeared. We want to ensure they're safe.'

'You'll have a drink, boys?' asked Sylvia, taking two mugs from a shelf. 'We only got gin. Sit yourselves down.'

We lowered ourselves upon a bench by the table. It was warm in there around the range, and we shed our coats and gloves.

'No Africans here, sirs,' said Gisele. She looked at the third. 'You see some Africans, Leonie?'

The short-armed woman shook her head.

'The cabman just told us he brought them here,' said the guvnor, taking the mug Sylvia handed him.

'No, sir,' said Leonie, as Sylvia scurried out the room. 'He must've made a mistake.'

'Do you live here, Miss Leonie?'

'We're staying here a few weeks,' she said with a smile, then had a sip from a wooden tankard. She was the only English one among them. 'Are they dangerous?'

'Are you sure they aren't here?' asked the guvnor. 'This is a large building.'

'No, sir,' answered Leonie, getting to her feet and putting the paper on the table. Her legs were almost as short as her arms, though her body was long and well-fed, almost bursting the seams of her thick dress. 'No, sir. We don't know anything about Africans.'

'Would you mind if we conducted a search? They might have found a way in. They might be hiding somewhere.'

Her voice turned hard. 'I told you they aren't here. Now, I think it's time you were off.'

We heard footsteps in the corridor, then a man stepped in and stood by the door, his arms folded over his chest. He was a meaty bloke: I could see from the way he carried himself he wasn't shy of using his muscles.

'We're trying to help them, Miss Leonie,' said the guvnor. 'They're in grave danger. Two people have been killed and I doubt they've many friends in London. Perhaps you are their friends. I can assure you that we are too.'

'The lady told you to leave,' growled the bloke.

The guvnor turned to me and nodded. I stood.

'What's your name, mate?' I asked the bloke.

'Nick,' he grunted. His hair was cut close, black but for a few dusty patches like he had an infection. He had no chin to speak off, his cheeks over-fleshy, his eyes darting and unsure.

'We're going to search the building, Nick,' I said to him. 'You can try and stop us if you like.'

He stepped across, blocking the doorway. In his hand appeared a knife.

'That's fine,' he said. 'I'll do that.'

I looked at the guvnor, who shook his head. 'Let's do this another way, then,' he said, crossing one leg over the other. He looked at Leonie. 'We know they're here.'

'Don't be soft, mister. I told you we never heard of any Africans. And I told you to go. So unless you want a fight with Nickie, you better hook it.'

'You came over on the boat from Calais with the Africans.

They told us about you. Now, if you don't bring them out to talk to us we're going direct to Mr Capaldi in Stockwell to tell him where they are. He lives on Albert Terrace, in case you don't believe we know him. He'll be glad to pay us at least a pound for such a valuable piece of information. And I suppose he won't be too pleased with you for hiding them.'

'Mr Capaldi?' said Leonie. 'Never heard of him.'

The guvnor laughed. He bent over and took the *Star* from the table.

'The lady said hook it,' grunted Nick, stepping forward with his knife held out before him.

The guvnor held up the front page. 'Look,' he said. 'First notice on the right.'

Leonie's nose wrinkled. Gisele glanced at it, then looked away.

'I'll read it for you,' said the guvnor, shaking out the paper. '*Piccadilly Hall. Capaldi's Wonders of the World, direct from Paris. Lobster Claw Lady, Tasmanian Pig Woman, Baboon Girl. Four weeks only. Touch them. Smell them. Hear them jabber. First show Friday 20 December, then every day 2 p.m., 4 p.m., 6 p.m., 8 p.m. Seven-year-old Child with a Giant Head. 3 p.m., 5 p.m., 7 p.m. Limited Time.*'

Chapter Fourteen

Sylvia stepped back into the room as he read out the notice. She'd changed out of her shirt and britches and wore a pink dress and a soft, blonde wig. A ferocious lavender odour filled our noses.

'It's you three ladies, isn't it?' asked the guvnor. 'You're Capaldi's Wonders.' He left it there for a few moments, looking at each in turn with his kindest eyes, his lips pressed together. Sylvia with the hair around her face, Gisele with her orange skin and mittened hands, Leonie with her white scalp and child-like limbs. 'I don't mean to offend you, really I don't. You're too elegant to deserve such cruel stage names.'

Sylvia fell into Nick's arms and began to weep.

'Oh, shut your face, Sylvia,' hissed Gisele. 'You got to get used to it.'

'I can't,' she sobbed, dusty tears starting to run down her pinked cheeks. Nick stroked her wig, whispering something in her ear.

'It's a fantasy invented to sell tickets, Miss Sylvia,' said the guvnor. 'You must never feel that name is you.'

'Don't you lecture us, mister,' said Leonie, putting her hand on Gisele's shoulder. 'You don't know anything about it. I *am* Pig Woman. That's my work.'

'Perhaps Miss Sylvia's different.'

'This her first exhibition,' said Gisele. 'Isn't it, Sylvia darling?'

Sylvia nodded, laying her head on Nick's chest. 'I know they're going to say terrible things,' she whispered. 'But I got my Nickie. Least he loves me as I am.'

'May I ask why you're here, Miss Sylvia?' said the guvnor. 'You don't seem to want to perform.'

'I need the money for my ma. Mr Capaldi offered me more than I could earn anywhere else.'

'And her brother's soft in the head,' said Gisele.

'Are they here with you?' asked the guvnor.

'New York,' said Sylvia. She looked up into Nick's face again.

'Have you got family in England, Miss Sylvia?' asked the guvnor.

She shook her head. 'We're going back one day. Nickie's got cousins there too.'

The guvnor watched them for a while. 'Is the large-headed boy here also?' he asked at last.

'He's not one of Mr Capaldi's,' said Leonie. 'Now, I think it's time you left.'

The guvnor clasped his hands behind his back and rocked on his feet. His tone became severe. 'Please bring the Africans, madam. It won't go well if I have to go to Mr Capaldi, you know that. And we *are* here to help them, you must believe me.'

Leonie glared at him for some time. Finally, she marched out the door and climbed the stairs on the other side of the corridor. We sat there in silence until we heard footsteps coming back down. It was Thembeka and Senzo, followed by Leonie. They looked ragged, tired.

'Thank goodness you're safe,' said the guvnor, taking each by the hand.

'Oh, William, Norman, thank the Lord you're here,' said Thembeka. 'Where's S'bu? We've been worried sick.'

'He's not with—'

He was interrupted by the sound of voices outside the kitchen window.

'Quick,' said Leonie in a hush. 'Hide!'

She opened the pantry door and waved us in. Thembeka and Senzo went first, the guvnor and me squeezing in after. The door was shut tight, the only light being four air holes cut into the top of the door.

We heard the knock outside, then voices and footsteps along the corridor.

'Please, sit down, Mr Capaldi,' said Leonie. Her voice was small through the little airholes, but we could hear the words clear enough. 'We weren't expecting you, else we'd have got some wine in.'

'Don't worry about that,' came Bruno's posh voice. 'I can't stay long. I only wanted to drop by to see that everything's in order before the opening tomorrow. Sold out for the next two weeks! You've done me proud, girls.'

'That's good,' said Leonie.

'Are you all prepared? You know what you're doing, Sylvia?'

We heard Sylvia sob and sniff. 'I reckon so, Mr Capaldi.'

'I can see you've been weeping. What's upset you, dearie?'

'Just don't like the name.' Another sniff.

'Ah! The name. But that's just for the idiots, poppet. You forget that. You're a beautiful girl. She is, isn't she, Nickie?'

'Yes, Mr Capaldi.'

It was a tight squeeze in there. I had the whole of the guvnor's front pressed up to mine, his hot breath on my chest.

My back was hard on the door, and I prayed that the latch would hold. On a shelf next to my hand were a couple of tins of condensed milk and a bottle of Sarson's. Thembeka was whispering something to herself, her head turned down to the floor; behind her on another shelf was a pile of sprouting spuds. Senzo was looking at me, his eyes narrow, his body rigid. I hoped he still had his gun. If Capaldi's men had killed already, they might do it again, but there'd at least be witnesses this time.

'Now, I wanted to introduce you to my son, Ralf,' we heard Bruno say. 'Ralf, these three lovely girls are Leonie, Gisele and Sylvia.'

'Pleased to meet you, ladies.' I recognized the voice of the boy I'd seen in the billiard room the other day. He was over-loud, trying to be confident.

Bruno went on: 'The main reason I decided to call this evening is that we're making a little change to the arrangements for these shows. As you know, I have a few performances on around the country right now. Capaldi's Wonders is my favourite of course, my lovelies, but it's too much for me to look after all of them, so I've decided that from now on my Ralf is going to be your manager. I'm teaching him the business. He looks young, but he has a man's head on his shoulders, I can assure you. Anything you need that Nick can't provide, you ask Ralfie. He'll talk to the theatre for you, make all the arrange-ments, go on tour with you as well. You're going to be stars, ladies! My Ralf'll do it all. Just make sure you don't give him any problems.'

'How old are you, Ralf?' asked Leonie.

'Sixteen,' we heard him say. Senzo moved his hand to his

nose, pinching it, then his head jerked forward as he held in a sneeze. Thembeka looked up at him.

'You're only a boy,' said Leonie.

'I'll guide him,' said Bruno. 'Ermano will give him a hand too. Don't you worry.'

I breathed out slow and shut my eyes. Someone'd passed gas. It was a strange kind of stew in that little larder: black and white, young and old, big and little, all pressed together like meat and spuds in a gravy of bad nerves.

'I don't know,' said Leonie.

'No, you don't,' said Bruno, his voice sharp now.

'He's a bit shy,' said Gisele.

There was a sound in the kitchen, like a scuffle. Then Bruno spoke again, but this time his voice was strained. 'Now, Sylvia. I got a little question for you. You answer me, all right?'

'Y-yes,' she said. She sounded scared.

'She'll answer, sir,' said Nick.

'You read about Musa and the old Quaker being murdered, did you?'

'Yes, Mr Capaldi,' said Sylvia. Her voice was muffled somehow, like she was being held. We all of us heard it. Thembeka's mouth tightened; the guvnor tilted his head to listen better.

'So tragic,' said Bruno. It sounded like he was right outside the larder door now.

'There's no need to frighten her,' said Leonie.

'I'm not talking to you,' growled Bruno. 'Now, Sylvia, answer me honestly. Have you seen the other three? Senzo, Thembeka and S'bu. D'you know where they are?'

Silence. The anger was rising in me now, cooped up in that cupboard, listening to them using their muscle out there. I wanted to get out and help, but I knew that would go worse for our friends.

'D'you know where Senzo is, Sylvia?' demanded Bruno, his voice tight and threatening.

We heard a gasp.

'Where's Senzo?' came another voice. It was Ermano, the brother with the ponytail who led us up from Capaldi's basement.

'Or the other two?' asked Bruno.

'She can't breathe, sir,' said Nick.

'Well?' growled Bruno.

'No, sir,' said Sylvia in a gasp.

'I sense there's something you're not telling me, my dear. Listen, you sweet girl, I only want to help. They're in trouble. The police believe they killed Musa and the Quaker. We need to protect them, so where are they, Sylvia?'

'They… they…'

'Yes?'

I slid my hand in my pocket and took hold of the pistol. The guvnor met my eyes. He seemed ready, his nose twitching, his fists clenched. Behind him, Senzo took hold of Thembeka's shoulder.

'We don't know,' said Leonie.

'They don't come here,' said Gisele.

'Please be quiet,' said Bruno, some warmth in his voice. 'Now, Sylvia. What is it you're hiding?'

'I d-don't know, Mr Capaldi.'

Silence for a few more moments. Then Bruno spoke again. 'Let her go, Ermano. Now, if you hear anything you tell me at once. No delay. Yes?'

The women murmured their agreement.

'Now, tell them about tomorrow, Ralf.'

'Oh, yeah.' The boy cleared his throat. 'I'll see you at the hall at midday. First show's at two.'

'Did you hire the carriage?' asked his old man.

'Oh, yeah. I hired a carriage to pick you up each morning and bring you home.'

'Food, Ralf.'

'And you'll get your supper there. Nick can get it for you.'

'Nick's got to stay and watch over them,' said his old man.

'Oh… of course. I'll get it.'

'No, that's not your job,' said Bruno. 'You ask at the theatre. They'll have someone bring it in. And did you tell Sylvia what she's got to do?'

'We teach her, don't you worry,' said Gisele. 'She's a good dancer.'

There was another silence.

'Ask Sylvia how she's feeling about it,' said his old man.

'How are you feeling about it, Sylvia?'

'I'm a bit nervy, Mr Ralf.'

'Bit nervy?' said Ralf, his voice forced. 'You'll be fine. Just stand there and relax.'

'There's more to it than that, Ralf,' said Leonie. 'She's doing the Highland Fling. And you must answer questions from the audience. We all got to know the stories.'

'Oh. Of course. Yeah.'

'Tell her she's going to be magnificent,' said Bruno.

'You're going to be—' began Ralf.

'Magnificent,' said father and son together.

Sylvia giggled. 'Oh, thank you,' she said, like it pleased her.

'Now, we must go,' said Bruno.

We listened as they said their goodbyes, as the footsteps left the kitchen, as the back door creaked and closed. Finally, the latch opened and we bundled out.

Chapter Fifteen

Gisele and Leonie stood by the range. Sylvia was fidgeting in the doorway, looking down the corridor.

'S'bu?' asked Senzo.

'Where is he?' asked Thembeka.

'We don't know,' said the guvnor. 'We were hoping he was with you.'

She spoke to Senzo, gripping his arm. His face fell.

'We'll find him,' said the guvnor, lowering himself with a creak to the bench. 'But first how about you tell us what happened at the Quaker Meeting House?'

Leonie passed a mug of gin to Thembeka, who took a big swallow and sat at the table. Her and Senzo both looked tuckered out, their eyes creased and worried. Thembeka wiped her face with her new tasseled shawl, Senzo scratched his belly, moving from foot to foot. He spoke quick to Thembeka. She turned to us.

'Two white men came,' she said, looking hard at the guvnor. She seemed out of breath. 'We'd never seen them before. We were playing cards. Musa was in the basement sleeping. Senzo tried to get out his pistol but they started shooting. Hit Mr Fowler. They made Senzo throw down his gun and told us to go with them. Then S'bu took out his gun, but they jumped on him before he could fire it. We ran off while they were fighting. We couldn't help him. They had two guns.'

'Does Senzo still have his pistol?'

She shook her head.

'Where was Mrs Fowler when this happened?' he asked.

'She was out buying food.'

'Well, she must have returned because she's missing too. How did you know to come here?'

'We were here for a night before Mr Capaldi took us to the boarding house.'

'And where was that?' asked the guvnor.

'I don't know, William,' said Thembeka. 'When we escaped, we walked a long time and found a church. The parson told us to go to the refuge and paid for the cab like I told you before. That's where we found you.'

As she talked, Nick passed around some fruit cake and Sylvia handed out the tea. I drank mine straight away, cupping my hands round the warm mug.

'D'you remember anything about the area?' asked the guvnor.

Thembeka shook her head. She talked with Senzo, then turned back to the guvnor. 'Little houses, pubs, shops. I don't know. So many streets look the same.'

'Didn't you think it was too dangerous coming here?' asked the guvnor.

Thembeka looked at Gisele, and her worried face softened. 'These folk are our friends.'

Both me and the guvnor turned our heads to Nick. He was Capaldi's man. As if to answer, he stepped over to Sylvia and put his hand on her shoulder. She lay her hand upon his and shut her eyes.

'Mr Capaldi won't be happy with you if he finds out, mate,' I said to him.

He shrugged. 'Best keep it secret, then.'

'Can you describe the men who killed Mr Fowler, Thembeka?' asked the guvnor.

She talked to Senzo for a little while longer. 'Two had very short black hair and whiskers and moustache. One of them hobbled. The other was a Chinaman, we think. Bald, also with a moustache. Tall and thick like you, Mr Barnett. The other two were a bit shorter.'

'You think one was a Chinaman?'

'He looked like one.'

'Clothes?'

'Dark overcoats, scarves.' She touched her neck. 'Bowlers. Find them, William. Please. Those men have S'bu.'

'We'll do our best. The police are looking as well.'

Senzo was sitting opposite me at the table. He held out his hand. 'Gun. Me.'

I looked at the guvnor, who shook his head.

'What have you heard, Nick?' asked the guvnor.

Nick shrugged. 'They don't tell me nothing.'

'D'you know who the men are?'

He shook his head. 'I only been working for them a couple of month. I only met Ermano, that's Bruno's brother, and a bloke called English Dave. I don't know any of the others.'

'Is Musa still in the Meeting House?' asked Thembeka.

The guvnor looked confused. 'Haven't you read the news?'

Her eyes narrowed. 'The news? Why?'

'You didn't…' said the guvnor, looking at Leonie.

'No,' she said quickly. 'We were waiting till they'd recovered.'

'What?' demanded Thembeka. 'Where is he?'

The guvnor looked at me now, his eyes fresh with tears.

Last time we had to break bad news like this, it was him who did it. It'd hurt him so bad he'd made me promise I'd be the one to do it next time.

'I'm real sorry, Thembeka,' I said. 'They killed Musa. They must have found him.'

When Senzo saw Thembeka's face, his own crumpled too. He dropped his head, a soft groan coming from him.

Thembeka just stared at me.

Gisele put her arms around her. 'Oh, my dear,' she whispered.

The guvnor touched Senzo's shoulder. 'I'm sorry, my friend.'

We sat there in silence, nobody drinking their tea, the cake left on the plates. Outside, a pigeon cooed. Another joined in. Nick chucked a bit of coal into the oven.

'Musa?' asked Thembeka, stiffening. It was like she'd just heard. Her eyes fell to the red tiles on the floor. 'They shot Musa?'

'No,' said the guvnor, his voice catching. 'They strangled him and... knocked his teeth out.'

Thembeka shivered and her face clenched like she had an awful pain in her guts. She spoke low and flat to Senzo. He was bent over, his elbows now resting on his thighs. He asked a question. She answered. He shook his head, said something else. Finally, he stood, clutching the edge of the table as he made his way out the kitchen.

'I found a letter in Musa's pocket,' said the guvnor, watching Senzo as he disappeared down the corridor. 'D'you know about it?'

Thembeka shook her head.

He took out his notebook and pointed at the page where he'd written the words. 'Can you tell me what this means?'

She read it slowly. 'That's our letter,' she said at last.

'What does it mean?'

'You took it from him?'

'The police have it now. What does it mean?'

She sighed for a moment. 'It's nothing. We've a cousin.'

'Here?'

She looked at the empty doorframe. 'In Paris. We were arranging to meet him.'

'Can you translate it for me?'

'Meet at…' she wiped her eyes, 'at Arch of Triumph Sunday at two.'

'That's all?'

'Yes.'

'No name?'

'We only know one person in Paris.'

The guvnor nodded and put away his notebook. 'I don't understand why you didn't go to the police when you escaped from Capaldi's boarding house.'

'Mr Capaldi's got friends in the police. He always told us they'd hunt us down.'

'They'll find out, all right,' said Nick, nodding his hard head. He was standing behind Sylvia, stroking the back of her neck. 'Dave told me Mr Capaldi pays off one of them to keep his cat-house safe. It's one of his relatives or something.'

'But you must tell the police what you know about the murders,' said Leonie. 'How else will they find S'bu?'

'Don't worry,' said the guvnor. 'We'll tell them what you've told us.'

Thembeka finished the mug of gin and wiped her hand across her lips. 'Find S'bu, William. Please. He'll be so scared. He's not as brave as he likes to pretend.'

'Norman and I will do whatever we can.' The guvnor stood and patted Senzo's arm. 'Tell Senzo that.'

She nodded. 'You won't tell them where we are, will you?'

'No, madam,' said Arrowood. 'I promise you we won't.'

Chapter Sixteen

We left them there and got a tram to the river. It was mid-afternoon and the puddles had turned to ice, the pathways slick. The guvnor was distracted. He was perched on the edge of the seat next to two women with baskets on their laps. I had a soldier next to me, his newspaper held open in front of him. The guvnor puffed on his pipe, his mind turning over in that monstrous buffalo head. Brixton turned into Kennington. As we passed under the railway lines on Westminster Bridge Road, I asked him what we were going to do.

'I don't know, Norman,' he said. 'I don't know what we can do.'

'We should leave it with Napper. The money's almost gone. We have to do some work that pays. I've got to eat, sir.'

'I can't do that, Norman. I promised.'

'Napper'll find S'bu.'

He looked at me and forced a smile. 'Will he?'

'He's not a bad copper.'

'It's not just that. I can't stop thinking about what we've done to them.'

'It wasn't our fault, sir. The guns were only meant to frighten them off.'

'I didn't mean that. I mean why they're in London. Why they left South Africa. Hamba's told me so much about conditions in India. You read the news in the paper, but it's different when you see a real person. It's different when you hear their stories.'

'We're not to blame for the empire.'

'We're part of it, whether we like it or not. This might be our only chance to make amends.'

When we reached Scotland Yard, a copper took us up to the detectives' office and opened the door for us. There was a bloke sitting on the other side of Napper's desk.

'What the devil?' said the guvnor under his breath.

'Ah,' said Napper, getting to his feet. 'You've come at just the right time. Let me introduce Constable Mabaso of the Johannesburg police.'

The African stood and turned to us, his movements controlled, his face severe. He was dressed in a worn mackintosh, darned in a few places, a navy police suit with no waistcoat, a thin yellow shirt and brown tie. His hair was tight to his head, his ears sticking out like oyster shells. I offered him my hand.

'Mr Barnett,' I said. 'This is Mr Arrowood.'

'Pleased to meet you, sir,' he said. 'I've just been hearing about you.' His English was perfect, his accent African. He had a sharp nose, pinched eyes. The skin on his face showed no sign of ever growing hair.

Napper asked us to sit, then explained.

'Constable Mabaso's just arrived from Johannesburg. He has an interesting story you might like to hear.'

Mabaso clasped his hands in his lap. As he spoke, his body remained still as a post, his face serious, his lips moving the least they needed to make the words. 'We have a criminal gang called the Ninevites in our district. They cause much trouble: ambushing stage-coaches, burgling houses, robbing workers of their wages. Maybe you've heard of them?'

'No, sir,' said the guvnor.

He tightened his mouth and had a small cough. 'They have a couple of thousand men, led by a man called Nongoloza and set up like an army: they even wear stolen military uniforms. They live in caves and old mine shafts in the hills around the city. Their men have infiltrated the mine compounds and prisons, where they recruit more members. A few months ago the Ninevites burgled the home of one of the owners of Robinson Mine, Mr Kruger. The thieves made off with a cart carrying the miners' wages and a quantity of gold bullion. Mr Kruger's child and a guard were killed. Detective Duffy of Langlaagte police station was appointed to track the raiders down. I am his assistant. We discovered they'd fled to Mozambique, where they met a French showman, Mr Monteuil, who was looking for natives to perform in Europe. They signed a contract with him and took a boat to Portugal, and from there a train to Paris. I believe they're now here, in London.'

The guvnor glanced at me.

'Detective Duffy died of dysentery on the boat coming over here,' said Napper. 'So until they send another detective, Constable Mabaso's in charge.'

'When will the other detective arrive, constable?' asked Arrowood.

'The boat takes about three weeks,' said Mabaso. As he shifted in his seat, I noticed a book jutting from his coat pocket. 'I sent a telegraph informing them of the situation yesterday, when I arrived in Southampton.'

'Until that time, the Colonial Office have asked us to give PC Mabaso any assistance he needs.' Napper paused to light a cigar. 'Even though he's only a constable.'

'I've been a police officer for fifteen years, sir,' said Mabaso slowly, his eyes fixed on the Scotland Yard man.

'But you're not a detective.'

'Blacks are not permitted to be detectives in South Africa, sir.' Mabaso looked at me, then at the guvnor. 'Detective Inspector Napper says that you've met the men I seek.'

'What are their names?' asked the guvnor.

'Musa Schoko and Senzo Nyambezi. Two of the four Zulus you were hired to protect. I hear Mr Schoko is dead.'

'Well, I don't know if it's them,' said the guvnor. 'I don't know their last names.'

'It is them, sir. I learned that Monteuil sold the contract to an English showman called Capaldi who brought them here.'

'So you aren't searching for the other two?' I asked.

'I don't know if they're involved yet.' He turned back to the guvnor. 'Do you know where Senzo Nyambezi is, sir?'

The guvnor's nose twitched, and I could see he hadn't yet decided what he should tell this stranger. 'I'm also searching,' he said at last.

Napper stared at him, a suspicious look on his mug. 'Did you talk to the vagrants?' he asked.

'Yes,' answered the guvnor.

'And what did you discover?' asked Napper, picking up his pen.

'A witness told us two white men with guns entered the Quaker Meeting House. Describe them, Barnett.'

I told them what we knew from Thembeka.

'A Chinaman, you say?' asked Napper, writing in his note-book. 'Could be Capaldi's men?'

'Could be,' I said. 'If they use a Chinaman.'

Napper stopped writing. 'What about the Africans?'

'We've reports of them at Charing Cross Station,' said the guvnor. 'Two of them, probably Senzo and Thembeka. The young lad wasn't with them.'

'Mrs Fowler?'

'No reports of her.'

'Who's the witness?'

'I can't tell you,' said the guvnor.

'What's that?'

'I can't tell you.'

Napper's brow wrinkled as he stared at his notebook, his pen clenched in his freckled hand. 'Can't or won't?'

'Both. They don't want to be involved with the police. We promised we'd respect that.'

Napper looked up and sighed. 'Tell me, Arrowood. This isn't a game.'

'No, detective. It's no game.'

'I'll have you both locked up.'

'You need us to help you. You've only two men.'

'Damn you!' exclaimed Napper, slapping the desk. 'If you're hiding anything that obstructs this case, I'll charge you.'

Arrowood nodded.

'Did they get on a train?'

'A child fell ill and I had to take the mother to the hospital,' said the guvnor.

'Did you ask around the station if anybody'd seen them?'

'We've been busy.'

'Doing what?'

'We're under no obligation to tell you about the cases we work on.'

'You are if they involve my case, Arrowood. There's a woman missing. She may be in danger.'

'You're only concerned with the white woman? What about the other three?'

'Haven't you been listening to what the constable said? They're criminals, Arrowood.'

'Senzo's the criminal.'

'The others are helping him.'

'S'bu's only a boy.'

Another copper came bustling through the door, whistling to himself. He pulled off his overcoat and dropped it on a desk. Mabaso'd sat through the little spat quietly, his hands in his lap.

'You need to find where Capaldi's other properties are and search them,' said the guvnor. 'They must have the boy. They might have Mrs Fowler too.'

Napper rolled his eyes. He jabbed his cigar hard into a bowl, dirty with dried porridge. 'Why would Capaldi's men capture Mrs Fowler?'

'They're witnesses to murder.'

'Then why not just kill them?' asked Napper. 'Why capture them? You can only hang once. No, there must be something else behind this. What d'you think, constable?'

Mabaso slowly turned his head. 'I'm just learning what's happened, sir. What about this Mrs Delacourte you mentioned?'

'We'll go there next.'

'Did they bring the gold to London?' asked the guvnor.

'It was never found,' answered Mabaso.

'They didn't have luggage when they escaped from Capaldi's boarding house,' I said. 'All they had was the clothes they stood in.'

Mabaso nodded. 'It's possible they hid it in Africa before they got on the boat. Luggage that heavy would have been noticed by Monteuil's people. He was paying their fares.'

Napper had a think. His thin, gummy eyes finally fell on the guvnor again. 'You haven't told me what you were doing today.'

'No, sir, I cannot.'

'Tell me.'

'Have you spoken to Mrs Fowler's family?'

For some moments, Napper glared at the guvnor, his eyelids half-closed. His chest rose and fell, rose and fell. 'My constable's questioning her servants and friends this afternoon. The superintendent wants her found: he might give me another constable tomorrow, and I hope to hear about offering a reward later today, if he can drag himself out of the chophouse.'

'Any other witnesses come forward?'

He shook his head.

'Would you like us to do anything for you?' asked the guvnor.

Napper gave a snort of laughter. 'You vex me, Arrowood.'

'A lot of coppers say that,' I told him.

Napper got up and reached for his hat. 'Right. Could you go to Charing Cross and find out if anybody saw where the other two went?'

'Anything to help, sir,' said the guvnor, pushing himself to his feet.

Chapter Seventeen

It was five in the afternoon when we reached Willows' and already dark. The coffee shop was busy with cabbies, Ma Willows' range being a great comfort from the icy streets. She gave our table a quick wipe with her dirty cloth and dumped a couple of bowls of mutton stew in front of us.

'How are the nippers, William?' she asked, laying her red hand on his shoulder. 'Still keeping you up?'

'They've a touch of fever,' said the guvnor, chewing on a bit of mutton bone. His stubby fingers were already wet with soup, his nails chipped and grimy.

'Try Fennings Cooling Powders. It worked for my niece's kids.'

'I'll tell Isabel.'

Rena grunted. She'd always held a candle for the guvnor, and wasn't too happy that Isabel was back in town.

'This soup is good,' said he. 'Is that a turnip?'

She peered at his spoon. 'Cabbage stalk. You hear about that lady got took by the Zulus?'

'That's our case, Rena, but it wasn't the Zulus who took her.'

'There's a copper comes in here said it was.'

'Don't listen to him. The police have no idea what happened to her.'

'She's been gone two day now. Probably—' She sliced across

her throat with her finger. 'And that other one with all his teeth smashed out. Here, you fancy a bit of plum pud? Just put it on today.'

'Coffee, Ma!' barked a coalman from the other side.

She lumbered off.

'We need another case,' I said. 'We aren't going to get paid anymore for this one and Napper's got Mabaso to help him now. Can you go and see if Scrapes has anything?'

'I will,' he said. 'But I'm not giving up on this one. Not while our friends are in danger.'

'But they killed a child. They're criminals.'

'Thembeka and S'bu aren't criminals. Mrs Fowler isn't either.' He lifted the soup bowl to his lips and drained it. 'If the killers were afraid of S'bu and Mrs Fowler because they're witnesses, they'd have just killed them then and there. So either they needed them alive for some reason or they escaped. That seems unlikely as Mrs Fowler would certainly have appeared by now.' He packed his pipe and thought for a while. 'Napper and Mabaso are talking to Madame Delacourte today, so we'll see what she says. For the moment, our best trail is Capaldi. We can't tell Napper about Thembeka and Senzo. There've been enough corruption cases in the police to believe what Nick told us is true.' He thought for a moment. 'When our friends reached London they were prevented from going out. That means they must have had one of Capaldi's men guarding them.'

'Nick?'

'They only stayed with the ladies in Gresham Hall for one night, then they were moved to a boarding house. If Capaldi's holding S'bu and Mrs Fowler prisoner, there's a chance he's using the same guard and the same boarding house. Now, let's just have a bit of that plum pudding then we'll go and see what else they can tell us in Brixton.'

We were back at Gresham Hall less than an hour later. Although the street was deserted, we could hear a little group of children singing 'O, Little Town of Bethlehem' from inside one of the houses. The guvnor paused for a moment to listen, his face wistful and sweet, his nose-breath drifting like pipe smoke in the frozen air. Then he clapped his hands and marched down the side alley to the annex. This time it was Nick who let us in.

'We need to talk to you, mate,' I said.

We stood in the corridor as he bolted the door.

'Come in the kitchen,' he said.

We followed him in there and sat down. The room was empty: a tallow candle sat in a jar on the big table.

'How well d'you know Bruno Capaldi?' asked the guvnor.

'Hardly at all. My ma's Italian. She knows his ma. I heard he was looking for someone to work for him. Never met him before then, and I only spoke to him five or six times even now.'

'Why didn't you tell him that we were hiding in the pantry?'

Nick looked at the ceiling where the sleeping quarters must have been; his jaws bulged and loosened.

'Me and Sylvia are sweet,' he said, looking into the hallway. 'I'd do anything for her, and she wants to protect them.'

'Does Bruno have S'bu and Mrs Fowler?' asked the guvnor.

'They'd never tell me something like that.'

'Can you find out?'

Nick screwed up his face. 'Ermano's the one who tells me what to do. Can't ask him, can I?'

'Did you guard the Africans?' I asked.

Nick shook his head. 'My job's to watch over the ladies.'

'But you came over from Paris with them?'

'That's right.'

'Was there another man guarding the Africans?'

'English Dave.'

'D'you know where we can find him?'

He shook his head again. 'I send Ermano a message if I need anything.'

'What about the boarding house the Africans were staying in?' I asked. 'D'you know where it is?'

'No idea.'

'We have a plan, Nick,' said the guvnor. 'But we need your help.'

He stood and went to the door. 'Sylvia needs me alive. I got to sleep now. Goodnight.'

The guvnor didn't move. He took out his pipe and set it ablaze, while Nick stood by the door.

'You're afraid,' he said at last. 'I'd be afraid too.'

'They'll kill me.'

'Not if we're careful, Nick. I understand, believe me I do. You want to stay as Mr Capaldi's guard for the rest of your life, and you want Sylvia to go on show as Baboon Girl for the rest of hers. Of course. You're happy with what you have.'

Nick stiffened. 'No! We got plans.'

'What plans?'

'When we got enough money we're going to New York, open a wig shop.'

'You think Mr Capaldi will just let you go?'

Nick frowned like he hadn't thought about this before. 'Why not?'

'You know a lot about his business. Have you seen any of his men leave?'

'I only been with him a few month.'

'And what about Sylvia? How old is she?'

'Twenty.'

'And how easy will it be for her to leave, d'you think?'

'She'd leave like that,' he said, brushing one hand over the other.

The guvnor gave a sad snort. 'You think that, do you? How long has Leonie been performing for Mr Capaldi?'

He shook his head.

'I'll wager she started when she was Sylvia's age, and I'll wager Leonie wasn't going to stay when she started either. That's what usually happens. But people don't leave freak shows, Nick.'

'Tom Thumb did. He's rich now.'

'Tom Thumb was famous all over the world, and he didn't work for Bruno Capaldi. I'll wager Leonie and Gisele aren't earning more than £2 a week. How much does Sylvia get?'

Nick glared at him.

'These types of performers don't leave, Nick. They begin to see themselves the way the public sees them, and then there's no place else they can be. You heard what Leonie said: "I *am* Pig Woman".' The guvnor spoke quieter now. He blew out a long train of pipe smoke. '"I *am* Pig Woman", Nick. One day that'll be your lovely Sylvia.'

'No. She don't like it.'

'Imagine how she'll feel tomorrow, the first time she goes on the stage as Baboon Girl. The people staring. The children with their mouths open in fear. All of them staring at the freaks.'

'Don't say that.'

'It's what they'll be saying, Nick. And drunken young coves making ape noises to amuse their friends, shouting the ugliest things. The respectable women with disgust in their faces. Will she look back at them? Or will she look up at the ceiling with tears in her eyes, praying she could just disappear. She'll feel like the most worthless person in the world.' Arrowood stepped over to Nick, and I watched with pride as he did what he did best: get into people's hearts. He shook his head, rubbed his eyes. He spoke in a whisper. 'It'll be the worst day of her life. And when finally the crowd leaves the room, when there's nobody left but the three women and you, she'll run into your arms and feel such relief. For a few minutes you'll comfort her, and then the next crowd of oglers will fill the room. She'll take her position in front of them and hear their insults again, see their faces, the frightened children, the drunken men, and this will carry on, performance after performance, day after day.'

'I'll care for her,' said Nick.

'Of course you will, but it can never be enough. What'll happen to her on that stage tomorrow will strike at her very self. You may stroke her. You may say soothing words, but it's her alone who'll have to battle with the spectators every time she goes on that stage. And that *will* change her. You've seen how Leonie has won the battle the only way she could, by *becoming* Pig Woman. When you become Pig Woman, how can you ever go back? How can you ever rediscover who you were? No, Nick, soon there'll be no way out. That stage will become her prison. She'll never feel beautiful again. By the time you've both saved enough to get out, it'll be too late.

She'll sit in that wig shop as Baboon Girl, and her only home will be the stage.'

Nick looked at me for help. He rubbed his chin that wasn't there; his jaws bulged; his eyes darted. He didn't know what to think.

I nodded, a sad frown on my mug. 'He's right, mate,' I said.

Seeing the guvnor's prediction confirmed, Nick sighed, his body drooping. Arrowood took his hand.

'The police might be posting a reward,' he whispered, nodding real slow. 'Maybe it'll help you buy that shop of yours.'

'What reward?' mumbled Nick.

'For helping find Mrs Fowler and S'bu. Sylvia needs a hero, Nick. Someone to rescue her. Are you that man?'

Nick nodded, his every muscle tensed and hard.

'I knew it,' said the guvnor. 'I knew you'd do anything for her, my friend. Now, we need to talk to Dave and we need your help. But I warn you, it's not going to be pleasant. Here's what we're going to do.'

Chapter Eighteen

Charlie Oysters spent most evenings watching the bathers from the spectator gallery of Lambeth Baths. He smiled when he saw us.

'Willam. Norman. What a lovely surprise. You ain't swimmers, are you?'

The guvnor shook his hand. 'No, Charlie.'

'Enthusiasts?'

'We need some oysters.'

Charlie's eyebrow arched. 'You having a party?'

Charlie Oysters was a big fellow. He was so wide he had to have two suits sewn together to fit inside, and he travelled from his shop to the baths and the pub in a wheeled chair that he was pushed around in by a pin-headed lad name of Cockle. A lot of people avoided old Charlie on account of his face, which was wide as a dinner plate and quite grey, his features swollen and melted from some illness he'd always refused to have named. He loved a party, did Charlie, though there were only certain people happy to have him around: he scared the kiddies and had been known to make a particular type of lady retch.

'It's for a case, Charlie,' said the guvnor. 'We need them now. D'you mind?'

Charlie took up his two sticks and we helped him to his feet, down the steps and out the door, where Cockles sat huddled on his wheeled chair.

'Shop!' barked Charlie.

It was only down the road and not much of a shop either, just a narrow path between two buildings covered over with a bit of corrugated iron. Stacks of oyster crates lined one side and that was about it. But Charlie knew his oysters better than anyone in South London.

Cockles pushed him inside and lit a candle.

'How many, gents?' growled Charlie.

'Half a dozen,' said the guvnor.

'You got me out the bloody baths for half a dozen!' cried Charlie, then he chuckled. 'Ah! You're codding me. Ha ha! Very good. Now, what d'you want?'

'Half a dozen,' said the guvnor. 'But they must be bad.'

Charlie looked at him.

'We aren't codding you, Charlie,' I said. 'We need to make someone wretched.'

He looked from me to the guvnor and sighed. 'Cockles, have a look in the bin, lad.'

Cockles scampered to the back of the shop, causing a rat to bolt toward the door. As it scurried past him, Charlie tried to spear it with a walking stick. The lad bent over into a barrel and rummaged around for a little while, pulling out shells and dropping them in a bucket. He brought it over and Charlie had a look through, examining one after the other under the candle and tapping them. He passed the ones he approved to me.

'There,' he said at last. 'Six.'

'Are you sure they're bad?' asked the guvnor.

'If they ain't you can have your money back.'

'How much?'

'Three bob.'

'Three bob!' cried the guvnor. 'But that's more than for good ones!'

'These is more rarer,' said Charlie.

'But they were in the rubbish bin! You're cheating me, Charlie, you scurf!'

'You don't got to take them, Willy. It's your choice.'

'I'll give you one and sixpence.'

'Two and sixpence.'

'For God's sake, Charlie. They're rotten!'

'You want them or not?'

'You blooming thief.'

Charlie began to roar with laughter. He slapped his thighs, his face wobbling and reforming, and roared some more. Cockles cackled in the dark at the back.

The guvnor opened his purse and fished out the coins, then banged them down hard as he could on the wet barrel top as served as Charlie's counter. Muttering to himself, he stormed out.

It was about ten, cold and dark with a wet fog, and I could see from his twitching the guvnor was thinking of going to the Hog. I needed to make sure he went home, as a whole night on the booze wasn't going to help us solve this case, so I took a tram with him back to Waterloo and followed him along Stamford Street.

'Go home, Barnett,' he growled at me as we walked. 'I don't need a chaperone.'

'It's on my way, sir,' I said.

'You're treating me like a child.'

'Ettie'll be on to me if I let you go drinking.'

'I'm not going drinking, I'm too tired. Anyway, I'm showing Isabel I've changed. I haven't been to see Betts since she returned.'

I kept pace with him. Finally, he stopped and whirled to face me. 'I'm not going any further with you following me!'

I crossed my arms and stood facing him. 'Suit yourself.'

After a few moments he turned and walked on. 'Bugger you,' he hissed.

I waited a few moments, then began to follow him again, grinning to myself as I heard him continue to mutter and curse under his breath. When we got to the pudding shop, he said over his shoulder, 'Well, you might as well come in now you're here. I suppose you want some of my brandy?'

We went through the shop, where Little Albert and his old man were still sorting out the last few punters, along the dark back corridor and up the stairs to the guvnor's parlour. Ettie and Isabel sat by the coal fire, while under the table knelt a little girl we knew. She was stroking the orange cat.

'Flossie!' cried the guvnor. 'What are you doing here?'

She peered up at him from her hiding place, her blue eyes big and full. 'I ain't going back to Mrs Driscoll's.'

'But you must. That's your home.'

'I ain't.'

'We tried to persuade her,' said Ettie. 'She won't budge. Mrs Pudding let her in when we were out with the babies. She was making up a fire when we returned. There was coal everywhere.' The glimmer of a smile came to her face. 'She was black as your hat.'

'Does Mrs Driscoll know?' asked the guvnor.

'We've sent her a message.'

'I ain't going back,' said Flossie again. The girl was only five years old. We'd found her living in a Soho alley with her brother Davy when we were working on the Gravesend Queen case that summer. She was a strong-minded little thing, had to be with all that had happened to her that year. She'd lost her ma and her brother and had nobody left in the world. Mrs Driscoll, one of the mission women, had taken her in. Apart from her, the four of us were the closest she had to family.

The guvnor knelt on the floor next to the table.

'But why, my darling? It's much better than an orphanage.'

'She's a witch. I seen her do spells.'

'Spells! Surely not. You must have misunderstood.'

'And she beats me.' The little girl pouted and looked like she might cry. She rubbed her nose.

'Oh, no. I'm sorry, my dear.'

'She can stay, William,' said Isabel. 'At least until we talk to Mrs Driscoll.'

He patted Flossie's head and, with a groan and a creak of his knees, got to his feet. 'How are the babies?' he asked.

'Sleeping,' said Ettie.

'Any change?'

Ettie frowned. 'Mercy won't feed. Leopold's taken a little milk, but not enough. They both just lie there.'

'Wailing?'

'Not so much. They're very weak.'

Isabel, who was staring at the glowing coals, spoke. 'The doctor thinks it might be—' She stopped, clutching her chest.

Ettie gazed at her sister-in-law. 'He thinks it might be typhus,' she whispered at last.

'But it can't be!' said the guvnor. 'How? There hasn't been any typhus around here since St Olave's. When was that? Eighty-nine? Ninety?'

'I'm sure it isn't,' said Ettie, her face frozen like a mask. 'That doctor of yours was trained years ago.'

'Typhus?' said the guvnor again. 'But why?'

'Their pulses are up and Leopold has some spots on his chest.'

'Lots of nippers have rashes,' I said. 'Neddy's sister's always breaking out.'

Ettie nodded, her grey eyes meeting mine. 'I'm sure it's just flu. The spots must be something else.' There was a little flitch in her cheek as she spoke, and I wished one of them would hold her. It wasn't something I could do, not after all as had passed between us, and not with the guvnor there anyways, but it seemed like she needed it just then.

'But what if he's right?' asked Isabel. 'What if Ettie's brought something back from one of her slums?'

'Oh, Isabel,' said Ettie softly, her fist clenched in her lap.

'That's where it always comes from.'

The guvnor stepped over and put his gloved hand on his wife's shoulder. 'They'll come through, Isabel,' he said. 'They'll be fine.'

She nodded, her eyes vague, but we all knew the danger. Babies were like the first ripe berries on the bush, and it seemed as every evil thing wanted a bite of them. There were so many little angels around us. Arrowood and Isabel had lost two. My sister stepped over when she was five, and my brother-in-law Sidney and his wife Pearl had Emily taken at four. Even little Neddy'd lost his brother two years back. Only Ettie, who'd never married, was free of the mark, but she was a nurse, her hands still bloody from the folk she'd cared for in Afghanistan.

Isabel opened the book she'd taken from the guvnor's collection and wiped her eye. Arrowood tried to press a brandy into my hand, but I didn't want to stay. Ettie walked me out to the shop.

'I'll just give them a moment,' she said as we made our way down the dark corridor strewn with sacks of flour and sugar.

'How are they getting on?' I asked.

'Not so well. Isabel says she still wants a divorce, but she's not doing anything about it. William's ever hopeful, but I watch him blundering about her and it makes me cringe. Her appointment about the scholarship's tomorrow, did you know?'

I shook my head. As we passed through the shop, the last few punters buying their pies, she whispered, 'Oh, Norman, I'm so worried.'

I took her hand from behind. She squeezed mine hard.

'How are you settling in?' she asked.

'It's warmer than my last place,' said I. 'There's a good family in the basement. The landlady's a bit of a riot.'

A few weeks ago I finally left the room I'd shared with Mrs B to move somewhere a bit smaller on Red Cross Street. I'd missed the rent too many times over the last year and reckoned it'd be the same again this year if I stayed. I needed to get out of that place, anyway, away from Rita's ghost. Though at first it was a comfort having her around, somewhere over the last year it'd changed, and if I was going to keep the love I'd always had for my old darling I needed to get away from that spirit that watched my every move.

'It sounds like just what you need,' she said, standing aside to let a couple of young fellows leave with their hot parcels.

'Maybe. We'll see.'

'Will you pray for them, Norman?' she asked. She was dressed smart, everything tight and tucked in, but her jaw was slack, her eyes full of care. Her usual determination and certainty were gone. 'I know you don't usually, but...'

''Course I will.' I held her eye for some time, feeling her loneliness. Then, when I could take it no more, I drew her close.

'Thank you,' she whispered.

As I walked back to the Borough, I thought about Ettie. I'd seen an aloneness in her that night I hadn't often seen before, and I remembered the time we'd kissed in the cab back from Newgate. That seemed a lifetime ago now, and the memory made me sad. I shook it out of my head as I pushed through the wet fog, but the feeling still hung around my heart. When I reached the Pelican, Molly gave me a kiss on the mouth and poured me a pint. It was busy in there, smoky and loud, and as she ran up and down serving the other punters, I leant my back against the bar and watched the folk of the Borough getting plastered. A bookie stood in a corner, taking bets for the weekend racing; a couple of sweeps were trying to get to know four showgirls who didn't want to know them. An argument started up over a domino game, and an old geezer took up his stick and swiped off another old geezer's hat. The victim grabbed his own stick and prodded the first bloke's dog, who let out a howl, then all hell broke loose. I'd normally enjoy watching the ruckus, but I was thinking about Ettie, about how the side of her I'd seen that night brought up feelings I thought I'd lost.

Molly came charging from behind the counter, shouting

for the boss, her black hair flying as she grabbed one of the blokes by the neck and threw him to the floor. I laughed. She was stronger than I thought.

'Get out, Percy!' she hissed, her face angry and strong, like Boudicca or someone. 'And you, Tom. Clear off, the both of you!'

The landlord appeared from the taproom. He helped Percy to his feet.

'Now, are you two gents going to shake hands and sit back down?' he asked.

'I told them to get out,' said Molly. 'You should bar them. That's the third time this week.'

'They're only battering each other, love.'

'I got enough to do in here without stopping them killing theirselves every half hour.'

Percy was already sat back down, stroking his grey-hound. I didn't like the way the landlord called Molly 'love', nor how he patted her rumple with his greasy grey cloth as he walked back to the taproom.

'You mind him doing that?' I asked her as she came back with three empty tankards in each hand.

'I'll say I do,' she said, dumping them with a clatter on the counter. 'They sit there all day buying no more'n a pennyworth, then they kick off like that. Why he allows them I don't know. They're only here for the fire.'

'I meant him poking you like that.'

She sighed and rubbed her brow with the back of her hand. 'I got a job, ain't I? Four or five girls come in today looking for work.' She laughed and pushed me on the chest. 'What's it to you anyway, Norm? You jealous or something?'

'Just don't like to see it.'

'Here,' she said, taking my mug and gulping it down so fast it dribbled down her chin and wet her grubby blouse. 'I'll get you another.'

I stayed till closing, then she wanted to go dancing at a place on Bankside. We knocked back a brandy within minutes of getting in there, watching as the press of punters jigged to the old fiddler sat on a box in the corner. The tables had been pushed to the wall, a pile of thick coats by the bar with a young girl guarding them. When we'd had another drink, we pushed our way into the crowd and for an hour we capered in the hot filthy steam of the Borough gentry.

As the fiddler began to play 'Morning Star', I had the strangest feelings of joy and regret following each other in waves. My eyes were fixed on Molly, and it seemed she was swallowed in the dance, as little aware of me as the strangers around us. She danced just like my Rita, with the same movements, the same blind abandon.

I remembered one of the first jollies we went on, to a little dancing place by St Saviour's Dock where they'd set up two fiddlers in the courtyard of an old stables. It was her and Molly and my mate Nobber and me, and we danced away like there was no tomorrow, until Nobber and me'd got tired and set ourselves down on a hay bale and watched the two of them go at it together for an hour at least, matching each other, collapsing into each other's arms when each tune finished, then straightening again when the bars of the next one struck up. It was a marvel, all right, watching those two girls dance and laugh, and on the way home Mrs B and me nipped into the churchyard and lay together for the first time, with Nobber and Molly at it somewhere else in the dark. Twenty years later, and I felt the joy of that night fill me again as Molly and me danced on, until I took her arm and pulled her close and placed my lips upon hers. Mrs B used to say to me, 'We'll meet again some day, you and me,' and I never understood what she meant until then. I was meeting her again through her best friend. It was Mrs B I was holding. Around us, all the folk moved and collided and spun while we held each other tight and kissed like we'd found the greatest love. Before the song ended, I took her hand and led her out into the frozen night.

Chapter Nineteen

We reached Piccadilly Hall at midday, where we waited at the stage door to meet Nick. He was to come out alone, making sure Ralf wasn't around lest he recognized me from my visit to his old man's billiard room. As we waited on the street, we listened to three thin soldiers singing 'Pretty Polly Perkins from Paddington Green', a cap in front of them on the pavement. One had his face half burnt off, another missing an eye, the last with such a tremble as you could feel it down the street. Folk on their way to lunch hurried past while horses glanced at them, sighing and nodding their long heads. As they neared the end, a hansom drew up on the other side of the road. In it sat Ralf.

'Quick, hide,' I said, pulling the guvnor behind a couple of horses stood by the kerb.

It was too late. Ralf caught sight of me and smiled. 'Mr Barnett!' he said, hurrying across the road. He wore a checked suit under his cashmere overcoat, his dimples and freckles making him seem younger than his sixteen years. 'You still looking for the Zulus?'

'I am, Ralf,' I said. 'You haven't heard anything, have you?'

'Dad thinks Madame Delacourte's got them. Did you see her?'

'The police are going to talk to her.'

'We're in trouble if they don't turn up soon. We'll have to pay the Aquarium out of our own pocket.'

'That's how the contracts work, is it, young sir?' enquired the guvnor.

'It always is. You have to pay up for lost revenue.'

I introduced them. When they'd exchanged hands, Arrowood asked: 'How much would you have to pay, if I might ask, Mr Capaldi?'

'A lot, that's all I can tell you.' The lad's eyes followed two young ladies as they walked past. 'They sold thousands of tickets. You here for the show, then?'

'We wanted to talk to Capaldi's Wonders,' I said. 'They came over on the boat with the Africans, didn't they?'

'That's right. I just took over as their manager.' He pulled a booklet from his pocket. 'Here, you can have one of these. We just had them printed.'

It was a souvenir pamphlet for the show, with a drawing of the three women on the front. Cost a shilling.

'Thank you, Ralf,' said the guvnor. 'I'll read it with interest.'

'Come in, I'll take you to them.'

The man on the stage door waved us through, and we followed Ralf along a corridor with heating pipes over our heads, up some stairs and through another corridor. It opened into a large room full of people carrying props and costumes. A whole brass band sat on the floor looking vexed. In the middle of the room was a cluster of clothes rails, around which chorus girls were changing their costumes. Ralf turned back to us.

'I do like going through here,' he said with a wink.

The guvnor poked me in the back, pointing at a clown leaning against the wall with a cigar in his mouth. 'That's Polichinelle,' he whispered.

'Ralf, my dear boy!' called the clown.

'Oh, Christ,' muttered Ralf as the fellow lurched across the room.

Polichinelle wore a yellow-and-blue hat, its crown like an upturned cone. His face was unshaved, the tip of his heavy nose hanging low over his wide mouth, around which he'd painted a pair of fat red lips. His narrow eyes were circled with black eye paint, and his neck was hid by a thick, stained ruff. The clown wore a strange yellow coat, stuffed so as his belly stuck out in a horn with big brass buttons down the front. On his spindly legs he wore red velvet plus fours.

'How good to see you, dear boy!' exclaimed the clown, taking Ralf's hand. 'How's that naughty father of yours?'

'He's very well, sir.'

'Polli! How many times must I tell you? Call me Polli!' He took a puff on his cigar. 'What are you doing here?'

'I'm managing our freak show. Father's teaching me the business.'

The clown laughed. 'How you've grown up. Such a shame. You were such an imp, Ralfie. And so afraid of me.'

'I'm not afraid of clowns anymore, Polli. You know where the ladies are?'

'Of course I do. I'm announcing them, didn't you know?'

Ralf nodded, but something about his face didn't look so pleased to hear that.

'Along that corridor,' said the clown. 'Last room on the right. And who are your friends, Ralfie?'

Ralf introduced us while the clown looked me up and down.

'It's an honour, sir,' said the guvnor, shaking the clown's hand for too long. 'I've seen you many times over the years. At the Alhambra, Cremorne Gardens, Crystal Palace. You're one of my wife's favourites.'

'Ah!' laughed the clown. 'A back-handed compliment.'

'No,' protested the guvnor. 'I didn't mean that. I think you're very funny. I was just saying my—'

'You're a big fellow,' interrupted the clown, turning to me. 'Eat a lot, do you?'

'Enough.'

His sly eyes seemed to blaze. 'I bet you do. Eat a lot of rough meat. A lot of flour, eh?'

A bell rang somewhere.

'That's me,' he said, touching Ralf's glove. 'I've some lovely cake in my room, Ralfie. Come see me later.'

'I might be busy,' said Ralf.

'You can make time for me, my boy.'

'How d'you know Polichinelle, Ralf?' asked Arrowood as he watched the clown totter away, touching the dancing girls on their necks and ringing a bell attached to his belt. The guvnor looked dazed, like he'd just met the queen.

'Dad used to manage him,' said the young showman. 'I know a lot of them that's on the stage. Here, come and talk to the ladies.'

We followed him to their dressing room. Before entering, Ralf stared at the door, chewing his lip. He took two deep breaths, raised his fist to knock, then dropped it again. His young face had lost its colour. He turned to me. 'Could you go first, Mr Barnett?'

'What is it, Ralf?' asked the guvnor gently.

The young fellow blew out his cheeks. 'Thing is… well…' He shut his eyes. 'I just can't look at them, Mr Arrowood. I know it's wrong and they're just ladies, really, but I can't do it. They're monsters. You can't say it otherwise.'

'You're afraid of them?'

'I get queasy just to look at them. Can't catch my breath, like. It isn't so bad when they're dressed normal, but… oh, I don't know what it is. I got to get over it, I know. Grow up a bit. I will get over it, just got to get used to them.'

'Good heavens, lad,' said the guvnor. 'Your eyes are too dominant, that's your problem. There are many ways of being human, you know.'

'I know. Don't tell Dad, will you? I don't want him to find out.' He stepped further from the door and looked back at me. 'You go on. Go in first.'

I knocked on the door. Nick opened up, his tight suit freshly brushed, his cap still on his head. When he saw Ralf behind us, he blinked, running his finger up and down his waistcoat buttons. He was scared, I could see it, and Capaldi's son being there didn't help.

'These gents just want to ask the ladies a few questions, Nick,' said Ralf over the guvnor's shoulder. 'Can you let them in?'

Nick nodded and stepped back. It was a small room with no windows. Leonie and Gisele stood by a looking glass. Gisele, the Lobster Claw Lady, had her hair brushed back and hid by an orange scarf. The rims of her eyes were blacked, which made her face seem more orange than before, and she wore a brown top with black specks.

Her hands, hid in gloves the last time we saw her, had no fingers, just a wide thumb next to a broad, knotted stick of flesh. She held a brush. Leonie wore a pink dress that showed her short, pink legs up to the knees and had no sleeves, so you could see her little arms too. She'd powdered her face and scalp so it looked whiter, and reddened her nose-holes. I suppose she did look something like a pig, but not unless you'd been told it. Sylvia sat on a sofa by the back wall, her blonde wig on, her eyes red and puffy. She clasped a handkerchief.

The guvnor introduced us like we'd never met them before. Ralf slipped in behind us and stood with his back to the wall, staring at the floorboards.

'Hello, Mr Ralf,' said Gisele.

'Hello, Gisele,' he said, his eyes flicking up to her for no more than a second.

'We'd like to ask you a few questions about the Africans you met on the Dover boat,' said the guvnor.

'Yes, sir,' said Gisele.

'I'll get you ladies some food,' said Ralf, and hurried out the door.

Nick shut it behind him.

'What's going on?' asked Leonie.

'We ran into Ralf outside and had to pretend we'd come to ask you questions,' said the guvnor. 'Mr Capaldi knows we're looking for the Africans. He even asked us to help him.'

'What's up with the boy?' she asked. 'Is he ill?'

'I suspect so,' said Arrowood as I got the oysters out my bag. Nick looked at them, his lip curling.

'Sorry, mate,' I said. When the guvnor had explained the plan to him the day before, Nick hadn't wanted to do it, but the guvnor told him there was no other way to get English Dave or one of the other guards to come, and we needed them to tell us the address of the boarding house. The Capaldis had to see him ill, and it had to be so bad they'd have no choice but to bring in another man till he was better. Nick still wouldn't have it, but Arrowood persuaded him that Sylvia wanted him to help S'bu, and that it was the only way of doing it so Capaldi wouldn't suspect him of betrayal. He still didn't like it, but finally he agreed.

'Is it safe?' asked Sylvia.

'He'll have food poisoning for a day or two, that's all,' answered the guvnor. 'We've all had it.'

'I'll look after you, sugar,' said Sylvia, coming over to her man and taking his arm. Though it was cold in that room, Nick's forehead was oily with sweat, his wretched eyes calm for once.

I opened the first shell with my knife. The smell was foul, and my eyes watered as I dug out the dry, brown flesh and held it out to him. He snorted, shook his hands, then took the shell and tipped it into his mouth. His bristly throat clenched. He shook his head wildly as it went down, then hurled the shell in the bin. Sylvia winced and stroked his back. He swallowed from a mug on the floor, then took the next one and swallowed that too. I held out the third, but he just stood there, his mouth slack, his thin eyes looking at me with hatred.

'Go on, mate,' I said.

'That's enough,' he growled.

I looked at the guvnor, who nodded.

Sylvia led him to the sofa and sat him down. He slouched back, shutting his eyes and crossing one leg over the other.

'What now?' asked Leonie.

'We wait,' said the guvnor, moving a bucket over with his foot.

Chapter Twenty

It didn't take long. After half an hour, Nick sat up clutching his belly. Five minutes later he grabbed the bucket and rushed out the room. Sylvia rose to follow him, but Leonie stopped her.

'We're on in a minute, darling,' she said.

'Norman will look after him,' added the guvnor.

As I went to find Nick, I noticed a basket of pig's knuckles on the floor outside the room. There was a note:

Have a good performance, ladies. I will
come see you after. Ralf.

I brought it in the room. 'He's run off,' I said.

The guvnor read the note. 'Would you send Mr Capaldi a message, please, Leonie. Say Nick's badly ill.'

Nick was in the passage that led to the privies, on his knees with his head hanging over the bucket. He retched out a great gush of pink porridge and oyster. After it hit the bucket, he coughed, spitting out a long tail of bile. I patted him on the back.

'That's it, mate. Get it out.' I wished I could tell him it'd get better, but we both knew it was about to get a whole lot worse.

Fifteen minutes later, the guvnor found us. Nick was sat on the privy now, his britches round his ankles. The bucket was on his lap.

'How is he?'

'Suffering,' I muttered.

'It won't last, Nick,' said the guvnor.

'Fuck off,' growled the poor bloke, spitting into the bucket.

'I don't suppose he'll want his pig's knuckle,' said the guvnor, keeping his distance. 'You stay with him, there's a good chap.' And with that, he hurried off.

I shut the privy door and went to sit on a crate in the passage. A few moments later, Polichinelle appeared. He was a little sweaty, a little puffed: he'd either just come off stage or he'd been rutting in his dressing room in his clown suit. I'd never seen his act, but everybody in London knew his name. He'd performed for the queen, for Gladstone, for Empress Sisi and her court.

'Hm,' he said, coming to a stop in front of me. 'You know, you have the most fearful hue, my friend. D'you suffer dyspepsia?'

'Me and half of London.'

As more wretched noises came from Nick, the clown bent and inspected my eyes. He smelt of wine and eggs, and close up I could see that he was a lot older than I thought: fifty-five or sixty, maybe. He had a whitish paint rubbed into the lines around his eyes and forehead. He straightened. 'Pains in the gut?'

I pointed to the left side of my belly. 'Are you a doctor as well as a clown?'

'I've studied nutrition with Mrs Crenshaw. What did you have for breakfast?'

'A bloater.'

He nodded in approval. 'Coffee?'

I nodded.

'I think you might have a fever in your kidney. Remove fats and farinaceous foods from your diet and reduce liquids. You may eat as much lean as you wish.'

'Yes, sir.'

He patted my arm. 'Fennel tea, twice a day. No more coffee, understand?'

Nick made a long, bubbling groan in the shithouse. 'Fuck it,' he whimpered.

'Bad oysters,' I said to the clown.

He looked at the privy door and shook his head. 'Allow him to fully purge, then give him some fennel tea.'

'We'll both have a cup,' I said. 'Have a little tea party.'

A terrible stench of corruption reached us. Polichinelle looked at the privy again, wrinkling his hooky nose. 'I think I'll use the audience facilities. Pray I don't get mobbed, my dear.'

Arrowood appeared ten minutes later. He pulled open the lavatory door to see Nick with his dignity gone, gobs of vomit on his waistcoat and his britches round his ankles. Drops of sweat spotted his forehead.

'Poor fellow,' said the guvnor. 'Don't despair. You'll pull through.'

'Cocksucker,' muttered Nick, not opening his eyes.

'We'd better get out of the way, Norman. Capaldi's men'll be here soon.'

We left Nick and went to the big waiting room where the brass band still sat on the floor and performers and stage-hands hurried here and there. We found a changing screen and pulled a couple of chairs behind it so we could watch the room without being too obvious.

Soon, Ermano appeared from the stage door, a bowler on his head and a brolly under his arm. He strode through in the direction of the ladies' dressing room.

'Stay hidden,' said the guvnor, waddling after him. 'He'll recognize you.'

Ten minutes later, Capaldi's Wonders of the World appeared, on their way to the stage for their first performance. Gisele lay in a huge glass tank decorated with starfish and stuffed trout, which was pulled on a cart by Ermano. She'd been painted a blazing orange, while her legs were curled in a brown fish-tail costume. Behind walked Leonie, stiff and proud in the absurd pink dress, her face with its cavernous black nostrils upturned. Her scalp was almost bare, and on her hands and feet were white leather gloves in the shape of hooves. She walked with her arm linked in Sylvia's, who had her hair combed so it stuck out in fans on all sides of her face, framing her jutting lips. She walked in silence, her rumple sticking out behind her in a dress short enough to show her furry legs. It looked like she was in a trance.

When they'd gone through to the stage, the guvnor found me again. 'Ermano's sent for English Dave,' he said.

'How's Nick?'

'Still in the privy. Ermano tried to get him up but there was no chance.' The guvnor sighed and shook his head. 'The fellow's a brute: he belted him around the face so hard it shook the floor.'

'Did he notice you?'

'He didn't even look at me. There are people everywhere.'

After half an hour the ladies returned from their perfor-mance, Leonie marching ahead, Sylvia behind with Gisele's hand on her shoulder. Ermano followed, talking to Ralf. His overcoat was open, revealing his bright red waistcoat. His face was still bruised blue and yellow, and I noticed he'd stuck his queer little pigtail into his collar where it wouldn't be seen.

It was about five when a bloke appeared I recognized. He was the bloke that arrived on a bicycle outside Capaldi's house, the one who attacked Neddy. Though he had neatly cut hair and a thick moustache, you could see right away he was a bully: he walked like the swell mob, pushing through the performers with his belly out, his shoulders back and his feet wide. You couldn't miss that rubbery scar that wormed across his face.

I kept back behind the screen as he paused to ask one of the dancers directions. She pointed down the corridor. He gave her a quick kiss and she laughed, pushing him away. He whispered in her ear, then cruised off.

Arrowood followed him. Now and then, a showgirl changing her costume by the clothes rails looked over at me sat there behind the screen. Nobody seemed to mind. There were a few other blokes sat around the big room just like me, and I remembered hearing that one of the showmen sold tickets to gents so they could watch the showgirls getting ready backstage. It made me feel dirty, and the next time one of the performers looked at me I felt my face colour. Get a grip, you twerp, I told myself. I stood and stretched my legs, feeling hungry. We'd missed our dinner again.

Some time later, Ermano passed through and disappeared toward the street. Then the ladies came back for their next performance, this time followed by English Dave. Ralf had vanished again.

The guvnor joined me.

'That's him, but we need to get him alone. There's too many people about here. He'll be with them until the show ends, so how about we get something to eat and return later?'

We found a coffee shop and ordered some cabbage and potatoes. The guvnor went around gathering the papers as lay about the empty tables. *The Times* and the *Daily News* reported on Constable Mabaso from South Africa tracking two bandits from Johannesburg thought to be Senzo and Musa, and the *Star* mentioned the guvnor, saying he was working with the Aborigines' Protection Society to find the Zulus. But that was it. No news of a reward being posted yet.

Lloyd's Weekly had a bit on Kitchener's campaign in Dongola. I didn't know why we were fighting in Sudan and I didn't much care: it was just another battle in our never-ending war with the world. I shut the paper and looked around the shop. On the next table were a mother and two boys, maybe seven or eight year old. They were sharing a single slice of bread. As we ate, the lads watched us, watched each spoonful as it travelled to our mouths.

'Isabel will have finished her interview for the medical scholarship by now,' said the guvnor. 'I wonder how she got on.'

'She's been studying long enough.'

'She was reading my Havelock Ellis, you know. *The Criminal*. I told you about it.'

I nodded but said nothing. I didn't want another bloody lecture on Havelock Ellis.

'D'you think it's a sign she's becoming interested in our work?' he asked, hope aflame in his piggy eyes. He dug his spoon into the spuds.

'How were the babies this morning?'

His face fell. 'No better. It can't be typhus. It just can't.'

I nodded. 'I'm sure it's just a fever. It'll break soon.'

He held my eyes for some time, then opened the *Pall Mall Gazette*.

'Well, well,' he said in a bit. 'There are more Zulus in town.'

'They're amaQwabe, sir.'

Ignoring me, he read out the article. '*Much curiosity has been excited by the arrival of the Zulu Princess Nobantu in the city. She is staying at the York Hotel, accompanied by two attendants. The princess is a strange-looking lady of the Zulu type. She wears a coronet of a gold colour instead of any other head-dress, and but scant clothing, her arms uncovered when indoors and her bodice lower than the current fashion. We are informed she is a bright and volatile person, with a fine flow of language and a quick wit. Last night, when she and her suite drove to Covent Garden for a pantomime, their carriage was mobbed by a ruffianly crowd who held the wheels so that they could peer into the windows. The princess appeared much less disturbed than an English lady would have been from such an indignity at the hands of Zulus. Mr Barber Beaumont is staging exhibitions of the Zulus in Brighton and Edinburgh, followed by three weeks in the Alhambra, London.*' Arrowood shook his head. 'That carriage ride must have been good publicity: I think Mr Beaumont's taken a leaf from the Barnum book. Isn't it odd the Capaldis didn't mention this Beaumont fellow as another competitor for their Zulu show?'

'Maybe he's an honest man.'

A couple of parsons on the other side of the room stood and left the coffee shop, leaving their plates of beef and dumplings half-eaten. The moment the door shut on them, the mother and sons moved to their table and began swallowing the left-overs as quick as they could.

'What are we going to do about English Dave?' I asked.

'We'll return to Piccadilly Hall to make sure he goes back with the ladies, then call at Gresham Hall later tonight. We'll have to get him to talk, Norman. If he doesn't know where S'bu and Mrs Fowler are, he'll know where that boarding house is.'

I sighed. I never liked it when we had to use force on a bloke, but we weren't getting any closer to finding S'bu and Mrs Fowler and I didn't see any other way.

'It might not even be Capaldi,' I said. 'It might be Delacourte.'

'Or Mr Beaumont, it appears. But we have to start somewhere.'

The guvnor chewed his lip for a while, then picked up the paper again. After a few minutes, he groaned and passed it to me, pointing at a story: Charles de Vere Beauclerc was suing his father, the Duke of St Albans, for causing him to go bald.

'What a world this is,' he sighed, stuffing his mouth with a quantity of cabbage. A thread of gravy oozed into his whiskers. 'D'you ever wonder who your father was, Norman?'

'Not anymore. I thought he might show up for Ma's funeral, but he never did. I stopped caring a long time ago.' I pushed my bowl away, winking at the smallest boy on the next table. He came over and took it. 'D'you think of yours much?'

'I can't help it with Ettie's face leering at me over breakfast each morning. He had that same disapproving look, even when he was trying to be reasonable. I've been reading Maudsley on temperament and it's got me worried we're tainted. And Mercy, of course. I hope she hasn't any of his blood.'

The guvnor's old man was a parson who spent the last ten years of his life tied to a chair in a private sanatorium. I'd never met him, but I imagined he was just an older model of the guvnor – an overfed round belly, short legs, a red, jowly face set in a balding ox's head. That sort of thing.

'Ettie isn't tainted and nor are you,' I said. 'You're a bit over-emotional, is all. Your nerves are nearer the surface. That isn't insanity, far as I know.'

He patted my hand and became thoughtful.

'D'you think I should get new teeth?' he asked at last.

Chapter Twenty-One

We were back at Piccadilly Hall as the last of the crowds emptied out on Great Windmill Street. It was about ten o'clock and the air was still, the clouds overhead thick and smoky. Frost covered the pavements; the horses tethered to the line of hansoms blew white from their muzzles. We waited behind a coffee stand about fifty yards from the stage door: after ten minutes, the performers began stepping out and disappeared along the road. Polichinelle stopped to sign the bills of a couple of odd gentlemen wearing jester hats and thick reefer jackets. At last, the doorman and English Dave lifted a trolley out. On his back, with his knees in the air and his boots flat on the planks, lay Nick, his arm crooked over his face. He groaned as the wheels clunked over the step.

'Careful, Dave!' cried Sylvia. She wore a long, red coat, a bonnet and scarf hiding most of her face.

'He ain't hurt,' growled Dave, turning the cart. 'Get a four-wheeler.'

Sylvia crossed to the line of cabs as Leonie and Gisele appeared at the door. We watched as they helped Nick aboard the carriage. As soon as they were moving, we got in a hansom and followed them down to the Embankment, over Vauxhall Bridge and onto the South Lambeth Road. When they turned into Capaldi's street in Stockwell, we asked the driver to stop. The guvnor had a think.

'We'll wait for them in Gresham Hall,' he said at last. 'There's nothing we can do while they're in there, and we need Dave on his own. It wouldn't do any harm to have a look round anyway, just in case they've got S'bu hidden there after all.'

It was nearing eleven when we arrived in Brixton. There were a few glimmers of light in the houses, but the front windows of Gresham Hall were dark. A couple of dogs were ravaging a manky pigeon in the gutter, a baby cried somewhere near, but there was nobody around to disturb us. We walked down the path to the annex at the back of the building.

I knocked at the yellow door a few times, but there was no movement inside so I got out my betty and had a fiddle with the lock. It was an old spring stock job and it clicked open in moments. We stepped inside the dark corridor and listened.

No sound. The guvnor lit his pocket candle and we began to search. The kitchen was cold: no sign of anyone being in there for hours. Aside from the stairs, there were two other doors in the corridor. One was a cupboard full of mops and brooms, the shelves stacked with Bibles and prayer books. The other led to the hall itself. The door wasn't locked, so we stepped in. The high, thin windows of the big room let in a faint glow from the streetlights outside. Chairs were set out in rows in front of a small stage, where stood a lectern. A harmonium sat on one side. We had a look in the two cupboards on either side of the stage. The smaller one held a ladder and a stack of chairs. The larger, big enough to walk around in, had piles of books on the floor, a little dresser, a few crates stacked against the far wall.

We went back into the corridor. Opposite the kitchen were the stairs leading to the floor above. We paused a moment, listening again. Somewhere outside in the cold a pigeon purred. The wind was strengthening, rattling the side door.

We crept up the stairs, the guvnor behind as always. At the stairhead, he gave me the candle. There was a short, dark corridor ahead, with a window on one side and a door at the other. A noise ahead made me freeze.

It sounded like a body moving, a soft rustle that appeared then just as quickly disappeared, leaving only the guvnor's wheezy breath on my back. Quiet as I could, I pulled the pistol from my pocket and walked on. The door on the right was ajar. I paused as I reached it, holding up the candle. A bed was against the near wall, with something like a pile of canvas on it. I took a step inside. The pile shifted and a face appeared, its eyes screwed up. I moved closer.

'Senzo,' I said. 'It's Norman.'

He shut his eyes, pulling the canvas sheets about him.

'Senzo!' hissed the guvnor. 'We told you to hide in the loft. English Dave's on his way.'

'Leonie said she'd make a noise,' came Thembeka's voice from behind the door. She was sitting on the edge of a mattress on the floor, clutching her thick shawl to her neck. Her eyes were only half-open. She nodded at the hatch in the eaves. 'The door's only there. We'd have time to hide before anyone came up the stairs.'

'That was a risk,' said the guvnor.

'It's too cold in there,' she answered. 'There's no proper floor.'

Senzo pushed himself upright, lowering his boots to the bare boards. He spoke to Thembeka as I checked the hatch: there was nobody there.

'Did you find S'bu?' asked she, rising to her feet. She'd been sleeping in her hat.

'Not yet, ma'am,' said the guvnor. 'I'm sorry.'

She told Senzo. He nodded, his sad eyes cast down.

'What can we do, William?' asked Thembeka. 'We must find him. He's only a boy.'

'I'm afraid you can't leave here. Until we find who killed your cousin and Mr Fowler, you're in danger.'

'It was Mr Capaldi's men,' she said. 'We're certain. The police must search his house.'

'They did search it. And you didn't actually recognize them, did you? We need proof. Now, listen. We've just been to Scotland Yard. A policeman's arrived from Johannesburg.' The guvnor stepped closer to see their faces better. 'Constable Mabaso.'

'Mabaso?' said Senzo, hopping to his feet. He spoke quick to Thembeka, his brow drawn over his eyes. She shook her head and replied. Senzo spoke again.

'He's here?' asked Thembeka. 'In London?'

'Yes. He's working with the police.'

'Does he know where we are?'

'We're the only ones who know.'

Thembeka walked to the window. The guvnor said nothing, waiting to see how they'd explain it. She spoke to Senzo again. He shook his head, then made a sound that could only have been a curse. They fell silent.

'Why's he tracking you?' asked Arrowood when it was clear they weren't going to speak. The candle was guttering: I spotted a hand-lamp on the floor and lit it.

'What did Mabaso tell you?' asked Thembeka.

'I want you to tell us.'

'First you tell me.'

He sighed. 'He said Senzo and Musa were in the Ninevite gang.' I watched Senzo as he spoke. Though he spoke no English, his head was pushed forwards, following every word, trying to make sense of it. 'He said they'd raided a mine owner's compound and killed a child and a guard. They stole a wage cart and some gold bullion, then fled through Mozambique to Portugal and then Paris. From there they came to London.'

She snorted, an angry laugh. Then, without looking away from the guvnor's face, translated it into African for Senzo. Again, they talked.

The guvnor checked his watch and sighed. 'Dave's taken the ladies to Capaldi's house. I'm parched. How about we all go downstairs and make a cup of tea? Norman can keep watch. We've a lot to talk about.'

When we were in the kitchen, Senzo started a fire in the burner. Thembeka got out the mugs. The guvnor helped himself to a bit of the cake we'd had before while I rolled a smoke. Nick's old straw mattress was upright against the wall; I leant against it, watching out the window in case anyone came up the path.

'Is it true?' asked the guvnor, standing with his bum to the burner. 'They raided that compound?'

'Yes,' said Thembeka. 'Sam and Musa. They are Ninevites.'

'Thieves,' grunted the guvnor. He studied Senzo, who stared back at him.

'The Ninevites are thieves, yes,' she said, the muscles in her jaw moving beneath the skin. Her eyes were hard, and I sensed she was tired of having to explain things to us. 'But your people are worse. You've stolen our land. You kill us in the mines. You beat us and imprison us for breaking laws we never wanted. The white man makes our boys dig gold for him. The Ninevites just dig some of it back.'

Arrowood said nothing for a while. Then he took a bite of cake and asked, 'Who killed Mr Kruger's child?'

Thembeka held her hands out to the cooker to get a bit of the warmth. 'Zixuko. A Ninevite lieutenant. He killed the boy and the guard, but he's dead. The other guard shot him.'

'Mabaso said it was your cousins who killed them.'

'Mabaso wasn't there. It was Zixuko.'

'Where's the money and gold?'

Again, she talked to Senzo.

'Go money,' said Senzo at last, looking at the guvnor. He brushed one hand against the other. He shook his head. 'Go.'

'What happened to it?'

'The Ninevites are an army,' said Thembeka as Senzo went back to making the tea. 'My cousins are only soldiers. They brought the gold to the caves and handed it over to the commanders.'

'Why does Mabaso say it was your cousins who killed the boy and the guard?'

She snorted, waving away the tea Senzo offered her and taking up Gisele's flask of gin. 'The police want someone to hang. Mabaso's just their dog.'

'Why did you come here with them, Miss Thembeka?' asked the guvnor, accepting a mug from Senzo.

She took a swallow of gin and grimaced. 'To keep an eye on S'bu. He's my nephew, William. He wants adventure, but he's not ready for it.'

'Why did S'bu come with you here?'

'It's a long story.'

'I want to hear it, if you don't mind.'

She took another swallow of gin. 'He was houseboy for an Afrikaaner. That's why he speaks Afrikaans, not English. At thirteen the family sent him away. The white families only want younger boys, you see. When they get too big they find another one. He went to Krugersdorp to find work. The master of one of the houses he called on was an agent for the mines. He offered him a job but S'bu said no. He didn't want to work underground. So many of our men never return from the mines, and he didn't want to be one. The agent had him arrested. Ten lashes and five months in prison for that.'

'Ten lashes? For refusing a job?'

'Why don't you know what's happening in your empire?' she cried, throwing her hands in the air.

The guvnor bit his lip, shaking his heavy head.

'I told you before,' she said, trying to be patient with us again. 'An African is not permitted to refuse work from a white man if he has no job. It's the Native Laws. He was put in a man's gaol. He was thirteen.'

'Disgraceful,' muttered the guvnor.

Senzo dumped some sugar in my tea and passed it to me. I kept close to the window, listening as I watched the path. Thembeka pulled her shawl closer to her neck. 'Ninevites control the prisons. They made S'bu join them. We brought him with us to get him away from them. It's no good for young boys in the army of the hills.'

The guvnor took a gurgle of his tea and looked at her for a while. 'Thank you for explaining that, Miss Thembeka,' he said at last. 'But Constable Mabaso's appearance makes things difficult for us. We have two different stories. Why should we believe you about the raid rather than him?'

'It's the truth,' she said. She looked at me, then back at him. 'Please don't tell Mabaso where we are. Please. They'll hang Senzo on the word of a policeman. That's justice in Natal.'

'But if the real murderer's dead, and the gold's with the Ninevites, why was Mabaso sent here? Surely it isn't worth it?'

'They like to hang anyone on a raid. They want to frighten the blacks and finish the Ninevites. And a white boy died, didn't he? They want blood.'

A sharp noise outside made us all freeze. I couldn't make out anything in the alley, so I shook my head. 'Must be a cat or something.'

'They're taking a long time,' said the guvnor at last. 'I hope they haven't gone to that boarding house you were in before you escaped. Are you sure you don't know where it was?'

She talked to Senzo, then shook her head. 'It was run by Mrs Farini. We don't know where it was. All we remember are pubs and buses and churches. All these streets look the same.'

Senzo drank his tea, while I rolled a fag for him and another for myself. The guvnor gave Thembeka a bit of baccy for her pipe and we all lit up and had a little smoke, thinking it over. It was then I saw the four-wheeler pull up at the entrance to the path.

Chapter Twenty-Two

Senzo and Thembeka hurried up the stairs to the loft as the footsteps approached outside. A key went in the door.

'It ain't locked,' came a bloke's voice as it opened. 'Not very clever, Nick, is it?'

'Leave him alone, Dave,' said Sylvia.

At first, Dave didn't see us. Nick's arm was draped over his shoulder. Nick himself was slumped and pale, his face wet, his eyes half-shut.

'Who are you?' asked Dave, stopping sharply.

'Mr Arrowood,' said the guvnor. 'This is Mr Barnett. We're friends of the ladies.'

'It's fine, Dave,' said Leonie, appearing behind him in the doorway. 'We know them.'

As Dave stood there trying to decide what to do, Gisele and Sylvia took Nick and led him past us into the kitchen.

'How is he, Sylvia?' asked the guvnor.

'He ain't being sick so often,' she said, straightening her wig under her bonnet. 'Poor darling.'

'How did you get in?' asked Dave. He was about my size, but uglier. He wore a pair of thick leather gloves.

'Housebreaking,' said the guvnor. 'Mr Capaldi asked us to help him find the Africans. We wanted to ask the ladies if they'd seen them. There was nobody here, so…'

Dave wiped the moisture off his moustache with the back of his glove. 'You seen the Africans, Leonie?'

'No,' she answered.

He stood back to let us out. 'Goodnight then, gents. It's late. The artists need their sleep.'

Behind us in the kitchen, Sylvia set the mattress under the window and helped Nick lay down.

'Of course,' said Arrowood, giving a little bow. I joined him, tipping my hat. Dave was thinking hard, probably wondering if there was something else he should ask us.

'Just one more thing, sir,' said the guvnor. 'We need to speak to S'bu, the youngster. It's rather urgent. Can you tell us where we can find him?'

He stiffened. 'I thought you said you're working for Mr Capaldi?'

The guvnor smiled. 'Yes, he asked Mr Barnett here to help him.'

'He did, mate,' I said. 'Ermano and Ralf were there. You can ask them.'

'Well, I don't know where he is. Now, it's time you went home, gents.'

I drew out my pistol. Arrowood did the same.

'Where are S'bu and Mrs Fowler?' he asked.

'You ain't with Mr Capaldi,' said Dave, his eyes on my gun.

'We decided not to help him after all, Dave,' said the guvnor in his most cheerful voice. 'We're from the Aborigines' Protection Society. Where's the boy?'

Dave looked me up and down, then his eyes fell on the guvnor standing behind. 'He ain't got the Zulus. He's had me out looking for them, you mug.'

Behind us we heard Nick retch.

'You were guarding them before,' I said. 'Where?'

'We use a boarding house in Vauxhall, but they run off. That's what started all this.'

'Where in Vauxhall?'

'Opposite the gas works on Wandsworth Road. Cross in the window. You can't miss it.'

'You found them at the Quaker Meeting House,' I said. 'You captured S'bu back.'

He shook his head and sighed. 'Not me, mate.'

'Your boss did.'

'I don't think so.'

'Then who?'

'Mrs Delacourte's men.'

I stepped forward and shoved my pistol in his belly.

'Where are they?' I asked again, my eyes level with his. Close up, I could see he was ragged from tiredness.

He held my gaze, the faintest smile on his face. He scratched the scar that wormed from his forehead to his cheek. He was a cool one, all right. 'Don't know, mate, but the other two are upstairs. As you already know.'

The guvnor flitched. 'How did *you*—'

'Nick told us, didn't he? Day after Mr Capaldi came here.'

'Then why doesn't Mr Capaldi capture them?'

'Why would he? They got nowhere else to go.'

'But they're witnesses.'

'Nick told us what they saw. A couple of blokes with guns. We got the descriptions. They're Mrs Delacourte's men.'

The guvnor frowned. He scratched his whiskers. 'Let's sit,' he said, pointing at the kitchen with his gun. I got behind

Dave, the pistol in his back, and guided him through. Leonie stood by the pantry watching us. Sylvia knelt on the floor next to Nick's mattress. We made Dave sit on one of the benches, while I stood behind him, the guvnor easing himself down on the other side of the table. Instead of speaking, he stared at the lamp for a few moments, pondering.

'The police went to search Madame Delacourte's premises yesterday,' he said at last. 'Has your master told the police that he's identified the murderers as her men?'

Dave shook his head.

'Why not?'

'He don't trust the coppers to do it right. Reckons they'll do the Zulus for the murders whether it was them or not.'

The guvnor pushed himself up and started to pace the sticky wooden floor. 'Where else does Capaldi keep people?'

'Sometimes they stay in the boarding house, but he prefers this place 'cos they use the hall out there to rehearse.'

I heard a noise in the corridor and spun around, pulling my pistol from Dave's back. It was only a cat, but in a flash Dave had my forearm in his grip. He gave it a sudden, wrenching twist.

A bolt of pain went through me, and before I knew it he held my gun in his palm.

'Stupid,' he whispered, jabbing it hard in my gut. 'Very stupid.'

He stood, facing me.

'Let them go, Dave,' said Leonie. 'They were just leaving.'

'I don't like being threatened, sweetheart.'

'Come on, Dave,' I said, just as cool as him. 'What are you going to do with the gun? You shoot me and my guvnor shoots you.'

188

'Least you don't get to do for me, Jumbo,' he growled.

'We were never going to shoot you, and you know it.'

For a few moments we stood in silence, the guvnor standing with his gun trained on Dave, Dave with my gun stuck in my belly.

'So what now?' I asked at last.

'Mr Capaldi gets to decide that.'

'I don't think so, my friend,' said Arrowood. 'You can't leave the ladies alone because for some reason I don't understand, your employer appears to insist on their being under guard. And you can't send him a message because there's nobody to take it.'

'We'll wait until tomorrow when Ralf comes.'

'You'd have to stay awake all night.'

'That's right.'

'Well, why don't we sit down at least?'

Dave nodded. The guvnor lowered himself onto the bench on the other side of the table. I sat opposite, Dave to my side, his gun now planted in my kidneys.

The guvnor looked over at Leonie. 'Why don't you all go up to bed? Nobody's going to get hurt tonight.'

'Do you know how stupid this is?' she asked.

'Yes, ma'am,' said the guvnor. 'But there seems no other way.'

Leonie shook her head. She looked from the guvnor to Dave.

'Go on,' said Dave. 'But leave Nick here.'

The three women shuffled out and slowly climbed the stairs, leaving the four of us alone in the kitchen.

'You look tired, Dave,' said the guvnor.

'I ain't tired.'

'Dark and puffy under the eyes, pale skin, drooping mouth. You look like you haven't slept properly for a while, my friend.'

Dave clicked his tongue.

'Your limbs are heavy,' said the guvnor in the voice he used to soothe the babies.

'What?'

Arrowood glanced under the table. 'Those legs look like lead.'

Dave glanced down, puzzled. 'Eh?'

'You're so tired, Dave. So tired.'

'I told you...'

'Your eyes want to close.'

'Shut your mouth, will you?'

'Mr Barnett and I will wake each other up if we fall asleep, but who'll keep you awake, my friend? How will you stay awake all night? You're so tired already. You didn't plan on this job, did you? Your arms are like dead weights. You want to shut your eyes, just for a moment. Go on. It's fine. We'll still be here.'

'Shut your mouth or I'll shut it for you.'

'You do look tired, mate,' I said.

He was blinking. He rubbed his eyes with his other hand.

'Were you working last night?' asked the guvnor.

Dave made no reply.

'Drinking?'

The hard man shifted on the bench, pushing the pistol tighter to my side.

'It's uncomfortable, being so tired,' continued the guvnor, his voice low and soft. 'The body yearns for sleep. The mind turns in on itself. The heart becomes irregular.'

Dave's eyelids lowered. He swallowed.

'You look whacked, mate,' I said.

'You can hardly keep your eyes open,' said the guvnor.

Dave shook his head and stood, pulling the gun away from my side. 'Go on, then, hook it. Both of you.'

I reached for my gun, but he jerked his hand away. 'Don't take the piss, mate. Now, get out.'

The guvnor paused. 'Is Mrs Fowler safe?' he asked.

'Christ. How many times d'you want me to tell you? That ain't us. Go and ask Mrs Delacourte.'

Chapter Twenty-Three

I went to collect the guvnor early next morning. Outside was grey and cold, carters and crossing sweepers hunched into their coats, scarves and shawls covering all but their eyes. Inside the shop, Mrs Pudding was mixing up the gubbins in the gubbins pot, the heat from the ovens just beginning to warm the place. The family hadn't cleaned up from the night before, and the little tables were strewn with crumbs and mouse pellets and dried smears of gravy. They used to be so clean, but things had changed in that family. They were dirty beggars these days.

'Morning, Norm,' she squawked, not even looking up as I wrestled to shut the sticky door. 'Not there!' she suddenly cried, throwing her stirrer at Little Albert. It struck his forehead, making him drop the metal tray that he was trying to balance on a stool.

'I told you not to do that, Ma!' he shouted, swinging his arm across the counter and knocking a stack of filthy bowls to the floor.

'Don't lose your rag with me, my boy!' yelled Mrs Pudding.

'Shut your hole!' roared Little Albert.

He was always her favourite son on account of him being a little slow-witted, but they'd been arguing a lot over the last few weeks, arguing in a way they never used to do. I didn't know what was up between them. Not wanting to hear any more, I hurried through to the back corridor.

There was no answer at the guvnor's door, so I let myself in. The window was wide open, the coals glowing in the grate. The guvnor's mattress stood against the wall, a stack of papers by the door. Both babies were in their crates on the table, and Flossie was underneath with the cat.

'Hello, darling,' I said, squatting down to see her proper. She looked a sight better in a dress and jumper than when we'd first met her: then she wore a sack with three holes cut in it.

Instead of answering, she held up a new dolly.

'That's nice. What's her name?'

'Annie,' said Flossie. 'Mrs Isabel gave it me. Her baby's real sick like Davey was.'

'You miss Davey, don't you?'

Her eyes fell. 'Yeah,' she whispered.

'You want a biscuit?'

She nodded. I straightened up and looked at the two babies. Leopold was asleep, all but his wide face buried under a stack of blankets. Mercy's pink eyes were open, gazing up at the ceiling.

'Hello, beautiful,' I whispered, stroking her clenched hand with my finger. She didn't make any movement, no twitch of her cheek, no ghost of a smile. Her skin was drawn across the bones of her face, her little lips like dried petals.

'Morning, Norman,' said Isabel, coming down the stairs. Her shawl was loose over her shoulders, her hair undone.

'They're no better?' I asked.

'Leo's been asleep since yesterday afternoon. Mercy, well...' She came to a stop at the bottom of the stairs, rubbing her raw nose. There was no life in her eyes. 'She just stares.'

'Any more news from the doc?'

'He told us to give them beef tea, but I told him they won't take it.' She stepped into the small pantry. I listened to her clink around in there for a few moments, not knowing what to say. The orange cat came out from under the table and rubbed its side along my leg, its back arched, a ferocious purr coming out of somewhere inside it. Isabel returned with a small cup. 'Maybe you can try.'

I pulled the chair up next to the table and brought a teaspoon of tea to Mercy's parched lips. She didn't respond, so I let a small amount fall into her mouth. It spilled out the corners of her lips and down her cheeks. I tried again with a full spoon. Again, it spilled out, but now she began choking. I was sure she was going to cry, but she just coughed and coughed, her eyes fixed on the ceiling, until all the tea had risen and rolled down her face. I turned my head, not wanting to see that cracked brown tongue jerk out of her sweet button mouth again.

'I don't think she can swallow,' said Isabel.

'It is typhus, then?'

She nodded, holding my eye. She wrapped her hand in the shawl and laid it on the side of her face.

'And the doc didn't have any medicine?'

'He said there's nothing that works. The apothecary suggested Jesuit's bark. Have you heard of it?'

I shook my head.

'It's from Peru, but it's very dear. He'd heard of someone having good results with it, but he couldn't swear by it.'

'Are you going to try it?'

'If we can find the money. It's forty shillings, he thinks. William has nothing at the moment, but he can ask Lewis, can't he?'

'Maybe,' I said, shifting on the hard chair: one side of me was hot from the fire, the other frozen from the open window. 'I hope so. You're looking thin, Isabel.'

'I've no appetite.'

'You've got to take care of yourself. They'll need you when they recover.'

The pause was over-long.

'I know, Norman,' she said at last.

'Shall I wake up Leo?'

'Let him sleep.'

I nodded. 'Is William in?'

'He's in the outhouse. He's been windy.'

'Did you see the scholarship committee yesterday?'

She sat forward like she wanted to appear enthusiastic, though there was no real energy in her face. 'Two hours I was in there. I think I did well enough. I answered their questions, but I was very tired.'

'What did they ask?'

'About my medical knowledge and my reasons for wanting to be a doctor. They wanted to know whether I'd be prepared to go to India. There are more female doctors there than anywhere else, apparently. Women aren't permitted to see male doctors, so they don't have much choice but to accept us. I wouldn't have to go. Mrs Anderson wants more women in England too.'

'She was there?'

She nodded. 'They asked about my home situation. One of the gentlemen wasn't happy to know I have a child, but I thought some of the others were sympathetic. They won't decide for a day or so. They were seeing other ladies.'

'I do hope you're chosen.'

'So do I, Norman. The more I've read, the more certain I am this is my calling.' Her hand waved at the babies. 'And after this…'

'They're only choosing one lady?'

'Yes, only one.'

The door opened and Ettie stepped in, followed by Reverend Hebden, the fellow who ran the mission she helped at. He nodded at me.

'Good day, Isabel,' he said, lifting his parson's hat. 'I've come to pray for the children.'

'Then do so, Reverend.'

Without another word, she got to her feet and climbed the stairs.

I didn't like seeing Ettie and Hebden come in together. I wondered how she could still talk to the dirty bastard. I'd never get over what they did, why she chose him, how he could stand so erect with his parson's hat and talk about love and sin as if he hadn't fathered little Mercy. I couldn't for one moment understand why he wouldn't claim that little angel as his own.

As the parson took up his stance over the ailing babies, Ettie beckoned me into the scullery. She took out a telegram and handed it to me. 'It arrived yesterday evening,' she said.

It was addressed to her.

DELIGHTED TO INFORM YOU HAVE WON WOMENS MEDICAL SCHOLARSHIP. PLS CONTACT MRS ANDERSON MONDAY NEXT FOR ARRANGEMENTS.

I shook my head, not understanding. 'Why's this come to you?'

'They've awarded it to me, Norman. My interview was on

Wednesday. I didn't want Isabel to know I'd applied in case it caused more bad feeling.'

'Congratulations,' I said, feeling that for once something had gone right in the world. Ettie had served in Afghanistan as a nurse and had been doing good work in the slums for the last few years. If anyone deserved this, it was her.

'How am I going to tell Isabel?' she asked, biting her lip.

'Just tell her straight. There's nothing else you can do.'

'But I can't tell her now, not with the children so poorly.'

'Does William know?' I asked, nodding at the outhouse.

'Only you, Norman.'

'Not Hebden?'

'No. And I told you that what we did is in the past. Reverend Hebden's promised to Miss Fitzhugh.'

'Of course he blooming is. Does she know he has a child?'

'No, and she mustn't.'

'You've a lot of secrets, Ettie. I'm not sure I like you this way.'

Her face fell, and I saw that I'd hurt her. Hearing the outhouse door squeak open, we moved back to the parlour and moments later the guvnor appeared. He glanced at Hebden but said nothing: the parson's hand was now on the crown of Mercy's head as he muttered a request for intervention. The guvnor patted my rumple as he passed, putting on his overcoat and hat, his gloves, his scarf.

'Come along, Barnett,' he said. 'We've work to do.'

Chapter Twenty-Four

The desk sergeant, a big-bellied bloke with a round, bald head, had us wait downstairs as he sent a lad to find Inspector Napper. We stood by the front door, watching as constables came in and out, some in uniform with their idiot hats perched on their heads, some in plainclothes. All wore thick gloves and grim, frosty faces. A PC bundled in a shivering brown fellow wearing a knitted coat bound by a rope around the middle.

'He stole an umbrella from Selfridge's, sarge.'

The sergeant shook his head and snarled. 'Name.'

'Henry Din, sir,' said the thief.

'Hindoo?' asked the sergeant.

'Christian, sir.'

'You're a Hindoo, I reckon.'

'My old man was from India, sir.'

'So you come all the way over here to steal umbrellas, do you?'

'I was born here, sir, in London.'

'You should go back there, boy, hear me? You think we want the likes of you in our place stealing from decent people?'

The door behind his desk opened and the superintendent appeared. 'A word, Farmerson,' he said to the desk sarge.

They went into the office and closed the door, leaving the PC and the umbrella thief waiting by the desk.

'That was a new trick you played on Dave yesterday,' I said to the guvnor.

'Well, any fool could see the man was exhausted. I've been reading Alfred Binet and his theory of suggestion. I was trying some of the techniques.'

'Isabel told me there was a medicine she wanted for the babies.'

'It's some kind of potion from Peru. Jesuit's bark and Jimson weed. The chemist wasn't sure if it'll work, but we have to try. They're so weak.'

'Where are you going to get forty bob from?'

He sighed and rested his head against the cold wall. 'We could pawn everything we own and still not get halfway. I owe the chandler and Mrs Pudding, and Lewis can't help. That shop has ruined him. You know he mortgaged his house again? And Scrapes is tight as a sparrow's ear so there's no point asking him. You don't have it, do you, Norman?'

'Wish I did, William.'

'If we could only get that reward.'

Half an hour later, Napper appeared.

'What news?' asked the guvnor.

'Come along. We've had some information.'

He wore the same brown suit and tie. A dark grease stain sat above his watch pocket. He pulled on his reefer jacket as he walked. We followed him outside, where we climbed into a Black Maria driven by McDonald, the young PC who'd been at the Quaker Meeting House. I sat next to the guvnor with Napper squeezed up against the window, his eyes wet with the cold.

'Where are we going?' asked Arrowood.

'Brixton. We've been told they might be holding the Africans in a place Capaldi uses. Mabaso's waiting for us there.'

McDonald gee-ed up the nags and they began to trot along the Embankment towards Westminster Bridge.

'Where did you get this information?' asked the guvnor.

'Mabaso got it out one of Capaldi's drivers,' said Napper. 'That fellow's a better policeman than I expected.'

'So Capaldi has them captured?'

'Didn't I just say that?'

The guvnor grunted as the carriage jolted in a pothole and turned onto the bridge. The tide was low, barges marooned on the mud and grit along the sides of the river. On the other side of the road, a wagon stacked high with Christmas trees had lost a wheel, and there was an angry queue stretching all the way past St Thomas's.

'Are you going to arrest them?' I asked.

'We'll hold them until we know whether it was them as killed Mr Fowler and the old one. If not, Mabaso'll take them back on the boat to face trial in Johannesburg. Now, tell me what you've discovered.'

'Not much more than you,' said the guvnor. 'What did you get from Madame Delacourte?'

'We searched her office and apartment on Thursday. Waste of time when Capaldi had them all the while.'

The guvnor held my eye: there didn't seem anything we could do. Even if we could prove Senzo and Thembeka didn't kill Musa or Mr Fowler, Mabaso was still going to take them, whether they were innocent or not.

'Are you going to arrest Capaldi for kidnapping them?' asked the guvnor.

'What good would that do? He's caught them for us.'

The guvnor shook his head. 'Any sign of Mrs Fowler?'

'She still hasn't returned home.'

'Did your superintendent approve the reward?' asked the guvnor.

Napper took out his marbles and began swirling them in his fingers. 'Not yet. I didn't get the extra constable yet either, but if we get one today we could finish it all off by the weekend. If he's in a good mood he might even let me take an afternoon off. There's a Crystal Palace match on.'

As we drove on south, me and him talked football while the guvnor stared out the window at the moving city. When we reached Gresham Hall we found Mabaso pacing up and down the pavement, his hands planted deep in the pockets of his police mackintosh. He'd got himself an old brown scarf since we met.

He led us down the side path, then stood aside as PC McDonald hammered on the door of the back annex with his truncheon. It opened almost straight off, and there stood Dave, his face twisted in a scowl as he took us all in.

'Mr Capaldi ain't going to like this, you stupid pricks,' he said, looking at me and the guvnor over McDonald's shoulder.

'I'm Detective Inspector Napper. What's your name?'

'Dave.'

Napper stared at him with eyelids half-drawn, breathing cold mist from his runny nose. 'Don't act the fool, man. Give me your name.'

'English.'

'Dave English. And you work for Mr Capaldi?'

'I didn't say that.'

'Yes or no.'

Dave filled his chest. 'Is that it?' he said. 'I'm busy.'

Napper pushed past him, the PC and Mabaso following. Dave sighed and stood aside. 'What did you tell them?' he asked me.

'We didn't,' said I. 'One of your lot told that African copper they were here.'

Dave watched as the three policemen looked into the kitchen.

'Where are the Zulus, ma'am?' asked Napper, disappearing into the room.

'Who are you?' came Leonie's voice.

'What Zulus?' asked Gisele.

The young PC stood in the doorway looking up from under his brow with his mouth hung open. It was clear he'd gone a bit queer seeing Capaldi's Wonders.

'Detective Inspector Napper, Scotland Yard. Tell me where the Zulus are.'

'We don't know,' said Leonie.

There was a bit of shuffling, then Napper came out and looked in the cupboard by the stairs. The door to the hall was locked. Next, Leonie appeared and was about to climb the stairs when Mabaso put his hand on her arm.

'No, mum,' he said. 'You must stay here.'

'Don't touch her, there's a good chap,' said Napper. He looked at Leonie. 'He didn't hurt you, did he?'

'Of course not.'

'Stay down here.'

Gisele appeared in the kitchen door now. PC McDonald backed to the far side of the corridor, where he stared at Gisele's floppy pink claws.

'What's the matter with you, boy?' she demanded, peering at him through her eyeglasses. 'You no seen a lobster before?'

The poor lad edged away further, till he was behind me.

'Shut that mouth of yours, boy,' demanded Napper, giving the lad a slap on the cheek. 'Don't be so rude. Now, get up those stairs.'

Leonie took Gisele's hand as the three coppers climbed to the floor above. 'Who's the black one?'

'He's from the South African Police,' answered the guvnor. 'He's been tracking them from Johannesburg. Says they stole some gold and killed two people, one of them a child. Did they tell you anything about that?'

She shook her head. 'Is it true?'

'The South African Police say so.'

We heard shouting from upstairs, and the sound of heavy boots. A few minutes later Senzo and Thembeka were brought down, their wrists in irons. Leonie, a head taller than Gisele, pulled her tight to her side, her knuckles white on her friend's arm.

Thembeka glared at me, fury in her eyes.

'It wasn't us, ma'am,' I said. 'It was Capaldi's driver.'

Senzo stood upright and strong, his eyes avoiding ours, blood running from his hair and down the side of his face. Both had on their coats and hats. Mabaso was behind, and then came Sylvia, wearing a thick man's jumper. Her eyes were bleary from sleep, her soft, blonde wig not quite straight on her head.

'What happened to him?' demanded the guvnor.

'He tried to strike me,' said Mabaso, his voice quiet, vexed. He tucked the scarf back inside his mackintosh and pushed Senzo along the corridor.

'Why are you arresting them?' asked Leonie. 'They haven't done anything.'

'Yes, they have, ma'am,' said Napper.

'They didn't kill Musa, no chance.'

'Then who did, Mrs…?'

'I don't know, but not them. They'd never kill Musa.'

'Well, don't you worry about it. We'll get the truth out of them.'

'I'm PC Mabaso from the Johannesburg police, ma'am,' said the African copper, tipping his hat to her. 'Do you know where the young one is? S'bu Kunene?'

'No,' answered Leonie. 'Nobody's heard from him.'

'How about Mrs Fowler, the wife of the dead Quaker?' asked Napper. 'D'you know anything about her?'

'Nothing. We can't help you. But Senzo and Thembeka haven't done anything, I can tell you. They're not like that.'

'They're wanted for murder in South Africa,' said Mabaso, his words slow and precise. His smooth cheek twitched: he rubbed his nose as if it was to blame. 'I'm here to bring them back.'

'They didn't kill the boy at the compound,' said Thembeka.

'We have a witness who says they did,' answered Mabaso.

'That's a lie.' She looked at Napper. 'You can't take me. I wasn't even on the raid.'

'You're an accomplice to murder, Miss Kunene,' said Mabaso. His voice had gone cold, his pinched eyes hard. 'Now, tell us where S'bu is.'

'We haven't seen him or Mrs Fowler since the day Musa was killed,' she said. 'Two white men came to the Quaker Hall. They shot Mr Fowler. S'bu took out a gun but they captured him. We escaped, and that's all we know. We've been hiding ever since.'

'What about Mrs Fowler?' asked Napper.

'She wasn't there.'

'You didn't see her?'

'She was shopping. And Musa was asleep in the basement when we escaped. The two men must have killed him too.'

Mabaso stepped close. She looked up at his face as he spoke low and firm. 'Is S'bu hiding here as well?'

She clicked her tongue and shook her head. Mabaso turned to Senzo and spoke in their queer language. Senzo shook his head, spoke back. Mabaso waved his arm at him, saying something strong. He began to cough, a wet, crackly hack, and took a hanky from his pocket to cover his mouth. Senzo watched him, his lip curling. When Mabaso spoke again, he was calmer. Senzo waved his hand and answered quick.

'What does he say?' asked Napper.

'The same as she,' answered Mabaso.

Napper grunted. He looked at Leonie and pointed at the door at the end of the corridor. 'What's behind that door?'

'The hall,' she said.

Gisele ducked into the kitchen and came back with the key.

'Keep them here, McDonald,' Napper ordered the young PC as he unlocked the door.

We followed him in to the great, cavernous hall. Napper looked around slowly while Mabaso strode the length of the room and checked the door to the street. Finding it locked, he marched back, his shoes soft on the parquet floor. He was a tall fellow, and thin, his stride stiff and quick, his ears sticking out from the brim of his hat. On either side of the stage were the doors to the cupboards that I'd had a look in the day before. As Napper sat at the harmonium and began to play a clumsy song, Mabaso opened the first cupboard, waiting for a little light to fill the place. After a quick look at the small space, he shut the door. He opened the second, the bigger one.

Immediately, he stepped back.

'Amasendi,' he said. He coughed into his hanky again.

Napper stopped playing. 'What is it?' he asked, crossing the stage as me and the guvnor hurried over.

Mabaso touched his chest, breathing heavy, then finally stepped forward into the cupboard where he squatted just inside the door.

'Please,' he said. 'A candle.'

Inside, among the piles of books and tracts, was a chair. And on the chair sat Mrs Fowler.

Chapter Twenty-Five

She gazed at the wall opposite, her yellow dress buttoned up to the neck. Her mouth was open, and stuck between her pale lips was a long-stemmed clay pipe.

'Is she dead?' asked the guvnor, straining to see in the dark little room.

'I think,' grunted the African copper.

I fetched the hand-lamp from the piano top. Napper lit it and squeezed in next to Mabaso. Now we could make out her face proper. Her skin was fine and pale, just the faintest violet hue to her well-fed cheeks. Her eyes were wide, one ball full of blood with a crust at the corner by her nose. Her hands were tied to the back of the chair with green ribbons, her ankles to the legs with blue.

Napper touched her wrist.

'Stone cold,' he said. He breathed heavy as he checked for a pulse. 'Nothing.'

'See how dry her eyes are,' said the guvnor. 'It looks as if she's been dead a few days.'

Napper moved the lamp through the air, examining each corner of the small room. From what I could remember, it seemed just the same as when I'd had a look in there yesterday: piles of books, a few crates filled with empty ginger beer bottles, a little chest of drawers with a candle stood on top in a sardine tin. Mabaso lit it and opened the top drawer, out of which he pulled a ball of string, a box of nails, a few tools.

As he slid open the next drawer, Napper stepped back into the hall.

'McDonald!' he yelled. 'Bring the prisoners in here!'

The young copper came through from the corridor, pushing Thembeka and Senzo afore him.

Napper pointed at the cupboard: 'How d'you explain this, ma'am?'

Thembeka looked past him into the little room where Mabaso knelt on the floor, searching for clues under the dresser. Her mouth fell open. She looked back at Senzo, whose face was grim. They exchanged words.

'Miss Thembeka,' said Napper again. 'Tell me what happened here.'

'S'bu?' said Senzo, stepping toward the cupboard. 'S'bu?'

'He's not here, lad,' said Napper. 'It's only Mrs Fowler.' Then, without warning, he clutched Senzo's jumper and pushed him up against the wall. 'Tell me what happened, damn you,' he hissed.

Senzo was a few inches taller than the detective, but he made no move to resist. His head touched the wall; his wide eyes looked down on Napper. He spoke in his own language.

'What's he saying?' grunted Napper over his shoulder.

'He's asking what happened,' answered Thembeka.

Napper let go of Senzo and turned to her. 'You've been here since she went missing. You tell me what happened.'

'We were on the other side, in the roof. We never came down here.' She jerked her head toward the ladies in the doorway. 'Maybe they saw someone?'

'Don't believe them, sir,' said Mabaso, stepping over to Mrs Fowler's body. He bent and picked something from the floor under the chair. 'Look at this.'

Between his long fingers was a red feather, just like the ones Senzo had worn around his neck when we first met. Thembeka frowned, her eyes flicking at her cousin. He shook his head.

Napper examined it. 'Anything else there, constable?'

'There's the ribbons tying her to the chair, sir. The newspaper reports said Mr Nyambezi wore feathers around his neck and Musa Schoko had ribbons on his hat when they appeared in the police courts.'

'They did,' said Napper, looking again at the feather.

Mabaso turned to the guvnor. 'Were the feathers like this one?'

'Well, they were the same colour,' said the guvnor, a troubled look on his face. He met my eyes. It wasn't just the ribbons. The clay pipe was the same type Thembeka was smoking in the Quaker Hall. 'I can't say if they're his.'

'And the ribbons?'

'Again, the same colour, but I really don't know if they're the same.'

'We didn't kill her!' cried Thembeka, moving from foot to foot. Her jaw was strained, her brow tight. 'You must believe us. We didn't kill her, sir.'

'Why should I believe you?' answered Napper.

'My oath on the Bible, sir. It wasn't us.'

Napper sighed and shook his head. 'If I believed every suspect who told me they were innocent, I'd hardly arrest a soul, Miss Kunene. Now come along, admit it. Your cousin killed that woman.'

'He didn't kill her, detective,' said Thembeka, taking Senzo's arm. 'He didn't.'

'Perhaps you helped him, ma'am.'

'No, sir.'

'Then it was S'bu.'

'No!' said Thembeka. 'He's only a boy!'

'If it wasn't him, it must be you two,' said Napper, raising his brow and scratching the tight bristle on his bonce. 'Look at the evidence. You both disappeared at the same time as Mrs Fowler. Her body is found in the hall where only you and the ladies have been staying. And this feather,' he held it up, turning it in between his thumb and forefinger, 'which your cousin was wearing, is found by her body. Help me, miss. Explain it.'

'We left the feathers and ribbons when we ran from the Quaker House,' she said, her voice ragged with despair. 'Someone put those there to make it look like us.'

'I'm arresting you both for murder,' said Napper. 'You'll hang for this.'

'No!' cried Thembeka.

'Hold on, Napper,' said the guvnor. 'I don't believe they killed her.'

Napper's eyes narrowed. 'How so, Arrowood?'

'If you were going to kill someone, would you leave the body in the same house you were hiding in? Especially in the cupboard of a hall used for public services? You saw yourself – that door isn't locked. Wouldn't the discovery of the body lead to a police search of the house? And wouldn't that be a stupid thing to do if you were trying to hide there, not to mention leaving all this other evidence?'

'They didn't consider the consequences,' said Napper.

'Nobody would be that foolish, detective.'

'They're Zulus, Arrowood.'

'AmaQwabe, sir,' I said. 'Other side of the river.'

'I'm just saying they acted on impulse,' said Napper, looking over at Mrs Fowler as if she was his ally in this. 'They didn't plan it out.'

'You don't think we can make plans?' demanded Thembeka.

Napper said nothing.

'Because we're Africans?' she added.

'Of course they can make plans, Napper,' said Arrowood.

PC Mabaso stood in the entrance to the cupboard, his arms crossed over his chest, his eyes fixed on the detective inspector. His face was severe and still.

Napper had coloured. 'Read your Havelock Ellis, Arrowood,' he said, then turned and strode clickety-clack across the stage. 'He explains it. Come along, McDonald. Let's get them locked in the van.'

'We didn't kill her,' pleaded Thembeka. 'I swear it, sir. We didn't know she was there!'

'Don't be an ass, Napper,' said the guvnor. 'They didn't kill her.'

'Come along, McDonald!' Napper barked.

'I'll help him take them to the station, sir,' said Mabaso.

'Yes, thank you. I can finish up here on my own.'

'Who was it told you the two prisoners were here, PC Mabaso?' asked the guvnor.

'One of Mr Capaldi's drivers. I don't know his name.'

'That was good work, PC,' said Napper.

There was a flicker of something in Mabaso's eyes, but his face was cold. 'Thank you, sir,' he said.

'How did you persuade him to tell you?' asked the guvnor.

'I followed him to the stables after he'd dropped Capaldi off. He was a weak fellow.'

'Did you assault him?'

'How he got the information isn't your affair, Arrowood,' said Napper.

'Did he mention S'bu or Mrs Fowler?' asked the guvnor.

'He said the Zulus were here, Mr Arrowood,' said Mabaso, stepping behind Senzo and putting his hand on his arm. 'I believed he meant all of them.'

'Pay him another visit once you've got these two to the station,' said Napper. 'See what else he knows. And McDonald, send the surgeon immediately.'

We watched as they took the two prisoners out. As the door swung shut, we heard Mabaso begin to cough again.

'Did they have the pistols on them?' asked the guvnor.

'No,' said the copper. 'We had a search.'

'There's something I must tell you, Napper,' said the guvnor. 'You won't like it.'

The detective sighed, lowering himself onto a chair in front of the stage. He pulled out a thin cigar and lit a match. When he'd got it going, he waved his hand and shut his eyes.

'Go on, then. If you must.'

'Senzo and Thembeka have been hiding here since Tuesday. We discovered this on Thursday but we didn't tell you.'

Napper's face screwed up and stayed that way for some time. Then his eyes snapped open. 'Go on,' he said.

'We were here yesterday evening. We searched the whole building, including those cupboards. Mrs Fowler wasn't here, dead or alive. Now, I don't believe Senzo or Thembeka could've left the building, not with the police and the Capaldis looking for them. The most likely explanation is that someone else brought Mrs Fowler's body here since then.'

'Or she arrived herself and then the Zulus killed her.'

Arrowood shook his head. 'She's been dead for several days. You saw how dry her eyes were. She was brought here some time between yesterday evening and now, and she was already dead.'

Napper took another puff and blew the smoke upwards to the ceiling. 'So, you knew they were here while we were searching all over town for them.'

'We did.'

'You allowed us to waste our time for two days while you kept this a secret.'

'We didn't know where S'bu or Mrs Fowler were,' said the guvnor. 'It wasn't wasted time.'

'And?'

'And what?'

'Why in damnation didn't you tell me?'

'They believe someone in the police works for Mr Capaldi. They were afraid he'd come for them.'

'Who?'

'They don't know.'

Napper stood. 'I'm arresting you both as accomplices to Mrs Fowler's murder.'

'No, sir,' said the guvnor. 'You're not going to do that.'

The detective blinked. 'And why not?'

'Because you need our help, Napper. You've rounded up two of your fugitives. There's only one left, but you've now got three murders to solve. You're in every paper already, and after today you'll be famous. The murder of a white woman and her husband. The arrest of two Zulus, no less, and who in Britain doesn't remember Rorke's Drift? You'll have all the press of the empire watching.' He shook his head. 'You cannot, you must not fail.'

Napper took a deep draw on his cigar, then raised one leg and gave the chair he'd been sat on an almighty shove. It slid across the floor, then tumbled head over tail to a stop. He dropped the cigar and ground it into the nice parquet floor with his boot. When he spoke, each word came out slow through his gritted teeth.

'Do not hide anything from me again. Understand?'

The guvnor nodded, then put his hand on the copper's arm. 'Don't underestimate the Africans, Napper.'

'We control almost a quarter of the world, for God's sake. Isn't that proof we're better made?'

The guvnor patted his elbow and smiled. 'It's proof our guns are better made, my friend.'

Napper pulled away. 'A *Daily News* man, are you? Well, I'm a patriot, and that's the end of it. Tell me what you think happened here.'

'May I have a look at the body first?'

Napper held out his hand. 'Don't touch anything. And before you say it, she's been throttled. The bruising around her neck's clear.'

Arrowood collected the lamp and waddled into the cupboard. There he put on his eyeglasses and examined Mrs Fowler, holding the flame up to her hair, her neck, her face. He studied the ribbons binding her wrists to the seat, her ankles to the legs. Then, with a groan and a burp, he got down on his knees and peered at her boots.

'Where's your magnifying lens, Sherlock?' asked Napper with a chuckle. The guvnor muttered under his breath. Napper gave me a wink. 'Are you trying to identify the type of clay on her boots?'

'What the hell's wrong with you!' barked the guvnor, looking up at the copper. 'Haven't you any decency? There's a dead woman here! Have some respect.'

'I was teasing, you bloody fool!' said Napper, his cheeks colouring.

'Well, your jokes are tiresome, detective,' muttered the guvnor. 'I'm afraid you're one of those unfortunate people who lack a sense of humour but don't realize it.'

'What's wrong with you?' demanded Napper. 'Why are you so blooming difficult today?'

'There's a taint in my bloodline,' said the guvnor as he studied Mrs Fowler's ankles with the hand-lamp. 'I was born with a mildly neurotic temperament, though nothing like my sister.'

Napper looked at me. 'I don't know how you can stand to work with him, Barnett. You ever thought about getting a job with us? You could make detective sergeant one day.'

'I might do that, sir,' I said.

'Right.' The guvnor, still on his knees, put the candle on the floor of the little room. He tried to stand up, but the effort seemed too much for his weak legs and he unbalanced, falling back onto the polished floor. Napper watched him, a distracted look on his red face. I'd have given him a hand up, but the copper was blocking my way. Arrowood rolled over onto his knees again, placed his meaty hands on Mrs Fowler's thighs and, with a groan, used her to push himself up to his feet.

'Don't touch the body!' cried Napper.

It was too late. Arrowood was already halfway to his feet when the chair tilted forwards, unbalancing him. He fell backwards onto the floor, crying out as the chair with Mrs Fowler tied to it landed on top of him.

'What the hell are you doing!' barked Napper. 'The surgeon hasn't examined the scene yet, you buffoon!'

'Oh, Lord,' groaned the guvnor, struggling to get out from under Mrs Fowler's cadaver. 'I've put my blooming back out now. Get her off me!'

'No! You damn well stay where you are! Do not disturb the scene one more inch.'

'What! Get me up, you fool.' Mrs Fowler's face was planted on his breast. He moved his arms and clutched her shoulders, but the chair legs were jammed between the set of drawers and the open door and he couldn't shift her. 'Lift it off!' he demanded. 'I'm in pain!'

'No chance! You stay where you are until the surgeon arrives, you fat baboon.'

'But that could be hours!' he cried from the floor. 'I'm not lying here till then! What's wrong with you?'

'It's your own fault. Don't you dare move.'

'Barnett! Help me up.'

Napper turned to me. 'I'll arrest you if you move that body.'

'I understand, sir,' I said. 'But he's done his back in. I've got to get him out.'

'He bloody deserves to lie there.'

'I know he does. He's always rude when he's in pain. That back gives him hell, it truly does, inspector. It's nothing personal. Maybe we can just put the chair back where it was? She's been dead a while. I know you're a careful man, sir, but now it's done it won't make much difference if she's down there or back where she was.'

'Get m—' the guvnor started.

'Shut your mouth!' I barked at him. 'He owes you an apology, inspector, and he'll give you one just as soon as we've got him out of there.'

Napper looked at me, thinking. He tightened his lips, and I could see he was about to nod when the guvnor started up again.

'Take this woman off me, Barnett! Don't listen to that blithering imbecile!'

We both looked down at him laid flat out on the floor, his grizzled red face clenched with fury, his bowler beside his ear and Mrs Fowler bent on top of him. The clay pipe had been knocked out her mouth and lay by his shoulder.

Napper picked up the lamp and slammed shut the cupboard door.

'Don't you dare leave me here!' came the guvnor's voice from within.

'I'm going to talk to the ladies,' said Napper to me. 'You stay out here until the surgeon arrives. Do not go in there.'

I sat on one of the hard chairs facing the stage, glad to take the weight off my feet. For a few minutes, the guvnor's muffled voice raged from behind the cupboard door, then slowly it calmed. I might have enjoyed his misery, but the weight of death around us these past few days was heavy, and I wanted the end of this case. My thoughts turned to Mercy and Leo. I had a bad feeling about those poor little mites. Fever in a baby was like the toss of a coin. I'd seen it too many times before.

'Norman,' came his voice, pleading now. 'It's dark.'

I rolled a smoke and lit it up.

'Norman, at least open the door.'

I choked down a sad laugh, then felt ashamed. What kind of brute was I becoming? Mrs Fowler was tied to a chair with the breath choked out of her. She seemed a good sort, more alive than her husband, that was sure. And poor old Musa had his teeth smashed out before they killed him. Whoever did that to him was some cruel monster and there was none of us going to sleep easy until he was caught. Three people were dead and a laugh had risen in my throat. I shook my head in shame and wondered, as I had so many times these last few years, if it was time to get out of this line of work, try and get some normal feelings back. I didn't seem to care about much anymore, and that was no way of living.

I rose, opened the door, and lifted the chair with Mrs Fowler off him. Then I helped him up.

He puffed and wheezed, his eyes screwed up tight. I had half an idea he might have been weeping in there, so I got out my box of Black Drop and gave him a couple, then led him over to a seat.

'Sometimes I think I'm cursed,' he mumbled, clutching his back. 'Like the good Lord just put me together to amuse himself. What with the gout and the wheezes and this blooming back. The damned nerves from my father. And his piles. There's blood in my stool again, did I tell you?'

'No, William.'

'D'you think he drinks, Norman?'

'Who?'

'The Lord!'

'Does the Lord drink?'

'Who knows? Go through and see what they're doing. I need to be alone a moment.'

In the kitchen, Napper stood by the range, Leonie, Gisele and Sylvia at the table. Nick was hunched on the mattress on the floor, his arms clutched round his knees. Under his eyes were puffy grey bags, his lips ridged and cracked. They were telling the copper they didn't know the body was there, didn't know who put it there, hadn't heard or seen anything. It didn't matter which way Napper asked the question, the answers were the same. Dave sat on a stool by the larder smoking a fag.

'D'you think it was one of the Africans, marshal?' asked Sylvia.

'I'm a detective, not a marshal, ma'am,' said Napper. 'The Africans could only have done it if they went out of the building or if Mrs Fowler came here. Do you think either could have happened?'

'Well, they were alone for most of the day,' said Sylvia, 'but...'

'But they'd never do that,' said Leonie.

'No, never,' said Gisele. 'It must be the lunatic, tying her to a chair with ribbons and all.'

'The murderers could come back tonight,' whimpered Sylvia. She wiped her nose. 'You got to move us, Dave.'

'I won't let anyone hurt you, darling,' said Dave.

'You saw what they did to that lady,' pleaded Sylvia. 'They'll come for us next.'

'Take something for your nerves, girl,' said Dave. 'That'll sort you out. Leonie, you got any pills?'

'I'll give you something,' said Leonie, getting to her feet.

'D'you think Mr Capaldi could have done this?' asked Napper.

'Well…' Leonie frowned. 'Thembeka and Senzo were afraid of him.'

'He says he kill them for not going on stage,' said Gisele. 'And Thembeka says his men killed Mr Fowler.'

'Mr Capaldi weren't behind the murders,' said Dave, dropping his fag to the floor and putting his heel on it. 'And he won't be too happy to hear you saying he were.'

'We didn't say that,' said Gisele. 'The detective asked.'

'Best you watch how you answer then, girl.'

'Don't call me girl, you big pillock.'

Dave's jaw clenched. He stared at her hard for a few moments, then shoved his hands in his pockets. 'We'll talk about that later,' he said at last. 'Gisele.'

Chapter Twenty-Six

We searched the pantry and cupboards in that part of the building, the room upstairs, the dark attic space where the wind squeezed and whistled through the tiles. There was no trace of any other ribbons or feathers, nor were Mrs Fowler's bonnet or scarf or Lewis's missing pistols anywhere to be found. The police surgeon, a tall grey fellow called Bentham, arrived about an hour after Senzo and Thembeka had been taken away, McDonald following him in with a gurney under his arm. They both wore rubbers shiny with rain.

'Ha!' said the old surgeon when he saw us. 'It's you two again. Still at it, then?'

'Yes, doctor,' said the guvnor, holding out his hand. 'It's good to see you again.'

'I heard you were involved with those bodies pulled from the river this summer.' His back was bent from so many years peering inside bodies, and he had to look up at Napper from under his tangled eyebrows. 'They're not as bad as people make out, you know.'

'Could we get on, sir?' asked Napper, opening the door to the hall.

The surgeon grunted and shuffled through. When he'd been shown poor Mrs Fowler, he asked the two coppers to lift her and her chair out into the main room. He took off his raincoat, then pulled over another chair and began his inspection, starting with an examination of her scalp, her ears, and her nose. He poked her eyeball with his finger, pulled back her lips and inspected her teeth. When he'd noted his findings, he felt around inside her mouth and assessed her violet cheeks with a magnifying lens. Mrs Fowler sat with dignity throughout it all.

'Did you get the prisoners back safely?' Napper asked McDonald as the surgeon did his work.

'Yes, sir. Desk sergeant received them.'

'Where's Mabaso?'

'He's there with them.'

'Good lad. I'll show you how to do a proper interrogation later.'

Bentham made more notes, then moved his lens to her neck. There he found the bruises.

'Finger marks,' he said. 'Her face is slightly livid and tumescent, although not a great deal. Veins in the eyes are visible, swelling at the back of the tongue, all consistent with asphyxiation. I'll need to open her up to be certain.'

The surgeon untied her wrists and ankles from the chair and tried to move her limbs. He shook his head. 'Her muscles have set in a seated position.' After recording more observations, his fingers approached the buttons of her blouse, and I was surprised to see a little tremble there. At first, he had some trouble undoing those buttons. He shook his hands out and tried again. This time he got them open, exposing her vest. Still sitting before her, knee to knee, he bent down further, lifting the vest and examining her sagging belly. Her skin there was browner than her face, and I realized she was wearing something to lighten her skin. Somewhere in her line there was blood from the colonies.

'How long's she been dead?' asked Napper.

'Between six and forty-eight hours, I'd say. The cold complicates it, but there are no signs of putrefaction. We can move her now.'

'Right,' said Napper. 'Let's get her to the van, McDonald.'

'Any idea where she was killed, Bentham?' asked the guvnor as we watched Napper and McDonald lift Mrs Fowler onto the gurney. Her body was bent stiff at the waist and knees like a number four, and it didn't lie proper on the narrow stretcher.

'It's obvious where she was killed,' muttered Napper, trying to straighten her legs. 'Give me a hand, lad,' he barked at the PC. 'Hold her ankles.'

'Don't do that, please,' growled Bentham, looking up from his notebook. 'She'll loosen up in time.'

'She'll fall off,' said Napper. He put his hands on her knees and tried to push them down.

'Stop it!' barked Bentham suddenly, a fury in his eyes. 'She's not yours to interfere with!'

McDonald stood back, looking from the surgeon to Napper.

'Well, don't blame me if she falls off,' said Napper, standing up.

'Turn her on her side.'

'What d'you think, Bentham?' asked the guvnor. 'Where was she killed?'

'I'd assume it was in the chair,' said Bentham.

'Why else would they tie her to it?' said Napper.

'Why else, indeed, detective,' said the guvnor with a nod. 'Why else?'

'If you have something you want to say then say it, Arrowood,' snarled Napper.

The guvnor stepped over to where Mrs Fowler lay on the gurney.

'Look at the skin around her mouth. D'you notice anything?'

Napper bent forward. 'A rash?'

Bentham used his thumbnail to scrape something from her cheek. 'Keratoses. She's been using arsenic to lighten her skin.'

'And do you see how she tries to disguise the blemishes with that zinc powder?' asked the guvnor.

'What of it?' asked Napper.

The guvnor pointed at her cheek. 'You see that there? What looks like a channel through the powder, from the corner of her mouth straight across about two inches toward the ear? And that dark dot at the end?'

'Get to the point, for God's sake.'

'When a person's throttled, is it likely that fluid would fall out of their mouth, Dr Bentham?'

'It's quite possible, yes. They gargle and retch. The saliva can't pass down the throat.'

'Well, here the spittle has rolled down the cheek, absorbing the powder as it went. Would you say, doctor, that the dark dot at the end of the trail is blood?'

'Yes,' said he. 'She has an infection of the gum. It would cause blood in the saliva.'

'I see. Now, I assume that for the spittle to run down her face in the direction of her ear, she must have been lying on her back when she was throttled. If she was sitting up straight, the way we found her, the spittle would have rolled down her chin. But there's no evidence of a track below her mouth, so she must have been tied to the chair after she was killed. A very strange thing to do, don't you think, gentlemen?'

Napper thought for a moment. 'There's another possibility. Maybe the killer ties her to a chair and then in a fit of rage he knocks the chair over. Then he strangles her before righting the chair.'

'Yes, that is a possibility,' said the guvnor slowly, scratching his chin. He looked at Bentham. 'Would there be bruising to the back of the head in that case, sir?'

'I think so,' said the surgeon. 'If she fell backwards, her head would probably have struck the floor before the chairback. Let me have another look.'

He took out his magnifying lens, turned her on her side, and examined the back of her head again, pulling her hair this way and that to see the skin. 'There's nothing here to suggest she's fallen backwards. No contusions.'

'What about the rigor?' asked Napper.

'Usually within six hours, but can be longer in asphyxia,' said the surgeon as I helped him to his feet. 'The lady could have been tied to the chair up to twenty-four hours after being killed.'

'Now, why d'you think she was tied to the chair after death, Napper?' asked the guvnor, stroking his chin. 'Any ideas?'

'To throw us off the scent, Arrowood. Don't talk to me like I'm a fool.'

The guvnor crossed his arms and watched the copper for a few moments. Finally, he sighed and said: 'Yes, but more specifically, if you believe she was killed while tied to this chair, you'll assume she was killed here. Our minds try and create coherent stories of the world we encounter, and the details we perceive in a situation are interpreted in such a way as to fit into those stories. William James has said it all. A dead woman tied to a chair triggers a story of her being killed while tied to that chair. It also makes us assume that she must have been killed in the place she was found, because if you wanted to move her body after death, you'd likely cut her off the chair. Far easier to transport that way. It's a trick to make you think she was killed here, Napper. A trick to make you arrest Thembeka and Senzo, and a clever one at that.'

'Shut your mouth, please, Arrowood,' said Napper. He turned to the PC. 'You'll have to come back when we've delivered her to the mortuary, McDonald. I want you to call on every building in this street. Find out if anyone's seen anything.'

They carried her out the front door and loaded her into the Black Maria. As we watched them roll away through the rain, the guvnor turned to me.

'He's got the evidence to hang them for this, Norman,' he said. 'And I'm afraid that's exactly what he'll do.'

Chapter Twenty-Seven

It was about three that Saturday when we reached St Martin's Lane. The place was busy with families coming out of the Christmas pantomime, the children of clerks and shop owners jabbering and quarrelling and getting in the way of horses and costers trying to get through. A crowd of women were leaving the Friends Meeting House, severe and silent as they tied their bonnets and pulled on their gloves. We squeezed past them into the vestibule, where the door to the office was open. There, a round fellow with a broad smile and a stiff collar gave us the name of a missionary in the Aborigines' Protection Society who'd served time in Natal. The address was back over the river in Camberwell.

We stopped in a coffee shop for some soup, then walked down to Blackfriars, where Madame Delacourte had her office. It was above a bicycle shop, where a giant yellow-and-blue sign cried DELACOURTE'S PRODUCTIONS. Silver stars flew out from her name and grew till they reached the eaves; elephants and crocodiles, monkeys and snakes curled round the words and spilled out over the brickwork. The street door was silver too, the frame blue. It was open. We went in, along an unlit corridor and up some thin stairs to a landing with three doors. The one ahead was open.

'Come in,' came a woman's voice as we reached the stairhead.

The room ran the width of the building, with three big windows looking onto the street. A long marble desk was to our left, stacked with ledgers and letters, a dirty pink blotter, a set of inkwells. Carved African men stood in a row holding spears and arrows, their heads over-large like poor Joe Merrick. Paintings of jungle scenes, of bright fruit and fire-eyed tigers, of waterfalls and half-dressed ladies hung from the walls. And over by the crackling fire stood a long white couch, on which lay Madame Delacourte.

'Madam,' said the guvnor, bowing with a sweep of his arm. 'I'm Mr Arrowood. It's a great pleasure to meet you.'

She looked at him for a few moments, her face absolutely still. Then her eyes turned to me. I nodded. 'Mr Barnett, ma'am. Assistant.'

She was a beauty, all right. A painted, lacquered beauty. In her long, pale fingers was a long black cigarette, its rose-coloured smoke curling up to the ceiling. Her hair was swept tight over the ears, bunched at the back, with a rising bun over her forehead. Her nose was sharp as a chisel, upturned, her nose-holes lying flat like apple seed. The skin of her arms and face was a deathly vinyl white, her lips a shining vermilion, while the veins of her neck, her arms, her hands, were painted the faintest blue. Around her throat was a green bow tie.

She sat with her legs up on the seat, her back propped against the arm, and it seemed to amuse her to watch us there, taking her in. She put the black cigarette to her lips. The end blazed; smoke drifted from her mouth. She nodded.

'So, gentlemen,' she said, her voice deep and lovely and not at all French. 'What are you here for?'

The guvnor bowed once more for good measure. When he

spoke, his voice had deepened too. 'We're private investigative agents, madam, working on the Zulu case. We'd like to ask you some questions, if we may?'

'Well, what would the harm be in that?' she answered.

'What indeed?' answered the guvnor.

'What indeed?' came another voice from behind the sofa. And who should pop his head up but Polichinelle. His face paint was scrubbed off revealing a bloke with pitted grey skin and a weak chin, the red-and-yellow three-pointed hat replaced with a brown fedora, the padded shoulders and horned midriff given way to a linen shirt and striped lounge suit.

He stood, a small white Pekingese in his hand that he dropped into the lady's lap. 'Hello, Mr Arrowood,' he said like they were best of friends. He winked at me. 'Mr Barnett. I hope you've been drinking that fennel tea?'

I smiled at him, holding my arms out. 'Can't you see me blooming?'

He laughed.

'You know these gentlemen, Cobbie?' asked Madame Delacourte.

'They work for Capaldi, dear heart.'

'No, sir,' said the guvnor, a little anxiety breaking through his words from seeing the famous clown again. He dabbed at his brow with his belcher, his hands aquiver. I remembered him being just the same when he found himself sitting next to Mrs Beeton in a train carriage the year before.

'We work for the Aborigines' Protection Society,' I said, giving him time to collect himself. 'We're trying to find the missing Zulu.'

'Only one?' asked she, moving her legs to allow Polichinelle to sit, while we remained standing in the middle of the room. 'I thought there were three.'

'The police have the others,' I told her. 'We're looking for the boy.'

'Then you should ask Bruno Capaldi.'

'He says you know where he is,' said the guvnor, putting his belcher away. The strength had returned to his voice. 'That you were responsible for the murders.'

She drew from her cigarette and thought. 'Why does he think that?'

'Because you're exhibiting some tribesmen from Borneo and don't want the competition.'

'Of course. Well, what a good reason to kill two people.'

'Three.'

Her eyebrows shot up. 'The papers said two.'

'Another body's been found. It's Mrs Fowler, the wife of the man who was shot at the Quaker Meeting House.'

'Where?' asked the clown.

'Brixton.'

'Well, it was nothing to do with me,' said the lady. 'It's just my friend Bruno making mischief. The police have been here already.'

'You've a reputation for violence, madam,' said the guvnor.

'Yes, I do.' She moved the dog off her lap and adjusted her dress. Outside on the street we heard a cobbler's gong. 'I am aware of you, Mr Arrowood. You're not so clean yourself.'

'Who d'you think killed them?' asked the guvnor.

'Bruno.'

'Why would he kill his own performer?'

She passed her cigarette to the clown, who took a puff.

'Bruno can be his own worst enemy. He has too much pride and doesn't like to be crossed. And that wife of his makes sure of it. Did you know he killed a waiter in France for bringing him a mushroom?'

'I heard it was a snail,' said the guvnor, lighting his pipe. 'D'you have any idea where he might be holding the boy?'

'I think he's probably floating past Foulness on his way to the Channel.'

'You think he's dead?'

'If Bruno's men killed the others, then the boy's a witness.'

'And if he's not dead, where would they hold him?'

'They use a place called Gresham Hall in Brixton for rehearsals.'

The guvnor nodded. 'That's where the body was found.'

'Then it was Bruno's men who killed her,' she said.

'Does he have any other places?'

'They also use a boarding house in Vauxhall and a warehouse by Lambeth Potteries.'

'How do you know this, madam?'

She smiled. 'I need to know what I'm competing with.'

'Do you know the address of the warehouse?' asked the guvnor.

She looked at Polichinelle, who passed the black cigarette back to her. 'It's on the high street, opposite the park,' he said. 'Between a tea merchant's and a chandler's.'

'Thank you, sir,' said the guvnor. 'Now, may we search your rooms, ma'am? Just to be complete, of course.'

'It's time for you to go, my darlings,' said the pale lady with a wave of her hand. And with that the tiny Pekingese leapt off the couch and began to bark at us with a mastiff-sized fury.

'D'you believe her?' I asked as we walked over Blackfriars Bridge.

'Yes,' he said, drawing the word out the way he does when he's not quite finished a thought. 'She appeared not to know two important facts.'

'She might just be good at covering her tracks.'

'I'm sure she is.'

'Don't trust her just because she's beautiful, William. We've made that mistake before.'

He nodded. 'Havelock Ellis says that, in medieval law, if there were two suspects for the same crime, the uglier one was considered guilty.'

My boot slipped in a bit of dung and I stumbled into the road, my hand landing on a cart full of cabbages.

'Steady on, mate,' grunted the carter, who couldn't have been more than twelve year old. 'You'll break them.'

The guvnor took my arm and pulled me back onto the pavement. 'I was watching her closely, Norman. When people hear something that confounds what they know, there's usually an immediate expression of surprise. It might not be obvious and it's often fleeting, a minuscule pulling down or a drawing up of the brow, for example. Well, that's what I observed with her when I said we were looking for the Zulu rather than the Zulus. The faintest line appeared on her forehead and then was gone.'

'She was surprised when you told her there'd been three murders too.'

'Her surprise was more visible in that case. Perhaps because it was a more brutal piece of news. The other thing that convinced me is that when people pretend not to know something that they do know, they either exaggerate that surprise, or else they make a little nod of the head. It's as if their unconscious is acknowledging the known fact before their mouth denies it.'

'From your Darwin book, I suppose.'

'It's something I've noticed.'

'D'you believe it's Capaldi?'

'I don't know. We'll take a look at the boarding house and the warehouse.' He pointed at a bus waiting at a stop just ahead. 'But first to Camberwell.'

The address we had for the Aborigines' Protection Society was a respectable three-storey house on a respectable paved street. A maid answered the door and showed us into a parlour, where sat a Reverend Druitt eating an orange in front of a coal fire. After the guvnor explained our interest in the Zulu case, he invited us to sit on his sofa.

'I was in South Africa at the same time as Mr Fowler,' he said, moving the tray from his knee to a side table. He'd been eating the fruit with a silver knife and fork. 'Delphine and I were terribly upset at what happened.'

'Do you speak their language, sir? The lady translates for us, but I'd like to understand what the gentleman says without her in the middle.'

'I'm afraid not. My church served the British community. So few of the natives could accept the Word.'

'You think the African missions are doomed to failure, sir?'

'Well... they can do other things. But convert Africa to Christianity? I think not.'

'You have a low opinion of the natives?'

He barked a laugh. 'Great warriors, I admit. But remember

what Dickens said of the Zulus: *The world would be better if they were gone*. If Spencer is correct, I'm afraid they *will* be gone one day.'

'Dickens said that?' asked the guvnor in surprise.

'Don't you read, Mr Arrowood?'

'Of course I read.'

A little canary in a cage by the window began to flutter its wings, and we all turned to watch it for a moment. 'Let's not discuss this,' said Druitt at last. 'I'm prone to melancholia in the winter. Now, my daughter speaks the native language well. She helped in the mission school.' He rang a little bell and the maid returned. 'Fetch Delphine, Mary. And take the tray. I'll finish my orange later.'

'Do you have any idea who's behind the murders, sir?' asked the guvnor. 'Any idea at all?'

'I didn't meet the Africans and poor Frederick was killed before we could discuss the matter. The obvious suspects would be the Zulus, of course.'

'They had the opportunity, but they don't seem to have a motive.'

'Ha!' laughed the missionary, waving his hand. 'Don't look for motive. Some little disagreement will have flared up.'

'You don't seem particularly upset about Mr Fowler, if I may say.'

'I officiated three funerals yesterday, Mr Arrowood. Grieving is for close relatives.'

'You weren't friends?'

'We worked together in the society.' He looked at me suddenly, even though I hadn't spoke. 'When souls leave this world to join the Lord, they go home. That's a good thing. Sadness is only weakness in disguise, and the devil will always exploit weakness, sir.'

The guvnor nudged me as he spoke, patting his purse pocket and nodding at Reverend Druitt. He never liked to ask for money from his betters. He somehow thought that made him their servant so he left it to me.

'Quite so, reverend,' I piped up. 'I suppose you know Mr Fowler was paying us to help the Africans using money from the Aborigines' Protection Society.'

'Indeed.'

'He paid us for two days and we've done that. But since we're still on the case, we need another payment.'

He burped into his hand. 'Well, I'd need to discuss that with the committee.'

'Thank you, sir. We charge twenty shillings a day. I think we'd need another three days.'

'Leave it with me, Mr Barnett.'

'Thank you, sir,' I said as a young woman stepped into the room.

'Ah, Delphine!' cried the parson. 'This is Mr Arrrowood and his assistant Mr Barnett. They're the private detecting agents looking for the missing Zulus. Mr Fowler hired them. They need some help translating.'

Delphine limped across to stand by the fire: poking out from under her skirts you could see one of her shoes built up about three inches. Her face was broad, her eyes small, and I reckoned she was six inches or so taller than her old man. A great bush of curls grew from her head. 'Do they speak iZulu or Fanakalo?' she asked.

'They're amaQwabe,' I told her.

'Then I think I should be able to converse with them. Father, may I?'

'Of course, my girl. You need to get out of the house.'

'I've been telling you that since we arrived,' she said sharply.

'Oh!' he exclaimed, his hand in the air as if he'd startled himself. 'Is it dangerous?'

'There's a murderer at large,' answered the guvnor. 'But we only want your daughter's help to talk to one of the Africans held at the police station, that's all.'

'But aren't they the murderers?' she asked with about as much emotion as a towel.

'I don't think so, miss. But until we know who did the killing, we can't be certain.'

She straightened her blouse, brushed down her skirt. The scowl on her face seemed fixed. 'I'll get my coat.'

'Not just yet, if you don't mind,' said the guvnor. 'We have to pay a visit first. Could you meet us at Scotland Yard at seven this evening?'

She looked at her old man.

'Yes, yes,' he said. 'Do you want me to come along, my dear?'

'No,' she said firmly.

He laughed and looked at us. 'The children loved her, you know. Gave her a mat when we left. She was very popular.'

As Delphine limped out the room without saying good-bye, I somehow doubted it.

Chapter Twenty-Eight

We walked up to the Oval and then on to Vauxhall, where we found the boarding house with the cross in the window near the station. Mrs Farini told us she hadn't seen the Africans for a week or so and let us upstairs to have a look at the rooms. They were empty. We walked further north to the Lambeth Potteries, the big works just before Lambeth Palace. All the way the guvnor moaned about his back and how tight his shoes were. It was a relief when, on the High Street, we found the place Polichinelle had told us about, a thin warehouse jammed between a ship chandler's and a tea dealer. Night had fallen, but in the dim moonlight we could see the tall chimneys rising from the factories behind, pouring out brown smoke into the murky sky. The doors were shut, the windows dark. A few of the other warehouses on the road were the same, but most had carts and wagons outside being loaded or unloaded. I hammered on the wide, arched doors. After a minute or so I tried again.

'Anyone in there, mate?' I asked a fellow in an apron who was smoking outside the tea merchant's.

'Big bloke left about an hour ago,' he said, pointing at the heavy padlock. 'Looks shut up.'

'Is there a watchman?'

'Don't know, mate. They come and go at all hours.'

'Can we get round the back?'

He shook his head. 'These are the only doors.'

We waited till he'd gone back inside, then the guvnor shielded me while I got to work. On the way, I'd fetched a set of skeleton keys I'd had since I was eleven or so and working for my Uncle Norbert. I took the keys from his locksmith shop after he fell in the river and died. He was a good bloke and that was a sad time for me and my ma. If my uncle hadn't gone to the other side, I'd never have got into the kind of trouble I got into around Jacob's Island, and no doubt I'd have become a locksmith myself rather than trailing around London taking beatings for the guvnor. But that's what happened: he fell between two barges one filthy night and my life was changed. All that was left of him were these keys.

I found one that fit, and with a bit of jiggling soon had the lock open. We stepped inside. It was an open space taking up the whole ground floor. The smell of spice filled the air. The guvnor lit his candle. Around us were bulging sacks stacked about eight foot high. A few small wagons stood near the door, with hooks and shovels hung upon the wall. To our right was a little office booth, and next to it some stairs.

We walked quiet as we could round the stacks, but there was nobody about. The next floor was the same: stacks of bulging sacks, the heavy stink of spices, the boards dusty and speckled with mouse droppings. Only one wall had windows looking onto the street. The others were bare brick.

Up we went to the top floor, where hundreds of ropes were stored, the thick ones in great, dead coils on the floor, the thinner hanging from pegs around all the walls. Cold air whistled through the roof slates, while outside the dark windows, over the rooftops and spires, trains rolled slow over the lines towards Waterloo. Halfway across the space was a rough wall with three doors, where a man sat sleeping on a chair.

The guvnor blew out his candle and pointed at the ropes. I crept across to the wall and took down a thin one. Then, slowly, we tiptoed across the dusty floor, testing each board for squeaks before putting our weight on them.

The bloke grunted.

We froze.

He was short and heavy, with a grizzled chin beard and a scarf wrapped round his neck. His legs were stretched out on another chair, his arms crossed. A club lay on the floor next to him. In sleep he seemed a puppy, but I knew from the dent on his skull and the stitching on his cheek that he was a rough.

He began to breathe again.

We moved forward. Now we could smell the gin oozing from his skin, the air around him warm and wet. We were a few steps away when the guvnor stood on something crunchy. The rough's eyes shot open, his head jerking this way and that as he tried to adjust his sight to the dark, but before he could rise we fell upon him, the guvnor jamming his belcher in the bloke's mouth, me looping the rope round his middle and pulling it tight to the chair so he couldn't move his arms. He struggled like hell, twisting his head furiously while the guvnor tried to keep the cloth in his gin-hole.

I looped the rope around the bloke again and again while he jerked and strained, tying him off quick as I could. He was like a wild beast, kicking away like blue hell. Arrowood squealed as he got a boot in his shins. I planted my fist in the fellow's belly and he went limp, heaving for breath: finally, I got his legs tied down too.

One last bit of rope around his head to keep the belcher in his mouth and we were done. A set of keys were in his coat pocket.

'Wait,' said the guvnor, sitting on the other chair to calm his wheezing. The rough was groaning and making noises in his throat, twisting his shoulders and rocking, but the bindings held tight. I stepped over to the stairhead and listened. There was no sound below. When Arrowood had caught his breath, he picked the gin-jar from the floor, sniffed it, and took a long swallow. He passed it to me.

'Let's see what's behind those,' he said, pointing at the three doors.

The bully'd gone still now: he knew there was nothing he could do.

I found a key that fitted the padlock on the first one. The guvnor stood behind me, the bloke's club in one hand and a candle in the other. I pulled it open.

Inside was a stack of mattresses, some empty chamber-pots, a table and a few stools. The little room had no windows.

Hearing a noise behind the second door, I nudged the guvnor and stepped across. He nodded, bracing himself.

When I'd opened the padlock, I ripped it off quick, expecting the door to burst open. But there was silence. It squeaked when I opened it. The guvnor brought over the candle and we peered in.

The candle threw its first glow into the room when there was a sudden noise and a flash of movement. A woman was coming towards us, throwing something. I jerked out the way just as a wobbling cloud flew past me and hit the guvnor in the chest.

He cried out in surprise, just as the woman raced past us and made for the stairs, a chamberpot breaking at his feet. Then another wave of filth came through the door, exploding over his shoulder.

'No!' he yelled as a second woman came hurtling out, screaming. She was tall, her face smudged and sooty, her hair long and knotted. Like the first, she wore an old overcoat, torn and patched, with nothing underneath. Her legs and feet were bare. And behind her came another, knocking me to the side and following the others to the stairs.

'Norman!' cried the guvnor, holding his arms away from his soaking Donegal as the women disappeared down the stairs. 'What in Christ's name?'

I collected the candle and lit it again, the women's cries becoming fainter as they reached the bottom and escaped to the street. We peered into the room: two mattresses on the floor, two broken chamberpots with their cargo thrown across the ground, a little table with two stools. The stink was so thick you could have shovelled it up.

'I wonder how long they've been in here,' I said.

'Get the other door open,' said the guvnor, his voice weak and blue. He took a canvas sheet from the floor and wiped at his jacket and waistcoat, trying to scrape away the solid matter. 'Why is it always me?' he muttered, coming out to stand behind me once again.

The last door was just the same as the other two. As I fitted the key into the padlock, there came a banging on the other side.

'Good day, sir!' a voice cried. 'Good day, sir!'

'S'bu?' I called. 'Is that you?'

'S'bu!' came his voice. 'S'bu!'

The moment I'd got the lock off, the door flew open and there he was, looking scared and young like the boy he was. They'd taken his clothes, just like they had with the women, and he wore only an overcoat. He was breathing heavy, his body jerking and trembling. The guvnor moved to put his arms round him but stopped himself. Instead he took the lad's arm.

'You're safe now, my dear. Don't worry.'

'Safe,' said S'bu, the tears starting to roll down his cheeks. 'Safe.'

I put my hand on his shoulder.

'Let's get moving.'

'Go,' said S'bu, his body stiffening, his eyes widening. 'Go, go!'

'We need to question this one,' said the guvnor, nodding at the guard.

'We need to get S'bu away from here before anyone else arrives,' said I, pulling S'bu to the stairhead. 'You can stay if you want.'

The guvnor hesitated, then followed us to the next floor. We were halfway down the final flight when we heard footsteps outside. Ahead of us the warehouse doors were open from the ladies' escape. Just as we reached the bottom, a big, solid bloke appeared on the pavement.

'Run!' I cried.

I rushed at him, S'bu behind me and the guvnor at the back. It was only as I raised my arms to shove him out the way I saw the dull steel in his hand. It was too late to stop: in a blind panic I threw all my weight at the geezer, feeling a sharp pain in my side as we both fell to the pavement. S'bu leapt over us, the guvnor stumbling on my legs.

I got my hands round the bloke's neck as he jabbed me in the face with his fist. Then there was a sudden crunching sound and the bloke screamed, going limp for just long enough for me to get off him. The guvnor pulled me up, and I saw the bloke's forearm propped across the edge of the kerb, bent where it shouldn't be. S'bu's foot was on it.

We ran. After a few steps I stumbled, clutching my side. I knew it'd be wet. I didn't know it'd be this sore. The guvnor took one arm, S'bu the other, and we hobbled and stuttered down past the churchyard and the distillery until we found a cab.

Chapter Twenty-Nine

When we reached Coin Street, Isabel was sitting in the parlour, the fire lit, a lamp glowing on the table. For once, the window was shut and it was warm. Ettie stepped out of the scullery, her pinny and hands black with coal dust.

'S'bu!' she said. 'They found you!'

'He's been through an ordeal,' said the guvnor.

'Hello, Miss Ettie, good day,' said the lad, looking from her to Isabel, who said nothing. He wore the guvnor's boots and my coat over his own, yet still he shivered.

'This is S'bu, Isabel,' said the guvnor. 'He doesn't really speak English. S'bu, this is my wife, Isabel.'

Isabel nodded, but there was no smile on her face. S'bu murmured a quick 'Good day', and then looked away. My wound was giving me hell, so I got out my Black Drop and put three in my mouth, picking up a mug from the table and washing them down with cold tea.

Ettie pulled a chair to the fire and led the lad over. 'Oh, my dear, you're cold. Warm yourself up. I'll get you a blanket.'

'They had him locked up in a warehouse,' I said.

'The poor soul,' said Ettie, sitting him down.

S'bu glanced at Isabel again, who looked at him in silence, her face hard.

'How are the babies?' asked the guvnor.

'What do you care?' snapped Isabel.

'Isabel, I had to go out. S'bu was being held prisoner.'

'You care for him, then?' she asked, scratching her face. 'Did you get the forty shillings? Did you ask Lewis?'

'He doesn't have any money. I'm trying to get the Quakers to pay us.'

Isabel looked at him in silence, her cheeks hollow, her eyes full of hatred. 'They need it now, William,' she said at last.

'I'm trying, Isabel,' he whispered.

'She's upset, brother,' said Ettie, covering S'bu's knees with a blanket. 'Leo had a convulsion.'

'Oh, my Lord. How is he?'

'They're both sleeping upstairs,' said Ettie. 'Flossie's there too.'

'Have they eaten?'

'Leo took some broth. Mercy still won't have anything. It just spills out of her mouth. She's very weak.' She blinked and peered at her brother. 'What in God's name have you been doing? Oh, my goodness. Get changed, will you!'

The guvnor looked down at his coat like he'd forgotten what the women had done to him when they escaped. With a sigh he climbed the stairs. No sooner had he gone than Isabel jumped up and rushed through the parlour door to the outhouse.

'She's been vomiting,' said Ettie. 'I hope she's not caught it.'

'Have you told her about the scholarship?'

She shook her head.

'They're sure to make an announcement.'

'I'll tell her soon. It's just such a terrible time.'

A sharp pain made me grip the table edge. Ettie noticed the blood on my hand. 'What's that?'

Holding my side, I lowered myself onto a chair. Ettie was already unbuttoning my waistcoat and shirt. I reached for the chloridine as she examined me.

The wound wasn't too deep, so she cleaned it with iodine and lathered it with Whelpton's. I grit my teeth, waiting for the medicine to dull the pain and watching the whorl of hair on the top of her head as she worked. I still couldn't get over the matter-of-fact way she'd told me what she'd done with the bloody Reverend Hebden. I wondered what she thought of me now. Her belly grumbled as her cold fingers spread the balm over my wound. Her woman smell surrounded me. I sensed she was angry, and it partly answered my question.

'You hungry, S'bu?' I asked, remembering he was there too. I made an eating sign. 'Food? Eat?'

'Ah. Yes. Eat. Yes.' He nodded with each word. A dog barked just outside the window and he jumped.

'You're safe, lad,' I said.

He nodded, but I didn't know if he understood.

'Thembeka?' he asked.

'The coppers have her.'

'Coppers?' His face didn't change.

'Did they hurt you?' I asked.

He screwed his eyes up, held his hands out to the fire.

'Did they hurt you?' asked Ettie.

He glanced at her, but it was clear he didn't know enough words to do any more. 'Thembeka,' he said again.

She got him a mug of ale and a bit of bread and cheese. He ate quick, his eyes on her and me, a sheen of fear still there. He gulped down the beer.

From outside, we heard Isabel puking.

'What does the doc say about the kids?' I asked.

'He doesn't know, Norman,' said Ettie. 'They'll either recover or they won't.'

The guvnor came down the stairs holding Mercy wrapped in a blanket. He'd washed his head and hands and put on some eau de Cologne. He wore his yellow summer suit.

'Let her sleep, William,' said Ettie.

'She needs to be fed,' he whispered. 'Look at her.'

The little face, swaddled in tartan wool, was a pitiful sight. The bones of her skull were almost visible through the tight, grey skin.

'She won't take anything, William. I've been trying all day.'

'She's burning up. At least wet her mouth.'

Isabel returned from the outhouse, a hanky held to her lips, and sat at the table next to me. Ettie brought through a cup of water and a cloth, which she dabbed at the little baby's lips.

Arrowood's eyes glistened as he looked down on the child's face. Isabel, turning to the window, began to weep too. S'bu watched them both, pain replacing the fear in his eyes.

Without looking up, the guvnor whispered, 'Norman. Go to Scotland Yard and fetch Delphine. We need to talk to S'bu.'

Ettie'd bandaged my wound and the chloridine was doing its work, so I found I could walk easily again. I got a hot spud from the potato man outside the station and crossed Waterloo Bridge, reaching Scotland Yard about ten minutes late. Delphine was waiting at the front, trying to ignore a weaselly fellow who was telling her a story.

'You don't mind helping us?' I asked as she limped along with me back to Coin Street.

'I'm happy to do it,' she said, though she didn't look or sound it. 'I get blue staying in the house all day. It's good to have a reason to go out.'

'You been in England long, miss?'

'Only a few months. I don't know anyone here.'

'You haven't any friends in London?'

She shook her head and said nothing more for the rest of the walk. That was fine by me: my head was drifting with chloridine, and I was carrying the sadness of the scene I'd just left heavy in my heart. By the time we reached the guvnor's rooms, Mercy was back upstairs and S'bu had on the guvnor's fair isle jumper and a pair of his britches, the legs too short, the waist too loose.

Arrowood got to his feet. 'Miss Delphine. So good of you to come.'

She nodded at S'bu, then peered at Ettie and Isabel as the guvnor introduced them.

'We wondered if you could ask S'bu a few questions?'

'Mr Barnett explained that already.' She turned to the lad and spoke the language that we were beginning to feel was familiar. He stood and offered her his seat. She refused, turning to the guvnor. 'Yes, Mr Arrowood, we can speak in Fanakalo. He's from Lower Tugelo, the same part of South Africa as we lived.'

'Ask him if he's hurt.'

They talked, both stood stiffly by the table. Isabel and Ettie watched from their chairs in silence.

'They didn't hurt him, but he's very thirsty,' she said.

I rose to get him another drink, while the guvnor continued. 'What did they do to him?'

Again, they talked. Delphine's face was pale and without emotion, S'bu's intense and anxious.

'They asked him questions, but he didn't understand. Then they left him in the room. He tried to get out, but they wouldn't let him. He wants to know if his friends are safe.'

When I gave him a mug of milk, he smiled for the first time since we found him. He drank it down in one.

'Tell him they've been arrested for murder,' said the guvnor. 'We're trying to help them.'

As she told him, S'bu was silent and still. He put the mug on the table. When he talked again, he held the guvnor's eye.

'It wasn't them,' Delphine translated when he'd finished. 'There were two white men. They had guns. Senzo took out his gun, trying to frighten them away, but they started shooting. They hit Mr Fowler. S'bu couldn't make his gun fire so he tried to run away. They caught him.'

'What about Musa?' asked the guvnor.

Delphine spoke. S'bu shook his head, raised his palms.

'He wants to know what you mean,' said Delphine.

'Did they kill Musa?' asked the guvnor.

Delphine spoke. S'bu swallowed. He asked her a question. She replied. His head moved slowly, a look of horror on his face. He spoke again.

'He's asking if Musa's dead,' said Delphine as S'bu sat heavy on the chair, his eyes fixed on the guvnor.

'Tell him yes,' answered the guvnor softly. 'Ask him who killed him.'

She sat at the table and asked him. His answer was muffled and low.

'Musa was asleep in the basement when the men came. He never came up. He wasn't there when they were shooting.'

'So when S'bu ran out, Musa wasn't there?'

Delphine spoke. S'bu shook his head. He pointed at the floor. 'Down. Down,' he said, the words broken by tears. He rammed the heels of his hands in his eyes.

'Did the white men go back to the Quaker Meeting House?'

'They put him in a carriage and took him to see Mr Capaldi, and from there to the place they kept him,' she said after asking him. 'He doesn't know if they returned later.'

The guvnor looked at me. 'So it was Capaldi's men, just as Thembeka thought. Ask him if there was a Chinaman there.'

Delphine spoke to S'bu. He nodded, uncovered his tear-wet face, and pointed at something on the bookshelf.

'What's he saying?'

'He says yes, like that.' Delphine stepped behind the sofa and took down a tin of rat poison from the shelf. She held it to the guvnor. It was red, with the name ROUGH ON RATS. On the tin was a picture of a Chinaman with his mouth open and a big black rat in his hand.

'My Lord,' murmured the guvnor, taking the tin. He examined it carefully. 'Look at this, Barnett!'

The Chinaman wore a red smock and short yellow trousers to his knees. On his head was a golden turrèt, out of which flowed a long pigtail like a snake. I looked at the guvnor's excited face.

'He's wearing almost the same clothes as Polichinelle,' I said.

'And Polichinelle was managed by Capaldi,' he said slowly. 'Well, that seems to seal it for Mr Fowler's killers.' He turned to Delphine. 'Ask him if he thinks Senzo or Thembeka killed Musa.'

As she translated, S'bu drew his head back. 'No!' he said, then spoke in Fanakalo again.

'He says they couldn't have,' said Delphine. 'Musa was Senzo's uncle. Thembeka's cousin.'

'Thembeka and Musa argued, didn't they?'

'She didn't want to come to London,' said Delphine after she'd asked S'bu. 'She wanted to stay in Paris. It was only that.'

The guvnor pulled out his pipe and got it going, the smoke drifting from each side of his mouth. It was packed in that little parlour. I stood by the wall, the guvnor in the middle of the room. S'bu, holding his head in his hands, was in the good chair by the fire, while Delphine, Ettie and Isabel sat at the table. Above, one of the babies coughed and began to cry. Isabel patted Ettie's hand and climbed the stairs.

Arrowood took out his notebook and showed Delphine the message he'd found in Musa's pocket. 'Can you translate that?'

'*Meet at hotel York. Thursday at two.*'

'Hotel York? Not Arch of Triumph?'

'Hotel York.'

'A hotel in York?' The guvnor looked at me. 'So Thembeka deceived us. I wonder who she knows in York? Ask him, Miss Druitt.'

S'bu shook his head. 'He doesn't know,' said Delphine.

'Maybe it's the York Hotel, in Waterloo Road,' I said.

'Good Christ, Barnett!' He turned to his pile of newspapers. 'Isn't that where the Zulu Princess is staying? What day was that report?'

A few moments later he found the article he'd shown me

the day before in the coffee shop. He was right. The Zulu Princess, Nobantu, was staying in the York Hotel with two companions, a woman and a man.

'Ask S'bu if he knows about the Zulu Princess staying in London.'

As Delphine spoke to him, his gaze fell to the floor. He sniffed, wiped his eyes, and replied in a low voice.

'No,' she said.

The guvnor took up his coat and hat. 'Let's get over there,' he said, wrapping his scarf around his neck. He looked at Ettie. 'Will you watch him?'

'What d'you mean, watch him?'

'If he wants anything. More food.' He pointed at the mattress against the wall. 'He can sleep on my bed.'

Ettie sighed and nodded. 'Tea?' she said to S'bu, miming drinking from a cup and saucer.

He shifted his head just slightly, but didn't answer. The fire held his gaze.

Chapter Thirty

The York Hotel was opposite the nurses' home on Waterloo Road. It wasn't a grand, chandelier-type affair, just a pub with three floors of rooms upstairs. Not really the place you'd stay in if you were a princess, but not too poor neither. The bloke at the bar gave us a watery smile, his eyes narrowing in what he must have thought was a welcome. He told us that last Monday the princess had gone to Edinburgh, where she was being introduced to the Duke of Fife.

'Could you tell us if anyone came here to see them?' asked the guvnor.

'Plenty of newspapermen. A few youngsters who'd read about them, you know the type.' He wiped down the counter with an old cloth. 'Three or four at a time, trying to impress their young ladies.' He glanced at Delphine, who stood next to me, her hands in her coat pockets. She glared at him.

'Any Africans?'

He nodded. 'There were a couple a week last Friday. No... Thursday. The twelfth it would've been.' He looked over the guvnor's shoulder at a lady who'd just arrived. 'Miss Walser, good to see you again. I've got you in number two at the back. You won't be woken by the carts again this time. Will you be eating?'

'I'd like to go straight up, Mr Deakin,' said the lady.

The guvnor turned to old Miss Walser. 'If you don't mind, ma'am. This is a matter of life and death. We'll only be a minute.'

'Well, if—'

'Thank you, Miss Walser. I knew you'd understand.' He turned his earnest face back to the barman. 'We're working with Scotland Yard on the murders in the Friends Meeting House earlier this week, Mr Deakin. What did these Africans look like? It's very important.'

'Well... black-skinned, both of them. The man wore earrings and feathers round his neck. Big, strong fellow. From the circus or something, I suppose. The woman did the talking. Spoke like a bloke, though. Shortish, I suppose. We thought they must be Zulus, just like the princess and her party.'

'Did they go up to her room?'

He shook his head. 'She'd gone to Canterbury. Overnight, like, to see the Cathedral. She was due back that day, but there weren't no trains. Broken rail or something. The two of them sat around all day over there in the corner, drinking away. Blimey, could they drink! Didn't believe me about her not coming back till gone nine in the evening, and my Lord they were jiggered by then. I told the princess when she got back the next day. She said I must show them straight up when they returned, but they never did come back. That's the strange thing. After waiting all that time, they never come back. Must have forgot or something.'

'Is she returning here after Edinburgh?'

'Twenty-third,' said the fellow. 'In the evening.'

'What day is it, Barnett?' the guvnor asked me as the three of us left the hotel.

'Twenty-first. She'll be back in two days.'

'Will you meet us at Scotland Yard tomorrow at ten, Miss Druitt?' asked Arrowood. 'I've an idea.'

'If it will help,' said the young lady, pulling on her gloves.

'But you mustn't tell anyone about S'bu. Will you promise me that? The police believe the Africans are the murderers. If they discover where S'bu is, they'll arrest him too.'

'Do you believe his story about what happened?'

'It fits what we know, and it's the same story as the other two told us. They had no opportunity to concoct it.'

Delphine rubbed her pea-sized eyes. 'If you want me to help you again, I do need to know if I'm helping the correct people. You said they're with the Ninevites. That's a bandit gang, Mr Arrowood.'

'You know about them?'

'Everyone in Natal knows about them. They steal from everybody, from white and black. The authorities believe they're rousing the Africans to revolution. They're showing the natives they can organize themselves and live without the whites.'

'Well, that's a different matter, miss.'

'I know, but the African officer said they'd killed a child.'

'They swear it was someone else.'

'But how can I be sure that's the truth?'

He pressed his lips together and studied her. 'You can't,' he sighed at last. 'Miss Delphine, do you believe that all of those African children you taught were savage killers?'

'Of course not. They were children.'

'Or that they'd grow up to be savage killers?'

'Of course not.'

'That's because you know them. But all the people of this imperial city understand about Zulus is that for twenty years since Rorke's Drift we've fought battle after battle with them. The newspapers and story books and exhibitions tell us only that they're a savage, warrior race. That they fight and kill. Rider Haggard said that Zulu history is one of superstition, madness and blood-stained pride.'

'That isn't true,' said she. 'He knows nothing about the people of Natal.'

'Neither does anyone else here. Nothing but the sort of thing Haggard says. Don't you think that'll influence the jury? The judge? Will they be free of those beliefs when presented with a Scotland Yard detective committed to the idea that Senzo, Thembeka and S'bu murdered three people?'

'I don't know,' said Delphine, raising her hand to a hansom approaching from Westminster. 'But I give you my word I won't tell the police about S'bu unless they ask me directly.'

'Thank you, miss,' said the guvnor as she climbed into the cab. 'We'll see you tomorrow.'

We stood by Waterloo Bridge as he pondered what to do next. The stars were out, though you could only just make out a twinkle here and there through the smoke above South London that night. 'I can't stop thinking about those women we freed from the warehouse,' he said, starting to walk back to Coin Street. 'What the hell was Capaldi doing with them?'

'Must be something to do with his cat-houses.'

'Yes, but why imprison them like that? Did they refuse to work for him? Had they gone to the police? That man is evil, Barnett. Out and out evil. He'll be looking for S'bu by now and it won't take him long to find where I live. We must take him to Lewis's.'

Lewis and the guvnor had been friends since they were kids, and though he was a filthy monster to look at, he was one of the kindest blokes I knew. A year ago he'd taken Willoughby in after the Catford case, and we knew we could rely on him to shelter S'bu. He answered the door in his dressing gown, a scarf tucked in the collar, a woollen nightcap on his head. He was the same height as the guvnor, also portly, also a glutton, but he had only one arm to the guvnor's two.

'My goodness, William,' he said, a troubled look on his face. 'You thought this was a day for your yellow suit?'

'A bit of an accident with my other one. I'll tell you about it later.'

Lewis looked past us to S'bu on the pavement. 'Another stray, my friend?'

Arrowood stood aside. 'He's called S'bu. He doesn't really speak English.'

'Pleased to meet you, S'bu,' said Lewis with a smile.

'Good day, sir,' said S'bu.

Lewis pointed at himself. 'I'm Lewis.' He pointed at S'bu. 'You're S'bu. I'm Lewis. Good day, S'bu.'

'Good day, Lewis,' said S'bu.

Lewis smiled. 'Come in, my friend. Get out of the cold.'

Willoughby was sitting by the fire in the parlour, warming his feet. He leapt up as we walked in, shaking my hand and the guvnor's, a smile of utter joy on his face.

'You come to see me, Norman?' he asked. 'You come to sit with us?'

''Course we have, mate,' I said. Willoughby, who was a little weak-minded, worked at Sidney's stables, and you could smell it on him. His nails were splintered and black; it looked like his jumper hadn't seen a mangle in months. Lewis wasn't a good influence on Willoughby's self-cleaning.

Willoughby looked at S'bu. 'What's your name?'

'S'bu,' I told him. 'He's African. He don't talk English.'

'Don't talk?'

'He does, but not like us.'

After the guvnor'd explained what had happened, Lewis nodded. 'Of course we'll have him. It's Christmas. The more the merrier.' He looked at S'bu. 'You. Stay here. Yes?'

'Yes?' said S'bu, low and tight-lipped. He wasn't sure about it all, you could tell.

Lewis made a sleeping sign, his hand flat against his tilted head. 'Sleep. Yes?'

S'bu nodded.

'How about a little brandy for the cold?' asked Lewis, already pouring from a bottle by his chair. He filled four tumblers, then paused. 'How old are you, S'bu?'

S'bu looked at him, not knowing what to do. He looked at the guvnor.

'About fourteen,' said Arrowood. 'Old enough.'

Lewis passed round the drinks. My side was smarting again, so I swallowed down another couple of Black Drop with the brandy.

'How are things at home, William?' asked Lewis.

The guvnor sighed. 'The babies are ill,' he said at last. 'The doctor thinks it's...' His nose flared and he shut his eyes.

'Typhus,' I said.

'No.' Lewis looked at me, his eyes wide. 'But... but not both?'

'Both,' I said. 'They're really not well. Isabel might have caught it too.'

'Oh, my Lord. I'm so sorry, William.' Lewis stepped to his old friend and grasped his arm. 'But they might recover. Lots do.'

'Lots do,' said the guvnor with a sad smile. 'I'm sure they'll come through. Look, you couldn't loan me forty shillings, could you? They need it for medicine.'

'I wish I could, William, but I've pawned anything of value. The bank own my stock. Until business picks up, I'm getting by on tick.'

'I know. I had to ask.'

Lewis patted him on the shoulder. 'I'll find you something to eat, though,' he said, and waddled out to the kitchen. 'Fetch S'bu some blankets, Willoughby.'

S'bu stepped over to the corner of the room and picked up the concertina that had been gathering dust there for the last few years. He sat on the stool, rested it on his knee, and began to play a jig. His eyes were shut, his lips moving like he was singing each note. Willoughby returned with the blankets and set them out on the couch, his head bobbing with the music.

When the tune finished, S'bu opened his eyes. We clapped. Then he seemed to remember Musa and his face crumpled.

Lewis came through with a dirty bowl of bacon rind and cold potatoes. The guvnor grabbed a bit before his friend had even set it down. Willoughby followed and then the guvnor took another for good measure. Lewis offered the bowl to S'bu, who shook his head. When I got to it there were only a few grey spuds left.

'You need to trim your whiskers,' Arrowood said to his friend. 'It's as if you don't have a face.'

'Ach,' growled Lewis, waving him away. He put his hand

to his chin and smoothed the mess down as best as he could. 'I've been too busy.'

'Too busy? You sit in that damp shop all day. There's a barber down the road. Or Willoughby'll cut it for you, won't you?'

'I cut it, Lewis,' said Willoughby.

Lewis nodded. 'Perhaps tomorrow. We'll see.'

S'bu yawned.

'Are you tired, mate?' I asked him. I pointed at the couch and then at him. I pretended to yawn. 'You. Sleep?'

'S'bu sleep?'

'Yes.' I pointed at the couch. 'You. Sleep there.'

He went to the couch, checking with me it was what I meant, then lay down with his head on the pillow. I set the blankets on top, while Willoughby took the brandy off him and swallowed it down himself.

We sat down for another drink while Lewis asked about the case. As we talked, S'bu just lay there under the blankets, watching us. He knew we were talking about him and Thembeka and Senzo, and I felt sorry he didn't understand.

'Capaldi's dangerous,' said Lewis when we'd told him all we could.

'Yes,' nodded the guvnor, taking a great swig of brandy and coughing. His eyes watered, his face went red, his hand went to his heart. 'His men killed Mr Fowler, but we just don't know who killed Musa and Mrs Fowler. The men might have returned later, we just don't know. Napper's convinced Senzo and Thembeka killed her, but good heavens it would have been difficult. She wasn't in the building the day before so they'd have to go, find her and then bring her back. Two Africans. Not easy to do without being seen.'

'Perhaps she called on them?' said Lewis.

'But she had no coat. And how did she know they were there? And why on earth tie her to a chair after she was dead? No, I don't think they killed her. Whoever did it wanted us to think it was them. That's the only conclusion I can come to.'

'What about the older one?' asked Lewis. 'Why would they bash out his teeth?'

'That's another puzzle. Perhaps they wanted information?'

'What information?'

'About the raid in South Africa, that's all I can think. But who knows? Thembeka's hiding something. She didn't want us to know they went to meet the princess.'

'What about Madame Delacourte?' asked Lewis. 'Was she involved?'

The guvnor blew his nose. 'We can't rule her out. Polichinelle was one of the men, but he knows both her and Capaldi.'

For a few moments, we thought it over. What a bloody tangle it was. And nobody was paying us either.

'I hope you still have my pistols?' asked Lewis finally.

'Ah, yes,' muttered the guvnor. 'Well, we're not quite sure, but don't worry, old friend. We'll get them back.'

Lewis slapped his forehead. 'I knew I should never have lent them to you! You'll have to pay me for them.'

'We'll get them back, Lewis,' said the guvnor, grabbing the last spud just before Willoughby got to it. 'I promise.'

Chapter Thirty-One

We parted at St George's Circus. The guvnor was on his way to the Hog, where he planned to play cards and take a mug of brandy and hot water.

'Don't stay out all night, William,' I warned him. 'We've too much to do, and I've had enough of rescuing you from a pool of your own piss.'

'Norman!' he exclaimed. 'What an unpleasant thing to say.'

'Listen to me. Please. This case is too difficult for one of your bank holidays. S'bu's in danger and Thembeka and Senzo'll be convicted if we can't solve this case. And your family need you sober, whether you know it or not. Those babies need you fit and able.'

He gripped my arm. 'Don't worry. What do you think I am?'

'I know what you are. You're the type of man who needs to hurt himself sometimes.'

'I need to think on the case, and I do my best thinking in the Hog.'

I didn't want to be his nanny tonight, so I watched him toddle up Waterloo Road towards Bankside. It was just gone ten when I gained the Pelican, Saturday night and the crowd in there was at their loosest and noisiest: a red-haired lad played the fiddle in a corner while folk talked and laughed and swayed like they had no troubles in the world. Whole families were in there, babes in their mothers' arms, kiddies whispering to each other and snatching gulps of their parents' booze, hunched old women with gammy eyes tapping the jig with fingers that weren't good for anything else. I spotted Molly working the counter. She was red-faced, hair tied back, her brown dress splashed with the gushing porter, while folk all around tried to get her eye and call out their drinks. Banging down a couple of mugs for a big-limbed lad who couldn't seem to get his money out his pocket, she leant over the counter and dug in there herself. He tried to catch a kiss as she counted out a few coins and put the rest in his hand.

A Welsh couple started dancing a jig in front of me: I pushed past them and found an empty space at the end of the bar. When she noticed I was there, Molly's eyes narrowed.

'Seven ales, beautiful,' said a bloke in a striped suit. He was Irish.

'What's up, Molly?' I asked as she poured them out.

'Thought we were going for cakes,' she said, her eyes on the barrel.

'Oh, Christ. I'm sorry. We've been working. I couldn't get away.'

'Couldn't send a message?'

I scratched my head. 'I forgot. But only 'cos of the case.'

Her eyes were brown, her neck strong and white, and I had a hunger for her that night. Starting to pour another, she looked up at me. 'At least you're honest, Norm.'

She didn't say it with a smile.

'It's not that I didn't want to. There's been three murders.'

She handed over a mug and started pouring another.

'I want to see you tonight. When d'you finish?'

She poured two more afore she answered.

'Couple of hours, Norm. But you better make it up to me.'

'You can take your davey on it, Moll.'

At last she smiled. I leant over the counter and gave her a kiss. Her taste was all cheese and gin, but I couldn't think of anything better.

The guvnor was late next morning. I waited with Delphine in the lobby of Scotland Yard, listening to the bells of Westminster calling Sunday service. Not much was going on in the station that early, just a few dirty old sods being released with sick on their trousers. The desk sergeant was a fellow I hadn't seen before, a thin, wiry bloke with a long, upturned moustache. Every five minutes, he blew his nose in a horrible, stained hanky, then wiped his lips on the back of his hands. I tried to have a chat with Delphine, but she was irritated with having to wait and answered each of my questions with a just a word or two. I gave up. It didn't bother me: I was tuckered out and floating in a cloud of Molly's joy. I thought maybe I even loved her. She was so like Mrs B in some of her ways, and there were moments last night, in the dark of her room, in the warmth of her body, that I felt I was with my old girl. It was the way she smelt, the feel of her arse on my hand, her hair on my chest.

Maybe that wasn't fair. As I sat there in the reception of Scotland Yard, arms crossed against the cold, I promised myself I'd try not to think like that. Molly was her own person, with a big heart and a wild soul. She deserved to be seen as she was. I wondered what Mrs B'd think about me taking up with her oldest friend. I hoped she'd be happy about it: I certainly needed a bit of warmth in my life.

About eleven, shouting arose from behind the door of the superintendent's office. The desk bloke stepped back and opened it a bit to have a listen.

'Don't treat me like a fool, Farmerson!' came the deep voice of the boss. 'You think I've forgotten what you did at the Asiatic Seamen's Home?'

'But that wasn't my fault, sir. It was the Oriental went for me, sir!'

We couldn't see them, but I knew from the voice it was the other desk sarge, the one who'd had a go at the Hindoo the day before.

'Don't answer me back! And even if he did go for you, how the hell did he end up in that state?'

'I explained it all back then, sir.'

'And promised it'd never happen again! But you *have* done it again, haven't you?'

'I swear I didn't touch the African, sir. I swear it on the Holy Bible. I never even went in his cell. Somebody else did it.'

The wiry desk sarge stepped away from the door quick, just before the superintendent appeared in his spotless blue uniform. His long face was flushed, the eyebrows hooked savagely. He stopped in the doorway, looking back into the office. 'Mr Nyambezi says it was you, Farmerson.'

'He ain't used to white folk, sir,' came the other voice. 'Happen he can't tell us apart.'

'He's from Nataland, you imbecile. Of course he's used to white folk.'

'He got it wrong, sir! I never touched the prisoner.'

'PC Mabaso spoke to him after you'd locked him up. He

confirms the story. You're suspended, sergeant. I'll have to bring charges.'

'No, sir. Please. I never touched him.'

'And I thank God you didn't go in the African woman's cell. Heaven knows what you would have done to her!'

'No, sir! I'd never touch a woman!'

'Go home and stay there until I call you. Now, get out!'

Moments later, Sergeant Farmerson appeared. He was bigger all round than the bloke on the desk this morning: a round belly, legs about a foot too long, his head pale and completely bald. He clutched his helmet in his hand, his worn overcoat over his arm. His eyes were cast down. The superintendent went back into his office and slammed the door.

The desk sarge patted Farmerson's back as he passed through.

'Be good, Jack,' he said.

'Fuck him,' muttered the suspended copper. He looked up at the desk sarge. 'Help me out, will you, mate?'

'I'll see what I can do.'

Still shaking his head, Jack stormed out the door.

The superintendent poked his head out the office. 'Do not get involved, sergeant,' he said. 'It was him, all right. You know what the man's like.'

'Yes, sir.'

The super stepped back into his office and shut the door.

'What's he been up to, sarge?' I asked the bloke at the desk.

'You a newspaperman?'

'No, I'm helping Detective Napper with the African case. Barnett's the name. I'm with Mr Arrowood.'

He looked at Delphine.

'She's with us, translating,' I said.

He rubbed his thick moustache and picked up a pen. 'Someone had a go at the African in the cell, that's all I know.'

'Is he hurt?' I asked.

'Just a few broken fingers and a smashed tooth. He'll survive.'

'That sergeant did it, did he?'

'You heard what the super said, didn't you?'

'Appalling,' Delphine whispered to me when he was back reading his paper again. 'They're just like the police in South Africa.'

The street door opened again and the guvnor stepped in. He was a pitiful sight: his step was unsteady, his nose swollen and red, the grey bags under his weepy eyes spongy and peppered with grit. He'd come direct from the Hog, that much was clear, and the wind as came in with him smelt so bad of beer I thought he must have slept in a barrel.

With a groan, he capsized onto the bench aside Delphine.

'You're an hour late, sir,' I said.

He burped into his hand and glanced at Delphine. 'Morning, miss.'

'It's usual to apologize, Mr Arrowood,' she answered.

'I'm sorry, madam,' he whispered.

Her nose wrinkled. 'Are you ill?'

'Yes,' he mumbled, burping again. He stared at the floor. 'Bless you.'

I sat back and chewed my lip. He'd poisoned himself again. Here we all were at the Yard, and I didn't know if he could work. I was so tired of his weakness.

Minutes passed as he sighed and burped and shifted in his

seat. Delphine looked at me again and again, but I could offer her no reassurance. He looked like a badly slaughtered pig. Even his bowler was suffering. I took out my box of Black Drop and put a couple of pills in his hand.

He shut his eyes. 'Thank you, Norman,' he mouthed, then placed them on his tongue.

I stood. 'Could you wait with him a moment, miss?' I said. 'I need to get him some coffee.'

'I'll be fine,' he rasped, trying to swallow the medicine. He coughed a pill up into his grubby hand.

Ten minutes later I was back with a bit of bread and marge and a mug of coffee. The guvnor's head rested on the wall, his eyes closed. Half one of the pills I'd given him lay snagged on his beard.

'Get that mumper out of here,' the desk sergeant called over to me. 'No sleeping in the station.'

I gave the guvnor's cheek a slap. 'Wake up, William.'

He moaned, squeezing his eyes together. I caught the pill as it fell from his beard.

I slapped him harder. 'Open your eyes or I'll pour this coffee in your lap.'

He half opened up, wincing like the light was too strong. His eyes were clouded with threads of blood. 'Oh, my head,' he said in his most pathetic voice. 'I think I've had a haemorrhage.'

'Open your mouth.'

I flicked the pill back in and poured a bit of the coffee onto his yellow tongue. He swallowed and opened his mouth again. I poured in more coffee. Then again. When we'd got halfway through the drink, I broke off a bit of bread, used the stem of his pipe to push it in his mouth, then poured on more coffee. He swallowed and choked.

273

'Leave me alone!' he muttered, trying to push my hand away.

'Open,' I hissed. He did as I asked. Bit by bit, I fed him half the bread. Finally, he sat up.

'No more!' he said in a fury.

'You damn fool,' I said.

'Don't talk to me like that.'

'I'll talk to you how I like.'

He gripped my wrist, digging his nails into my flesh. His yellow, bloodshot eyes glared at me in fury. 'Who the hell d'you think you are?'

It seemed like he was trying to pierce my skin. I tried to prise his fingers away, but he wanted to see me in pain. I brought my arm back and slapped him hard as I could across the face.

He groaned, letting go and slumping on the bench.

'Now you behave yourself, William,' I whispered in his ear. 'Open your mouth.'

He did so, and slowly I fed him the rest of the bread. Delphine watched in disgust. As I neared the last of it, Napper came striding in with Mabaso.

'Oh, you're here again, are you?' he said when he saw us. He lifted his bowler and raked his stubby fingers through his tight orange hair. 'Well, I suppose that's lucky. We've had another development.'

'What's happened, inspector?' I asked, stepping across to hide the guvnor from him.

'It's Sylvia,' said Napper. 'She's gone missing.'

Chapter Thirty-Two

'When?' demanded the guvnor, using my arms to pull himself to his feet.

'Last night. We had a message from Miss Leonie this morning. I'm just having a word with my super and then we're off to meet them at Piccadilly Hall. They asked if we could bring you. I don't know why.'

With that, Napper and Mabaso marched past the desk, knocked on the door, and entered the superintendent's office.

The guvnor shook his head. 'Sylvia? But why?'

'You good now?' I asked him.

'The pills are starting to work. Do I need to apologize?'

I raised my eyebrows at him.

He sighed. 'Thank you for helping me. I was at the end of my tether last night, Norman. My mind wouldn't settle, not for a moment. This case gets more tangled the more we discover. I've developed a spasm.' He pointed at his kidneys or his liver, somewhere in that vast region. 'Just here. I don't know if I've grown a tumour. My mother had one in the same place. And I am so sorry, Miss Delphine. Your time is precious, I know. I hope we haven't kept you from anything?'

'Church,' she snapped.

He nodded, then looked back at me. 'Don't blame me, Norman, please. You know I need to relieve the infernal irritation somehow. And something occurred to me last night when I was in my cups. Remember that tin of rat poison that S'bu was pointing at? The one with the Chinaman in the red-and-yellow costume that we thought must mean it was Polichinelle he'd seen?'

'I do.'

'Well, Mr Wu came into the Hog last night.'

'You didn't take the pipes again, William.'

He waved my question away. 'We were fools, Norman. Polichinelle'd never do an armed raid dressed in his clown outfit. I've noticed my mind is sometimes overwhelmed by one unusual element and it prevents me thinking clearly. It was never Polichinelle on that raid. You see, Mr Wu also has something that the Chinaman on that tin had. What d'you think that is?'

'Just tell me, William.' I knew he was right about the clown and was vexed I hadn't seen it myself.

'A ponytail. Every drawing of a Chinaman you ever see has one. And who do we know on this case has one?'

'Ermano.'

He clapped me on the back and smiled. 'It was Ermano.'

Napper came out the door, Mabaso following.

'Come on, then, you two,' he said, his boots clicking on the floor.

'Could we just have a quick word with Miss Kunene and Mr Nyambezi?' asked the guvnor. 'Miss Druitt's offered to translate.'

'It'll have to wait,' answered Napper.

'I see,' said Delphine, standing.

'I'm very sorry, miss,' said the guvnor. 'It seems we've wasted your time.'

'So long in the cold for nothing,' said Delphine. 'You're lucky I'm quite desperate to occupy myself.'

'It's the nature of murder investigations, I'm afraid. Could we ask your help later? Either this evening or tomorrow?'

'As long as you don't send me home again, Mr Arrowood.'

'I promise,' he said with a bow. 'And I do apologize.'

We walked up Whitehall towards Leicester Square. It was Sunday lunchtime, the place dotted with families out strolling. Outside Morley's Hotel was a newspaper boy with a stack of papers flung over his shoulder. 'Missing woman found dead!' he cried. 'Latest on the Zulu murders! Missing women murdered! Three dead now! Get it here!'

A queue had formed up toward Duncannon Street, and every few seconds a punter dropped a coin in his hand and took a copy. As we passed, a young black fellow in a thick overcoat greeted Mabaso, taking him by the arm and stopping him.

'Three dead now!' cried the paper seller again, handing over the papers one by one. 'Calls to bring in Sherlock!'

The guvnor stopped. 'Who's calling to bring in Sherlock?' he grunted at the boy.

'Get your purse out and find out,' said the boy. The queue laughed.

'Holmes's never bothered with murdered women,' snapped the guvnor, looking up and down the queue, trying to catch someone's eye. 'Where was he on the Ripper case, eh?'

'He was likely never asked,' said a short fellow with a silk rose in his button-hole.

'He would have done if he was,' agreed a proper-looking woman.

'I doubt it,' said the guvnor. 'And I'll wager anything he *was* asked.'

'Come along, Arrowood,' said Napper. He looked around for Mabaso, who was laughing and clapping the African fellow on the arm. The stranger threw his head back and laughed himself. Mabaso's body had lost its tight control, his long limbs loose now, his face shining with delight. He was like a completely different bloke.

'Constable!' barked Napper.

Mabaso muttered something in the bloke's ear, who laughed again, then hurried to catch up with us.

'I didn't think you knew anybody here,' said Napper.

'I just met him, sir,' said Mabaso, his face severe again. He hacked into his hanky, his eyes watering.

'Didn't look like it,' said Napper.

Mabaso said nothing as we walked on.

'Did PC McDonald discover anything when he called at the houses around Gresham Hall?' asked the guvnor.

'Nobody saw anything. Now tell me what you've learned since we last talked.'

Napper marched ahead, the guvnor and me following and Mabaso behind with his hands rammed in his pockets. He was coughing worse than the last time we'd seen him. His scarf was wrapped thick around his neck, his ears like mug handles. He looked so cold I shivered just to look at him.

The guvnor told them about Thembeka playing us false over the note, and about them visiting the hotel. Still wary that Capaldi had a copper on the inside, he didn't tell him about S'bu.

'But why would they hide their knowledge of the princess?' asked Napper. 'Any ideas, Mabaso?'

'They'll have read about her and called on her because they missed home,' said the constable in his careful voice. 'That's what I think. They didn't know the lady or else they'd have gone back.'

We passed up the side of the Square and turned down towards Piccadilly. 'But why hide it?' asked Napper.

'My people don't lead the police to another's door. They don't trust them, even when they need them.'

'Do they trust the black officers?' asked Napper.

Mabaso began to cough again. He held his hanky to his mouth, covering his nose. When he'd caught his breath, he replied, 'They despise us, sir. For working with the colonial authorities.'

'Are you still convinced it was they who killed Mrs Fowler?' asked the guvnor. Although the shops were all shut up for the Sabbath, there was a queue outside Lyons' tea house, kids with scrubbed faces spilling out onto the kerb, the boys in little suits, the girls in Sunday dresses. We stepped onto the road to get past.

'All the evidence points to them,' said Napper, his boots click-clacking as he walked.

'But what motive did they have?' asked the guvnor.

'The motive isn't important. These chaps are used to killing. It means little to them. Am I right, Mabaso?'

'Yes, sir.'

'Senzo Nyambezi's already killed two people in South Africa.'

'He says it wasn't him,' said Arrowood, getting out of breath at the quick pace.

'He also says the deaths here weren't him,' said Napper. 'But why's he always there when people are killed?'

The guvnor shook his head. 'How d'you explain Sylvia disappearing?'

'I don't know, Arrowood!' snapped Napper as we crossed Coventry Street. He turned back to Mabaso. 'It's true about you having different rules for killing, isn't it, constable? Ellis says that something that's a crime here wouldn't be where you're from.'

'The authorities have the same laws against killing as here,' answered Mabaso. He cleared this throat. 'But in the home-steads they do things differently. They follow the old ways.'

'Why the devil would Senzo kill Mr Fowler?' cried the guvnor. 'The man was helping him, for goodness' sake!'

'Sir, just because we are of the same people does not mean I know his mind.'

'It would be insane.'

'Perhaps he is insane,' said Mabaso, walking careful round a pile of dung spilled onto the pavement. 'They were arguing on the boat, the ladies told us that. Let me interrogate Senzo, sir. I know how to get information from these Ninevites.'

'We'll see,' said Napper.

As we approached the theatre, the pavements became busier, folk spewing out of cabs and buses, excited about their Christmas outings. A ragged woman was selling mince pies from a tray around her neck. An old soldier who sat in a wheeled chair with one of his legs missing sold saveloys from a griddle, while next to him a loudmouth couple had a vat of hot wine on the bubble in a little metal cart.

'But what argument could be so serious for them to kill Musa?' asked the guvnor.

'Have you heard of the Qwabe succession dispute, sir?' asked

Mabaso, only now coming up level with us. He had a queer way of walking on his toes like his heels were tender. 'It split the Qwabe people. There have been feuds ever since between those who support Meseni and those who are with Siziba. Murders, violations, riots at beer parties. You have no idea how hot the feelings are. I believe Musa was with Meseni. Senzo and Thembeka are Siziba.'

'But Musa was Senzo's uncle!'

'The dispute split families apart,' said Mabaso, shaking his head. 'These fellows will fight if one of them breaks wind. As for Mr Fowler, well, he no doubt just got in the way.'

'But Senzo and Thembeka said two white men killed Mr Fowler. I'm inclined to believe them.'

'Well, I'm inclined to believe Constable Mabaso,' said Napper. 'He understands their minds better than we could. But we need to find the boy. He's in on it too.'

'Capaldi's men captured him,' said the guvnor. 'Thembeka said they fell upon him.'

'She's protecting him, Mr Arrowood,' said Mabaso. 'She's deceiving you.'

Chapter Thirty-Three

Nick opened the dressing-room door and stood aside to let us in. He looked a bit better than the last time we'd seen him, but his eyes twitched and his face was pale.

Gisele and Leonie were sat in front of a long looking glass, getting ready for the show.

'Tell us what happened, Miss Leonie,' said Napper.

'We woke up and she was gone,' said she, her powder brush in her hand. 'Just disappeared!'

'She was take in her nightclothes,' said Gisele, her orange face full of worry. 'Her house dress is missing, and her shoes.'

'Perhaps she ran away?' suggested the guvnor.

'She doesn't know anybody in England,' said Leonie.

'You saw and heard nothing?' asked the guvnor.

Both ladies shook their heads.

'What about you, Nick?' asked Napper.

'Nothing,' he answered with a frown. 'I was sleeping in the kitchen, by the door.'

'The door was locked?'

'Yes, sir. They must have a key.'

The guvnor turned to Leonie. 'Where's Dave?'

'He left after we found she'd gone. Went to tell Mr Capaldi.'

'Was he there overnight?'

She nodded.

'Could it be Bruno?' asked the guvnor. 'He must have a key.'

Leonie shook her head. 'We've four shows this afternoon, and we're sold out every day until the middle of January. They're going to lose a lot of money.'

'Could be him, though,' said Nick. 'She goes missing, it's in all the papers, they sell more tickets. Then she comes back.'

'But it might be the murderer!' exclaimed Gisele.

'We have the murderers in gaol,' said Napper. 'This is something different.'

Leonie spoke angrily. 'Senzo and Thembeka didn't kill that woman.'

Napper flushed. 'Leave the policing to me, ma'am,' he snapped.

'Then what are you going to do to find her?' asked Leonie, wringing her hands. 'She's in danger. They'll kill her like they killed the Quaker lady. And we'll be next.'

'We'll go to see Mr Capaldi and find out who else could have had keys. I'll apply for another warrant to search his premises. It may be as Nick says, but I can't see him doing it in the middle of a run. Madame Delacourte would make more sense, but we've just searched her building too. We'll concentrate on the keys for now. Maybe one of Mr Capaldi's men is working against him.'

'Or maybe S'bu?' said Nick.

'No, Nick,' snapped Gisele. 'How can you say? He just a boy.'

'I don't know!' cried Nick, throwing his hands in the air. 'I'm worried half to death for my poor Sylvia.'

'It's not impossible, though,' said Napper. 'He might think Sylvia's disappearance would convince us the killer's still out there and we'd then release the two prisoners.'

Nick nodded like his life depended on it.

'Perhaps she ran away, Nick,' said the guvnor in his softest voice. 'I'm sorry to say it, but isn't it possible? She hated the shows. She was weeping about what the audience said. She didn't want to be Baboon Girl.'

Nick spat in a bucket on the floor. 'She'd never leave me like that. She's nuts on me.'

The guvnor went over to Nick and took his shoulder. 'I know she is, Nick. I know she is. But perhaps she hid her despair from you because she knew it was too dangerous to get you involved. Capaldi would have killed you if you'd been caught. Perhaps she ran away *because* she loved you.'

At that moment, the door opened and young Ralf Capaldi walked in. He stopped when he saw the coppers, his gloved fingers touching the pockets of his cashmere overcoat. His eyes travelled over each of us men, lingering on Mabaso for a few extra moments, avoiding the corner of the room where Leonie and Gisele sat.

'Hello?' he said when he'd managed to find his words again. 'What...'

Napper stepped forward. 'We've met before at your father's house, Mr Capaldi. Detective Inspector Napper. This is PC Mabaso from the South African Police.'

'Yes, sir,' said Ralf, backing towards the door. He looked like he might be sick. 'If it's about the Zulus you ought to speak to my dad. I don't know about them.'

'It's about the disappearance of Miss Sylvia.'

'Of Miss Sylvia?' He was in the corridor now, just out of sight of the two women.

'Didn't you know?'

'Sylvia disappeared?'

'Dave went to your house to tell you this morning, Ralf,' said Leonie from her chair.

'I was out all night,' said Ralf, his eyes on Mabaso again. 'What d'you mean disappeared?'

Napper explained what'd happened.

'But we've a show in twenty minutes!' he spluttered. He swung round to Nick. 'Nick, where is she?'

'Don't know, sir. It's like the police says. She just disappeared.'

'But did you search the building?' he asked, pulling off his calfskin gloves and twisting them in his fists.

'We did search, sir.'

'Maybe she just went out for a walk. Maybe she's there now. Nick, go back, will you? She'll be there waiting for us. I'll st— no, you stay here and look after the ladies. I'll – no.' He turned to Napper. It was clear poor young Ralf didn't want to be alone with Sylvia nor with Leonie and Gisele. 'I'll come with you.'

'You go, sir. We'll come along later.'

'But I… I can't.' He turned to the guvnor, a pitiful look on his smooth, rosy face. 'Mr Arrowood, could you…?'

Napper answered. 'No, I don't want him examining the scene before I arrive. Send Nick.' He looked over at the guard. 'Don't disturb anything. Just see if she's there and come straight back.'

'Yes, sir,' said Nick, getting his overcoat.

'Hurry, Gisele,' said Leonie. 'We're on soon.'

The two women began to apply their paint again.

'But what am I to do about the show?' asked Ralf, his voice

high and reedy. His pale and perfect skin had pinked. 'We've two hundred and fifty people in there waiting to see three Capaldi's Wonders. They'll want their money back. Oh, my God, Dad'll be furious.'

'Send him a message, son,' said the guvnor. 'He'll know what to do.'

'He said I wasn't to come running to him when I had a problem. I got to prove myself with this show. I got to fix things. Oh, Lord, I'm so blooming unlucky, on the second night, too. Why did this…' As he spoke, he was staring at the guvnor. His eyes narrowed. 'Mr Arrowood, could you…'

'Could I what, lad?' asked the guvnor.

'Could you take Sylvia's place?'

'Take what?'

'Sylvia's place, sir.'

Arrowood looked at him, bewildered. He opened his eyes wide, then squinted at Ralf. He rubbed his pitted nose.

'Take what?' he asked again.

'Please, Mr Arrowood. I wouldn't ask if I didn't have to. We need three Wonders, not two. They'll go mad.'

The guvnor looked at him in horror. 'You mean as Baboon Girl?'

'You can do it, sir. Please help, please, Mr Arrowood. There's hundreds of people out there.'

The guvnor turned to Leonie, who was dabbing charcoal powder at the entrance of her nose-holes. Gisele was putting orange enamel paint on her arms and neck. He frowned and looked back at Ralf. 'But I don't look like a baboon.'

'I don't look like a pig,' said Leonie, lifting her head and examining her nose in the glass.

'But I'm nothing like a baboon! Barnett, tell them.'

'We'll paint your face, Mr Arrowood,' said Ralf. 'Don't be afraid. The ladies do it every day.'

'I'm not afraid, I just don't look anything like a baboon.'

Napper had the widest smile I'd ever seen on his face. 'You do look like a baboon,' he said.

'You have the arse,' I told him.

'I do not.'

'Trust me, sir,' I said, trying not to smile. 'You're close enough.'

He looked at me like I'd betrayed him. Finally, he turned back to Ralf.

'I don't understand why you're asking me this, Ralf.'

Napper stepped over to the door. 'Well, I hate to miss the show, but I've got an appointment with a magistrate. Come along, Mabaso.'

The two coppers disappeared into the corridor, shutting the door behind them.

'We can brush your whiskers so they stand up,' said Ralf. 'Shave your moustache off. Please, Mr Arrowood. You can do it. We've only two performances today.'

'No! What d'you think I am?'

'Just one performance then,' pleaded Ralf. 'I'm sure Nick'll bring Sylvia back before the next one.'

'I'm not even a woman!'

'You can wear Sylvia's dress,' Ralf went on. 'You're about the same size. I'll find you a wig. Leonie'll do your face. Have you got hairy legs?'

'No.'

'He does,' I said.

'Perfect,' said Ralf. 'Please, Mr Arrowood. I'm desperate. I'll give you Sylvia's money. I'll give you more. Twenty shillings.'

The guvnor sniffed. He looked at me for help, then went to stand by the door, looking at the ladies like he'd been hit in the face by a trout. He pulled out his pipe and got it going. He shook his head and sighed again.

'Forty,' I said.

'No, Norman!' he cried. 'I'm not doing it.'

'The medicine, William,' I said.

He bit his lip, drawing hard on his pipe. He shut his eyes and tapped his walking stick against his boot. Finally, he sighed. 'Only for one performance,' he said.

'Can you sing "The Fishermen Hung the Monkey, O!"?' asked Ralf.

'I know it *and* I'm a very good singer. I take lessons.'

'Can you dance the Highland Fling?'

'Of course,' answered the guvnor as if it was something that no gentleman, even a poor, fallen one, should be asked.

Ralf held out his hand. 'It's a deal, Mr Arrowood.'

'One more thing, Mr Ralf. You have to tell me what happened at the Quaker Hall on the night of the murders.'

Ralf swallowed, his hand mid-air. 'I don't know what happened.'

'Of course you do, son,' said the guvnor. 'Your father told me he had no secrets from you. He said you were his right-hand man.'

'He did? He said that?'

'Exactly those words. So, tell us. Why did he have Mr Fowler shot?'

'He didn't. It wasn't anything to do with him.'

'Then why did your uncle Ermano shoot him?'

'My uncle…' Ralf's mouth had gone dry. He took a flask from his pocket and had a long swallow.

'We've three witnesses. Detective Napper's keeping it secret for the moment, but he'll be arrested in due course. And your father for giving the command.'

'I don't know anything.'

'Of course you do. Thembeka and Senzo have identified him. He's already done for, so you're not betraying anyone. Listen, Ralf, if it was self-defence, then nothing will happen to him. That's the law. But if it was deliberate murder, then…' The guvnor paused, clutching his forehead, his jaw dropping. 'Oh my goodness. It *was* deliberate. That's why you won't tell me! Oh, my Lord, you poor lad. Having to keep a terrible secret like that. Trying to protect your uncle from the gallows. Oh, you poor thing. You're too young, Ralf. Much too young.'

'It weren't his fault!' cried Ralf. 'One of them Zulus pulled a pistol on him. He thought they were going to shoot him so he pulled his out, then Mr Fowler jumped in front of him at just the wrong time. The witnesses'll tell you the same. It was self-defence.'

'The murder of Musa wasn't an accident, Ralf. His teeth were beaten out of this mouth.'

'That wasn't him. We didn't know about that till we saw it in the papers, I swear it. When Mr Fowler was shot they got out of there as quick as they could.'

'Why did they take Mrs Fowler and S'bu?'

'They didn't! Father's been in a rage ever since, thinking it'd all come back on us. Dad even bashed up Uncle Ermano about it all.'

A short bloke appeared in the corridor. 'Ten minutes, Mr Capaldi,' he said, then turned and disappeared.

'You better get ready, Mr Arrowood,' said Ralf. His voice was quiet now, unsure if he'd done the right thing. 'I'll wait out here.'

'Money first, Mr Ralf,' I said.

Ralf took out his purse and counted out two quid. 'I'll give you a knock,' he muttered. He turned to me. 'You can go out front if you want to see the show, Mr Barnett. I might join you later.'

I saluted the lad, then turned and marched down the corridor. I bought a hot brandy from the drinks counter and made my way to the hall where Capaldi's Wonders were to perform. It was jammed in there, old and young, rich and poor, all standing waiting to see the freaks. I sipped my brandy and waited for the show.

Five minutes later, the band started up and the crowd fell silent.

Chapter Thirty-Four

Polichinelle, dressed in his yellow-and-red clown costume, skipped onto the stage to the cheer of the crowd. A single electric spotlight was on him. He rang the bell attached to his belt, then jumped as if he'd had his arse pinched. Folk laughed. He put his finger to his ear and turned his head like he'd heard something off-stage.

'What's that you say?' he asked. The punters cheered again. It was his phrase. I only knew it from Neddy, who used to say it a lot, and always with that same finger to the ear, pretending to hear something just out of reach.

'Ladies and gentlemen, I have a treat for you. From the four corners of the world, the most wondrous, the most monstrous, the most educational, the one and only Capaldi's Wonders!'

To great applause and cheering, the curtains behind him opened to reveal Gisele painted orange and lying in her glass tank with starfish hanging round her. A woman in black next to me gasped.

'THE HUMAN LOBSTER!' cried Polichinelle.

Her legs were in the fish tail costume, her top half in the orange vest. The tank was half-full of water, rising to about her waist. She raised her hands so the punters could see her deformities.

There were gasps and mutterings all round the room. A child began to weep.

'This creature was discovered by the captain of a tea clipper off an isolated island in the Samoan seas,' said Polichinelle, going to stand behind Gisele's tank. 'When she's out of water for more than two hours, she begins to turn blue.'

'Show us!' yelled a bald fellow in the middle.

'Get her out!' yelled another.

The clown silenced the chatting in the room. 'I'm afraid we cannot do that, sir. You see, for her being out of water's like you being in a fire. She shrieks like the Catholic martyrs. People have gone mad when they heard her shriek. I heard it once and had to spend two months in a monastery.'

I chuckled and lit up a fag.

Polichinelle moved back to centre stage, ringing the bell on his belt. He cupped his hand to his ear. 'What's that you say?' he asked the crowd. He waved his other hand around, encouraging the audience, then cupped his ear again.

'WHAT'S THAT YOU SAY?' roared the crowd.

The clown laughed. 'Next, ladies and gents, the one and only in the world. The most beautiful... TASMANIAN... PIG... WOMAN!'

Leonie appeared from the side of the stage and clumped over to join Gisele. She wore her stage costume: over-tight dress of soft pink, white gloves and boots with leather hooves sewed to the ends, a curled tail stuck to her rumple. Her face and scalp were painted a whitish pink, her wide nose-holes darkened with charcoal.

'I don't like it, Mama,' said a girl of six or so behind me.

'You're not supposed to like it,' said her mama.

I moved away to the side of the room and took a swallow of my brandy.

'This beauty was first discovered by a missionary about a hundred miles from the penal colony of Hobart,' announced Polichinelle. 'He came across her in a forest where she was eating mushrooms straight from the ground. All we know is that she's the daughter of a Greek chap named Hercules who ran a pig farm on nearby land. Nobody knows who her mother is.'

'Kiss me, darling!' yelled a wag near the front.

His mates around him laughed.

'Go on, then, sir!' shouted a gent from the middle of the crowd. 'Get up there!'

The wag climbed onto the stage. He looked an ordinary sort of bloke, a shopman or something, and it was clear he'd had a few drinks. He stumbled towards Polichinelle, who slapped his face hard. That got the biggest laugh so far, but the bloke didn't mind. He turned and took a bow, then advanced towards Leonie, his arms out. Though she tried to push him away, he pulled her close and planted a kiss right on her lips. Cheers filled the room. He got to one knee.

'Marry me, my princess!' he shouted.

'Ugly princess, more like,' called out a rough-looking fellow in front of me.

Oh, they liked it, this crowd out to find a bit of magic that Christmas.

'Marry me, piggy!' demanded the drunken bloke, still on one knee.

He was struggling to his feet when Leonie stepped forward and kicked him in the face. He shrieked, falling on his back. The crowd liked that even better. Showing a strength you wouldn't think he had, Polichinelle grasped the fellow by the back of his coat and threw him off-stage into the first row of punters.

When the uproar had died down, Polichinelle rang the bell attached to his belt and cocked his head.

'WHAT'S THAT YOU SAY?' roared the crowd.

'Some say she's the missing link,' he said, his voice serious now. 'Living proof of Mr Darwin's theory of the descent of man. From a Mexican tribe of snake-eaters who say they found her living with bats up a tree in the deepest, darkest Mayan jungle. Hold your breath, ladies and gentlemen, boys and girls, while I present to you... THE... BABOON... GIRL!'

The guvnor appeared, stepping out from the curtains. He peered into the dark of the hall.

'What the bloody hell is that?' muttered a croaky young woman.

Sylvia's ballet dress came down to his knees. His legs and arms were exposed, and it looked as they'd used charcoal to make the hairs thicker. They'd shaved his moustache off, and the hairs on his cheek, and smoothed away the blotches of his face with some kind of purplish powder. They'd left his side whiskers and the hair round his jawbone and neck, but had starched it so it stuck out like a fan around his face. He walked stooped, his arms dangling toward the floor, his bum padded with a cushion.

All around, people were whispering and muttering.

'It's hideous, Charles,' said an old woman to a young bloke next to her.

'I'll get nightmares, I shouldn't fancy,' murmured a boy of about eleven or so to his ma in front of me.

A soldier by the stage poked the guvnor in the belly with a walking stick. Arrowood swatted it away and loped over to Leonie. He looked out at the crowd with a pout and a sneer. I laughed. He wasn't half-bad as a baboon.

'That ain't a lady,' growled a grizzled old bugger wearing a battered top hat. 'They must think we're fools.'

The opening chords of 'The Fishermen Hung the Monkey O!' started up, and the other stage lights turned off, leaving only the guvnor in the spot as he began to sing the famous song:

> *In former times 'mid war and strife,*
> *The French invasion threatened life,*
> *And all was armed to the knife,*
> *The Fishermen hung the Monkey, O!*

As he sung, he staggered back and forth across the stage, his rumple out, staring at the punters left and right. I looked around at the couples dotted here and there and wished Molly were here. The guvnor sang on:

> *They tried every means to make him speak,*
> *They tortured the Monkey till loud he did squeak*
> *Says one that's French, says another it's Greek.*
> *For the Fishermen then got drunkey, O!*

The crowd cheered, mugs and pots were raised, folk took great gulps of their booze. And as they drank, the chorus came along, and the whole room sang:

> *Dooram a dooram a dooram a da,*
> *Dooram a dooram a da*
> *Dooram a dooram a dooram a da,*
> *Dooram a dooram a da*

The kiddies all round were staring at the guvnor with wide, fascinated eyes. Verse by verse, Arrowood acted out all the words of that ugly song, the torture, the hanging, the head-shaving, the ear-severing. And as the monkey was slowly mutilated, the kiddies' smiles turned to fear, and then horror.

When the final chorus ended, a dozen children were sobbing, the parents on their knees comforting them. Without a pause, the band began to play the Highland Fling, and Leonie and the guvnor began to dance.

When it was all over, dozens of punters crowded round the stage, the children feeding the three performers fruit, touching Gisele's hands, stroking the guvnor's legs and tugging at his whiskers. Polichinelle stood at the side with a cigar in his mouth, watching it all.

I got myself another brandy and waited in the vestibule for the guvnor to become himself again. The wound in my side was playing up, so I swallowed down another couple of Black Drop as I watched the punters empty out of the hall.

After a while, the guvnor put his hand on my shoulder. He was back in his yellow suit, his Donegal coat, his bowler. He'd combed his whiskers down, but there were still smears of purple around his chops where he hadn't wiped careful enough. I didn't like the look of him so much without his moustache.

'Nick says there's no sign of Sylvia in Brixton,' he said. 'God only knows where's she's got to.' He looked around, surveying his public. 'How was I?'

'Better than I expected.'

He nodded. 'I was excellent. Say it, Barnett.'

'You were better than I expected.'

'I was excellent. Say it.'

I stood.

'Say it.'

'You were excellent.'

Finally, he smiled. 'Yes, I was, wasn't I? I didn't look anything like a baboon, though, did I?'

'Of course not. Sir.'

'Right, let's go,' he said, tapping my ankles with his stick. 'The road to solving this case lies in discovering what happened to Mrs Fowler. We need to have another look at the last place we know she was alive.'

Chapter Thirty-Five

The door of the Quaker Meeting House was open, and the same smiley fellow we'd seen last time sat in the office.

'Did you find Reverend Druitt?' he asked, shaking our hands.

'Yes, most helpful, sir,' said the guvnor. 'You heard about Mrs Fowler, I suppose?'

'The poor woman,' he mumbled. 'It was in the evening papers. Was it the Africans what did it, Mr Arrowood?'

'The police are still investigating. That's why we're here, sir. Would you mind if we had another look in the main meeting room? There are a few details…' The guvnor paused by the hooks. 'You've left her coat there?' he asked.

'Oh, what a dummy,' said the chap. 'I should've sent it to her house. I'm forgetting everything these days. But would you mind if I left you to it? I've quite a bit to do before locking up.'

The guvnor searched Mrs Fowler's coat pockets again. He pulled out her gloves, her hanky, the fold of acid drops and pamphlet on the Bombay plague. 'Where are her scarf and bonnet? They weren't on her body,' he said, hurrying into the large meeting room. He'd changed since his performance, his steps quicker, his eyes more alive. There was no trace of his earlier disgrace. He pointed at the far wall. 'You take that side. Look everywhere, every nook and cranny.'

I searched in the piano, under the burner, in the cupboard and all round the benches and chairs, while the guvnor did the same on the other side. As he had a look around the double doors, I lit a candle and climbed downstairs to the tiny room where Musa had been sleeping before he was killed. I examined the empty bottles and broken chairs, the stack of old curtains and shelves of books that looked as if nobody'd opened them for twenty years. On the floor were his blankets. I picked them up and shook them out. Five ribbons, green and blue, fell to the floor.

I took them upstairs, where the guvnor sat on a chair in the middle of the room, smoking his pipe, his stick between his legs. He took the ribbons, studied them, and shoved them in his pocket. 'We'll have to search the rest of the building.'

I helped him to his feet and we spent the next half hour examining every room. The smiley bloke unlocked those we'd not been in before, but we found nothing. The Quaker appeared again as we reached the bottom of the stairs.

'One question, sir,' said the guvnor.

'Yes, Mr Arrowood?'

'When we discovered the murders, there were a pair of driver's gloves, a hat with ribbons, and a feather necklace on a bench in the main room,' he said. 'Did the police take them?'

'I kept the gloves in the office,' said the bloke. 'But I didn't see a hat or a necklace.'

'Was it you who found the gloves?'

'Yes, the day after the murders. But there was nothing else on the bench.'

'May I see them?'

The Quaker took us to the office and opened a drawer. It was empty but for Thembeka's coachman's gloves.

'Is there anyone else who could have taken the other things?' asked the guvnor.

'It must have been the police. Nobody else was allowed in until the next day, and I was the first in.' He pulled his watch out. 'I'm afraid I have to close the building now, sir.'

'Of course. Thank you for your help,' said the guvnor. His hands touched the stiff gnarls on his turnip. 'Fetch my hat, will you, Barnett? I think it's in the meeting room.'

I looked at him: we were standing not two foot from the door to that very room.

'Oh, for goodness' sake,' he grumbled. 'I'll fetch it my blooming self.'

I held the door open for him, just to show willing, and he waddled over to the long table in the centre of the room to collect his bowler. Just as he turned to come back, he stopped, looking at something above the doors. Then, without a word, he hurried over to the basement door and brought out the stepladder as was stored at the top of the stairs.

He dragged it over to the double doors.

'How did I not notice that before?' he asked as he began to climb.

I stood back to see what it was. The doors from the vestibule weren't built into the main wall, but instead into a recess that projected into the hall about three foot. On either side were narrow walls, one of which contained the doorkeeper's window. Above the double doors, forming the roof of the recess, was a platform about three foot deep and six foot wide, with coving on three sides and the main wall on the other.

I held the ladder till he was at the top. With a groan, he stretched, reaching out for something just out of sight.

It was Mrs Fowler's scarf. When he'd come down, I mounted the ladder to have a look myself. The little roof above the door formed a shallow rectangular box, the coving making a wall around it. There was no way of seeing anything inside it from the floor.

'You think the murderer hid it in there?' I asked as I reached the floor.

'Her coat and umbrella were in the hallway. Why hide the scarf and not the rest?' He asked, gazing at me with his big cow eyes.

Arrowood was silent as we walked to get a tram. There were no seats, and we had to stand for the first half of the journey. The other passengers were wrapped up in coats and double coats, their breath white, their noses running in the wintry carriage. He held the scarf in his hand, gazing at it, pulling on it, considering it, as folk pushed past him to get on and off. Now and then he took a sniff. As I gripped the rail against the judder and lurch of the tram, my thoughts turned to Molly. I felt happy just remembering her smiling face, her hearty appetite, the pleasure she took in having a lark. Though it hadn't been long, I felt such a need for her sometimes it made me restless. Maybe I did love her. Maybe I did.

It was only when we reached Kennington Park that he spoke. 'We've two reports that Mrs Fowler wasn't there when her husband was killed. Miss Thembeka says she hadn't returned when they fled, and S'bu says she wasn't there when he was captured. Yet her coat was there when we discovered the bodies a few hours later. What do we make of that?'

'She came back after they'd gone.'

As a nun rose to get off the tram, he dropped onto her bench, next to a maid with a cat on her lap.

'If what S'bu said is true. Now, S'bu and Thembeka also said that Musa was in the basement asleep and didn't come up during the fight. So here's what I think happened. Either Capaldi's men returned or someone else arrived after they'd left with S'bu. Whoever it was discovered Musa and killed him. Mrs Fowler arrived while the killer was there. She removes her coat and gloves, puts away her umbrella and is about to remove her scarf when she hears something. She goes through to the meeting room and catches the killer in the act. "Ah!" she screams. He pounces on her and…' The guvnor made a strangling gesture with his grubby paws.

The young maid sitting next to him was listening in, her face screwed up in concentration. A navvy who stood next to me was nodding, his eyes fixed on Arrowood.

'The most logical explanation for us finding her scarf above the doors is that her body was hidden there. With the coving it wouldn't be seen from the floor. The murderer escaped and returned later to move the body. When he pulled her down, the scarf was left behind. It's not something the killer would notice if they climbed up the ladder just enough to pull her off.'

The maid nodded, poking an aniseed twist into her mouth. The cat lay on its paws, its head up, also thinking about the case.

'And you might have noticed that, for the body to fit in the space, you'd need to bend her legs into about the same shape as if she was sitting.'

I pictured the size of the space and nodded. 'Clever, sir.'

'Yes, Barnett. Thank you. I must say being on stage's been a tonic. They loved my singing, didn't they? My thinking's been sluggish the last few days, but now I feel like lightning's going through me. It's every bit as good as Mariani wine.'

'You should join a theatre group.'

'D'you think so?' he asked, the idea distracting him for a moment. He filled his chest, lifting his head as if delivering a soliloquy. Finally, he gave a shudder. 'Anyway, I don't think the killer planned that part, although it might have given him the idea of tying her to a chair later.'

'Why didn't they take her at the time?' I asked.

'It was broad daylight. There were so many people about in the street what with the fire just down the road. How could they get her out and into a carriage without being seen?'

'They couldn't,' said the maid. 'No chance.'

'But they left Musa and Mr Fowler without hiding them,' said I. 'Why hide Mrs Fowler?'

'That,' he said slowly, 'is what we need to understand next.'

Chapter Thirty-Six

It was about nine that night when we reached Gresham Hall. Nick let us in. Leonie and Gisele were at the kitchen table eating a bit of cold mutton and beans. They were out of their costumes now, like ordinary people again.

'Has Sylvia returned?' asked the guvnor.

Leonie shook her head. 'Heaven knows where she is.'

'They could be doing anything to her,' said Gisele.

'Did you ask Mr Capaldi to move us, Nick?' asked Leonie. Her face was bloodless. She moved the meat around the bowl with her fork.

'He said no,' said Nick, standing with his legs against the range. 'I'll keep you safe.'

'You didn't keep Sylvia safe.'

'And Dave'll be here soon too.'

'Did Detective Napper come to look around?' asked the guvnor.

Leonie nodded. 'He didn't find any clues.'

'Well, he wouldn't,' said the guvnor, lifting the lid of the pot on the stove and peering inside.

'Why not?'

'Because Sylvia wasn't kidnapped. D'you mind if I have some of these beans?' he asked, a bowl already in his hand. 'I don't mind it cold.'

Nick glanced at the guvnor, then at Leonie. He seemed frozen.

'She wasn't kidnapped?' asked Leonie.

'Who'd kidnap her?' asked the guvnor as he spooned the wet beans onto his plate.

'Madame Delacourte,' said Gisele and Leonie at once.

'To spoil your show? Well, I suppose that might be possible.'

'It's got to be her,' said Nick.

'Not your master, Nick?' asked the guvnor.

'It could be him too,' he said, his voice quiet.

'Tell me, was her wig missing?' asked the guvnor, settling down at the table.

Nick swallowed.

'Nick?' asked Arrowood without looking up.

The bloke shrugged.

Leonie rose. 'Let me have a look.'

We watched the guvnor eat as we waited for her to come back down. Finally, she appeared at the door.

'It's gone,' she said.

The guvnor just nodded.

'So what does that mean, Mr Arrowood?' asked Leonie.

'It means she left of her own accord,' he said.

As he spoke, Nick watched him from the corner of his eye.

'I suspected as much when you said that she left in her night clothes, but that she'd taken a dress. A kidnapper's unlikely to take the extra time to search for her dress, though I suppose it's just possible they grabbed one if it was nearby. I assume it was by her bed?'

'Yes, on the chair,' said Leonie.

'Hm. But to take her wig? That wig was very important to

how she presented herself to the world. What would a kidnapper care about that? Particularly if they were going to kill her. And if she pleaded for it, you'd surely have woken, given that you two were sleeping in the same room.'

'Maybe they knew her,' said Leonie.

'She didn't know anyone here in London. No, my friends, she took the wig herself.'

'Why?' cried Nick, suddenly angry. 'Why would she leave me?'

The guvnor stood, put his bowl in the sink, and wiped his mouth on his sleeve. He stepped over to Nick, brushing some crumbs off the guard's lapels. 'Why indeed, Nick,' he whispered, looking into his eyes. 'Why indeed.'

Nick stood straight and still, his eyes flicking this way and that.

'Did you know that a person's emotions can be transmitted through the air, Nick?' asked the guvnor.

Nick frowned.

'Yes, Le Bon writes about this. It's how crowds turn wild. And once you know it can happen, you start to feel it. I don't know how it happens. Some say it's due to magnetism, but it might just be our unconscious noticing clues that our conscious mind's too busy to perceive. You're not worried. You might say you are, but you aren't as worried as you should be with a murderer on the loose. You haven't been since Sylvia disappeared.'

'I *am* worried!' cried Nick. 'I'm scared half to death!'

The guvnor tilted his head and looked at him for some time. 'No,' he said at last. 'I just don't feel it. You know what I think? I think she's run away and you know it. You might even be planning to join her, maybe after you collect your next wages, whenever that is. But why did she go without you, I wonder? Perhaps you're being extra careful. Perhaps she's gone first because she's the easiest for Capaldi to hunt down, given her unusual looks, and you're going to wait a few days to make sure he hasn't tracked her down. If she hasn't been found after a certain time, you're going to join her and flee to America. If she does get found, then she'll be brought back here. They'll chastise you for not guarding her well enough, no doubt, but you'll end up guarding her again. You and her can then plan another escape in some other way. Something like that, Nick? Clever to cover yourself in case of failure, I must say. Very clever. I'm only guessing, of course.'

Nick just looked at him.

'We'll see you tomorrow or the next day, ladies,' said Arrowood, putting on his bowler. 'Stay close to Nick and Dave tonight and you'll be safe.'

And with that we were gone.

It was about ten when we reached Coin Street. The guvnor was excited about returning with the money for the babies' medicine, and I was happy for him. Since Isabel came back, he hadn't had much chance to prove himself to her, so this was important. The shop was closed, but Mrs Pudding had left a couple of dried-up kidney pies in the oven with a note for the guvnor to take them if he cared. He did, and we bore them triumphant through the back passage and into his rooms.

We both knew it was bad the moment we stepped in. The ginger cat lay on the mantel, watching us. Isabel sat in the good chair by the window, her eyes puffy and pink. Ettie was moving about in the scullery.

'Isabel,' whispered the guvnor, hurrying towards his wife. 'What is it?'

She didn't even look at him.

'Isabel? Speak to me.'

She shook her head. The guvnor straightened, looking at the two boxes on the table. In one, under a pile of blankets, lay Mercy, her head tossing from side to side.

The other was empty.

'Where's Leo?' whispered Arrowood.

'We lost him this afternoon, William,' said Ettie, stepping back into the parlour. She laid her hand on Isabel's shoulder. 'The fever took him.'

The guvnor collapsed onto a chair, covering his face with his hands. Isabel placed her own hand on top of Ettie's. In the other she clasped a hanky so tight it shook.

A great clucking arose from the next-door hens, and, one after the other, the neighbourhood dogs started to bark. Outside in the dark alley, someone tapped on the window. I opened the curtains and held the candle up to the glass. It was Reverend Hebden again.

'Can you let me in?' he asked in his booming voice, pointing towards the shop.

I looked over at Ettie, who nodded. A tear rolled down her cheek.

I made them tea and stood in the parlour for as long as I could bear it. When I finally stepped onto the street, my body was seized with exhaustion and my heart with hopelessness. I knew it was going to happen. I'd dreamt it earlier in the week as I lay in a restless sleep with Molly at my side. I'd dreamt it and pushed it out of my mind, hoping that'd stop it coming true. I never believed in premonitions, but I couldn't help the sense that by dreaming it I'd brought it forth, just the same way I did with Uncle Norbert and Mrs B.

The Pelican was about to call last orders that Sunday night, and the counter was three deep with pissed-up Cockneys wanting one last dose of holy water before another week of toil. A hunched old woman in a hooded cloak sat alone in a corner, a mug in her hand. She stared at a creased Christmas card, opening and reading it, closing it and gazing at the picture, a smile alternating with a look of such sorrow. A boy of twelve or so was helping the landlord, filling the mugs from a barrel as his boss took the money and poured out the gin and brandy. It was hot enough in there, hot and anxious; I counted out my money, hoping to take the edge off my sickening desperation.

'Half pint of gin,' I said when I'd got the landlord's attention.

He poured it out and handed it over.

'Molly in tonight?' I asked as I gave him the coins.

He shook his head. 'She ain't well. Maybe tomorrow.'

'Where is she?'

'How do I know?' he said, looking over my shoulder at the woman behind. 'Yes, mate?' he asked.

I took the flask over to the other side, where there was a space on the wall, and had a long drink. There was a bitter mood in there tonight. On the table next to me, three ladies were complaining to each other about the privy in the court where they lived. Across the room, a bloke was ranting about something to do with permits, his hands out wide, his eyes glaring as his mate shook his head and cursed. A fellow in a sailor's hat took a swing at a lascar over the shove ha'penny board and a bit of pushing and shouting started up among the other folk waiting to play. Looking round that pub I could not see a laugh or a song or a bit of tenderness in the whole place. I swallowed my gin. Where was Molly? I couldn't understand how the landlord put up with her going off sick again. I'd bet half the women there would have fancied the job she had, here in the warm with a steady wage. Better than the factory and the street, that was sure.

Molly had a room with her sister in the basement of a building just in front of the boiler works on Tabard Street, so I put the flask in my pocket and walked down Borough High Street, hoping she'd still be awake. I'd only been there once, the night we went dancing; her sister was off somewhere with her fellow so we'd had the place to ourselves.

The gin had given me a bit of comfort, and I saw some beauty in the Borough that night. Frost coated the trees outside St George's, and the moonlight picked out the sleeping bodies on the steps of the church. A horse trotted past Borough station on its own, a saddle on its back and reins dragging along the icy road. A couple of dogs were sniffing around the urinals on Great Dover Street, while two jiggered ladies sang 'The Violet I Plucked' as they staggered along the road. Black Mary's song again. As they disappeared round the corner, I remembered the scene at Coin Street and the sadness fell over me again. Poor Leo. Poor Isabel. I'd be back there tomorrow, amongst it all. Christ, I hoped Molly would be awake.

The house was in darkness. I went down the steps to the basement window and tapped. A sheet was hung across it as a curtain. There was no sound.

'Molly,' I said, tapping on the glass again. I didn't want to wake her if she was sleeping, so I had a swallow and stood there for a few more minutes. Then I thought maybe she'd appreciate a bit of gin, so I tapped again.

'Molly,' I said, louder. As soon as I heard my voice, I regretted it. She was sick, and I was waking her up for myself. I hoped there'd be no reply. Out of the brown sky, a cold rain began to fall. Now I wanted nothing more than to go back to my room and be alone, and was just climbing the stairs when I heard a shuffling inside.

'Who is it?' came a woman's voice from within.

'It's Norman. Is Molly there?'

'Norman? Is that you?' The glow of a candle appeared behind the sheet. It rose in one corner and I saw the flame, and behind it the face of a woman, a sleeping cap on her head, a thick jumper and scarf below.

'I don't want to wake her. They told me she was ill.'

'Hold on.' The curtain dropped, and it went dark. Moments later the basement door opened.

'I'm her sister, Ann,' she said. She was a few years older than Molly, taller and more bony. 'She told me about you, Norm. You're Rita's husband.'

'You knew Rita?'

'Not too well. Sorry to hear about her.' The flame lit her head from below: her face was craggy and brown.

'Is Molly there?' I asked, moving closer against the wall as the rain got heavier.

She hesitated, glancing at the street over my shoulder. 'No, she ain't,' she said.

'She ain't in hospital, is she?'

'She's working.'

'I've just been at the pub. She's not there.'

She nodded. 'She does other work.'

'She didn't tell me.' I was going down, I could feel it. Something wasn't right. 'What work?'

'You better ask her.'

'What work?' I asked, the vexation rising in me.

'Ask her, Norm. It ain't my business.'

I put my foot in the doorway. 'Why the secret? Just tell me, will you?'

She looked down at my foot. 'Back off, will you? She'll be in the pub tomorrow. You talk to her.'

I looked at her tired face again in the flickering candlelight, the strands of grey hair falling from her cap, her worn-out eyes. I took my foot away.

''Night, mate,' she said softly, and shut the door.

I finished off the gin and dropped off quick, waking in the early hours with the wound in my side aching, thinking about Molly and what she was doing out so late at night. Why hadn't she told me she had other work? I went through the reasons she could have and didn't like any of them, and then those thoughts tumbled into others, into who was killing people, why those women were locked up in Capaldi's warehouse, what was going to happen to Thembeka and Senzo and S'bu. On top of it all I was worried about the guvnor and how he'd react to the death of Leo. He saw himself as Leo's father, did so the second he picked up that child, and I knew Isabel wanted him to, whatever she said. Though the two of them might never be a loving couple, they were already a family, a vexed, confused one, but a family all the same. But the guvnor did have a weakness, a taint from his father, and I'd seen him descend into his own world of rumination and bitterness and melancholy before. It was after the Betsy case. For months he didn't work, barely left his rooms, fell into debt. That was when Isabel left him. I didn't know how many times a man could have a nervous breakdown and recover, and I didn't want to find out.

I fell asleep just after the knocker-upper tapped on the window next to mine. When I woke again the grey daylight had crept into my room. I looked at my chair, my washstand, my set of drawers. I'd planned to buy a rug for the floor this Christmas, but we hadn't been paid and the money I had would only last a few more days. An anger rose in me. When would things change? I wondered, as I had so many times over the last few years, if I should try and find a steady job. Molly'd suggested it last time I saw her. A steady job. Molly. Where the hell was she last night?

Chapter Thirty-Seven

I had a bowl of porridge at Willows' and arrived at Coin Street about nine. The Puddings were boiling and baking, a few wet punters sitting at the thin tables guzzling spotted dicks and mutton pies. Ettie greeted me at the door. They'd set up the parlour for the laying out: the mirror was covered with a bit of muslin, the clock stopped, the chairs pushed back against the wall. The guvnor's mattress had gone upstairs. On the table was Leo's box, and there lay the baby boy in a long white dress. A ha'penny covered each eye. He was still.

We looked upon him for some time without speaking.

'How's Mercy?' I asked at last.

'She's taking milk now.' Ettie nodded. 'The doctor believes there's a good chance she'll recover, but we must all pray for God's mercy. Why he would take Leo I cannot understand. To give Isabel two miscarriages and then this.'

'How is she?'

'As you'd expect.'

Arrowood came down the stairs wincing, taking one step at a time. His haemorrhoids were at him again.

'Norman,' he said as he tackled the last few steps. He was in his Sunday best, a silk tie, a pair of Lewis's old shoes.

'William,' I nodded.

'I'm staying here,' he said. 'The case is over for me.'

'No!' exclaimed Ettie. 'Don't be so weak. You must carry on. They need your help.'

'I can't do it,' he said, soft as a cat. He took Ettie's hands. 'I just...' A grimace came over his face and he hurried out to the scullery.

We heard movement above, then Isabel's boots on the steps. We both watched in silence as she descended. She wore a black shawl over her usual brown dress. Her eyes were red, her pupils tiny pinholes.

'Did he say he was giving up the case?' she asked, no strength in her voice.

I nodded.

'I don't want him here. Tell him he must go to work.'

'Isabel...' Ettie said, but stopped. She didn't know what to say.

Arrowood stepped back from the scullery, a mug in his hand. 'He was my son too, Isabel.'

'No, William. He wasn't your son. He was Luther's son. You've no right to claim him. He was mine and Luther's.'

She was breathing hard, twitching her nose as she tried not to weep.

'I think you should finish the case, brother,' said Ettie.

He looked about to speak, then changed his mind. He nodded, put the mug down, and collected his coat.

'Get the medicine, Ettie,' he said.

It was Monday morning, two days before Christmas. The roads, still muddy and slick from the overnight rain, were full of delivery carts taking food and gifts to the big houses all over town. Delphine had agreed to help us again, so we went

318

to Camberwell to collect her and see if her old man had talked to the committee about getting us more payment. He hadn't and, seeing how we weren't too pleased to hear it, offered to let us use his carriage that day instead.

As we crunched and skidded through the muddy streets, the guvnor explained to Delphine what he wanted her to do. 'Will you remember that?'

'Of course,' she said, looking offended. She touched her bonnet. 'It's not complicated.'

The desk sergeant who was there last time told us to go straight upstairs to the detectives' office. All the desks were occupied by plainclothes officers, all writing reports. In a corner sat Mabaso, reading the book he always carried in his pocket. He sat up when he saw us enter.

'You've taken your time,' said Napper, not looking up from whatever it was he was writing.

'Did your men take any of the Zulus' possessions from the Quaker Meeting House?' asked the guvnor, dropping into a chair. 'In particular a hat with ribbons and a necklace of feathers?'

'No. Why?'

'They were there when we found the bodies but they've gone missing.'

'Well, it's probably a souvenir hunter. They're always nicking things from the crime scene. Now, I suppose you want to know what clues we found of Miss Sylvia's disappearance?'

'We're not interested in that, Napper,' said the guvnor, sitting on the chair in front of his desk.

The detective's eyebrows rose. 'Oh? How so, Arrowood?'

'She ran off by herself.'

'Ran off, did she? And how do you know that?'

'I had a feeling for it.'

'A feeling?'

'Nick'll disappear next. He'll go and join her.'

'Oh, really. Well, maybe you'll change your story when you hear what we discovered in Gresham Hall.' Mabaso took out a hanky and began to cough. Napper looked at him for a few moments, then picked a cigarette end from his desk and held it out. 'A French cigarette, found under Miss Sylvia's bed. Yet none of the ladies smoke cigarettes.'

Arrowood looked carefully at the butt. He sniffed it. 'Interesting.'

Mabaso kept coughing, finding it harder each day to catch his breath.

'Can I get you a drink?' asked the guvnor.

The constable shook his head, his eyes closed.

'Whoever it was stole three pounds from Miss Leonie's purse,' said Napper. 'Money she'd been saving. The cigarette suggests someone connected to Madame Delacourte, wouldn't you say?'

'It does, indeed,' said the guvnor.

Napper took back the butt with a smile. 'We've requested the warrants.'

'Well, you're certainly moving forward,' Arrowood said, placing his palms on the desk. 'Learn from this, Barnett. The work of a master. Now, sir, I want to try something, with your permission. It might provide more evidence for you about the prisoners. Something to make your chances of a conviction more secure.' He turned to Delphine. 'I'd like to introduce Miss Druitt. She used to live in Natal.'

Napper rose and shook her hand. 'A pleasure to meet you, miss. You were here before.'

'Yes. I speak Fanakalo, sir. It's a language from Natal.'

'Ah, well, we already have someone who speaks that language. Constable Mabaso.'

The African copper was on his feet now. He bowed his head. Delphine spoke to him in his tongue.

'Ma'am,' he said, and sat back down.

'I want to interview Thembeka and Senzo,' said the guvnor. 'Miss Druitt will listen and do some translating for us.'

'As I said, we already have a police officer who can do that.'

'But they know he can speak their language,' said the guvnor. 'They don't know that Miss Druitt can. Now, this is what I want you to tell them.'

Ten minutes later, me, Delphine, and the guvnor entered an interview room in the basement, a place we'd been once before with a couple of officers from the SIB. Napper sat at a table between Thembeka and Senzo, whose hand was wrapped in a brown bandage. One of his bottom teeth was gone, his lip swollen and scarred. Thembeka's hands were clasped upon the table top.

'Ooh, is this them, sergeant?' asked Delphine as she stepped through the door. She wore a smile we'd never seen before on that unhappy mouth, and spoke with a light, engaging voice. Me and the guvnor looked at each other in surprise: all he'd asked her to do was to pretend she couldn't understand their language and let him do the rest.

'Yes, ma'am,' said Napper. 'These are the two murderers. Miss Thembeka Kunene and Mr Senzo Nyambezi.'

Delphine was staring at Thembeka. 'What, she as well?'

She covered her mouth in a childish manner, her eyes big and surprised. 'The lady?'

Napper chuckled. 'Yes, both of them. You don't think they look like killers?'

'Who is this girl?' asked Thembeka, turning to Napper.

'This is Miss Whitehead, the daughter of Lord Whitehead, Duke of Southampton and member of the Privy Council,' said the copper, rising from his seat. 'A great friend of our Commissioner, as it happens. Miss Whitehead's never met an African before and very much wanted to see you before you… Well, before the trial.'

Thembeka looked at Delphine. Delphine's broad face flushed, and she seemed lost for words. She looked at me with panic in her eyes.

'Well?' asked Thembeka.

'Can I touch them, sergeant?' asked Delphine suddenly, glancing at Napper.

The guvnor looked horrified. 'No, Miss Whitehead!' he exclaimed.

Napper turned to Thembeka. 'Do you mind, Miss Kunene?'

'Tell her to go away,' she hissed.

Senzo asked Thembeka something. She answered him with a roll of her eyes. He shook his head.

'What did they say?' asked Delphine. Her face was burning now, her body rigid.

'I don't know,' answered the copper. 'The man doesn't speak any English.'

'Ask him if I can touch his hair, miss,' Delphine said to Thembeka.

'Get out of here, girl,' said Thembeka. 'This is not an exhibition.'

I met the guvnor's eyes. He shook his head, as baffled as I was. Delphine now stepped over to Senzo and held out her hand: 'I adore your hair, sir,' she said, louder now. 'May I touch it?'

Senzo moved his head back, scowling. 'Mampara,' he muttered, or something like that.

'No, miss,' said the guvnor. 'Stop asking, please.'

'We're facing execution, you foolish girl,' said Thembeka, crossing her arms over her breast. 'And you ask if you can touch us? Get out of here.'

Delphine opened her mouth to speak, then her face fell. Arrowood took her arm and led her out the door. After she'd stepped into the corridor and out of sight, he turned back. 'Oh,' he said. 'I just had one question, Miss Thembeka. May I?'

'Are you helping us or are you with him?' asked Thembeka, nodding at Napper sat beside her.

'I don't believe you killed Mrs Fowler,' said the guvnor. 'We're trying to find out who did, but we need more information from you. When I asked you to translate the letter, you deceived me. It wasn't about a meeting in Paris, it was about meeting Princess Nobantu at the York Hotel here in London.' Here he paused. He smiled just a bit, tilting his head and looking at Thembeka. She looked at me. Still, the guvnor said nothing.

Napper blew his nose.

Senzo began to speak. Thembeka answered. He spoke again. And then nobody spoke.

Finally, the guvnor asked, 'Why did you lie to us about the princess?'

'My cousin knows her from a long time back. He wanted to see her. But she isn't a real princess, she just talks like one because she worked for the governor's sister. It's only to sell more tickets.'

'But why didn't you tell us that?'

Again, Thembeka and Senzo talked. Thembeka looked back to the guvnor. 'Mr Capaldi has people inside the police. The princess has nothing to do with our case, but he would have found out and he might have thought she knew where we were. We didn't want him making trouble for her. His men are violent.'

'Have you met her before?'

She shook her head. 'My cousin was working on her kraal when he was younger.' She glanced at Senzo and lowered her voice. 'He thinks he can marry her. I don't think so.'

'Did he know she was coming to London?'

'We heard when we were in Paris. It's why they signed the contracts to come to London. I didn't want to come here. We had many arguments, but Monteuil convinced Musa and S'bu that London would be better. He said there were more black fellows here. They thought Monteuil was going to take us, but, of course, he'd sold our contract to Capaldi.'

'How did you hear the princess would be in London?'

'She's doing exhibitions. We're doing exhibitions. Everybody knows everything in this world.'

'Is she also with Mr Capaldi?'

'Mr Beaumont. Another showman.'

'She didn't tell you she'd be coming?'

'No.'

Through these last exchanges, Senzo was watching the guvnor carefully. If you didn't know better, you'd swear he understood every word.

Chapter Thirty-Eight

We went up to the waiting room while they locked Senzo and Thembeka away. Delphine's head was down, her face quite white now.

'Miss Druitt,' said the guvnor.

'Yes, yes, I know,' she said, staring at the floor. 'I feel so ashamed. It's just… I completely lost my nerve. I'm not used to being asked to do something like that. She was glaring at me, and I had this awful feeling she knew everything, she knew what we were up to. I didn't know what to say. I was afraid I'd ruin it. Then I remembered my cousin. She visited us in Natal last year. She's from Hampshire. She did exactly that with our housekeeper. Almost exactly those words. It was all I could think of doing to pretend I didn't know anything about her people or her language. It was stupid.'

'It was insulting,' said the guvnor.

'I know!' she said fiercely. 'I feel awful. I need to apologize.'

Just then, Napper came up from the cells and led us up to the detective's office. There was another copper sitting on the other side of the room, a cigarette in his hand, a mug of tea in front of him. Mabaso still sat where he'd been before, his book in his hands. As he shut it, I noticed his fingernails were smooth and perfect as a princess.

'What are you reading?' asked the guvnor.

'Frederik Douglass,' he said, a cold fury in his eyes. 'A narrative of his life as a slave.'

'Ah, yes. What d'you think of it?'

'It angers me.' He spoke slowly, fixing his glare on the guvnor.

'Of course.' Time seemed to slow as the guvnor nodded. His blood-raddled eyes watered. 'But at least you don't have slavery in Natal.'

Mabaso snorted and shook his head. 'It's not called slavery, but we are not free, Mr Arrowood. Your people want to take charge wherever you go. It's a fault in your nature. I think my people see it more clearly than yours.'

'Miss Kunene has told us something about it,' said the guvnor with a frown. 'My father saw Mr Douglass speak, you know. He was a great orator. It's hard to imagine how a man like that could be a slave.'

'But easy to imagine how others could be?' asked Mabaso quickly. He stifled a cough by clutching his chest.

'That's not what I meant.'

'No?'

'Say, constable,' said the detective on the other side of the room. He wore a dusty suit, his hair greased down over the shiniest forehead I'd ever seen. 'From Natal, are you? Are you behind the Boer or the British?'

'The Zulus,' said Mabaso.

'The Zulu war was over fifteen years ago, lad,' laughed the detective. 'Keep up.'

'Yes, sir.'

'So, the Boer or the British?'

Mabaso continued to hold the shiny detective's eye, but said nothing more.

'So did your little trick work?' asked Napper, pulling out a chair for Delphine to sit. 'What did they say?'

'Miss Kunene told Mr Nyambezi that you knew she'd deceived you about the letter.' Her face was its usual stony self now: Miss Whitehead had truly gone home. 'He said Constable Mabaso had probably looked at it. He wanted to know if you suspected anything. She said she wasn't certain but didn't think so. Then he said they had to get out before you talked to the princess. She told him he had to forget about the gold, and that they needed you, Mr Arrowood, to prove they didn't kill anyone or they'd be hung.'

Mabaso pulled his hanky from his pocket, covered his mouth, and began to cough again.

'Did you try liquorice like I told you?' asked Napper.

Mabaso shook his head as he hacked away. His eyes were going pink.

'Brown's Bronchial,' said the guvnor. 'That's quite good.'

We watched as the coughing went on. When he finally pulled his hanky away, there was no missing the blood in it, and for a moment none of us spoke. Mabaso shoved the cloth back in his pocket and stared at the floor.

'Brown's Bronchial,' said Arrowood again. 'Try it, constable.'

I didn't reckon it would do much good. Seemed like the poor bloke had consumption. He was thin enough.

'Thembeka mentioned the gold?' asked Napper, turning back to Delphine. 'From the raid in South Africa?'

'I don't know, sir. She only said "the gold". That was all.'

The guvnor was thinking, his stubby finger tapping his hooter. Napper leant back in his chair, smoking a cigar and revolving his marbles in his hand. His face was split in a great, ugly grin.

'I told you they were up to no good, Arrowood,' he said with a triumphant waft of out-smoke. 'Didn't I tell you that?'

'Yes, Napper,' said the guvnor, looking puzzled still.

'And didn't Constable Mabaso also tell you that?'

Mabaso sat upright, his back arched. He gave a sharp nod.

'Yes, Napper,' said the guvnor. I could see from his cloudy eyes that he was somewhere else.

'You're a treasure, Miss Whitehead,' said Napper, getting to his feet. 'I think you might just have helped us solve this murder.'

'I'm glad I could be useful,' she said. 'Can I see her, Detective Napper? I want to apologize. I was rude.'

'I'll tell her,' said Napper. 'Don't you worry about it. There's a reward, you know. Twenty pounds. Mrs Fowler's family have just posted it.'

'Well, a reward would certainly be useful.'

'Really?' said Napper, perplexed. 'Don't you…'

She frowned. 'Have you forgotten I'm not Lord Whitehead's daughter, sir?'

'Oh, yes, of course.' He laughed. 'By jiminy, you're a good actress.'

She smiled for the second time that day, revealed a dimple that had no business on her face. 'Thank you, detective.'

'It would have to be divided, of course.'

'Ah,' she said, her face falling again.

'Would you mind if I questioned Senzo and Thembeka again, sir?' asked the guvnor, coming out of his daze. 'Separately this time, and would you mind helping once more, Miss Druitt?'

'I don't think so,' said Napper before Delphine had a chance to speak. He rose from his chair and collected his overcoat from the hook on the wall. 'If anyone's to question them it'll be us, but there's no point. They'll only make up another story. Now we know there's a connection between them all, we'll call on the princess and make her think her lover has already told us about the gold. Then, when we have more information, we'll interrogate the prisoners again. Come along, Mabaso. You're about to meet a princess.'

'The hotel said she's not back until Christmas Eve,' said the guvnor. 'She's in Edinburgh.'

'What time?' asked Napper, halting in the doorway.

'She's arriving on the evening train.'

Napper thought for a moment, then looked at the African. 'You might as well have the rest of the day off then, Mabaso. Take in the sights, or something.'

'Yes, sir.'

Napper turned to the guvnor. 'I suggest you find something else to do now. I'll call you if I need anything. And I don't want to see you at the hotel when the princess returns. Leave this to us. Understand?'

'I understand what you've said, detective,' said the guvnor.

'And you agree?'

The guvnor took a packet of mints from his pocket and popped one in his mouth.

'No,' he said, and walked out the office.

Chapter Thirty-Nine

It was a bit of luxury taking the Druitts' carriage to Elephant and Castle. When we reached Lewis's house, Willoughby let us in, happy as always to see us. S'bu sat in the parlour in front of the fire, wearing one of Lewis's silk dressing gowns. He smiled to see us, but it wasn't a strong one. The boy needed to get back with Thembeka and Senzo.

'Good day, ma'am,' he said, getting up and giving Delphine a bow.

'Good day, sir,' she replied, bowing back.

'Good day, sir,' said S'bu to the guvnor and me.

'Good day, sir,' said Arrowood, taking his hand. 'How are you?'

'Very well, sir. How are you?'

'I taught him that,' said Willoughby.

'Why aren't you at the stables, mate?' I asked him.

'All the cabs out,' answered Willoughby. 'Sidney says I got a holiday.'

'You being lazy, then?'

He laughed his wide mouth, tight-eyed rumble. 'Being lazy, Norman. Being sleeping. Being snoring!'

We laughed some more. What a joy it was to be around old Willoughby.

'Where's Lewis?' asked the guvnor.

'At the shop,' he answered. 'He just gone.'

'Right, Miss Druitt,' said the guvnor. 'Tell S'bu we've been to see Princess Nobantu and we've spoken to Senzo and Thembeka. Ask him why he didn't tell us about the gold.'

She talked to him, then turned back to us. 'He asks what Senzo and Thembeka said about the gold.'

'No, we're asking him what *he* knows. Tell him if we don't find who killed Musa, Senzo and Thembeka could hang. We need to know about the gold because the killer might have been trying to get the information from Musa.'

Again, she asked him. As he spoke, he jerked his hands in the air, staring hard at her: it was clear he was frightened.

'He thinks the Ninevite officers took the gold.'

'Why did Senzo and Thembeka visit the princess?' asked Arrowood.

Again, they talked.

'She's a prostitute from Johannesburg,' said Delphine when they'd finished. 'He says Senzo's in love with her and she used amandiki on him to make him follow her. It's a type of magic.'

'Was S'bu also on the raid?'

He shook his head when she asked him.

'Then why was he fleeing with them?' asked the guvnor.

For some time, they talked. Delphine nodded, asking for more details. Finally, she turned back to us. 'When he was in prison he joined the Ninevites. It was the only way for a boy of his age to be safe in there. After he was released, he went to live in their city in the caves. He looked after the horses.'

'I do!' said Willoughby. 'I look after Sidney's horses. Tell him, miss!'

Delphine explained this to S'bu, who smiled and shook Willoughby's hand.

'Go on, Miss Delphine,' said the guvnor. 'What else did he say?'

'One of the lieutenants wanted to lie with him,' she said, no trace of embarrassment in her face at all. 'S'bu refused. The man started to cause him trouble, bullying him. One day, S'bu broke a bottle in the man's face. He knew he'd be punished, so he ran away. Thembeka gave him shelter, but the Ninevites came looking for him. It was the same time Thembeka was hiding Senzo and Musa after their raid on the Kruger compound. The Ninevite leaders blamed them for the death of Zixuko. They were both being hunted, so they took S'bu with them when they fled.'

'And Thembeka? Why did she flee?'

There was more talking.

'She's his aunt. She thought she had to look after him.'

Willoughby brought through mugs of porter and handed them round. The guvnor had a long swallow and a longer think.

'So, perhaps the person who took a hammer to Musa's teeth was one of them?' he said at last. He looked at Delphine, who was wearing a moustache of beer foam above her lip. Her eyelids twitched, one after the other, then she swallowed the whole mug in one long gulp.

'Are the Ninevites all black?' asked Arrowood.

'Most, but not all. I've heard they've a Scottish bookkeeper.' Delphine looked into her empty mug, then tipped it over her mouth for the last couple of drops. 'You know that's a traitor punishment?'

'A traitor punishment?' repeated the guvnor, holding out his mug for Willoughby to refill.

Delphine did the same. 'It's what they do when someone betrays the gang, they knock out his teeth. It's a Ninevite punishment.'

'Are you sure?'

She nodded. 'Other times they slice open the throat with a knife. It's a warning to others.'

'So Musa was killed by a Ninevite for something he did.' He thought for a moment. 'Thembeka didn't tell us it was a traitor punishment. Is it possible they didn't know, Miss Druitt?'

She shook her head. 'Everyone in Johannesburg knows what it means. You see these men without teeth pulling rickshaws, doing laundry, working on the railways.'

'Then why didn't she tell us?'

Delphine shrugged and took in more porter. Arrowood shook his head, not wanting to admit what now seemed all too possible: that Senzo and Thembeka were involved in Musa's death.

'I suppose it could have been someone in the princess's party,' he said at last.

'You got a horse, miss?' asked Willoughby, wiping the beer from his chin.

'No,' she said. 'I have a bicycle.'

She said it with such anger that Willoughby flitched. He looked at her, his eyes wide with fright. Then, for the first time, Delphine laughed, and I saw she had a little evil inside her. She laid her hand on his arm. 'Do you have a horse, Mr Willoughby?'

He stepped away from her. 'We got fourteen. At the stables. I look after them.' He looked at me again, not knowing if he should keep talking.

'He's good with them,' I said. 'He works with my brother-in-law.'

'Precisely,' she said, as if confirming it was true.

The guvnor looked at S'bu and smiled. S'bu finished off his beer and smiled back. He nodded, then his face became serious. He spoke again to Delphine.

'He wants to know about Senzo and Thembeka,' she said, getting to her feet. It was clear the two mugs of porter had made her tipsy. 'Then I must go. Father's arranged a blooming dancing lesson for me.'

We stopped in the Hog on the way back to Coin Street. Betts stood at the bar, a torn dressing gown over her corset, a pipe in her mouth. The lascar Hamba was sitting against the wall, chatting away in his broken English to her, while Old Loyle sat in his usual table in the corner, a flask of red wine before him. One of his Pomeranians had died a few weeks back, and its empty collar still hung from the leather strap that tethered the other three lying on the floor at his feet. It was mid-afternoon, and a few dockers were finishing up their ales afore stumbling off to their evening shifts. We shared a bowl of oysters at the counter, but he said nothing more as we ate. It was usual for him to keep his mouth shut when he was working on a case in his mind, but the death of Leo and the way Isabel'd spoke to him had dulled him. I finished off my porter and took out my gloves.

'We doing anything this afternoon?'

He shook his head. 'Let me think.'

'Don't stay here long. Your wife needs you.'

'Does she?' he asked, banging his mug on the counter. Betts filled it from the barrel and swept the shells into a bucket.

I patted him on the back and left him there.

The landlord of the Pelican was sorting the fire out again, while the old regulars sitting around the hearth moaned and grumbled about the cold.

'In the kitchen,' he said, digging out the coal.

Molly was cutting up carrots and dropping them into a vat of boiling water.

'Where you been, Norm?' she asked with a smile.

'Been looking for you.'

'My sister told me you was around.'

'Where were you last night?'

She didn't reply, and I watched her get a handful of spuds from a basket and start cutting them up, skin and all. They still had mud on them from the fields.

'You don't wash them?' I asked.

'Don't do the punters any harm.'

'You got another job?'

'I do.'

I took a crust of bread from the table and had a bite. She dumped the rough choppings in the water: she wasn't going to tell me what she was doing last night lest I prised it out of her.

'What is it?' I asked.

She wiped her brow, moving a bit of hair out of her eyes. 'You sure you want to know, Norm?'

'Reckon I'm going to have to.'

She turned and looked me full in the face, the knife in her hand. 'When I need a bit extra, I go to a house on Bankside.'

I looked at her for some time. 'A baudy house?'

'You got a problem with that?'

I reckon I knew already, but hearing it made me go cold.

'But you got this job.'

She nodded. 'And a mountain of debt to clear.'

'You didn't tell me that.'

She put the knife down and stepped toward me. 'We haven't done much talking yet, have we, mate?' She was speaking soft now, her eyes damp, and it seemed she wanted to touch me. I stood back.

'You didn't tell me that,' I said.

I turned and walked out.

Chapter Forty

I'd been sitting in Mrs Butterworth's beer-house for half an hour when Neddy burst in. He grinned when he spotted me, a little dog following him on a bit of string. He'd picked up a scar on his forehead since I last saw him.

'I forgot you moved, Mr Barnett,' he said, grabbing the last bit of cheese off my plate. 'I been in all the pubs on the High Street.'

'This is my local now, mate.'

He nodded, looking around. It was an ordinary place, the front room of Mrs Butterworth's home with a hole knocked in the wall to her kitchen where she sat doing her knitting. The floorboards were bare, the fire warm enough, the punters friendly. I'd spent a lot of time here since I moved.

'What happened to your face? Not those lads from Broadwall again?'

'They was waiting for me when I picked up my money. Didn't get it, though. Here.' He pulled a muffin out his pocket.

'Thanks, mate. You want a drink?'

'Mr Arrowood wants you to meet him at the Town of Ramsgate in Wapping. He already left.'

I finished off my mug and stood. The little dog stared up at me with shining black eyes.

'Whose is that?'

'Mine,' said Neddy. 'He ain't got a name.'

I buttoned my coat and put on my gloves. 'You coming? It's a bit of a walk.'

''Course I am,' said Neddy.

I ate the muffin as we walked up Red Cross Street toward the river. There we crossed London Bridge, the boats packed so tight in the Pool you could hear their sides scraping and knocking in the wind. The pub was on Wapping High Street, down the road from the River Police building. It was a place I'd known too well when I was younger, but it had changed: they'd knocked through the back wall and added another room, toffing it up with long mirrors and glass lights. They'd even nailed a bit of canvas to the chairs. The punters hadn't changed though, mostly Russians and Spaniards, spending their earnings afore the next boats sailed. Ladies and young blokes were there to help them spend that money, either latched on to their sailor for his whole time ashore or floating, hoping to pick up a bit of company for the day.

The guvnor sat alone reading the *Daily News*. He still wore his black tie, his Sunday best.

'They've got all the details of Mrs Fowler's death already,' he said. In front of him sat a bottle of Vin Mariani and the knotted ends of a few saveloys. 'They're not questioning Senzo and Thembeka's guilt.'

'How's Isabel?'

'She hasn't risen from bed.' He shook his great, swollen head to dislodge the dirty tear gathered in the corner of his eye. 'Are you coming to the funeral tomorrow? Christmas Eve, for God's sake.'

'I'll be there,' I said, laying my hand on Neddy's shoulder.

The guvnor nodded. Bit his wet lip. When he spoke again his voice was urgent. 'Something occurred to me that should have occurred before. You know I wondered why Thembeka hadn't told us that Musa's death was a traitor killing?'

I nodded.

'It's just occurred to me that Mabaso would also have known it was a traitor killing.'

'And he didn't tell Napper,' I said, wondering how it was I hadn't thought that myself.

He stood. 'Let's get to work, Norman.'

'Where are we going?' I asked as I followed him out to the street, Neddy hurrying behind with the little dog.

'To the office of the Castle Mail Packet Company.'

The street was busy with wagons and carts going to and from the dock. Horses snorted, snot spraying from their noses, their shoes clattering on the cobbles. Cabmen yelled at each other to get out the way, groups of sailors on the ran-tan laughed and argued, while coffee stalls, hot potato sellers, eel women and trotter girls bawled out over the cold riot of noise. The guvnor was in a hurry, waddling ahead, holding his bowler to his head against the wind. The office was on the wharfside in Shadwell Basin. He walked straight through the doors, into a long room filled with blokes in suits from Nichols sitting at desks and counters.

'Yes, sir,' said a fellow with oily hair sitting on a high chair by the door. 'Can I help you?'

'I'm Inspector Arrowood,' said the guvnor. 'This is Mr Barnett. May I ask your name?'

'Mr Lilly, sir. Office manager.'

'Pleased to meet you, Mr Lilly.' The guvnor held out a letter to him. Though I couldn't read the writing, I could see it had the Metropolitan Police header on it. 'We're helping Detective Inspector Napper of Scotland Yard on the multiple murder case you've probably heard about. The one involving the Zulus.'

'Ah, yes, sir,' said the bloke, dropping his spectacles from his forehead to his eyes and having a quick read of the letter. He nodded and handed it back.

'I need some information about a passenger from Port Natal. A Police Constable Mabaso.'

'Certainly. What date did he arrive?'

'Around the seventeenth or eighteenth of this month.'

'Well, the *Hawarden Castle* was scheduled to arrive in Southampton on the seventeenth, but they had very favourable conditions. It arrived three days earlier, on the fourteenth.'

'Southampton?'

'Yes, sir. The passengers disembark there. Our warehouse is here because most of the cargo is brought to London on another boat.'

'Would you mind checking your passenger list for me?' asked the guvnor.

The bloke marched over to a desk near the back and mumbled to a swarthy fellow, who rose and searched the shelves behind him.

'Did Napper give you a letter of introduction?' I whispered to the guvnor.

'A bit of Scotland Yard notepaper fell into my pocket from one of the other desks,' said the guvnor under his breath. 'I didn't want to trouble Napper to fill it in himself.'

The clerk pulled down a ledger and handed it to Mr Lilly. The office manager opened it and found the right page. His finger traced down the page. 'Yes, Mr Mabaso. Police Constable of the Langlaagte Police.'

'And he arrived on the fourteenth?'

'Yes, sir. At 3.45 p.m.'

'When did the boat leave South Africa?'

Mr Lilly read from the page. 'Twenty-sixth of November. It takes three weeks or so.'

The guvnor straightened his back and looked at me. 'Why didn't he go to Paris, Barnett? When our friends left Mozambique, their destination was Paris. Their contract was only sold to Capaldi while they were there, and that was only a couple of weeks ago. How did Mabaso know to come here?'

'If I may, sir?' said Lilly. 'There are no direct sailings to France from Port Natal.'

'I see. Of course. Now, his superior Detective Duffy died of dysentery on the boat. Can you tell me where and when that happened?'

He turned the pages again. 'This is the doctor's report, but there's nothing about a death. Deaths are always recorded here.'

'So Detective Duffy disembarked at Southampton?'

Lilly checked the ledger again. 'No, sir.'

'Did he get off the boat on the way?'

Lilly frowned. Again, he leafed through the ledger. 'Let me see. East London, no. Port Elizabeth, no. Cape Town, no.' He looked up. 'Those are the only stops. Let me just check something...' He walked back to the swarthy man and talked to him. They both looked through the ledger. Finally, Lilly nodded and returned to us. 'He had a ticket, but isn't recorded as having boarded, nor of disembarking.'

'Are you sure, Mr Lilly?' asked the guvnor. 'Would you mind checking that one more time?'

'Let me ask the captain,' said the office manager. 'He's upstairs with the directors.'

The guvnor sat on the bloke's chair as we waited. As the minutes went by, the clerks murmured to each other, telegraphs arrived, boys were sent with messages. Neddy's little dog edged over and stood between the guvnor's legs, gazing up at him with moony eyes. As the guvnor leant over to pat it, it turned to show him its backside, tail stuck up straight as a cock-stand. The guvnor shook his head, then did what the dog wanted, scratching the bit of fur where its tail joined its body. The dog's back leg shot out in the air, jerking with pleasure.

'He always does that,' said Neddy.

'I don't like it,' said the guvnor, taking his hand away and straightening.

'Nor me,' I said.

'He can't help it,' said Neddy.

'How are those sisters of yours?' asked the guvnor.

'Abi's going into service,' said the lad. 'Can't wait to get rid of her. She eats *so* much, and she don't try to sell those matches. Ma says she's got three legs. And why must I share the bed when she can share with Ma? She's always got nits. She won't be shaved. I can't wait to see the back of her.'

The guvnor'd usually be laughing by now, but he wasn't even listening. He was gazing out the window at the dark basin, his face solemn. Leo's death lay heavy on him, and what Isabel said had swiped out all his hope.

'Where's her service?' I asked.

'There's a lady fixing it up for her. You know she's got to give her the first three months wages for it? It's a blooming swindle!'

'Don't curse, boy,' growled the guvnor.

'Sorry, sir.'

'You tell her to be careful,' said I. 'You must go with her, make sure it's a proper house and not one of those rackets.'

'I know, the Maiden Tribute. Miss Ettie told me already.'

Mr Lilly appeared with the ledger under his arm. 'Detective Duffy never boarded the boat, and there were no deaths on the voyage. The captain confirms it.'

'Are there any other boats he could have been on?' asked the guvnor.

Lilly took down another ledger and looked through it. After some time, he shook his head. 'He wasn't on the later or earlier boats.'

'Are you the only shipping company serving South Africa?'

'Yes, sir.'

'Well, I'll be jiggered,' said the guvnor. 'Mabaso did say he died of dysentery on the boat, didn't he, Barnett?'

'Napper said it. Mabaso didn't correct him.'

'And Mabaso said they were sending another detective. Well, well. I think we need some answers, don't you?'

'We do, sir,' said Neddy. 'We need some answers.'

We reached Scotland Yard about four that afternoon. Napper made us wait about half an hour, then came down to see us.

'What is it now, Arrowood?' he grunted. He looked awful. His nose was red and runny, his hair like an orange sponge, his suit in need of a good brushing. 'We've got our murderers, whether you like it or not. The only thing left is to discover whether the gold's here in England.'

'Did you question Senzo and Thembeka about it?'

'They're both sticking to their story it was taken by the Ninevite commanders. But we'll question the princess when she returns. Meanwhile, I have a murdered lady in Shepherds Bush to tend to.'

'Is Mabaso here?'

'I told him to take in the sights. He'll be back to interview the princess when she returns. Tomorrow, did you say?'

The guvnor grunted.

'Not that it makes much difference to me. The way they treat us is shameful. You know detectives don't get a single damn rest day, I suppose? Not even Christmas. Even factory workers get rest days. The Chief Inspector could show a little understanding, but oh no, that would take a little too much initiative.'

'You don't seem to admire your superiors, Napper,' said the guvnor.

'I suppose you take holidays whenever you want?'

'At least you get paid, Napper,' I said.

The doors to the street shot open and two PCs dragged in a navvy with no boots.

'We've some new information,' said the guvnor, watching the fellow as he was taken through to the cells. 'I wanted you to know immediately.'

'Well, this makes a change,' answered Napper. 'What is it? And hurry, I'm busy.'

'What did Mabaso tell you about Detective Duffy?'

'He died of dysentery on board.'

'Are you sure?'

'Of course I'm sure.'

'We've just been to the shipping company. Duffy had a ticket but never boarded the boat.'

Napper blinked, his head twitching as he tried to understand what that might mean. 'And?' he asked at last.

'Mabaso deceived you.'

'So? Duffy never got on the boat. He had dysentery.'

'Mabaso said he died on board.'

'What's your point, Arrowood?'

'He also said he'd sent a telegram requesting another detective the day before we met him. That was the eighteenth.' The guvnor uncapped his pipe. 'Why didn't he send the message before he left, if he knew Duffy wasn't coming?'

'He might not have known until it was too late.'

'The ship stopped at East London, Port Elizabeth and Cape Town. Why not from there?'

'You tell me, Arrowood.'

The guvnor lit his pipe. 'He arrived in Southampton on the fourteenth. He sent the telegram on the eighteenth. Why did he wait four days?'

Napper had his marbles out of his pocket and was twiddling them furiously. 'You know what I think?' he said at last. 'He wants to solve the case himself, bring back the Zulus on his own. He wants to prove he's as good as any Englishman. It was clear from when he first arrived he thinks he's a few levels above his station.'

'Very possibly. But there's one more thing you should know. Before Musa was killed he had all his front teeth knocked out with that hammer. Did Mabaso tell you that the Ninevites do that in Natal?'

'No.'

'It's what they call a traitor punishment. The gang do it to a person who's betrayed them. According to Miss Druitt, it's very common to see such men in Natal. Mabaso didn't tell you?'

Arrowood watched him steady as he puffed on his pipe.

'Ha!' exclaimed Napper. 'That proves it was Senzo who killed him. I was right. But that bloody Mabaso wants all the credit to himself, the bloody jumped-up hound. They won't allow him to be a detective so he's trying to prove a point. I'll send a couple of constables over to bring him in.'

'Wait, Napper. He might be more involved in all this than we realize. Here's what you must do. Send a telegram to the Langlaagte police station. Tell them Duffy hasn't arrived. Ask them where he is.'

'Why should I do that?'

'Because if they think Duffy's here, then we have another missing person.'

Chapter Forty-One

Napper had the telegram sent, then ordered us to wait in the reception while he sat in his office pretending to work. A reply came about two hours later, and we stood as the desk sarge took it upstairs. Napper was down five minutes later, the paper clenched in his hand.

'The Langlaagte Police says Duffy left for England on 26 November. Mabaso must never have sent a telegram at all!'

He summoned McDonald and hailed a four-wheeler, giving the driver an address on Lambeth Road. It was already dark, the Thames rolling black under Westminster Bridge, the little lights of steamers and tugs like candles in the air.

'Here, McDonald,' said the guvnor, leaning forward. 'Remember when you brought Senzo and Thembeka back to the station from Gresham Hall?'

'Yes, sir,' answered the young PC.

'Did Mabaso visit Senzo alone in his cell?'

'He wanted to question him.'

'Did you check on the prisoner after?'

'No, sir.'

'And that was the same day Senzo was assaulted, or was it the day before?'

'Same day, sir.'

Napper was glaring at the lad, his fingers clenched around his precious marbles. 'Why didn't you tell me, boy?' he hissed.

'I didn't think I needed to, sir.'

'The kaffir was assaulted that same day, you imbecile! That's why Mabaso volunteered to help you take them back to the Yard.'

'But that was Sergeant Farmerson!'

'Farmerson denied it!'

'The super said it was him, sir.'

'Don't trust everything the superintendent says. I told you that.'

'But the prisoner himself said it was Sergeant Farmerson who beat him, sir, and the sergeant's done that sort of thing afore, sir!'

'Tell me, lad,' said the guvnor. 'Did Farmerson treat Mabaso with respect?'

'No, sir. He called him a savage, and a few other things besides. He's always the same with the foreigners. Only the other day there was a Hindoo brought in and—'

'Farmerson would be the perfect person to blame,' he interrupted. 'I think Mabaso told Senzo to say it was him. Perhaps he threatened to hurt S'bu or Thembeka if he didn't. The prisoners have been hiding what they know about Mabaso since they arrived, anyway. They're holding a secret about the gold that was stolen in Natal, and Mabaso's involved in some way.'

McDonald's mouth fell open as if to speak, then he winced, looking at the ceiling of the cab.

'Don't worry, lad,' said the guvnor, giving his knee a squeeze. 'You'll learn.'

We followed the tramlines to the Lambeth Road, where we pulled up outside a lodging house. A thin woman holding a candle let us in and led us to a room at the back. When there was no answer, she got out her keys.

The room was empty but for a portmanteau with a spare suit and a pair of drawers in it. Mabaso's book lay on the mattress.

'D'you know where he is, madam?' asked Napper.

'He don't tell me where he goes.' She was wearing a pair of boots as looked like they'd been bought that morning, and a shawl as seemed too pricey for a boarding house like hers. The stink of sweat and onion fitted her well enough.

'Listen, when he returns, I want you to send a message to me at Scotland Yard.' Napper reached in his pocket and pulled out a penny. 'Send a boy. But you mustn't tell Constable Mabaso that I'm looking for him. Understand?'

'What's he done?' she asked, taking the coin.

'It's police business.'

'He's done something bad,' she moaned, twisting her pinny in her hand. 'I knew it. First time I saw him, I knew he was up to no good.'

'He's a police constable, madam. Just do as I ask, please.'

'He always seemed so quiet. Will he kill me?'

'Only if you don't do what I ask.'

'Eh?'

'Just do it, madam.'

'Can't he stay?' she asked, pointing at McDonald. 'Tell him to stay. I can't fight him myself.'

'You don't have to fight him.' Napper squeezed past her and hurried back down the corridor. The woman grasped McDonald's arm as he tried to follow.

'You stay, son,' she murmured. 'There's a good lad. Don't leave me alone all night.'

'Sorry, missus,' he said, pulling free. 'My boss says I got to go.'

When we were back on the street, Napper turned to us. 'I need you to watch the building. When Mabaso returns, follow him and send me a message.'

'We don't work for you, detective,' said the guvnor. 'McDonald can stay.'

'What, in his uniform? Mabaso'd spot him a mile off.'

'You're in plainclothes,' said the guvnor. 'You stay.'

Napper shook his head. 'I have to circulate Mabaso's description. If we get it to every PC on the beat, he'll soon be found. There can't be many Africans in yellow shirts around town.'

'Then send another plainclothes man. This isn't our job. We've been working unpaid for the last week.'

Napper fingered the boil on his neck, then pulled his scarf up over it. A mangy brown dog came padding over and sniffed at his boot: he gave it a kick and it scurried away with a whimper. 'If we discover that Mabaso's in on the killings, I'll make sure you get a share of the reward.'

'How much?' I asked.

'Five quid.'

'Each?'

'No.

'The reward's twenty,' I said. 'Who gets the rest? You?'

Napper flushed. 'I'm the detective. And I promised Miss Druitt.'

'Equals,' I said. 'Five quid each, else we go home.'

He turned and strode off down the street, PC McDonald trotting after him.

'Does that mean yes, Barnett?' asked the guvnor.

'Don't know, sir.'

He sighed. 'Right. The princess returns on the Edinburgh train tonight at eight. I wouldn't be surprised if Napper tried to arrest her too, so we need to talk to her before he does. You stay here. I'll send Neddy to relieve you. Come straight to the Elephant and Castle pub when he arrives.'

I waited in the doorway of a boarded-up shop just down the street, keeping my eye on the lodging house. It was dark, just after six, and kids were coming back from school, some in groups of two and three, others with their mas or grandpas. An hour or so passed, the rain began to fall, and I found myself thinking about Molly again. I realized I felt something like contentment when I was with her – in her face, her laugh, the glow of wildness as followed her around. Quickly I'd come to crave the warmth of her body as a cure for the cold ache in my bones. Where I grew up on Jacob's Island, half the women worked the streets when money was short. Not my ma, on account of her face being so badly burned, but she'd have done it if she had to. Still, I didn't like to think of Molly with other men, even for money, and it chafed that she kept it from me. I wondered if I was just another punter to her, paying in memories rather than coins. As I stood there in the dark, sheltering from the rain, questions came to my mind as quickly as I tried to shove them away. Did she really have such money troubles that she had to do that? What had she done to owe so much? Did she toss them off? Put them in her mouth?

How many greasy Charlies had spent inside her between the times she saw me? I felt my teeth grinding. I cursed under my breath. Don't think of it, I told myself as I stamped the cold out of my feet. There's nothing you can do about it right now. Keep your eyes out for Mabaso. Keep ready in case he takes you by surprise. I crossed the street where a bloke was selling hot potatoes and ate one in my doorway as I watched folk coming back from work. Some held boxes with what must be Christmas gifts, others baskets of food. A filthy bloke with a cough like a mastiff's bark dragged a sorry Christmas tree along the road, yelling, 'Lovely tree! Two bob! Make me an offer!' He stopped by me.

'Take if off me hands, will you, mate?' he growled.

I shook my head and had another bite of my spud.

'Just bloody take it!' he barked, spittle flying out of his mouth. He seemed crazed, and for a moment I saw him as one of Molly's punters, and she with her hand on his ulcerated cock-stand.

'Fuck off,' I hissed, hurling my spud at him. It struck his neck. He yelped and ran off down the road, his tree jumping and scraping behind him.

I took up my spud from the gutter, picked off the mud, and had another bite. Neddy arrived just then, two scarves around his neck and the sailor's cap on his head. A bruise had come up round the scar on his forehead, but he seemed cheery enough.

'Mr Arrowood wants you to meet him at the Elephant and Castle,' he said, taking the spud from my hand and having a bite.

'I know.'

He held the spud out for me.

'You keep it, Neddy. Where's that queer dog of yours?'

'Flossie's got him.'

'You shouldn't have left him there. They got too much going on, mate. Why didn't you leave him at yours?'

'I can't do that. Ma'll eat him.'

'Don't be soft, Neddy.'

'She done it afore when I had Dolly. I swear it. She pretends she didn't but she did.'

'She never did. That dog ran away.'

'She did. I found the bones in the ditch.'

I shook my head. 'You know what you're looking out for?'

'Black bloke with stick-out ears and a yellow shirt. I'm to follow him.'

'How are you going to send us word?'

'I got to find a boy and tell him Mr Arrowood'll give him a penny when he delivers the message.' He took another bite of the spud. 'It ain't got any marge.'

I nodded at the potato man on the corner. 'Bloke's a skinflint. Here, those boys give you any more trouble?'

'I'm keeping out of their way. Picking up my money in the morning now.'

'Looking forward to Christmas?'

His face darkened. 'You know that money I was saving for Christmas dinner? Well, Ma only went and found it. She went on a bender.'

'The guvnor told you to leave it with him, didn't he?'

That didn't help. He looked at me like I'd robbed him myself.

'Sorry, son,' I said. 'Your ma shouldn't have nicked that

money. It ain't right. You're a good lad. You do your best to look after your sisters and it ain't fair.'

'I wish she was dead. She ruins everything.'

'She can't help herself, Neddy. Least she stuck by you.'

Neddy's eyes fell. His old man walked out when he was five and was never heard of again. The guvnor was the nearest he got to a father.

'I wanted us to have beef and mince pies for once,' he said. 'We'll never have a proper Christmas long as there's a bottle of gin somewhere in London.'

I gave his shoulder a little squeeze. 'Right, now don't do anything stupid. Keep well back and don't let the bloke see you. He's a copper, remember, so you need to take extra care. Don't go inside or try and overhear him. You promise?'

''Course.'

I handed him a couple of mint imperials from my pocket and left him there.

The Elephant and Castle was on Newington Butts. Outside, a group of women from the Temperance Society was singing carols at every thirsty sinner trying to get inside. One of them put her hand on my arm.

'Join us,' she said, her eyes twinkling with kindness.

'I'm working.'

'Be sober-minded, be watchful,' she whispered, bringing her face up too close to mine, 'for the devil prowls like a lion seeking someone to devour.'

'Thanks for the warning, ma'am,' I said, tipping my hat. 'Merry Christmas.'

The guvnor was at the counter. He drained his mug and handed it me. I held it up for the barmaid.

'Ettie's arranged for the funeral tomorrow at four.' He shook his head. 'Christmas Eve. I don't know how Isabel will manage.'

'Her family coming?' I asked as the barmaid slid our drinks over.

'They never visited Leo once so I doubt they'll bother now he's dead. Best get it over, anyway.' He drank his porter down in one. All the skin of his face seemed to sag and stretch, from his watery eyes to the hair of his neck. He shook his head again. 'Let's finish this case, Norman.'

'What are we going to do?'

He scratched his oxters. 'If the princess has something to do with the gold, then they didn't all arrive in London at the same time by coincidence. Senzo worried that we'd found out about it, which can only mean that the Ninevite leaders don't have it. It means the gold's somewhere else, somewhere that he didn't want us to know about.'

'You think it's here?'

'It's possible. What I'm puzzling over is why they didn't tell us Musa's death was a traitor killing.'

'So we didn't suspect he was killed by an African.'

He nodded. 'Did they kill him? Or S'bu?'

'Or someone with the princess?'

'Her party left for Edinburgh the day before the murders.'

'What about Mabaso?' I asked. 'He's the only other one.'

'But if it was him, why would they hide it from us? The whole country thinks they're the murderers. They could be executed.'

357

'He's a police officer. Napper'd never believe them over Mabaso.'

'But they could at least speak out.' He tapped his hooter with a finger. 'Or... perhaps Mabaso also knows about this gold, and they fear exposing him would bring it to light.'

I nodded as I lit a fag.

'I'm not convinced he wants to solve the case himself to impress his superiors. Getting on the boat without Detective Duffy and then lying about it is too much. They'd never forgive him for that. No, Barnett, the fact he didn't tell us about the traitor killing suggests a different story. There's a secret, most likely about the gold that was stolen from the mine owner's compound. That secret is known by all of them and involves the princess. None of them wants the police here to know. If that's the case, it might be that Mabaso doesn't want the police in South Africa to know either.'

I thought on it for a moment as the guvnor ordered us each a brandy.

'You think he did something to Duffy to stop him boarding the boat?'

'I think he killed Duffy. If he was alive and in South Africa, his station would know.'

'He could have had an accident on the way to the boat.'

'Then Mabaso would have reported his disappearance much earlier. I think we'd best assume Mabaso's a bad apple, that he knows the gold isn't with the gang and that he wants to retrieve it himself, either to impress his superiors—'

'He wouldn't kill a detective for that—'

'—or because he wants that gold himself.' He pulled his watch out. 'Quarter to eight. The Edinburgh train doesn't arrive for another fifteen minutes. Ah!' he said, looking over my shoulder. 'Miss Druitt. So kind of you to come.'

She was packed out for the cold, her brown overcoat bulging with wool. A severe brown hat was on her head, a severe black scarf tied round her throat. She looked around the pub like she'd never been in one afore.

'Are we having porter?' she asked the guvnor.

'No time, I'm afraid,' he said, getting to his feet. 'First we're going to talk to S'bu again, then we'll call on the princess. Now, here's what I want you to do…'

We walked down Walworth Road as he explained, and were at Lewis's house on Wansey Street five minutes later. Lewis answered my knock.

'It took you long enough!' he barked. 'Where've you bloody been?'

'What's wrong?' asked the guvnor.

'He's through here,' said his friend, hurrying into the parlour. Willoughby stood in the doorway to the kitchen, his face pale.

There, on the sofa, lay S'bu. His face was battered, his bottom lip swollen like a sausage and oozing thick blood. His breath came in whistles through his nose, plugged as it was with thick, bloody snot. One eye was shut, the flesh around it purple, and below it looked like his cheekbone was caved in. His good eye turned to us.

'I've called for the doctor,' said Lewis, his voice breaking. He lowered his bulk onto the chair by the fire.

The guvnor knelt by S'bu's side. 'Oh, my dear boy. What's happened to you?' He raised his hand to touch the lad, then stopped, not knowing where.

'It's lucky we came back when we did or I don't know what

would've happened,' said Lewis. 'There was an African. S'bu was on the floor. He was stamping the poor boy in the face. We might all be dead if I hadn't had that.' He nodded at a pistol on the mantel. 'He ran off when he saw it. I'd just brought it from the shop. It wasn't even loaded.'

'Describe him.'

'Short hair, tightknit. Raincoat. Yellow shirt.'

'That's Mabaso. The constable I told you about.'

Delphine came into the parlour with a basin of water and a cloth. She took the guvnor's place and began dabbing at S'bu's face, her movements gentle as a sparrow. She spoke soft as she did it, and slowly S'bu's breathing calmed, his hands stopped shaking, his eyes lost their terror.

At last, he spoke. She nodded. He flitched as she touched his lip, then allowed her to clean it. They talked like this for some time, while me, the guvnor and Lewis sat watching. Willoughby stood by the fire.

Eventually, she rose.

'He says Mabaso wanted to know where the gold was. S'bu said the Ninevites had it. Mabaso wouldn't accept it. He was stamping on his face.' Delphine fingered a curl that sprung out from beneath her bonnet. She sighed. 'S'bu told him he didn't know, that he wasn't on the raid. Senzo and Musa didn't tell him anything about the gold.'

'Did Mabaso ask anything else?'

'He asked him if Princess Nobantu had the gold, but S'bu didn't know that either.'

'How's he feeling?'

'He's afraid. D'you have any laudanum?'

Lewis took a vial from the drawer and handed it to her.

She let a few drops fall on S'bu's tongue. Willoughby brought over a mug of ale and helped him drink.

Tears began to roll down the lad's face.

'If we had any doubts about Mabaso, we don't anymore,' said the guvnor.

'He must be a Ninevite,' said Delphine.

'He's a PC with the South African Police, Miss Druitt,' said the guvnor.

'The Ninevites are everywhere. They have soldiers among the native police, the guards of the mining compounds, the prison officers.' Delphine corked the vial. 'Everywhere.'

'Good God. Why didn't you tell us this before?'

'I thought you knew about them. . .' She touched S'bu's hand. When he didn't flitch, she stroked it with her finger. This wasn't the cold, severe young woman we'd seen before. This was a different Delphine.

'Ask him if Mabaso's a Ninevite.'

She spoke to S'bu. He answered softly through his tears.

'He doesn't know,' she said, letting fall another few drops of laudanum on the poor lad's tongue. Willoughby helped him take more ale.

'Oh my Lord!' cried the guvnor. 'Neddy!'

Chapter Forty-Two

We hailed a hansom on Newington Butts and drove as fast as the horse would take us to Lambeth Road. It was almost nine when we arrived. The doorway I'd left him in was dark and empty: Neddy was nowhere to be seen. We hurried up the street to Mabaso's lodging house.

'Open up!' I bellowed, hammering at the door. There were no lights within. I hammered again.

'What is it?' came the woman's voice just as the guvnor caught up. He held the railings, wheezing and panting.

'It's the agents. Let us in. It's urgent.'

The lock turned, the bolt slid back, and we were in. There was no light in the corridor.

'He ain't here,' said the woman, taking the key from her pinny.

Mabaso's room was empty, the portmanteau in the same place, still open as we'd left it. I lit a candle on the window sill and had a look round.

'Did he come back?' asked the guvnor.

'No. What's happened?'

'Did a boy come?'

'No, sir.'

'If Mabaso returns, send a message to Detective Napper at Scotland Yard as soon as you can. But don't take any risks. Don't let him catch you. He's dangerous.'

'Why? Tell me what he's done!'

Arrowood turned back to the front door, where Delphine waited quietly, her eyes on everything. 'Please, just do it, madam.'

We searched that street, checking every doorway, every set of basement steps, asking in every pub. Neddy was nowhere to be found.

The guvnor was beside himself; he couldn't stand still, his head jerking this way and that, looking up and down the dark street again and again. 'What the hell's that fiend done with him?'

'Perhaps he was scared,' said Delphine. 'It's so dark.'

'Yes. Yes.' Arrowood was already marching north. 'He'd have run back to Coin Street.'

The pudding shop was shut when we arrived. We hurried through to his rooms. The orange cat leapt off the good chair, purring loudly and rubbing its side on the guvnor's leg. Upstairs, we could hear Ettie's low, scratchy snore.

The guvnor lit a candle and climbed up. I heard some murmured words. He came back down with Ettie.

'He's not here, Norman,' he said.

'Hello, my dear,' said Ettie to Delphine.

'Mabaso must have him,' said the guvnor, wringing his hands.

'But why?' asked Ettie. She wore a nightdress, her undertrousers tucked into thick socks, a jumper over the top. 'He's of no use to him.'

We all knew that didn't mean anything. Mabaso might have taken him to an alley to try and beat some information out of him. His body might already be in the mud at the bottom of the river.

'He's a brute,' said the guvnor. 'He hurt S'bu quite terribly, and it might have been him who battered Musa too.'

'You think he killed Mrs Fowler?' I asked.

He nodded. 'Though I still can't understand how he moved her body across town without being seen. Hard enough for a white man to do that without witnesses.'

'He must have had help,' said Ettie.

'I didn't get the impression he knew anyone in London.'

'But how much do you really know about him?' asked Ettie. She placed her hand on his arm. 'William, be calm. You don't know Neddy's in danger. If he came back here I wouldn't have heard him knock. I was abed at eight. Have you called on his mum?'

'I'll do it now,' I said, heading for the door.

She stopped me. 'You get a drink and something to eat. I'll go.'

The guvnor still couldn't settle. I lit the lamp as he paced the small room, then went to put on the kettle. Miss Druitt examined the guvnor's shelves of books on the psychology of the mind.

And then there was a tapping at the window.

The guvnor was there first, lifting the cloth and peering out into the black alley. From behind, I saw his shoulders lift.

'My Lord,' he muttered, lifting the catch and pulling up the window sash. 'Neddy. My boy. Thank goodness.'

He leant out to pull him in and moments later Neddy's sailor's cap appeared at the window, then his head, his dirty hands on the ledge. The guvnor gave one more hoik and the boy landed with a tumble on the floorboards. Arrowood took him in his arms.

'I'm sorry, Mr Arrowood,' said Neddy, his face pressed to

the guvnor's coat front. 'There was a gent. He kept walking past me, looking at me funny. I thought he was...'

'An African?'

'No, sir. A dirty great man. I...' He pulled away from the guvnor's embrace, his eyes full of tears. He caught his breath, then whispered. ''Cos that boy got snatched on Bankside. I got... got scared, sir.'

'You did right to come back, lad,' I told him. 'There's some nasty sorts out late.'

His filthy, bruised face went tight as he tried not to weep.

'Nothing's more important than you being safe,' said the guvnor.

Ettie returned just then. She'd thrown her coat over her nightclothes. 'Oh, Neddy. Thank the Lord. Are you hurt?'

He took off his cap and bowed his head. 'I'm a bit hungry, miss. And thirsty.'

She stroked his cheek and smiled. 'The biscuit tin's in the scullery.'

'Where's my dog, Miss Arrowood?'

'Upstairs with Flossie, darling. They're sleeping.'

As he scampered off to the scullery, the guvnor picked a pile of papers from the table. 'Any mail?'

'Nothing for you.' Ettie rifled in the pile he held and took out a telegram. 'Just this for Isabel.'

He took the white envelope and turned it over. 'The medical scholarship?'

'Probably.'

He put the pile down and checked his watch. 'We must go. Neddy, you return home. Come and see me tomorrow for your money. Did you get the medicine, sister?'

'I've given her a dose already. Are you going to see the princess?'

He nodded. 'Her train should have arrived over an hour ago.'

'Will Mabaso be there?'

'I don't think so. I told Napper and him she was returning tomorrow. I wanted to talk to her first.'

'Tell me what I've missed,' she said, crossing her arms over her chest and standing in front of the door. Seeing he was not to be let out, he quickly he told her where he'd got to in his thinking about Thembeka and Senzo, the princess and Mabaso.

'D'you think she'll tell you anything?' she asked. Her belly gurgled. She ignored it.

'We'll try the same trick with Miss Druitt as we did in Scotland Yard. Hopefully they'll let something slip.' He looked at our young translator. 'That's if you don't mind helping us a bit longer, miss?'

The young woman shook her head. 'This is the most interesting thing I've done since we moved here. I've nothing to do these days but dancing lessons and entertaining father's friends.'

'Just don't pretend to be your cousin this time.'

'But will the same trick work again? The princess might just throw me out.'

'I can't see what other choice we have.'

'I have an idea,' said Ettie. 'Where did you say they're performing?'

'The Alhambra,' I said.

'Delphine and I will go up and see them first,' said Ettie. 'Wait ten minutes, then you and Norman arrive. We'll pretend we don't know you.'

Ten minutes later, we were in the bar of the York Hotel. There were a few out-of-towners in there eating a late supper, but not many others. The bloke we'd talked to before wasn't there, instead a big-eared lady of about my age wearing a high-necked black dress. We sat at a table and watched as Ettie talked to her, Delphine at her side. At first the woman shook her head, but Ettie talked some more, pointing at her briefcase, her eyes bright, her tongue quick. Finally, the woman nodded and pointed at the stairs.

A young girl who looked like she'd been supping on Dalby's Calmative was cleaning the tables. When she came to ours, the guvnor put a penny down. He pointed at it.

'That's yours if you tell us which room the princess is staying in.'

The girl swallowed, then glanced back at her boss, who was fiddling with one of the beer barrels.

'Room seven,' she said at last, each word quiet and slow. 'Don't you tell her I said.'

We waited ten minutes, just as Ettie ordered. Then, as the landlady tried to fix a leak coming out the barrel, he snuck up the stairs. I had to wait till a punter ordered something from out back afore I could get past and join him.

The door to room seven was shut. I knocked. It was opened quick by a bald African bloke with a bushy beard. He wore a tweed suit.

'How can I help you?' he asked. He spoke with a thick African accent. 'Are you with the artists?'

'No, sir,' said the guvnor with a bow. 'I'm Mr Arrowood. This is Mr Barnett.'

'Newspapermen? Come back tomorrow.'

'We're friends of Senzo Nyambezi and Thembeka Kunene.'

He looked down the corridor, then at me and the guvnor again. 'Who?' he asked.

'They've been arrested,' said the guvnor. 'They asked us to deliver a message to the princess.'

'Wait,' he said, and shut the door.

A minute later he opened it again. 'Come inside.'

The room had three narrow beds side by side. An African woman with a long neck perched on a chair under the gas lamp, while another, shorter woman, stood by the window. Ettie and Delphine sat on the ends of two of the beds, each with a sketch pad on their lap and a pencil in their hand. Two trunks were open by the window, full of beaded costumes and queer instruments. A small fire warmed the room.

The long-necked woman asked us something in her own language, testing to see what we knew. Her eyes were aslant, a sore on her lip. She wore a small coronet atop her black hair, and over her shoulders was a thick tartan shawl.

'I'm sorry, madam,' said the guvnor. 'I don't understand what you're saying.'

'We haven't met a single person in this country who does,' said the princess. Her voice was upper class, sharp and correct. You could tell she'd worked for a governor's sister, as S'bu'd told us. She cleared her throat. 'What is the message, sir?'

'Are you Princess Nobantu?' asked the guvnor.

'I am.'

'I'm Mr—'

'Arrowood. I heard you. What do you have to say?'

The guvnor nodded at Ettie and Delphine. 'I can see you're busy. We can wait downstairs if you prefer.'

She looked at Ettie and spoke again in her own language.

'I'm sorry,' said Ettie with a frown. 'I don't speak your language either.'

The princess laughed. 'I'm sorry. I've been talking with my friends all day. I asked if it would disturb you?'

'No, but if you could try to remain still,' said Ettie, lifting her pencil.

'Talk,' said the princess, turning her head side on to us.

'Did you know that your compatriots Senzo Nyambezi and Thembeka Kunene have been arrested?'

'It was in the newspapers.'

'They've been charged with murder. If convicted, they'll hang. They need your help.'

'How can I help? Didn't they kill a woman?'

'I don't believe they did, Your Highness. I believe it was a policeman from Natal named Constable Mabaso.'

She didn't move, not even a twitch. There was nothing to be read in her.

'Has he been to see you?' asked the guvnor as Ettie and Delphine continued to sketch her.

'We've been in Edinburgh.'

'But you know him.'

'I read the newspapers. I know he's here to arrest those who raided the Kruger compound.'

'Will you help us?'

Without moving her head, her eyes darted to the woman by the window. She was smaller, in plainer clothes, an intense look to her face. The bloke was looking at her too. The princess spoke in African. The bloke added something, while the small woman nodded. She looked down at her feet, chewing her lip. She spoke. The princess nodded, then looked back at the guvnor.

'I don't understand how we can help.'

'Constable Mabaso's looking for a certain cargo from your country. I think you know what it is. His only way to find it is through you.'

'I don't know what you mean, Mr Arrowood,' said the princess.

'Would you mind just looking at the window again, Your Highness,' said Ettie. 'It always looks better in profile.'

The princess adjusted her head.

The guvnor was silent for some time, a pained smile on his codfish lips. The bearded bloke got nervy, shifting on his feet.

'You must explain, sir,' said the princess at last.

'Senzo Nyambezi told us about this cargo,' said the guvnor.

'What did he tell you?' asked the princess.

'He told us where it is, and that you also know.'

Again, the princess talked in her language. The small woman replied quickly, a fling of her hands.

'Where did he say this cargo is hidden, Mr Arrowood?' asked the princess at last.

The guvnor laughed and shook his head. 'You don't really want me to say in front of the two artists, do you? Now, I believe Mabaso will come to you tomorrow. He's been told you arrive on the evening train. When he does, the police will be waiting to arrest him.'

'Why are the police not here now, Mr Arrowood?' asked the princess. 'Why you?'

'They're looking for Mabaso right now. Will you help us? All you have to do is wait here for him to arrive, then cooperate with the police.'

'Will the prisoners be released?'

'Only if we catch Mabaso and it can be proved that he's responsible for the murders. You must understand that the police need to convict somebody. If it isn't the real murderer, they'll have no qualms about charging your friends.'

The princess spoke again to the small woman. Finally, she nodded. We arranged a time to meet them the next day, and left Ettie and Delphine to struggle with their masterpieces.

Chapter Forty-Three

Mercy was wailing upstairs when we arrived at the guvnor's rooms.

'Ettie!' cried Isabel, hearing us arrive.

'She'll be back in ten minutes,' the guvnor called up to her. 'Shall I get the baby down?'

There was no reply. Instead, her feet moved across the floorboards. After a moment, Mercy's wails got quieter, until she was silent. Flossie was sitting under the table, her arms wrapped round Neddy's little dog. It watched her with its dark eyes, like it was afraid she'd abandon it.

'Hello, darling,' said the guvnor, getting to his knees.

'Hello,' said the girl in her gruff voice. 'He ain't got a name.'

'Didn't Neddy take him back?'

'He said I got to look after him till tomorrow.'

'You must go to bed. It's late.'

She must have been very tired, for she crawled out from under the table, the dog still in her arms, and climbed the stairs. She'd been sharing a bed with Ettie since she arrived.

'Has that woman she was living with answered your letter yet?' I asked.

He shook his head. 'She can take as long as she wants. I like having her around. It makes it easier somehow.'

I made the tea. As we sat drinking, listening to the clock on

373

the mantel, the guvnor stroked the orange cat. Fifteen minutes later, Delphine and Ettie returned.

'What did they say?' he asked the moment they stepped into the room.

'Nothing useful when you were there,' said Delphine. Her eyes were bright, her cheeks rosy.

'They began to quarrel when you'd gone,' said Ettie, taking two digestives from the biscuit tin and biting into them both like a sandwich.

'The man wanted them to move to another hotel so that Mabaso couldn't find them,' said Delphine, also taking two biscuits. 'He said he'd kill them.'

'Why?' I asked.

'They didn't say. But the small woman said they needed Senzo to get the gold.'

'Why?' asked the guvnor, helping himself to a biscuit. 'Where is it?'

Delphine shook her head and finished her digestives. 'That's all she said.'

I handed her a cup of tea. She put in four spoons of sugar and stirred. She looked at the biscuits again.

'Help yourself,' I said.

'Thank you, Delphine,' said the guvnor as she dived in. He turned to Ettie. 'Now, what story did you spin them, sister?'

'I told them the Alhambra needed a picture of the princess for their bills. She wasn't sure about it because of the hour, but I said we'd been drawing the other performers all day and she was our last. I told her they'd sell more tickets with good billboards. The small woman told her to sit for us.'

'But you can't draw,' said the guvnor. 'Didn't they realize?'

Ettie looked at Delphine and smiled. Delphine's face darkened.

'They weren't entirely complimentary about our pictures, were they, dear?'

Delphine ignored her. She gulped down her tea and did up her coat. 'Do you need me tomorrow, Mr Arrowood?'

'Could you meet us at Scotland Yard at ten?'

'My father's having the committee over for dinner, but that should be fine.'

And with that she stomped out the door.

Ettie smiled. 'They told her a child could have made a better picture.'

The three of us laughed. It was only then I noticed Isabel standing at the bottom of the stairs. Her face was twisted with fury.

'Oh, my darling, I'm sorry,' said Ettie, rushing to her. Isabel pushed her away. 'How are you? Did you sleep?'

'The parson came,' she said, glaring at the guvnor, her eyes set in deep, grey sockets. 'The burial ground can't do the funeral tomorrow after all. Too many bloody influenza cases. They've moved it to the day after tomorrow. Half past eleven.' She turned and climbed stiffly up the stairs. 'And your daughter needs feeding, Ettie,' she said without turning back.

I went direct to the Pelican. I don't know why, nor what I wanted from Molly. I was confused and vexed, but I had a need for that woman I couldn't escape. It was Monday night, getting near closing time. I got a beer from the landlord, and had just sat at a table when the door opened and Molly stepped inside.

'Back, are you?' she asked, her pipe in her mouth. Her strong arms carried a basket of turnips.

'I don't know why,' I said.

'Nor do I, Juggins.'

Juggins. There it was again, the sound of my dear Mrs B in my ear. The sound of my life.

'You finishing soon?' I asked.

She dropped the basket onto the counter, moved the curls from her face, and looked round the pub. 'We'll be shut in half an hour. I'll see if he'll let me go now.'

Fifteen minutes later, with a pint of gin in my pocket, we arrived in my room. I lit the paraffin lamp and watched Molly as she looked round. It was cold and bare and unlovely, but it was home of a sort. I knocked at Mrs Kosminski's door upstairs and borrowed enough coal for a fire, then set about getting it going while Molly rinsed out my two mugs and poured us drinks. For some time we sat with our boots on the fender.

'Why d'you do it?' I asked at last.

She sighed, and when she started to talk I realized she'd had a few drinks already. 'Me and Ann got a stack of debt. Not through our own fault, but debt it is.'

'So what happened?'

'We wanted to buy a little beershop. Wanted to be our own people for once. I've been under blokes like that pasty bastard in the Pelican all my life. I know there are good ones, Norm, but I'd say I've lost my faith in people.'

I nodded, had a sup, lit a fag.

'The chandler on the corner agreed to borrow us the money to get the lease. He's the one everyone goes to. So on the day we need the money we sign our names, he hands over the money, and on the way back, 'tween his shop and our room, we get robbed. Four fellows with scarves over their faces. It was like they was waiting for us.' She shook her head, staring into the hot coals. She had a swallow.

'You think he'd set it up?'

'Don't matter what I think. We lost it all and now we owe him. Got to pay him back ten bob a week. That's why I do it. Ain't got no other way of paying.'

'Does your sister work in the same place?'

'Her arthritis is too bad.'

The bells of All Hallows rang down the road. Mice moved behind the walls. Molly took up her pipe and we sat there puffing away.

'Why didn't you tell me?' I asked at last.

'You'd have run a mile, mate.' She laughed sadly. 'You did.'

She pulled a piece of chocolate wrapped in Christmas paper from her coat and broke it in two, giving me half. It was the good stuff, creamy and silky on my tongue. I hadn't had chocolate that fine for a long time, and I let it melt in my mouth, thinking about what she'd said, enjoying the warmth of the fire on my feet and the looseness that came with the gin. She was right. I didn't know how to touch her now I knew what she did, how to read her.

'It's good chocolate, Moll,' I said, wondering how I could tell her what I was thinking.

'One of the blokes on Bankside gave it me,' she said, then paused. 'I do him every week.'

Spit filled my mouth, and I noticed the smoothness of the chocolate had given over to something grainy and rancid, like it'd been made with bad marge. I wanted to spit it out, but I knew this was a test of some kind.

She poured more gin into my mug. 'Wash it down with that,' she said with a smile. 'Gin can take away the taste of anything.'

I swallowed it down, looking at her smirking face in the dim light, unsure what she was doing.

'What d'you think of me?' I asked her.

'I'm fond of you, Norm,' she said, raking her fingers through her curls. 'I like being with you. I feel easy.'

'Am I like one of your punters?'

'What kind of a question is that?'

'I mean, can you be with a man proper without the other men tainting it?'

'Tainting it?' she asked, putting her hand on my leg. 'What d'you mean?'

'Can you forget them when we...'

'When we touch each other?'

'When we're fucking.'

'How can you ask that?'

'How can you expect me to understand if I don't?'

'Can't you see how I feel about you, darling?'

I looked into her brown eyes. The glow of the fire softened her nose and cheeks, wiped away the creases and lines that life had given her. My old man stiffened in my britches, my body remembering the last time we lay together. I felt my breath shorten, and though I couldn't see what she felt, I nodded, hoping I would if I just let go a bit.

I wanted her.

I reached out and touched her hair. We kissed, her fingers running down my neck. I stood and took her hand. By the bed I unclothed her, then she unclothed me. We pressed our bodies together, the cool of her skin on mine, my lips on hers,

378

hungry and forgiving and lonely. She pushed me onto the bed, and suddenly all that mattered was her breath, her skin under my fingers, and the scent of lavender on her neck.

After, we lay together, the room warmed from the little coal fire. Her head was on my chest.

'You got to be around more, Norm,' she whispered.

'Yeah,' I murmured.

She pushed herself up, her elbow digging into my side, and staggered across the room, more pickled than I thought she was. Picking up the flask, she took a few gulps straight from the bottle. A little fart escaped from her bum. 'I think you got a mouse,' she said with a laugh.

'Does it feel different when you do it with me?' I asked.

'Different to who?'

'Your punters.'

'Oh, Lord, why'd you ask such questions? Did you ask Rita that sort of thing after you'd had a shove?'

'She weren't a judy, Moll.'

'I ain't a judy. What's wrong with you, saying things like that after we've been so close?'

'If I didn't ask, I'd be thinking about it.'

''Course you're different, Juggins,' she said, finishing off the gin.

'How?' I asked.

'Strewth, you don't stop, do you? I don't know how Rita put up with you.' She got back into the bed and curled up aside me, her head on my shoulder, her arm over my belly. 'I wish she was still alive, Norm. I miss her so.'

I looked down the length of her back, at the ridges and knuckles of her spine to the crack where her bum started. I knew then that she was using me to get to Mrs B just as I was using her, and I didn't want that. We couldn't lead each other back to when we were happier.

'Pull the blanket up,' she murmured, and kissed me on the chest.

I felt the cold draught creep through the broken panes of the windows, and knew that it was over between us.

Chapter Forty-Four

I met the guvnor outside Scotland Yard at ten the next morning. Delphine was already there, sitting in the reception area in her overcoat and gloves.

'When'll he be back?' the guvnor asked the desk sergeant, the same wiry fellow with the upturned moustache who'd been there when his mate got the boot.

'Couldn't tell you.' He blew his nose. 'Don't know where he is.'

It was four hours before Napper arrived. Arrowood pushed himself to his feet and began explaining what we'd discovered on visiting the princess. Napper nodded.

'I thought you said she was arriving this evening?' he asked, his freckled nose already wrinkling.

'She returned yesterday.'

'You said this evening.'

'Are you sure?' asked the guvnor.

'Of course I'm sure!' roared the detective. Over his shoulder I could see the desk sarge wincing. 'You misled me again, you damn scurf! Well, this time I'm going to charge you for obstructing my inquiry.'

'You still need us, Napper.'

'You're wrong there, Arrowood.'

'We're about to discover the truth of the gold and what the

hell Mabaso's up to. We can do it, Napper. We'll play Miss Druitt's trick on Senzo and Thembeka again, this time using what we know from the princess and her people. Take us down to interview them.'

Napper looked at Delphine. 'No.'

'Don't be a damn fool. The blind's working: each time we do it we learn something new. This is when we solve the case, Napper. When *you* solve the case. This is your chance for recognition. It's been in every paper all week. Take us down to talk to them now and let's get it over with.'

'They aren't here,' said the detective, glancing back at the desk sarge. He swallowed, stepping over to the stairs.

'Aren't here?' said the guvnor. 'Where are they?'

'I released them this morning.'

'Released them? What in the Lord's name did you do that for?'

Napper turned back in a fury.

'As a lure for Mabaso! It's them he wants. They know where the gold is.'

'But—'

'I've two constables following them,' snapped Napper. 'As soon as Mabaso tracks them down, we'll pounce. Last night I sent a message to every editor in town that the prisoners would be released this morning. It's in all the morning editions, haven't you seen? The paperboys have been shouting the news from every street corner.'

'What if he doesn't hear? What if he's in hiding?'

'He'll hear, all right. Someone must be helping him. One or other of them will have heard the news.'

'So where are they now?'

Napper turned to the desk sergeant. 'Any news?'

'Not yet, sir,' said the bloke. He blew his hooter again.

'I've a police carriage outside with McDonald,' said Napper. 'As soon as they send word we'll set out.'

'They'll go to the York Hotel,' said the guvnor.

'You don't think they'll lie low for a while?'

'They've no money. They won't go to Gresham Hall in case Mabaso looks for them there. They won't go to Capaldi. They tried to see the princess before. They'll try again.'

We arrived at Waterloo twenty minutes later. Napper told PC McDonald to wait by the police van while the four of us went inside. The bloke we'd talked to the first time was at the counter reading a paper. He looked up.

'Detective Inspector Napper,' barked Napper. 'Scotland Yard.'

The manager stepped aside as we bustled up the stairs and along the corridor. The door was locked: Napper pounded on it, yelling, 'Police! Let us in!'

He put his ear to the door. He pounded again.

'Stand aside,' said Napper.

'No!' cried the manager, pulling a bunch of keys from his pocket. He pushed past us and unlocked the door, jumping out of the way as soon as it clicked open.

On the floor, tied back-to-back to an iron heating pipe, were the small woman and the bald, bearded fellow. The princess was gone.

A torn sheet was bound around their heads. I cut it off with my knife, then pulled another bit of sheet out of each of their mouths. They gasped, coughing and wheezing, their chests heaving.

Their two trunks had been emptied, all their contents strewn across the beds and floor in a big mess of dresses, shirts, drums, pipes, shields, cooking pots and beads.

Delphine talked to them as I cut their wrists and legs free. The answers were quick and urgent, the man and woman rubbing their limbs as they talked. I heard Mabaso's name.

'Mabaso?' asked the guvnor as he helped the short woman to her feet.

'Mabaso,' she said.

'And a white man,' said the bloke, then groaned as Napper helped him to his feet. Dark blood matted his thick beard. 'They've taken Nobantu. You said the police would protect us!'

'I didn't think he'd come until after the evening train.'

'Where did they take her?' asked Napper.

'The Castle Mail Shipping Company,' said the bloke.

'Is the gold there?' asked Napper.

'Yes,' said the fellow. He opened the window and spat blood onto the street, his every muscle strained and tight. 'He has a gun. He'll kill her. You must go now!'

'Was Senzo with him?' asked the guvnor.

'No, but—'

The woman interrupted him. He nodded as she spoke, then addressed us. 'They need two marks. Senzo and the princess must both sign to collect the crates.'

'Does Mabaso know that?'

The African shook his head. He spoke to the woman. She tutted.

'Where's the Castle Shipping Company?' asked Napper.

'Shadwell New Basin,' said the guvnor. He turned to the hotel manager, who stood in the door. 'Did you see them leave?'

'No, sir. The boat train was cancelled this morning and half the blooming passengers were waiting in the pub for the next one. It was like the Lord Mayor's Parade.'

'But you allowed them up?'

'This one told me they were expecting someone.' He nodded at the bald fellow.

'Not him!' said the African. 'Not Mabaso.'

'How's I bloody supposed to know that?' demanded Deakin, a hot temper come over him.

'Would anyone else have seen them leave?' the guvnor asked.

'Try asking Clive, the crossing sweeper out on the corner there.'

'One more thing. If any other Africans come in looking for the princess, I want you to tell them they've gone to Shadwell Basin to retrieve their luggage from the Castle Mail Packet office. Tell them the princess left with a black police officer.'

'And don't tell them about us, you understand?' added Napper. 'Don't say anything else at all.'

'What's all this about?'

'Just do it,' said Napper.

Clive was on the pavement leant against the wall of the hotel. He was eating an onion, and wore the most tattered coat I'd ever seen, a top hat with no rim, a boot with no toe.

'African couple, yeah?' he said. 'About midday? Come staggering out with a big English fellow. That lady was right jiggered, I tell you.'

'How did they travel?'

'Had a coach, didn't they?'

'Describe it.'

'Green four-wheeler, bit battered up.'

385

The guvnor looked at me. 'Bill blooming Craft, Barnett. That's who's been helping him. Bill blooming Craft.'

We left Delphine in Waterloo and made our way to Wapping. PC McDonald drove the horses hard, ringing the bell as we went through the busy streets. As we were thrown about on the benches inside, clutching tight to the leather straps to avoid crashing into each other, the guvnor told Napper about S'bu being beaten by Mabaso.

'You knew where he was all along?' spluttered Napper. 'You let us search for him?'

'You didn't search very hard, Napper. We did, and we found him.'

Napper glared at him. 'I hope I never see you again, Arrowood.'

'I think he went after S'bu because he didn't get enough information out of Senzo.'

'Who's this fellow Craft?'

'Bill Craft,' I told him. 'The cabman who picked up Senzo and Thembeka after they fled the Quaker Meeting House. He's the one took us to Gresham Hall.'

'That must be how Mabaso knew they were hiding there,' added the guvnor.

'He said he got that from Capaldi's driver,' said Napper.

The wheel hit a pothole, a bone-breaking jolt that sent us all into the air. The guvnor lost his grip on the strap and flew onto my lap, skidding off my britches onto the floor, his legs in the air.

'Agh!' he cried as he landed. 'My blooming back!'

'Careful, constable!' bellowed Napper, rubbing his elbow.

I gripped the guvnor's arm but he shook it off. 'Don't touch me! It's agony!'

'You just going to lay there?' I asked him.

'For the time being,' he said, glaring at me from the floor. He winced as we hit a kerb. 'Christ almighty. Does he know how to drive?'

''Course he knows how to drive,' said Napper, a smile on his face as he looked down on the guvnor. 'You should have held the strap.'

'I did hold the damn strap!'

'Not very well. Now finish what you were saying.'

'Have you any chloridine, Barnett?' asked the guvnor.

I pulled out my Black Drop and tipped out a couple of pills. 'Only these. Open up.'

He stuck his grainy purple tongue out through his patchwork teeth, and I dropped the pills into his great cavern of a mouth. 'Drink!' he demanded.

I shook my head.

'How did this Craft fellow come to be helping Mabaso?' asked Napper.

Lying at our feet with his belly rising like the dome of St Paul's, the guvnor continued. 'When he tracked Thembeka and Senzo, he must have found Craft's cab the same way we did. Not only did Craft take him to Gresham Hall, but Mabaso must have offered him work. You only need to talk to Craft for a moment to know he's a crook. The cove would do just about anything for a few coins.' He shifted the sack of potatoes that was his rumple and groaned. 'Oh Lord, that hurts. He said it was Capaldi's driver who told him about Gresham Hall so you didn't know he knew Craft. He didn't want Craft to give the game away.'

Napper nodded, looking down on the guvnor in a superior way. 'So Craft probably helped him take Mrs Fowler's body to Gresham Hall too.'

'Ah!' cried Arrowood as we lurched into another hole. 'What the hell's that idiot doing up there?'

Napper brought out a hip flask and had a swallow. He looked at the guvnor, who gazed back at him from the floor. Napper looked away and had another sip. The guvnor licked his lips, looking like a mongrel who's sniffed a bloater.

'Give him a bit, will you, detective?' I asked.

Napper smiled, and, from some height, tipped his flask over the guvnor's open gob. Some of it got in, the rest went on his chin. The guvnor cursed, wiping his face, licking his hand. 'I hope you get a bad back one day, Napper.'

He opened his gob for more.

It took well over an hour to get to Wapping that Christmas Eve. The traffic was diabolical, with folk getting in the way of the horses and jamming the pavements as they searched for what they lacked afore the feast. It was almost dark when we arrived, the fog descending as London's dwellings began to light their fires. The entrance to Shadwell Basin was on New Gravel Lane. Three great steamships were moored in the basin opposite the offices, two dark and still, the other with its lights on and a couple of sailors busying themselves on deck. The Castle Mail Packet Company was the only one of the buildings that wasn't shut for the holiday. By the time we pulled up, the Black Drop had done its magic, and the guvnor was off the floor.

Mr Lilly rose as we entered. The room was almost empty,

only a woman sweeping and a young fellow with a full beard doing some copying at the far end of the room.

'Good evening, sir,' said the guvnor. 'This is Detective Inspector Napper of Scotland Yard.'

'Mr Lilly, office manager,' said the oily-haired fellow, pushing his spectacles to his forehead and climbing off his high chair with a bump. The cracks of his lips were stained purple: on his desk was a half-eaten mince pie. 'How can I help you?'

'Can you tell us if Princess Nobantu travelled on your ship?' asked Napper. 'She would have arrived a week or two ago.'

'We did carry her, yes,' said Lilly. 'As I told you two before, we're the only shipping company that does the route, so unless she flew…' He raised his eyebrows and laughed like a randy gull. You could smell the booze on him. Seeing us stood there stony-faced, he stopped, hitched up his britches, and put on a serious voice again. 'There was a good deal of interest from the newspapers when she landed. Her manager, Mr Beaumont, made sure of that.'

'Has she been here today?' asked Napper.

'Not that I know, sir.' He slurred his words a bit and looked shamefaced from it. Pressing his moustache down with his fingers and squeezing his lips, he said, 'The owners did visit and allow us an hour for wine and pastries of the season. Bean!' he barked over his shoulder.

The young fellow at the back who'd stopped writing to watch us, replied, 'Yes, sir?'

'Did the Zulu Princess call today?'

'No, sir.'

'Are you holding any of her luggage in your warehouse?' asked Napper.

'Let me see,' said Lilly, crossing to the ledgers. He stared at the shelves for an age, before finally pulling down his spectacles and staring again. He took one down and opened it, running his fingers up and down the pages. 'Yes, a chest and five crates. Not yet claimed.' He peered at Napper. 'What's in them, detective? Not a tiger, I hope?'

He laughed again, a gob of snot coming out his nose. Wiping it with the back of his hand, he glanced at the younger clerk, who laughed a little late.

'Did she arrive on the same boat as Constable Mabaso?' asked the guvnor.

He shook his head. 'She arrived in England the week before him. I believe she was performing in Bristol before arriving in London.'

'Has anybody else tried to collect her luggage?'

'No, sir. They'd need a signed letter from the princess and...' He peered at the ledger again. 'And a Mr Nam... Namba... zezi.'

'How would you know the signatures were authentic?' asked the guvnor.

'We have a copy of both signatures in our records. Security is one of our principles, Mr Arrowood. People must be able to trust us.'

'What time d'you shut?' asked Napper.

'Six o'clock, sir,' answered Lilly. 'The owners gave the rest of the staff the afternoon off.' He pulled out his watch and peered at it. He looked like he might cry.

'Are you open tomorrow?'

'Christmas is the only holiday in our year.'

'So if the princess wanted her luggage—'

'She'd better arrive in the next hour and a half.'

'Is the warehouse secure?' asked the guvnor.

'They shut the dock gates at seven; no vehicles in or out without permission. Four watchmen patrol the basin overnight and we've the strongest locks money can buy on the doors.' Lilly stroked his wine-stained lips. 'A lot of valuable cargo comes from South Africa, you know.'

The guvnor looked at Napper. 'What d'you want to do?'

'We wait,' said the copper.

We hid the police van in a stables behind the office. Napper and the guvnor decided to station themselves in the director's office at the back, where there were a few glowing coals still left from the day. It had a window looking into the big clerking room. A box of mince pies was on the desk, and half a bottle of port.

The guvnor licked his chops. 'D'you mind if I—'

'I'll take them for the cupboard,' said Mr Lilly, gathering them up.

'You and McDonald wait on that boat opposite,' said Napper to me. 'If they arrive, let them enter. Come down, but keep hidden. Make sure they don't try to escape through the front door. We'll guard the back.'

'D'you think Senzo'll be with them?' I asked.

'Who knows?' said Napper. 'I'll be happy if we catch Mabaso. He's a lot to answer for, that fellow, and to think I gave him the benefit of the doubt. I told you about him, Arrowood. I told you.'

'Told me what?' asked the guvnor, biting a mince pie. Heaven knows where he got that from, as Lilly still had the manager's box under his arm.

'That they're a violent race.'

'Show me an English criminal who wouldn't kill for a crate of gold,' said the guvnor, catching a bit of crust as fell out his mouth.

'I'm not talking about criminals.'

'Yes, you are.'

'What the hell's wrong with you? Everybody knows what they're like. They keep fighting us!'

'We keep fighting them.'

'You're a damn fool, Arrowood. A controversialist. You're no better than those buffoons at Victoria Park.'

'You're the damn fool, sir,' said Arrowood sharply. 'I wonder you've ever caught a crook with a brain like that.'

Napper stared at him for a few moments, his lip curled. 'Mr Barnett, take your employer to wait on the boat,' he said at last. 'McDonald, you stay in here with me.'

'Don't be childish, Napper,' said the guvnor. 'It's freezing out there.'

'Get out. And keep hidden.'

The ship opposite the office was a tea clipper. One of the sailors had seen the police van, so he allowed us aboard and showed us where to stand to keep out of the way as his mate washed the deck around us. On the other side of the boat, a single winch lowered boxes onto a barge, but that was the only work being done this late on Christmas Eve. We were about fifty foot above ground, and would have had a good view of the dock gates on one side and the warehouses on the other if it hadn't been for the brown fog. It had come down thicker while we'd been inside, cold and gritty and choking in your gullet. We could just make out the shipping office opposite, and on the road a trough for the horses and a row of empty carts. Along the edge of the basin were a line of streetlamps, a solitary man with a loose cap following them until he was swallowed by fog. Somewhere over by the locks we could hear the soft grunt of the pumping station, and in the air the stink of the animal charcoal works hung heavy. There was no hint anywhere on the dock that it was Christmas tomorrow.

The guvnor fiddled in his pocket and handed me a sugar mouse. He pulled out another and bit into it.

'How's your back?' I asked.

'Can't feel it,' he said. His belly gurgled and groaned. He gripped a cleat on the rail and swung back and forth. 'I need something better than this to eat. And a good tot of brandy. How's that woman you've been seeing?'

'I'm not seeing her anymore.'

'Ah… well, I'm sorry.'

I nodded, my hands jammed in my coat pocket. 'I thought she was someone she wasn't.'

'She misled you?'

'I misled myself.'

He put his hand on my arm and looked up at me. 'You've been making some bad choices since Mrs Barnett died, Norman. Are you lonely?'

The question made me start. Was I lonely? How could he ask that? What use would it do to decide whether I was lonely? I'd spent the last two years avoiding that word, and I wasn't going to start thinking about it tonight. I breathed long and slow. Somewhere in the fog a horse snorted. Nearby church bells rang out the half hour.

A few moments later, the young clerk stepped out the office and made his way to the gates. He was wrapped up in a thick coat, a bowler, a scarf over his face. Heading home for Christmas.

'What are you going to do after the funeral tomorrow?' asked Arrowood when he realized I wasn't going to answer him.

'I'm going to Sidney's for dinner. What about you?'

'We were going to see Lewis, but not now. We'll sit at home and look after Isabel.' He burped. 'Why is there so much sadness, Norman?'

'There just is, William. There just—'

He gripped my arm and pointed. From the direction of the dockyard gates, two figures were appearing from the fog. It was Thembeka and Senzo.

Chapter Forty-Five

We crouched below the gunwale, watching through the gaps as they made their way along the cobbles. Their faces were part-covered in scarves and they wore broad-brimmed hats they didn't have before, but we knew it was them. When they reached the row of carts, they paused and waited, watching out in case anyone should be following. They moved on.

A curse came from the bargee on the other side of the clipper. Thembeka and Senzo stopped, peering over in our direction. There was no chance they could see us through the rails, though the bloke swabbing the deck was in clear sight.

An empty wagon then appeared, approaching from the opposite direction where the warehouses sat silent. The two Africans stood aside to let it pass, but the driver pulled up and spoke to them. His hat was low over his eyes, his collar up.

'Who's that?' whispered the guvnor. 'Is it Mabaso?'

We could hear the flow of their conversation, the low muttering like the murmur of the boats in the black water. There was a silence, Senzo stamping his feet, the driver sitting back.

'Well?' barked the driver, suddenly loud enough to hear.

Thembeka nodded.

A woman burst from the fog from the same direction the wagon had come, walking fast toward them. As she got nearer, we saw it was Princess Nobantu.

Senzo called out as he saw her approach. She ran forward, talking quickly as the driver climbed down from his seat and tied his horse to a post. Senzo tried to put his arms around her, but she stepped back and went to Thembeka instead.

All four of them entered the shipping company office. As soon as the door shut, we hurried down the gangway onto the dockside and crept up to the window. The princess was talking to Mr Lilly, Thembeka and Senzo watching from the side. The driver had his back to us.

'Go in?' I whispered.

'Wait until Napper makes his move,' said the guvnor.

'What's he waiting for?'

'Mabaso.' Arrowood turned, looking each way up and down the dock. 'Damn it. If he's out there somewhere he'll have seen us already.'

Mr Lilly went back to the ledgers and took down the one he'd looked at before. Next, he pulled out the drawer of a filing cabinet and found some papers. He asked a question. The princess answered with a shake of her head.

The office manager then put a document on the desk and handed Senzo a pen. He signed it and passed the pen to Princess Nobantu. She reached out to sign, but her hands shook and she dropped it. Mr Lilly returned it to her. She signed her name and stood back.

Mr Lilly blotted the document, then held it under the lamp. His face puckered. He took up the other paper from his desk and studied that. He shook his head and handed the pen back to the princess. She signed again. Again, he checked.

Finally, he took a key from his watch pocket, went to a wall cabinet, and unlocked it. He brought out a bigger key, put on his coat, and turned to the door. The driver turned too.

It was Bill Craft.

We ducked under the window and scurried to the row of carts, hiding there as the five of them came out. Craft untied the wagon and led the old white horse after them as they marched away from the gates towards the row of warehouses further down the basin. A few moments later, the office door opened again, and there was Napper and PC McDonald, peering through the fog. When the wagon turned a corner and disappeared from sight, we all four hurried after them.

At the intersection, Napper had a look round the corner.

'He's unlocking the warehouse,' he whispered. We waited out of sight for a few more moments. 'They're in.'

'The driver?' I asked.

'Him too.'

We all had a look now. The alley had warehouses on one side and another basin on the other. There were no big ships moored there, but in the gloom we could just make out the shapes of dumb barges in the black water. Under the haze of a streetlamp stood the empty wagon and the old nag. About a hundred yards past the wagon was another junction.

'Where are those constables who were supposed to be following them?' asked Napper, looking back.

'Must have lost them, sir,' said McDonald.

'Shall we go in?' the guvnor asked.

'We wait until Mabaso appears,' said Napper.

'Maybe he's in there already, sir,' said the PC.

Napper pointed past the warehouse to where the alley joined another. 'We'll go round the back and take a position down there. You stay here, Arrowood. If he appears, we approach from both ends and arrest him. Wait till you see us move. If he doesn't appear, we follow the wagon.' He turned to the PC. 'Can you get the van out quickly?'

'Yes, sir. Stables aren't locked.'

Napper and the PC went back past the office and disappeared down another alley. A few minutes later, Craft backed out of the warehouse pulling a trolley loaded with small crates, each about the size of a baby. He stopped by the wagon and he, Thembeka, Senzo and the princess lifted them one by one onto the back as Mr Lilly stood watching. When they were finished, Lilly pulled the trolley back into the warehouse and locked up the doors.

'Merry Christmas,' he said, nodding his head at each of them.

'Thank you, sir,' said Thembeka.

Fearing they would see us, we drew back behind the corner, hearing Mr Lilly's footsteps approach on the cobbles.

He turned the corner, starting when he saw us. The guvnor shushed him softly and waved him on. He nodded and walked past.

Carefully, we looked round the corner again. The princess, Senzo, Thembeka and Craft stood by the wagon in silence. The princess stroked the old horse. Somewhere in the fog, a man coughed.

'There, at the basin,' whispered the guvnor.

A head had appeared in the cradle of a fixed ladder rising from the water to the dockside.

'He must have a boat.'

We watched as the figure climbed the rungs, his chest coming into view next, his hips, his legs. Finally, he stepped out onto the cobbles. Though it was murky and dark, the figure no more than an outline, we knew from the way his ears stuck out it must be Mabaso. He looked up and down the alley, then hurried over to the wagon.

Napper and the PC, truncheons in hand, burst through the fog at the far end of the warehouses, running towards the wagon. We moved too, our guns in our hands.

For a moment, Mabaso froze. Then, instead of retreating back to the ladder, he darted around the horse. Quick as a cat he was behind Senzo, wrenching his arm up his back, his other hand at his neck.

'Mabaso!' yelled Napper, reaching them just before us. 'Put it down!'

It was only then we saw it: Mabaso was holding a long blade to Senzo's gullet.

'Stand back, gentlemen,' said the African copper calmly.

'Don't, please don't,' pleaded Thembeka.

Senzo was shaking, pulling his head back away from the blade. His mouth was open, his lips still scarred and swollen.

Thembeka tried to take Mabaso's arm.

'No!' he yelled, pushing the blade harder into Senzo's throat.

She backed off. 'He's been punished enough, Mabaso. Please. No more.'

'Leave it to the courts, constable,' said Napper, dropping his truncheon and holding his hands in the air.

'The court's already heard his case,' said Mabaso. He coughed again. 'He's guilty.'

'What court?' asked Napper.

'The Ninevite court.'

'That's not the law here. Put the knife down, there's a good

399

lad. He'll get his punishment. Don't get yourself into any more trouble, eh? You've done enough.'

'You don't understand,' said Mabaso.

'Then explain it to me,' said Napper.

Mabaso grimaced, an expression so full of pain I felt my skin prickle.

Then he sliced the blade across Senzo's neck.

The princess screamed.

Senzo stood for a moment, his hands moving to his throat. Blood began to surge through his fingers.

Before we could react, he collapsed onto the cobbles. Mabaso stepped toward Thembeka, the knife still in his hand.

I fired.

He gave a startled cry, clutching his belly, and as he stood there looking at his hands, McDonald smashed his truncheon onto the back of his head.

Thembeka was already on her knees, her fingers trying to knit together the gash in Senzo's neck, but the blood was coming faster now.

She muttered something over and over as the blood spread over the cobbles, perhaps a prayer, perhaps a last message to him. Senzo stared up at her face now, his hand gripping her coat. His legs jerked. His mouth shot open.

Then he went slack.

Thembeka buried her face in his breast, sobbing, her shoulders heaving. The princess knelt behind, putting her arms around Thembeka.

Mabaso lay upon the ground behind her, his breath coming in short jerks, his face wrought with pain.

'Well, you spared the courts some time there, Barnett,' said

Napper, wiping his hands on his trousers. He was trying to sound jaunty, but his voice trembled.

I looked at the pistol in my hands. 'He was about to kill her.'

The guvnor said nothing. He stared at me.

'Get the van, McDonald,' said Napper.

'He was about to kill her,' I said again. I'd never felt so cold before. My whole body was shivering.

The guvnor stepped over and took the pistol from my hand. 'He'd killed three people, Norman. You had no choice.'

'Hold up your arms,' Napper said to Craft as the PC scurried away.

'I just drove him around, sir!' said Craft. 'I didn't do nothing!'

'That's enough for me,' said Napper, putting the wrist irons on him.

We waited for the police van on the foggy dockside, listening to Thembeka sob softly on the floor. Napper went over to check the basin where Mabaso had climbed up from.

'Little steam launch,' he said. 'That was how he was going to get the gold away.'

The van arrived and we lifted Senzo's body into one of the small cages. Craft was pushed into the other. Mabaso was lying on his side, clutching his knees to his chest, coughing. He cried out in pain as we lifted him onto the floor of the van.

The princess helped Thembeka climb aboard, then sat with her on the bench, holding her hand. Finally, McDonald whipped on the horses and we left Shadwell Basin.

As we rolled through Wapping, the pubs spilling out with folk from all four corners of the world, Mabaso breathed his last.

'Still think he was trying to impress his superiors, Napper?' asked the guvnor.

'Don't be a fool, Arrowood. He was after the gold all the time.'

'Have a look in his pocket.'

'What?' asked the detective.

'Barnett, have a look in his pocket.'

I bent down. Mabaso's mackintosh was greasy with blood. In the pocket I felt a pistol. I pulled it out and handed it to Napper, who held it up to the lamp inside the van. It was one of Lewis's.

'That proves Mabaso was at the Quaker Meeting House between Senzo and Thembeka running off and our arrival,' said the guvnor. 'Check the other.'

I bent again. Sure enough, I found one of the other missing pistols.

'So,' said Napper, crossing his arms. 'He was trying to make me believe it was Senzo and Thembeka who killed Musa and Mrs Fowler, when all the time it was him.'

'He was a clever fellow,' answered the guvnor. 'He even used your prejudice against you.'

Napper sniffed, glancing at the princess.

'Bullets?' asked the guvnor.

I checked the guns: they were fully loaded.

'Interesting,' said the guvnor, then sat back and watched the busy night.

Nobody spoke for some time. Finally, Napper said, 'For God's sake, Arrowood. Just say what you're thinking.'

'Why didn't he use the pistols? He might have escaped. He had a boat.'

'What does it matter? We've got the gold. We've got the murderer.'

'Not of Mr Fowler. That was one of Capaldi's men.'

Napper sighed. The guvnor glanced at me. We both knew the copper was going to pin that one on Mabaso as well, but I could see that Arrowood had no fight left in him to argue. Capaldi would have to wait for another day.

We drove on in silence. Down Wapping High Street, past St Katherine's Dock, around the Tower. It was early evening, and Thames Street was high on Christmas spirit. Minstrels and carollers and oompah bands rang out from every corner. Old men in soldiers' uniforms and paper chains around their necks begged from the crowds of folk filling their baskets from the butchers', the wine merchants', the costers' wagons. Parents took their kiddies to the pantomime, while dippers moved through the currents like flies, preying on the happy gents who'd been in the pub all afternoon. As we stopped and started, Thembeka's sobs grew quieter. The princess sat upright and stiff, stroking her, staring out at the tumult.

Napper drew down the window and called up to the driver as we neared Blackfriars. 'Waterloo, constable.'

He sat back on his seat.

Princess Nobantu asked Thembeka something in her own language. Without looking up, Thembeka answered slow, her words broken, her voice barely more than a whisper. Anger appeared on the princess's face. They talked for a few minutes, Thembeka finally covering her face with her hands, shaking her head.

'So you were working with Mabaso all the time, ma'am,' said Napper to the princess. 'I should have guessed.'

She shook her head. 'No, sir. Mabaso captured me from the hotel. He knew the shipping company required two signatures, so he had that white man take me to the dock and keep me there until Senzo arrived at the office. I was to get the gold released. Mabaso was going to take it away in the boat.'

'He knew Senzo would arrive, did he?'

'He knew they'd been released from gaol and that they'd come looking for me. He told my friends in the hotel he was taking me to the shipping company. He knew Senzo would follow us there.'

'Why did you agree to do it?' asked Napper.

'At first he said he would kill me if I didn't,' said the princess unhappily. 'At first.'

'He thought you were arriving in London tonight,' said the guvnor. 'Why did he come to your hotel so early?'

'There was a report in the newspapers this morning saying we'd arrived yesterday.' She drew in a big load of breath, pulled her shawl tight around her long neck, and turned to Napper. 'Are you finished with us now, detective?'

'Yes,' said Napper. 'And count yourself lucky.'

'Thank you, sir.'

'What about me?' I asked.

Napper waved my question away. 'There'll be an inquest, but you'll be fine. You were assisting me. He was about to kill Miss Kunene.'

The guvnor patted my knee, but I knew from his face that he was troubled. I was troubled myself. I'd never killed a man before, and had a bad feeling I'd been too quick to pull that trigger. I went through it again and again in my head, trying to convince myself Mabaso had been about to kill Thembeka, but there was a doubt I couldn't shift.

We climbed down at York Road and watched as the Black Maria turned and took the two coppers and their quarry back over the river. A two-wheeler was approaching from the west, driven by a couple of lads on the ran-tan shouting insults at everyone they passed.

'William!' came a voice from across the road. We turned to see Ettie, pushing her perambulator. She waited for a night soil cart to pass, then crossed over to us. 'Mercy wouldn't settle. I thought some air might do her good.' She smiled at Thembeka. 'Hello, again.'

Thembeka gave her a quick hug. 'Hello, Ettie.'

Noticing her forlorn expression, Ettie frowned. She turned to Princess Nobantu. 'Good evening, Your Highness.'

The princess looked puzzled.

'May I introduce, Ettie,' said the guvnor. 'My sister. I'm afraid we played a trick on you, Your Highness. She's not an artist. The woman she was with speaks Fanakalo. We wanted to know what you were saying to each other.'

'Ah,' said the princess. 'I wondered why neither of them could draw.'

'I'm sorry,' said Ettie. 'What happened?'

The guvnor quickly explained. When Ettie'd heard I'd killed Mabaso she touched my arm. 'I'm so sorry, Norman. You must feel awful.'

'Mabaso wanted to kill Senzo and Musa, didn't he, Your Highness?' asked the guvnor. 'It was more important than getting the gold.'

The princess looked at him, her lips pressed tight together

as people dodged and bustled around us on the pavement, heading for the station and home, or out to Bankside to drink and dance.

'Well, they're all dead now, Mr Arrowood,' she answered at last.

'Why?' asked the guvnor.

She shook her head.

'You don't have to worry,' he said. 'We're not going to report this to Napper. He wouldn't be interested anyway. But we've worked ourselves to the bone trying to get to the bottom of this case. We've tried to do our best.'

She put her arm around Thembeka and squeezed her. She thought.

'Come into the hotel,' she said at last. 'I need a drink.'

Chapter Forty-Six

We parked the perambulator by an empty table in the back corner, out of the way of the loud crowd by the bar. Mercy was sleeping. When we were all seated, the guvnor asked, 'So, was I correct, Your Highness? Was Mabaso here to kill Senzo and Musa?'

'Yes,' she said.

'For betraying the Ninevites.'

'No,' said the princess, her eyes shining with sadness. 'For betraying our people. Senzo and Musa were native intelligence officers. They were spies.' She paused, looking at Thembeka. They held each other's gaze.

The guvnor blinked, looking from one to the other. 'Spies? For who?'

'They worked for the colonial authorities,' the princess continued. 'They're paid to spy on the blacks, to report any signs of protest or rebellion.'

'But...' Arrowood shook his head. For once he had no idea what to say.

'*One who comes with the horses*, that's what we call a government spy,' the princess continued. 'Would it surprise you to know there are many Africans who don't want the British to rule us?'

Ettie shook her head.

'We don't want to be told where to work, who to work for, where we can and cannot live. We want our land back. The whites in Natal are terrified that we'll come together and rise against them, and so the colonial authorities watch us. If a movement begins to grow, they stamp it out with great and sudden force. You are a violent people, you know.'

'That's not fair, Your Highness,' said Ettie.

'Really, Miss Arrowood? Look in your papers. You're fighting all over the world. Just this year you've had battles in Sudan, Zanzibar, South Africa and the Gold Coast colony. War is in your nature.'

'Commerce is in our nature,' said the guvnor.

'War and commerce come together in the empire. My people have suffered, and we cannot hide our eyes as you can.'

He nodded. He wasn't insulted or surprised: I'd heard him talking about these things in the Hog with Hamba and his Lascar mates many times. It's just that there was no satisfaction in ending this case and I could see he found that hard.

The princess continued: 'The government are afraid of the Ninevites because they're well organized and have many men. The Regiment of the Hills, that's their other name. They even wear army uniforms. Senzo and Musa had managed to get inside.'

A small gob of spit had formed at the corner of her lips as she spoke. She took a lug of brandy and pulled off her coat. Warmed from the fire, I did the same.

'But the Ninevites are a gang of bandits,' said the guvnor. 'Why shouldn't the police investigate them?'

She laughed softly. 'Things are never just one thing. Just as commerce can come with violence, crime can come with rebellion.'

'But Delphine said they rob your people as well,' said the guvnor.

'Yes, they're criminals. But they show the people that blacks can defy the government.'

'They break the law, Your Highness,' said Ettie. 'That cannot be right.'

'If your choice was to slave in the mines or become a bandit, what would you do?'

'I wouldn't kill innocent people,' said Ettie.

'It's a shame your empire doesn't have your principles, Miss Arrowood.'

'Who was Mabaso?' asked the guvnor.

'A hero,' she said softly, fingering the handle of her mug. Thembeka was listening careful, but her head was bowed like she was ashamed. Ettie signalled to the barmaid for brandy; I took out my pouch and rolled a fag. The doubt I'd had the second I pulled the trigger was suffocating.

The princess took my baccy from the table. 'May I?' she asked.

I nodded. Feeling short of breath, I took my air in slow, holding it, letting it out.

The princess spoke as she rolled. 'A month ago Senzo and Musa gave information to the Natal authorities about a group of rebels working with the Ninevites to build up an armoury on the coast. The leaders were executed, the arms taken. The Ninevite commanders knew somebody had passed on the information and Senzo and Musa were afraid they'd be discovered. That's when they were sent on the Kruger raid.'

She paused as I offered a match for her fag.

'Did they shoot the guard and the child?' asked Ettie.

'I don't know. There were six men on the raid. The other four bandits were killed by the guards, so I suppose we'll never find out. When Senzo and Musa found themselves the only ones left, they saw a chance to escape South Africa and make themselves rich at the same time. Mabaso said they might even have shot the other bandits themselves. Anyway, Senzo knew I was coming to England to do exhibitions with Mr Beaumont. He asked us to transport the gold and meet them here. I didn't know then that they were government spies or I'd never have agreed.'

'When did you discover this?' asked the guvnor.

'Today. Mabaso told me everything.'

'Did he mention Mrs Fowler?'

'The white lady?'

'Who was killed, yes.'

'She arrived when he was executing Musa. She said she was going to get the police. If she did that, then he wouldn't find Senzo. He had to kill her.'

'No, he didn't,' said Ettie. 'He chose to kill her.'

'There are always casualties in war. Do not judge my people for fighting yours.'

'You called him a hero. He killed an innocent woman.'

'Many of your colonial heroes are men who have killed innocent people. I doubt you were ever this concerned about their victims.'

'Actually, I...' Ettie began, then stopped. She dropped her eyes. If there was one thing you could say about Ettie, it was that she was honest with herself.

'Why did he risk taking her body across the city?' asked the guvnor. 'Why didn't he just leave her there with the others?'

'He told me he had to make a quick decision. He was in the Meeting House with three corpses and had to get out quickly. If he tracked down Senzo and killed him there'd be a fourth murder, and that would mean more of a chance of being caught. He decided to make it look as if Senzo killed the lady, then Senzo would be executed by the British courts. That would be safer for Mabaso, and since he was working with the police, he could arrange it all. He hid the body somewhere until he could find a way of moving it.'

'How did he know they were hiding in the Meeting House in the first place?'

'He read about the court case in the paper. He paid a white boy to go to the court and follow them.'

'Did he kill Mr Fowler?' asked the guvnor.

She shook her head. 'The gentleman was dead when he arrived. He didn't care who did it. He thought it would complicate things for the police.'

'Why didn't he just kill Senzo in the police station? He was alone with him in the cell.'

'It was safer to leave the courts to execute him.'

The guvnor nodded slowly. He pulled a cigar from his pocket and lit it. Ettie took a gulp of her gin. She was troubled.

'How can you be sure what Mabaso said was the truth?' asked Arrowood at last.

'I knew the rebels were betrayed by someone,' answered the princess, pulling her shawl higher around her neck. 'That was common knowledge. When he explained it in the carriage after he captured me, it all fitted together, the risks he took to find them, the way he spoke. I saw truth in his eyes. But I only knew for sure when he killed Senzo. He could have tried shooting when he saw you running to us. He had two guns. Maybe he'd have had a chance of getting the gold if he killed you as you ran. But the Ninevites do not use guns for their punishments. They cut the throat open or destroy the teeth.'

'Did you know they were spies, Miss Thembeka?' asked the guvnor, his voice soft and gentle.

She'd been watching the baby sleep, but now she looked up. Her face was grey, the strength gone from her voice. 'They told me in Paris.'

'And you stood beside them?' asked Ettie.

'It wasn't so simple, Miss Arrowood. S'bu needed me. He wasn't involved. Has he been found yet?'

'He's safe,' said the guvnor. 'We tracked him to Capaldi's warehouse. Mabaso gave him a beating, but he'll survive. He's staying with a friend of mine. I can take you to him tonight.'

'Why did Mabaso try to kill you, Thembeka?' asked Ettie. 'Are you also a spy?'

Thembeka caught my eye, but said nothing: it told me all I needed to know.

'You had to do it, Norman,' said the guvnor, putting his hand on mine. 'You couldn't risk it. Not after what he'd done to Senzo.'

'The judge would have sentenced him to death even if you hadn't,' said Ettie.

The serving girl came over with two bowls of oysters. Everyone began to eat, all except me and Thembeka.

'What will you do now, Miss Thembeka?' asked Ettie.

'I don't know,' she said. I'd never seen her so tired, so uncertain, and I wondered what Senzo really was to her. 'I've had enough of showmen. They only use us. I didn't like performing in Paris, all the shouts, the stupid things they made us do.'

'Then you and S'bu must join us,' said the princess. 'We're doing three weeks at the Alhambra here in London, then our contract with Mr Beaumont is finished. We're going to manage ourselves. We'll tell them the real history of our people and what is happening now in South Africa. Half the show in Qwabe costume and half in English dresses and suits. We'll write our own pamphlets, perform the dances we choose. No cooking. No pretend battles. No yipping. We'll present ourselves the way we really are, and we'll take all the money. There are so many cities we can go to.'

'What about Mr Capaldi? We have a contract.'

'He won't pursue it,' said the guvnor. 'After what we saw in that warehouse, he won't want to attract any more attention.'

'But are you sure this is permitted?' asked Thembeka. It was the same question she'd asked the guvnor the second time we met. She just couldn't seem to believe it.

The princess smiled. 'This is not South Africa. There are no native laws here.'

When Thembeka still didn't look convinced, the princess turned to us. 'It's true, isn't it?'

The guvnor nodded. 'You can manage yourselves.'

'Chang and Eng did it,' said the princess. 'They left their manager and ran the shows themselves. They made a fortune.'

Still Thembeka didn't seem to believe it. She rubbed her nose and sneezed, and with it came a sob. Ettie passed her a hanky.

'We're stronger together,' said the princess. 'And we'll make a lot of money. Talk to S'bu.'

'Yes,' said Thembeka, dabbing her eyes. 'Yes, we will join you, but only for a year. I don't like performing. I don't like people looking at me. I'll do it until I've saved enough to buy a beershop. My sister and I used to sell beer in Johannesburg, you know? That's what I want to do. Buy a beershop here in London.'

'Of course,' said the princess, touching her hand. 'Whatever you want.'

Thembeka's eyes narrowed. 'Would it be better to have two shows?'

'Two shows?'

'I know some ladies who perform as Capaldi's Wonders. Big crowds. They're unhappy with their manager. Maybe they want to join us too.'

The princess smiled. 'Yes, ask them. We'll build a new Barnum's.'

The princess's companions, the bearded man and the short woman, arrived from upstairs just then, and they all began talking in their own tongue. Though Thembeka's eyes were strained with sorrow, it seemed important she make plans then and there for herself and S'bu.

Chapter Forty-Seven

Ettie took Mercy back to their rooms, while we hailed a four-wheeler and brought Thembeka to Lewis's house, where she was reunited with S'bu. There were tears in both of their eyes as they embraced. Lewis set out another mattress and we left her there. Not feeling ready to go back to my room, I returned to Coin Street with the guvnor. It was past eleven. Isabel was awake, sitting in the good chair by the fire, a mug of gin on the table and a telegram in her hand. She seemed relieved to see us return, and even managed a trembling smile.

'It's good to see you up,' said the guvnor, hesitating in the middle of the room. His instinct was to go to her, kiss her, touch her hand, but now he didn't know what to do.

'How are you doing, Isabel?' I asked as I hung up my coat.

'Managing.' She breathed in deep. 'I'm sorry your case ended the way it did. Ettie told me.'

'Thank you,' said the guvnor. He removed his scarf, his bowler, his overcoat. 'Did you hear from your family?'

'I don't think they'll come.'

'Lewis and Willoughby are meeting us there,' he said as Ettie stepped inside from the outhouse. 'I think Scrapes also.'

Isabel bit her lip and shut her eyes tight. Ettie stepped over and took her hand. 'Can I get you anything, my dear? Some tea?'

'No, thank you,' whispered Isabel, opening her eyes again. She took a sip of her gin.

'What's that?' asked the guvnor, pointing at the envelope. 'Your sister?'

'The hospital.'

'Ah,' he said, but asked no more. It was clear Ettie'd told him she'd been offered the scholarship over Isabel.

'What did they say?' asked Ettie, taking her pipe from the mantel and setting a match to it.

Isabel passed it to her sister-in-law. Ettie held it under the lamp and puffed away as she read it. She looked up.

'This is wonderful,' she said quietly. 'Congratulations. You deserve it.'

'Thank you, Ettie,' answered Isabel. There was only sorrow in her voice.

The guvnor took the telegram from her and read it himself. He looked up. 'But this is marvellous. I can't believe it.'

'Why?' asked Isabel. 'Didn't you see me studying? Didn't you think I had a chance?'

'No, I can't believe that both—'

'We were all hoping so much that you'd win the scholarship,' interrupted Ettie. 'You deserved it. You worked so hard.'

'Yes, of course,' said the guvnor softly. 'But—'

Ettie cut him off again. 'You'll have to decide when you feel up to it. You must tell them about Leo. They'll understand.'

'You'll make a fine doctor, Isabel,' I said. Out of the corner of my eye I saw Ettie frown at the guvnor and shake her head.

'Help me with a cork, brother,' said Ettie, leading him into the scullery.

'Tell me about the case again, Norman,' said Isabel as they left the room. 'Distract me.'

I sat at the table and started to explain all that had happened that day. Soon, brother and sister returned with some Allinson's, a plate of cheese, a fresh bottle of brandy. For a while, Isabel listened close, asking question after question. But as the bells of St Andrew's rang out at the end of the street, we lost her again and she fell silent.

Soon after, I said my goodbyes, promising to return the next morning for the procession.

'I'll take you out,' said Ettie, pulling on a shawl and collecting the keys from the mantel. She led me down the passage, into the cold pudding shop. The only light in there was a dim glow coming through the window from the streetlamp. She cursed as she barked her shin on a bench.

'Why didn't you want her to know you'd been offered the scholarship too?' I asked.

'I turned it down. They offered it to her instead.'

'But you want to be a doctor. You're perfect for it.'

'Actually, I'm not. I realized that more than anything I want to work for the mission.'

'For Hebden?'

'Oh, Norman, he's not such a bad man as you think. I don't judge you for lying with a woman, so why do you judge him?'

'He's supposed to have higher morals.'

'He's just a man. But that's not why I want to work for the mission. I have a calling. I believe the Lord wants me there.'

A thin bloke rushed past the window. Two others chased him.

'Did you do it because Isabel lost Leo?'

'Of course not. I didn't know they'd choose her instead.'

'Really?'

'Really.' She turned to the door and unlocked it. 'William told me you've met a woman. A friend of Rita's?'

'I've seen her a few times.'

'I'm glad,' she said, gripping my forearm. 'You seem so lost sometimes.'

I looked into her handsome, grey eyes, feeling comforted and challenged at the same time. I wished she wouldn't do that.

Thoughts were spinning in my head as I walked home, and when I crossed Blackfriars Road onto Southwark Street a great wave of tiredness came over me. It was half an hour before midnight. Here and there people slept in shop doorways under piles of sacks, pretending not to hear the laughter and shouts of the folk staggering home from the pubs. Up ahead, a copper on his beat was approaching from London Bridge, taking particular care to prod each sleeping pile with his truncheon and telling them to move on.

'Give it a rest, will you, mate?' I said as he got near. 'It's Christmas. They'll only lie down somewhere else.'

'Mind your own business,' he growled. 'Unless you want a night in the cells yourself.' He was Irish, and I could see from the way he shuddered that he was sickening with something.

'Merry Christmas, mate,' I said, passing him. He'd probably be here doing just the same tomorrow night.

The lights were still on in the Pelican, and even from fifty yards off I could hear the sound of singing inside. I thought about Molly, about my cold, empty room.

I put my hand on the door. Inside, the same woman from before was singing Black Mary's song again: '*Only a violet I plucked, when but a boy…*'

The pub fell silent.

I turned and went home.

At nine o'clock next morning, I was at Scotland Yard. It was quiet. I wore my dark suit. The desk sarge wished me Happy Christmas and rang up for Napper.

'Thought you'd be here, sir,' I said when he appeared.

'It's my bloody superintendent. Wanted some of us in this morning, the rest in the afternoon. At least I get half a day holiday, I suppose.'

I held out the packet of chocolates I'd bought for Molly a couple of days back. 'Happy Christmas.'

He looked at them like I'd brought him a bomb. 'Eh?' he said at last. 'For me?'

'From Mr Arrowood and me. For putting up with us. You're a decent copper.'

'Well… Well, thank you.'

It seemed to make his muscles tense. He glanced at the sarge, then back at me. 'You want a quick brandy across the road?'

The pub was almost empty. When we were sat down with a drink, he said: 'Craft told us everything. Mabaso found him the same way you did. He followed the Africans' trail from the Quaker House to Charing Cross, and learned from the sweepers they'd got into Craft's cab. Craft told him they were hiding in Gresham Hall, just as he told you. Mabaso knew they were there a few days before he told us.'

'Enough time to take Mrs Fowler.'

'That's right. Craft helped him collect Mrs Fowler's body and take it to Gresham Hall the night before we discovered it. Seems he's a dab hand at picking locks. Been in stir three times for burglary, has our Mr Craft.'

'He told you that?'

'We encouraged him. He knows he'll dodge the murder charge.'

'Did he get paid well?'

Napper's eyes were on a young lady selling winkles from table to table. When she turned her head, her gave her a nod.

'He wouldn't tell us. I doubt he was in it for the good of Africa, though.'

'I doubt it.'

'That's how Mabaso got around without being seen. Craft hid him too, when he disappeared.' He hoiked up his britches. 'Oh, and Nick did go missing two days after Sylvia, just as your guvnor said he would. Seems like he was right about a few things, after all.'

I nodded. I wanted to ask him about me shooting Mabaso but at the same time didn't want to make him think about it too much.

'We're due the reward. I'd like to take it to Mr Arrowood today.'

'As a Christmas present?'

'If you like.'

He shifted on the bench. 'It'll take a few days.'

'You going to do anything about those three women Capaldi had prisoner?' I asked, standing and buttoning my coat.

He shrugged. 'What can I do? We don't know who they are or where they've gone.'

'You could raid his cat-house.'

'I'll ask the superintendent.'

'Promise?'

He nodded. 'He's off with his blooming family. Insists on us working while he stuffs himself with turkey and pudding.'

At half ten, I was back at Coin Street. The hearse was parked outside the pudding shop, Leo's tiny coffin already lying there. The Puddings were in their dark overcoats, Mrs Pudding holding Mercy tight to her breast. I waited by the black horses until the guvnor appeared with Flossie. They stood by the second carriage as Isabel stepped out of the shop with Ettie holding her arm. Arrowood touched her shoulder as she passed, and she gave him a weak, trembling smile. The two women climbed aboard, followed by Mrs Pudding and Flossie. The undertakers whipped on the horses, and the guvnor, Mr Pudding, Little Albert and me walked behind. It was Christmas morning, 1896. We'd never see the Africans again, but within a year the British would be at war with the Boer. It was Christmas morning, and we were going to bury a child.

Historical notes

The Arrowood books are narrated by Norman Barnett, a white man born in the slums of Bermondsey. As such, the story is filtered through his perceptions and understandings. For much of the background detail regarding the situation of black people in Britain in the 1890s, I relied on two books in particular: David Olusoga's *Black and British: A Forgotten History*, and Peter Fryer's *Staying Power: The History of Black People in Britain*.

Multicultural London in the 1890s

The largest immigrant groups in London at this time were Eastern European Jews and the Irish, both of whom formed communities in the East End. As a result of the British Empire and London's status as a major port, there were also people from many other parts of the world living and working in the city, including those from continental Europe, China, South Asia, Africa and North America. Black people had lived in London since the Roman Empire in the third century AD. In the Victorian period, black migrants from Africa, America and the West Indies came as sailors, soldiers, medical and law students, missionaries and entertainers, among others, and worked in a wide range of jobs in the city. Although scattered throughout London, there was a small black population near the docks in Canning Town. Before slavery was abolished in the British Empire in 1833 and in the United States in 1865, black visitors from America also came as anti-slavery campaigners and fugitive slaves. Slave narratives, such as those by Moses Roper and Frederick Douglass (which PC Mabaso reads in the story), were very popular at this time.

Zulus in London

The four primary African characters (Thembeka, Senzo, Musa and S'bu) were inspired by the true story of five men from Natal (Somanquasane, Inconda, Maquasa, Istri and Inaquala), who appeared in Westminster Police Court in 1879. They had been arrested for refusing to appear at the London Aquarium for the showman, Mr Farini, with whom they had a contract. As in the novel, Farini had been keeping them prisoner, refusing to allow them out in case it affected the ticket prices. Their court appearance was reported and discussed in many newspapers, including the *Illustrated Police News* where I first came across it. As in this novel, a translator from the Aborigines' Protection Society aided them, and the magistrate dismissed the case.

The Princess Nobantu character is inspired by a real woman who arrived in London in 1880. The Zulu Princess Amazulu stayed at the York Hotel in Waterloo with a 'suite' of two women and four men. She was the subject of great interest in the press, and travelled to Brighton to give daily receptions at the Aquarium. The article Arrowood reads out to Barnett is an amalgamation of two articles from the *Edinburgh Evening News* and the *Globe*, published in January, 1880.

Conditions in Natal

Much of my understanding of the people of, and situation in, Natal is based on Michael Mahoney's book *The Other Zulus: the Spread of Zulu Ethnicity in Colonial South Africa*. Natal contained a number of chiefdoms, including Zulu, Qwabe, Thembu and Chunu. In 1837, the Boer invaded and set up a republic called Natalia, which was then taken over and set up as a British colony called Natal. This led to an influx of British settlers. By 1879, the colonial authorities had taken 80 per cent of the land for the government and white settlers. Africans, left with only 20 per cent of their original land, were confined to 'reserves' set out for 'natives'. The best farming land, and all the lucrative diamond and gold mines in the area, were given over to the settlers. As a result, the traditional homesteads could no longer support the native population, and young men and women were forced to leave home to look for wage labour as servants or in the mines and docks. This situation was made worse by a five-year drought that began in 1888, and a rinderpest epidemic in 1896 which decimated cattle herds.

Natal had significant powers of self-government, although just about the only people allowed to vote were white. A range of 'native laws' were passed which only applied to the black population. The Masters and Servants Law of 1850 made it a criminal offence for an African to break a contract and leave a job they didn't want without their employer's permission, while later pass laws in some areas made it an offence to refuse work when it was offered. The pass system meant Africans could only get permission to live in a town if they had employment, while the compound system meant mineworkers were required to live in compounds on the company's land, where they were always under the oversight of their employers. The 1891 Native Law Code outlawed both adultery and sex between unmarried women and men, and made it illegal for a woman to leave the homestead without the permission of a male guardian. As a result of these laws, 30 per cent of black workers in the Rand faced police prosecution in some years, whilst in 1905 it was estimated that about 40 per cent of Africans in Durban had been arrested.

South Africa employed black police officers to enforce laws directed at the black population. These police officers were unpopular and had a reputation for brutality. In the latter part of the nineteenth century, colonial authorities and the settler population were increasingly worried about an uprising against the whites, and, in 1897, they began to develop a network of African spies (Native Intelligence Officers) to collect information on the black population, focusing particularly on political sentiment, leadership and possible plots against the government.

The Ninevites

A real bandit gang who operated from caves and disused mines in the hills outside Johannesburg from the 1890s onwards. I've relied heavily on Charles van Onselen's writing on this topic. Their leader was 'Nongoloza' Mathebula (aka Jan Note), and at one time their membership reached almost one thousand. The gang was organized on military lines and had its own legal system. They lived off a variety of crimes, including robbing African workers of their wages, seizing wage carts on their way to mining compounds, stopping coaches and robbing passengers, and burglary. They were also known for getting back at bosses who had cheated or abused their workers. Members of this gang were mostly migrant workers from Zululand and Natal who had come to the Rand in search of wage labour. Life as a black labourer in South Africa was hard due to low wages and the native laws described above that led to large numbers of black men being imprisoned. The Ninevite gang offered an alternative, and had members amongst the black police, the compound guards and the prison system, where they set up widespread prisoner networks. These were the origin of the infamous 'Numbers' gangs still found in South African prisons.

British perceptions of Africans

Despite the success of the anti-slavery campaigns, racism was a feature of life in Britain in the Victorian period, and black people were often subject to abuse when out on the street. Negative stereotypes were perpetuated by the popular blackface minstrel shows, and are easily found in newspapers of the time as well as in the works of popular writers such as Conan Doyle, Trollope and Dickens.

Generally, white people were considered superior, a view that was promoted in the 'racial sciences' of the day by writers such as Robert Knox, James Hunt, Arthur Gobineau, Thomas Carlyle and members of the London Anthropological Society. These pernicious ideas can be found woven into the writings of Victorian criminal anthropologists such as Havelock Ellis, who is referred to in the novel. Social Darwinists and many anthropologists argued that the fact that the British Empire had taken over the land of African countries was proof that white British people were superior. These so-called 'scientific' reports have since been proved biased and based on completely inadequate evidence. Although these ideas were dominant at the time, we should remember that there were always ordinary white people in London who welcomed black people and rejected these racist ideas. There were also writers such as Robert Dunn and John Stuart Mill who criticized the methods and conclusions of the race scientists. There were also significant black writers and campaigners who lived in or visited England during the Victorian period and argued for equal rights, black pride and self-government in Africa. Some of those involved in the Pan-African movement included Edward Blyden, James Africanus Beale Horton, Celestine Edwards and Sylvester Williams.

In 1879, Rorke's Drift and subsequent Anglo-Zulu battles gave the impression that the Zulus were a warrior race, and this was promoted in the fiction of the day. The article quoted in the book, *Might As Well Be Zulus*, containing the quote from the Earl of Derby, was published in 1880 in the *Shields Daily News* (and reported by many other papers).

British Empire

In the 1890s, the empire covered India, Australia, New Zealand, Sri Lanka (then known as Ceylon), Hong Kong, Malta and parts of Africa. As a result of the 'Scramble for Africa' by European nations, by 1900, a third of Africans were British subjects. In Britain, there was a good deal of popular support for, and pride in, the empire, and newspapers regularly ran reports from the colonies and detailed the military campaigns. However, there was much debate about day-to-day actions and policies of the British army, corporations and government in the colonies, examples being the arguments for and against the slave trade, and the actions of the British authorities in the 1865 Morant Bay uprising in Jamaica. Aside from the opposition to empire from huge numbers of colonized peoples who fought the British, there was also some general opposition within Britain, for example from the philosopher Richard Congreve, the Chartist Ernest Thomas, and the travel-writer Wilfrid Blunt, as well as in the pages of the *Bee-Hive* journal and the *Daily News*.

Ethnic exhibitions and freak shows

Freak shows and exhibits of non-white people could be extremely lucrative in the Victorian period. 'Ethnic exhibitions' or 'human zoos' were staged throughout the nineteenth century, often in small theatres and halls, in which customers could watch people from non-white cultures perform in reconstructions of native villages, where they would engage in cooking and other cultural practices, and perform songs and dances. In the 1890s, larger exhibitions were held in London at Alexandra Palace, Crystal Palace and Earls Court, including the 'Empire of India Exhibition' and the 'East African Village and Great Display by the Natives of Somaliland' in 1895, and 'Savage South Africa' in 1899. In the latter, two hundred Africans, including fifty Zulus, were brought over to act out the Matabele War and pretend to live in a specially constructed 'kraal'. Lions, tigers and elephants were also transported for the exhibition. While these exhibitions attracted large numbers of visitors, there was also some opposition. The Aborigines' Protection Society campaigned against the South Africa show for exploiting Africans.

The descriptions of Capaldi's Wonders in the story owes much to John Woolf's book *The Wonders*, which describes the business and lives of freak show performers in great detail, as well as Matthew Sweet's *Inventing the Victorians*. Woolf argues that while in earlier periods these sorts of shows were often exploitative and cruel, particularly those associated with fairgrounds, in the late Victorian period there were better opportunities for freak show performers to make a decent living, and the more famous of them became rich and were feted in the European courts. Chang and Eng, who were conjoined twins, did indeed take control of their own shows, and made a lot of money. Sylvie is inspired by Julia Pastrana, a famous performer who had hypertrichosis, which caused excessive hair growth, and gingival hyperplasia, which affected her teeth and lips. She exhibited in the mid-nineteenth century under many names, including 'Baboon Lady', 'Apewoman' and 'Nondescript'.

Chinese stereotypes

There were a number of racist stereotypes about Chinese people in Victorian times, depicting them as dirty, carriers of diseases, criminal and dangerous. One myth was that they ate rats. The tin of rat poison in the book is based on an American brand 'Rough on Rats', which can be seen here:

https://www.tolerance.org/classroom-resources/texts/rough-on-rats

Other real characters

Elizabeth Garrett Anderson was the first woman to qualify as a doctor in Britain (in 1865). She set up the New Hospital for Women in London, and, in 1874, the London School of

Medicine for Women. Charles de Vere Beauclerck, who sued his father, the Duke of St Albans, for his baldness, was described in Andrew Scull's *Madness in Civilization*.

Typhus

Typhus was three times as deadly as typhoid fever. It was predominantly a disease of the poor, although those caring for the sick could also become infected. There was no known treatment at the time, and doctors could only recommend rest, fresh air and good diet. On the suggestion of my editor, Finn Cotton, I invented an expensive fake remedy for typhus that people might have been tempted to buy in the absence of any proven medicine. My remedy was made of Jesuit bark and Jimson weed, plants used in traditional Peruvian medicine and which therefore might well have been expensive. Jesuit bark was used to treat malaria and Jimson weed for inflammation and convulsions, although to my knowledge they were not used for typhus.

Song lyrics

'The Fishermen Hung the Monkey, O!' – the lyrics to Ned Corvan's nineteenth-century music hall song were found on the songfacts.com website.

'The Violet I Plucked from Mother's Grave' – Mary Jane Kelly (Black Mary) is widely believed to be the last victim of Jack the Ripper. She was heard singing this song by the last witness who saw her on the night she was killed. The lyrics were found on the traditionalmusic.co.uk site.

Sources

Many thanks to the British Newspaper Archive in the British Library. I relied on many other sources for the historical detail. The main ones were:

Alfred Binet, *Animal Magnetism*. 1887. Kegan Paul, Trench & Co.

Christine Bolt, *Victorian Attitudes to Race*. 1971. Routledge & Kegan Paul.

Havelock Ellis, *The Criminal*. 1890. Walter Scott Publishers.

Peter Fryer, *Staying Power: The History of Black People in Britain*. 1984. Pluto Press.

Judith Flanders, *Victorian Christmas*. 2014. https://www.bl.uk/romantics-and-victorians/articles/victorian-christmas

Lee Jackson, *A Dictionary of Victorian London*. 2006. Anthem Press.

Lee Jackson, *Palaces of Pleasure. From the Music Halls to the Seaside to Football, How the Victorians Invented Mass Entertainment*. 2020. Yale University Press.

Lee Jackson, The Victorian Dictionary. http://www.victorian-london.org/index-2012htm

Paul La Hausse, *'The Cows of Nongoloza': Youth, Crime and Amalaita Gangs in Durban, 1900-1936*. Journal of Southern African Studies, 1990, 16, 1, 79-111.

Gregory B. Lee. *Dirty, Diseased and Demented: The Irish, the Chinese and Racist Representation*. Journal of Global Cultural Studies, 12, 2017.

Michael R. Mahoney, *The Other Zulus: The Spread of Zulu Ethnicity in Colonial South Africa*. 2012. Duke University Press.

David Olusoga, *Black and British: A Forgotten History*. 2017. Pan Books.

Charles van Onselen, *The Small Matter of a Horse: The Life of 'Nongoloza Mathebula 1867-1948*. 1984. Ravan Press.

Charles van Onselen, '*The Regiment of the Hills': South Africa's Lumpenproletarian Army 1890-1920*. Past & Present, No. 80 (Aug., 1978), pp. 91-121.

William Osler, *Typhoid Fever and Typhus Fever*. 1901. W.B. Saunders & Co.

D. Renshaw, 'Prejudice and paranoia: a comparative study of antisemitism and Sinophobia in turn-of-the-century Britain' *Patterns of Prejudice*, 2016, 50 (1), 38-60.

Matthew Sweet, *Inventing the Victorians*. 2002. Faber & Faber.

John Woolf, *The Wonders: Lifting the Curtain on the Freak Show, Circus and Victorian Age*. 2019. Michael O'Mara Books.

Acknowledgements

Many thanks to the people who have made this book possible. To Vincent Wells for his comments on an earlier draft, to my editor, Finn Cotton, for his close reading of the book, his insightful comments and his help in negotiating tricky issues, to the sensitivity consultant for raising important issues, and to Jon Appleton for his careful copy-editing. My huge gratitude to my agent, Jo Unwin, for all she has done and continues to do for the Arrowood books, for her advice, grounding and unfailing encouragement. Thanks also to Joe Thomas and all those at HQ for their hard work behind the scenes, to the British Library, and to all those readers who have been so kind in their support of the series.

Read more of Arrowood and Barnett's adventures...

OUT NOW!

ONE PLACE. MANY STORIES

ONE PLACE. MANY STORIES

Bold, Innovative and
empowering publishing.

FOLLOW US ON:

@HQStories